FML & WTF

Two Books in one by Scarlett J Rose

A Word from Scarlett:

Dear Reader, I'd like to thank you first off, for purchasing this book, it's a double whammy of the first two books in the FML series, of which there was only going to be one A standalone book – FML.

That was until Libby started up her nagging, and then Zane began his whining – we're getting to you Zane, quit ya bitchin'!

FML started out as, well, an idea, as most of my stories do. Poor Mel was stuck in my head until her story came out. there were quite a few times when I was stuck, but after brainstorming with some fantastic fellow authors (Susan, Joanne, Cheryl, Chiara… I'm looking at you bitches! *Love you girls!* ;)) I got cracking and often didn't stop until the wee hours of the morning, when I had to get up for work, or coming back from work in the wee hours of the morning and sitting on the computer until the sun was shining, the magpies warbling, and the husband unit was getting up with his disgruntled greeting of 'why haven't you been to bed yet?'. I know he understands that when the Muse has control, he has to wait – he knows I love him to the ends of the universe and back.

WTF, and OMG, (Zane's story) were never going to be part of the deal, until Libby glared at me from the pages. Her story came flowing through the month of November, 2017, when I was taking part of National Novel Writing Month (aka, NanoWriMo or That Month I think I'll Write Fifty Thousand Words of Crap and Hope It Makes Sense.)

Though her past is a little dark, Libby powered forward to the end goal of having her story told. I'm glad I was able to brig both Libby and Mel's stories to the wold, I just hope I can do the same for Zane when he starts talking to me again… what a Diva!

Again, A huge thank-you to my dear readers, and friends who have helped me to get Mel and Libby's stories out there

May you enjoy these humble stories, have a laugh, cry or a giggle-snort, all work, as long as you enjoy the journey!

Happy Reading!

-Scarlett J Rose

January 1st 2018.

FML

Scarlett J Rose

Dedication:

This one is for my Mum, Kaye. Her love and support is priceless and I'm proud and honoured that fate gave her to me for my Mother.

I'd like to thank my beta readers, Cheryl Riddell, LeAnne Rodgers, Joanne Effendi, Chiara Beltrami-Gottmer, Kat Stewart and Helen King.

To my editor, Susan Horsnell, I really need some more mirrors in my books… right? ☺.

Without you gorgeous gals, I'd never have gotten this done!

My life was like some psychotic mutant cross breed of Notting Hill and Bridget Jones's Diary. I worked in a second-hand bookstore and I was a blonde British girl trying to find the love of my life. The only difference was, I had no handsome(ish) Brits after my pudgy British arse, I didn't smoke like a chimney, but on occasion I did drink like a fish. and yes, my mother did like to send me her off cast clothing that looked like they were right out of the nineteen-forties.

Oh, and I lived in L.A. Movie capital of the world.

It took a twisted turn, however, the day my gay roommate managed to convince me that going in to a movie studio for Extras Casting was a good idea.

If I had known what my life would be like after that fateful day, I would have told him to sod off and cut his bollocks off for dragging my arse out the door.

Fuck. My. Life!

Chapter One.

He was worse than a bloody alarm clock, at least you could turn one of those off. Zane, well, he was always on. Literally. Always. On. He was also one of the biggest, loudest gays I knew, including my baby brother. As camp as a row of tents.

Flamboyant with multi-coloured highlights in his peroxide-blond hair, more shoes than I could ever wear in a lifetime, not that my meagre wages at the bookstore even accounted for a shoe budget after my rent, utilities and food had been taken care of for the week.

I groaned and tried to snuggle deeper into my blankets, trying to hide from the hurricane disaster who was bounding with, well, boundless energy into my room. He leapt on top of my bed, jumping up and down like a Kangaroo on speed, yelling, "Ooh Melinda! Wakey, wakey hands off… oh right, girls don't have snakey's… Wakey, wakey, hands off your pussy… oh wait… eww."

He stopped jumping long enough for me to grab my pillow and toss it at him.

"Bugger off, Zane," I muttered, trying in vain to recapture my sleep. I gripped the covers tight, knowing the bastard's next move.

"Uh-uh-uh sweet cheeks, you promised." He gripped the blankets and tugged. For such a slight framed guy, he had a heck of a lot of strength. He whooped with victory as the bedding was ripped from my hands, cold air from the apartment's air conditioning causing goosebumps to pebble my skin.

"Gah," I grumbled. Sitting up, I blinked blearily at him as he moved to my window and ripped open the curtains. Another bright and sunny L.A. day beckoned.

This was supposed to be my day off. This was supposed to be the day I lazed my arse around the house, getting up when I wanted to, eating all those terribly fatty foods which gave me an arse like a Heffalump, despite my attempts to work it off by walking… fifty metres to the bus stop before getting on the bus, and, after getting off the bus, another fifty meters to work before plonking my arse on a seat behind the counter to sell second-hand books.

"What did I promise again?" I asked, scrunching my eyes against the light. I threw my arm over my eyes, trying to hide from the nasty sunlight like a vampire. The bed bounced as Zane flopped down beside me. His cologne drifted across my nose, making my allergies twitch.

"You, my sweet dumpling, promised me you would come with me to a casting call for extras at Valleyrock Film Studio. Where you and I will both be discovered, become famous stars and die at the ripe old age of twenty-seven from tragic drug overdoses. Then, we will get posthumous stars on the walk of fame." His arms flailed in the air before he clapped his hands and rubbed them together.

"That's a nice dream, can I go back to sleep now?"

"Nope, now get that luscious *arse* out of bed, my sleeping British beauty, and make yourself beauty-licious. I bet as soon as they hear your beautiful, and refined, British accent they'll swoon over you."

"You do realise I sound like a terrible Bridget Jones, right?"

"And you do realise, Renee Zellweger is actually an American, don't you? Her accent was a put on." he pulled open my closet as he continued. "And, she had to put on weight for the role."

"Your point?" I asked, finally sitting up, knowing I wasn't going to win this battle.

"My point is, darling, that you have everything our lovely Renee had *after* she became Miss Jones for the film. You are a natural, you don't have to change." He pulled out a dress I knew would accentuate my ass and tits. I raised an eyebrow at his choice.

"Now don't you go all *Dr Spock* on me sweetie."

"Don't you mean *Mister Spock*? God, Zane, for a gay nerd your *Star Trek* knowledge needs serious work." I pushed myself up from the bed and snatched the dress from his hands.

"I was more a Star *Wars* fan, you know *R2D2* had a filthy mouth? Hence all the bleeping going on. Now, shoes," he smiled.

"Not the black ones, the heel is loose." I warned as I padded to the bathroom.

"Don't worry about that, I'll fix it."

I shook my head as I pulled my PJs off, and jumped under the warm spray. Knowing Zane, I had about a minute of hot water.

It was less. Thirty-seven seconds to be exact.

Fuck. My. Life.

Chapter Two.

I could feel the left heel wobbling as we walked through security at Valleyrock Films.

"I told you these heels were no good," I hissed under my breath as we were ushered towards a large group of hopeful extras.

"Don't worry, it's still attached. Maybe the chewing gum has gone soft in the heat." Zane said, preening in front of a pane of mirrored glass alongside one of the studios

"*Chewing gum*? You bloody well fixed my heel with chewing gum?" I whispered angrily, when I actually wanted to scream at the man. This day couldn't get worse, could it? I was having major boob sweat from the Californian sun, my heels were about to break, and we had almost missed the bus because of said heels. The bus driver had glared at us with disgust at having to wait for my sorry arse. If looks could kill, he'd be serving two life sentences. I was about to let go with another tirade at my housemate, when a woman sashayed up to our group.

I didn't know hips were capable of swinging that way. Her business suit screamed *I'm important,* and her strict, tight bun hairstyle was so severe, it almost made her Botox injections unnecessary.

"All right, extras this way please." She cast an eye over our group, before sniffing and turning away, striding over the deep blue carpet of the hallway. Like a group of lost ducklings, we followed her. Posters of Valleyrock Films previous movies adorned the walls, some even had the signatures of the stars scrawled on them in various shades of thick ink. We followed Miss Prissy-Pants down the hallway until we arrived at a set of double doors.

The group was ushered through, and invited to take a seat at a long table where stacks of forms were laid out in front of each seat.

"Please take a seat and fill out these release forms, if you do not sign, you will be asked to leave the premises immediately."

Zane went all caveman, grabbed my hand and dragged me to a seat. As I filled out the forms, my eyes swept over the usual legal mumbo-jumbo, understanding nothing, but *legal action may be taken.*

"All right, now before we send you off to a set for work, we're going to sort you into groups. These groups will be sent to a set where you will work as extras for the day. We have a few simple rules." She spoke as she collected the forms and passed them to a lackey. "Listen to what you are directed to do by the production team, failure to do so will result in instant termination. Do not disrupt the set, remain in character until the director calls *Cut.*" She glanced around the room, ensuring she had out attention. "And, most importantly, *do not* interact with the main actors on or off set. They have a job to do just like you, but unlike you, they get paid a lot of money for their work, and don't need to deal with slobbering try-hard extras."

I leaned over and whispered softly to Zane "Did she just insult us?"

He chuckled. "That's what they do best honey."

"You two," she snapped. "Is there a problem? Have a question?"

I suddenly felt like I was back in high school, with my tenth-grade English teacher snapping like a rabid dog over note passing.

"No Ma'am," I mumbled, feeling about an inch tall under her glare.

"Very good, let's keep it that way. Now let's get you sorted into appropriate groups."

Our group was divided. I was sent off with a small group of men and women, Zane with another and a third group in yet another direction to a studio somewhere on the other side of the massive lot. We were escorted to a large building, a hand-written sign attached to the small entry claimed this was 'Set 25' and the movie being filmed was *A Duke to Remember*. I'd heard about this film, it had two of the hottest upcoming stars in Hollywood as its headliners - Adam Jacobs and Kira Holsworthy.

"Oh, my gosh! I wonder if Adam Jacobs will be on set," a young woman giggled nervously.

I simply concentrated on stepping one foot in front of the other in my murderous heels. I had much bigger problems to worry about than coming face-to-face with a hot movie star, especially if these damned heels decided chewing gum was a poor substitute for superglue.

We entered the set, my eyes drinking in the expanse of coiled cables running to lights and cameras. A desk filled with monitors was attended by a man wearing a large set of headphones with a mic attached. Gaffers and Grip were running around setting this and that right on the set beyond. There was a beautiful ballroom beyond the cameras. A chandelier hung from the top of the set, and looming above it all was a camera on a boom, set up and ready for an overhead shot. I watched as it panned over the empty ballroom set, the image being displayed on one of the larger monitors as the operator played with the controls via a joystick.

Off to one side of the ballroom's floor, a group of people were working on setting a banquet table. A large fountain-tiered-style punchbowl was being filled with a red liquid, I wondered if it was actually punch, or just food-dye-coloured water.

"These are the extras?" a flustered-looking young man asked our escort.

She nodded.

"Good. Come on, let's get you into costume."

We were quickly ushered to a room away from the bustle of the set and taken over by a group of costume workers. I was pushed into a frilly light blue dress, a shade of blue which was almost white, and would probably have sparked an epic, and totally pointless debate, on Facebook as to what colour it was.

It was blue, a very pale, light blue. Riddle solved.

The costume girl looked at my shoes. "Those are fine, leave them on."

Before I could protest, and tell her my shoes were in a bad way, I was pushed to the next room, where I had makeup liberally applied to my face. My hair was pulled every which way from Sunday, and piled into some sort of Victorian up-do. As soon as my hair and makeup was done, I was ushered back out to the main room. Extras were being moved to a small, out-of-the-way space where another flustered-looking assistant was pairing us up, and explaining the scene.

"All right, in this scene, Duke Reynolds is dancing with the beautiful debutante, Lady Cunningham. All we need you to do, is dance or mill about in the background. Look British, look posh, look like you're having a good time at the party, but no breaking out in a funky-chicken style dance or you're out." He paired me up with a young man who grinned and said hello, I reeled at the scent of his breath, and almost retched at the sight of his teeth. And, they say us Brits have terrible teeth, this bloke would put even my uncle Sam to shame, and he had *no* teeth.

We were all manoeuvred into positions, Smelly Breath guy, and me were placed on the sidelines. I was thankful, there was no way I could dance in my murderous heels.

"You two, you in the white dress, and your partner," the director called out to us. I pointed at myself, unsure if he was really calling us out or not.

"Yes, you two, get on the dance floor. I want you two to waltz around." He waved his hands about as if they were a pair of dancers themselves. I gulped, I knew this was a bad idea. A very, very bad idea.

Fuck. My. Life.

Chapter Three.

Mr. Stinky-Bad-Breath, I soon discovered, had grabby hands as well as poor oral hygiene. He pulled me close against him, and I could swear the boy had something dancing around in his pants. Perhaps it was a hamster, or some other sort of small rodent. Whatever it was, it was unimpressive to say the least as he kept pressing himself against me at every opportunity he got as we danced around the fake ballroom, practicing before the director called in the stars.

The two stars of the movie entered like a royal couple, everything stopped for them. The director rose from his chair, and kissed Kira on each cheek, before he took her hand and guided her to the centre of the ballroom where he wanted her positioned.

"Now Kira, darling, this is where the duke comes in and sweeps you off your feet. But remember, you are a virginal debutante, unaccustomed to the wiles of a rugged, good-looking man like this. So, lots of pretty smiles, and see if we can't get some natural blushing going?"

Kira smiled, her surgically enhanced chest catching the eyes of the males on, and off, set as she took a deep breath and got into character.

I looked over to Adam Jacobs, and was surprised to see him watching me. I quickly averted my eyes as Mr. Grabby-Feel-Me-Up ran his hand down my back and groped my left arse cheek. I swatted him away with my hand, but he went back for another grab just before the director shouted for us to take our places. Grabby-Hands turned, and grinned at me, as we waited for the calls for cameras to start rolling, and the action to take place.

We started moving at the appropriate calls. Grabby-Hands held me close, rubbing himself against me with every step of the waltz. I don't know how he managed it, but he made a beautiful dance feel dirty, and not in a good way either. I tried to keep in character, my face stoic, a fake smile at the corners of my lips as we passed the first, and second cameras. Above us, the whirring of the boom camera caught my attention as it hovered overhead, taking shots from above. I felt self-conscious of the low neckline of my dress which exposed a good portion of my bosom. The whirring continued above us, and I wondered if the damned operator was getting a good look down the front of my dress.

I don't think my girls had ever received so much attention.

The scene moved quickly, with Adam taking Kira's hand, and directing her around the dancefloor.

"Hey," Grabby-Hands whispered as he whirled me around the dance floor. "I want to try something." I started to protest, but he cut me off. "This will be awesome, just trust me."

Famous last words, no way in hell was I going to trust this asshole, but he gave me no time to stop him as he pushed me out into a spin. I took two steps before my heel caught on the bottom of my long dress. Time slowed as I heard the distinctive sound of material tearing, my *good* heel giving way. Shocked gasps from other extras filled the air as I stumbled toward the buffet table, crashed into it, and sent the damned thing tumbling into me. Glasses shattered as I fell to the floor, the surface of the table sliding at an angle to crash onto the floor at my arse. I turned away from the carnage when I heard something heavy sliding towards me, there was no way I could move in time to avoid the large punchbowl.

Cold, red liquid drenched me. I gasped in shock at the chill. There were bloody ice cubes in the *punch!* Hooray for attention to detail. I mean, who really looks at the food in a movie?

I sat in total shock, my sodden clothes stuck to every curve of my body, my white bra stood out against the soaked material, and of course, being cold, my nipples decided they wanted to stand to attention like two pointy soldiers.

I.

Was.

Mortified.

I sat in the puddle of punch, scattered hors d'oeuvres and shattered glass, drenched from head-to-toe. Until the tittering laughter of Kira-fucking-Holsworthy broke the mood. I wiped the mess of saturated hair from my face, ruining my makeup.

"What the fuck have you done to my set?" the director screamed as he stormed toward me. "You," he turned to the real culprit, Grabby Hands. "And you, get the fuck off my set, you'll never work on Valleyrock films again!" He pointed to the door.

I scrambled to my feet, the rest of the dress' skirt ripping as it was partially caught under the top of the destroyed buffet table. I turned around and tugged on the ruined material which was now stained a light reddish-pink from the liquid. Another burst of laughter came from the bitch actress, starting up another round of chuckles, snorts and chortles from the entire set.

I turned and glared at her, she was leaning against Adam Jacobs. He wasn't laughing, at least he had the decency to look sympathetic. I tugged violently at the last shreds of the destroyed dress, ripping it from its prison, and wrapping it around my waist. I hobbled away from the cruel laughter, my ankle screaming in pain with each step I took. I hung my head, embarrassment an understatement, as I left the set. After dragging myself out of the dress, I pulled my old clothes back on, sniffling as I wrestled my clothes over my damp and sticky body. Yes, it was real punch in that damned bowl.

I looked at the ruined dress, and the pair of heels I was happily abandoning to their fate.

Traitorous bastards. I'd changed my mind, if anyone asked me what colour the fucking dress was now, I'd say it was fucking red.

I left the costume change rooms, and walked across the set to the exit. I turned and cast a last glance over the mess I'd left. Totally not my fault.

I passed someone in the shadows, I ignored them, uttering the magic words that had become my mantra

"Fuck. My. Life."

Chapter Four.

I managed to hobble home, and submitted to misery in the shower. Sitting on the cold tiles of the shower, I dissolved into an ugly cry of epic proportions. Ignoring the insistent buzzing of my phone on the vanity, I let the water run cold. Snot ran down my face to be washed down the drain, joining the growing clog of years of hair, and other bodily fluids.

For the rest of the day, I hid myself away from the world, and its bitchy actresses, with a bucket of ice cream as my only solace. I rested the cold bucket on my swollen and sore ankle. I was certain I'd sprained wearing the heels of death.

I sat on the couch, watching some corny chick-flick, my mind not really following the story, and the ice cream melting in the bucket. My ankle throbbed, but everything else felt numb. And, not in a good way.

I jumped, when the door burst open to allow Zane's grand entrance. The ice-cream tumbled to the floor, its semi-melted gooeyness slowly spreading out onto the carpet.

"Jesus fucking Christ Zane!" I sat up, and leaned forward, trying to scoop the melting ice cream back into its bucket. "Could you possibly be a little less gay when entering a room? I mean, do you need to bloody well have a goddamned flash mob precede you every time you enter a room, or is that some kind of requirement for gays?"

"Wow…" Zane stopped and studied me. "Someone turned the bitch-switch to eleven." He shut the door, and walked to the side table, where he dropped his keys into a bowl. "Okay, you have a BJ thing going on. Your eyes are puffy and red, and I can tell you're in a mood, so spill sweet cheeks, what the heck happened?"

I sighed. "It was a total, utter, fucking disaster. The arsehole I was paired with for a dancing scene, couldn't keep his bloody hands off my arse. Then, he tried a dance move my heels weren't cut out for. I crashed into a huge banquet table, and spilt an entire fucking bowl of fucking punch all over my-fucking-self. Add to this, I twisted my bloody ankle, was laughed off the fucking set and told I would never work in the film industry again. Yeah, great fucking day." I sighed again, and leaned my head against the backrest of the sofa.

"Oh sweetie," Zane said softly. He stiffened for a second, then looked at me, his eyes wide and his face paling with some sense of realisation "Oh, my god, that was *you?*"

"What do you mean, *that was you*?" My body tensed, a feeling of undeniable dread forming in the pit of my stomach. Zane avoided my glare. "Zane, tell me what the fuck is going on. Right now."

"Ah… I think I hear the washing machine beeping." He stood to make a hasty escape.

"ZANE!" I yelled, trying to grab at him. I stood on my good foot, and stepped in a puddle of ice cream I'd failed to rescue from the floor. My foot slid out from under me, and I flopped back on the couch with a grunt. On the battered coffee table, my phone vibrated with an incoming text.

I sighed, ignoring my sticky and cold foot to check the phone. Libby, one of my friends back home in England, had sent me a text, along with a *YouTube* link.

"OMG girl! Talk about awkward, and with that hottie watching everything happening to you!" I shook my head,

frowned in confusion and selected the link. Within seconds it had opened to my phone's *YouTube* app.

"Extra goes down!" the title announced. I watched as the video loaded, and began to play. It was the set from the film, I was dancing with the arsehole. Then, I was spiralling out of control, my arms windmilling as I tried to regain my balance. I watched in horror as I crashed into the buffet table, the red punch splashing over my body, instantly soaking the thin material of my dress, and making my light bra very prominent against my body. Hot tears pricked my eyes as I watched the worst day of my life unfold in front of me again. And what was worse, I'd looked at the number of views this had received.

Already, it had topped one million views.

My wet arse had been seen over a million times.

I'd been embarrassed over a million times.

I'd been laughed at a million times, okay probably *more* than a million times.

Like an idiot, I looked at the comments. Why did I do that? I really shouldn't have. Many of them, of course, were not very flattering. There was more than one comment about my body shape, or me being a stupid bitch who couldn't dance- at least they got that right. I can't dance, and right now, I *felt* like a stupid bitch.

I closed the *YouTube* app, not wanting to relive my worst moment in time. My phone vibrated again, and again with more texts from friends, laughing their arses off. They had no idea how bad I felt.

The ice cream I had tried to use as an alternative to Prozac was completely deficient in its purpose. Feelings like this, needed to be numbed with alcohol. Lots, and lots, of fucking alcohol.

I was about to join the statistics of people who drown their sorrows in a bottle.

Fuck. My. Life.

Chapter Five.

The next morning, I awoke to a pounding headache, a sour taste in my mouth, and a stomach that began to heave as soon as the sweet scent of Zane's chocolate-chip pancakes hit my nose. I rushed to the bathroom where I fell to my knees, and fervently prayed to the gods of porcelain. Once I had finished bringing up the ugly, and foul-smelling contents of my stomach, I noticed I had a new text on my phone.

Unknown Number: I'm very sorry for what happened yesterday, you didn't deserve to be treated that way. I Hope you are all right, and I would like to make it up to you.

The number had also been blocked, so I guessed it was a private number. I had no idea who had my number, or who would take the time to apologise. Surely it wasn't the director? He was super pissed, and I had read in those wonderfully trashy tabloids, the ones you read while bored witless at work, that he had something of a temper. I groaned as I hugged the porcelain throne. The loo was my best friend at this moment in time, and I needed it to bring me back to the land of the living. Or, pancakes, my aching stomach rumbled at the scent of Zane's cooking. It was in utter conflict, again it wanted to heave, but it also wanted to be filled with the sweet, chocolatey disasters that were Zane's pancakes.

I struggled to my feet, and looked in the mirror. Ugh. I was a national disaster zone all on my own. My hair resembled a poorly put together bird's nest, the only things missing were feathers, poop, and starving half-naked chicks roosting in the destroyed bun. Dark circles marred the space beneath my very red eyes. I could still taste vomit, mixed with an aftertaste of alcohol which had not yet been processed. I groaned, splashed water on my face and pulled the pins from my hair, yanking out long golden strands in the process.

"Bollocks," I muttered. I grabbed the tube of toothpaste, and brush, and began scouring the revolting taste from my mouth. When I was all minty, and fresh again, I staggered blearily into the kitchen where Zane was humming some nameless tune.

"Can someone turn the lights down?" I scowled while trying to shield my eyes from the horrible sun. *Now I know what a vampire feels like* I thought to myself.

Zane turned and placed a plate of pancakes in front of me, along with a bottle of aspirin and cold orange juice. "Thanks, you prick." I muttered, remembering him leaving me in the lurch about my fifteen seconds of fame. My phone had blown up overnight with texts, and Facebook notifications. It vibrated on the table beside me, the ringtone overly loud in my head. It was Mrs. Phillips, the owner of the bookstore where I worked. Today was supposed to be my day off, she worked the weekends. I worked on weekdays, and on weekends only if there was an emergency. Today being a Sunday, I wasn't expecting to work. Fate, however had other plans... *fickle bitch.* I groaned before I answered it, the incessant ringing bringing the thumping back to my head.

"Ah, Melinda, I have a family emergency. My sister is in the hospital, and I have make sure she is all right. Can you please come into the shop today?" The older widow was sweet and kind. She'd helped a poor British girl, who had fallen on hard times, when the man she'd fallen in love with, and followed across the Atlantic to the States, had cheated on her with a Chinese girl, followed by a Russian girl, then an African-American girl. I'd found the pictures on his phone when I'd mistakenly taken his, we'd had the same model phones for whatever stupid reason. Then, I'd come home to our apartment to find him with *all three women* in our bed. I packed my bags and was out of there before the asshole could beg me to stay and join in.

I owed this woman so much. I'd seen the 'help wanted' sign in her shop window. I had no money and nowhere to live. She put her faith in me, gave me a job, and a room in her little two-bedroom apartment until I was back on my feet. So, when she called and needed me, I always answered with a yes. No matter how hung over I was, no matter how much the world thought of me as a running joke, the answer was always, yes.

"Of course, give me time to have a shower then, I'll get over there and open up." I looked at the old Mickey Mouse clock which was Zane's most prized childhood possession. It was almost ten already. The store opened at ten, but today it might be a little late. Obviously, I had a key, and knew the alarm code, having opened and closed the store every weekday for the past two years.

"Oh, thank you Melinda. Could you please do the inventory on the romances today? I was hoping to finish but then this cropped up."

"No problem." I smiled, even though she couldn't see me. I ended the call and put my phone on the table.

"Everything okay, baby-cakes?" Zane asked, as he sat down opposite me with his own stack of pancakes.

I glared at him. "You are in the bloody doghouse, boy-o. Yesterday was all your fault." I jabbed my fork at him.

"Sweetie, I'm so sorry. I just didn't know how to break it to you." He had the decency to look abashed. "I don't think you should worry about it, I mean no-one really knows who you are, right? So, don't stress, this will all blow over quickly, and you'll be relegated to one of those 'Fail Army' videos on *YouTube*." He sliced into the stack of pancakes, the melted chocolate chips dribbling onto the plate.

"You're not off the hook, Zane. You owe me for dragging my arse to that bloody studio in the first place."

Zane sighed theatrically. "All right, fine. I'll cook, and clean for the week. Fair?"

"Fair," I agreed. He knew how much I hated cooking, and cleaning, being domestic in any way, shape or form. Though I had been well trained by my mum, I had become lazy after my breakup with Asshole Ex. I guess I was still in a mourning period, well that was my excuse for my laziness, and I was sticking to it.

I devoured my pancakes, my rebellious stomach settling with the excess of sweet, gooey goodness from the molten chocolate chips and pancake mixture. It was never quite cooked all the way through, but enough so you didn't get sick. I downed the orange juice, and moved to wash my body of the shame and horror of yesterday's escapades, and aftermath of my pity party.

Within twenty minutes, I was riding the bus three blocks to the book shop. Ten minutes after arriving, I had the shop open, and welcomed my first customer. I smiled sweetly as the young woman and her boyfriend ambled around the shop. He was looking for a book his English literature class was reading, and I knew we had copies in the back section. His girlfriend, was glued to her phone the whole time she was in the shop. I was sure I heard the click of a camera as I turned to greet another customer when they entered the shop. The bell jingling over the door merrily covered another possible click from the girl's phone.

Little did I know I was in for a long day. The bitch was tweeting my location to the world.

Fuck. My. Life.

Chapter Six.

I'd never seen the shop so full of people, they certainly weren't previous customers. Everyone had their phones out, and were videoing me as if I'd do something stupid. Some asked me what happened, others asked me to do something funny. I flipped them the bird, and told them to bugger off unless they wanted to buy a book.

Four-thirty rolled around, and the large group of gawkers had trickled down to a few actual customers, late Sunday shoppers. I was buggered, my body ached, and I had missed lunch because of the vultures who were perched in front of the shop, waiting for me to leave. I swore there were actual paparazzi types out there. I wondered why the hell they'd waste their time with me? I was a nobody, a clumsy girl who'd embarrassed herself, and managed to get it filmed, and shared with the world. I moved to the electrical switchboard and began to flip the lights off, preparing to close up for the night. The door opened, the bell jangling as a man in a baseball cap, high-collared jacket, and dark glasses entered.

"Sorry, we're closed, you can come back tomorrow," I said as I moved between the shelves filled with musty, second-hand books to usher the intruder from the store. I stopped when he took off his glasses, and looked at me.

Deep green eyes regarded me with a look of… *longing, desire, lust, all of the above?*

Holy shit. I'd seen those eyes before.

Modern Art, James's Diary, Kissing Mr. Perfect, Bratva, A Dangerous Love.

All movies which starred leading man, and Hollywood heartthrob, Adam Jacobs.

Who was right now, at this very fucking minute, standing in my workplace, surrounded by musty books, and holding a bunch of roses.

Adam.

Fucking.

Jacobs.

"Uh…" I said articulately. Not.

"Hi." He smiled. It was one of those genuine smiles, the kind that wins Academy Awards and Golden Globes. The ones an actor can't fake, because they go from the lips, to crinkle the nose (if they don't get Botox injections), and the eyes (Again, if there's no Botox involvement).

"H-Hi," I stammered, unsure as to what to say next. My body trembled a with nerves, and my brain had gone from a little mental fart, to total fucking nuclear meltdown.

"I wanted to apologise for yesterday. Tony was out of line, it was obviously an accident. I had no idea it was being filmed, and never imagined it would be leaked and be put online." He smiled again and offered the roses to me.

"Uh…" Yep, I was back to that. My power of speech was gone. I had nothing, nada, zilch, standing in front of this godlike vision of a man.

"I'd like to make it up to you by taking you out to dinner." He stood holding the roses I still hadn't accepted.

"I… I, don't know what to say…" I stammered, my hand finally reaching out for the roses.

"Well," he grinned. "Yes, would be a good start." He chuckled, breaking the spell, he held over me.

I giggled, unable to stop the embarrassing chuckle from escaping my lips. I miraculously regained my senses, and gazed at him.

"Yes, and thank-you, the roses are lovely." I brought the colourful bouquet to my nose and inhaled their delightful scent. My father would have been tickled pink at the perfection of the blooms. I could see they were greenhouse grown, each one checked and inspected at each stage of growth for any imperfections. "I need to close up, and I'll be right with you." I turned and rushed around the store, going through the closing routine. I placed the day's takings in the safe in the back room, while Adam-fucking-Jacobs leaned against the counter and waited, his cap pulled down low over his face as he looked through an old copy of *War and Peace*.

I grabbed my bag and headed back to him. I could barely believe Adam Jacobs was taking me out for dinner, surely this had to be some cruel joke of the universe? Something was going to happen, there was a niggly feeling in the back of my brain. Something would happen, and it wouldn't be good.

"Ready?" he asked, as I came to the front of the shop, grabbing the keys to the front from my bag.

"Yep." We left the shop and while I turned to lock the door, my stupid mouth voiced my uncertainty. "So, are you sure you want to take me out? I mean I'll totally understand if you don't, after all you're-" I turned and he cut me off with a finger pressed to my lips. My heart hammered in my chest. Adam Jacobs was touching me. Adam *Fucking* Jacobs had his finger pressed against my lips to hush me, and my flapping mouth,

"I'm certain, Melinda." He smiled

"How… how did you know my name?"

He lowered his eyes to the floor and seemed a little sheepish. "I had a friend in casting look up your information in the Extras files, it's how I got your number as well. Then, I saw someone had tweeted you were working in this bookshop."

Wait. He'd looked up my information? "Well, that's not creepy-Stalker-type behaviour at all." I snorted. I double checked the lock, then slipped the keys into my bag. My hand brushed over the small can of mace I kept for emergency use. For stalkers, and bad guys, who wanted my purse or my non-existent virtue.

"I know, I'm sorry, I just…" He rubbed the back of his neck, his cheeks flushing a bright cherry red.

Well, fuck me, this huge Hollywood star is actually blushing. "Just what?"

"I saw you on set, you looked like someone I'd like to get to know better. All through the scene, I was messing up my lines, because I couldn't think clearly after I saw you. Then, your accident happened, and I tried to catch you as you left, but I wasn't fast enough. I wanted to make sure you were alright, you were limping." His words seemed to come out in a rush.

I smiled. Maybe he wasn't so creepy-stalkerish after all. "Wow." I shook my head in amazement before my blue eyes met his green. "Of all my friends who have seen that damned video, you're actually the first person to ask if I was alright. Well, apart from my roommate. He doesn't count because he didn't tell me when he first knew, bloody prick," I grumbled.

Adam chuckled, held his arm out for me to intertwine mine with, and we walked down the street towards a small diner nearby. I'd eaten there a few times before and knew their food was edible. Nothing five-star like Adam Jacobs was probably used to, but it didn't give you the squirts, unless you ate there on a Wednesday when one of their new cooks was on.

We slid into a booth and placed our orders, all the while Adam kept his baseball cap on, pulled down over his eyes. He hunched over in the booth, seeming to be uncomfortable in the place.

"Hey." I leaned forward and reached out to touch his hand to get his attention. "We can go somewhere else if you're not okay here?"

He gazed at me and smiled.

"No, I'll be okay. I just need to keep an eye out for paps."

"Paps?" I was unsure what he was referring to.

"Paparazzi."

"Oh, right. I think I had a couple hanging around the store today. I can't believe how many people were in there, all on their phones, asking me this and that, taking pictures of me. I had to tell them all to sod off or buy a book, they all buggered off after that." The waitress approached and began pouring coffee. She smiled, her eyes on Adam as she poured. Her distraction was my undoing. Hot liquid quickly overflowed my cup, which was near the edge of the table, and cascaded into my lap.

I squealed when the burning liquid hit my thighs and stood up, brushing it from my jeans. The waitress gasped when she realised what she had done, and quickly dabbed at the hot liquid, now dribbling down my jeans and into my shoes, with a cloth.

"Oh, my God miss, I'm so sorry!" she apologised.

"It's okay, just a little scald." I spoke through gritted teeth. "Is there a bathroom where I can clean up?"

"Sure, in the back." The waitress directed me to the bathrooms and I hurried away, my thighs burning. Thankfully my snatch missed out on the coffee bath, or I'd have had more to say to the waitress. I glanced down, it looked like I had pissed myself.

I peered at myself in the mirror. "Bloody hell." My face was pale and my eyes sparkled with unshed tears of pain. I gingerly unsnapped my jeans button, and pulled the zipper down. It had been a while since I'd groomed down there, with no boyfriend, and no date prospects, I'd gotten lazy. Sunbathing was out of the question, I burned to a crisp if exposed to the Californian sun for more than forty minutes, so I never wore swimsuits. I carefully dabbed cold water on the reddened area where the coffee had soaked through my jeans and scalded me.

There was a knocking at the door, Adam's voice calling out to me. "Melinda, are you okay in there?"

"Yeah, I'm okay, just cleaning up," I called back.

"Do you need me to come in there?" he asked through the door.

Wait… what? I thought nervously, we'd only met each other not even an hour earlier.

"No, no, I've got it, I'm alright." I turned to toss the paper towel into the waste bin. My jeans were around my ankles and somehow, thanks to my feet being trapped in layers of blue jeans, I managed to lose my balance. I squealed in fright as I fell towards the basin, banging my head against the ceramic.

"Bollocks!" I shouted out as I crumpled to the floor. My head throbbed where I'd knocked it, and my ass hit the cold tiled floor of a bathroom, which at second glance, was not very clean.

The door burst open. I jumped, my hand on the swelling bump, and my eyes locked onto the green of Adam's. He frowned down at me, concern all over his face, before his mouth split into a cheeky grin.

"Well, Melinda, if I had known all it took to get your pants off, was a cup of coffee, I would have brought you one earlier." He chuckled before he helped me up, and righted me. Then, pulled my jeans up, despite my protests, and checked over the growing egg on my head. I looked down at the wet marks on my jeans. Adam smiled, removed his jacket and tied it around my waist. "Come on, let's get you home." He put an arm around me, guiding me from the diner. I heard someone call my name, and looked up, to be temporarily blinded by several camera flashes.

"Oh shit, paps." Adam growled. He pulled his phone from his pocket and pushed a button, a speed dial number. "Yeah, need an extraction, right now," he said before disconnecting the call and turning to me. "Sorry, we might have to cut this short." He sounded sad for some reason.

"Yeah, I guessed as much." The cameras continued to flash, and paps called out irrational questions like *"How long have you been with Adam?"* Or, *"Did you meet on the set?* "And, *"What's it like knowing his reputation as a playboy?"*

The paps continued to harass us as we were rescued by four burly guys with earpieces, and stern looks behind their aviator-style sunglasses. We were hurriedly ushered into a dark-tinted car.

"I'm sorry, they've got your scent now, they'll harass you for a story.". Adam spoke with regret while he sat next to me on the backseat of the car, and looked through the window at the passing paps.

Oh... goodie, just what I need!

Fuck. My. Life.

Chapter Seven.

The car pulled up outside my apartment building, Adam climbed out before I could open the door, and opened it for me. I was surprised, and stared at his offered hand in a moments confusion before accepting it. I wasn't expecting him to be such a gentleman. He gently helped me from the car, and I felt the warmth of his hand on the small of my back.

"What number?" he asked as we walked up to the security door.

"Three C," I answered while sliding the front door key into the lock. Adam followed me in, and walked up the three flights of stairs, his hand still warm on the small of my back. I felt tingles rushing up and down my body as his hand shifted with each step up. We stopped at the landing of my floor. I could see my door two down on the left. Adam slid his hand from the small of my back to my side, pulling me against him. My breath caught as I felt his hard, muscular body against mine. His warmth seeping through the tee-shirt he wore. I could smell his cologne, sweet, but spicy and so very manly. I couldn't help but take a sneaky sniff as he pulled me to his side, my own arm going around his waist. I didn't want to leave his side as we stopped at my door.

"Well, this is me." I felt slightly awkward. I stepped away from his arm, and reached into my handbag for my apartment key.

"Melinda," Adam spoke from behind me.

I glanced at him shyly. His sunglasses were perched atop his baseball cap, and his green eyes sparkled with desire. His gaze fixed on my lips before flicking back to my eyes. He eased me around to face him, and pressed me against the wall. His head lowered, and his lips smashed against mine, tongue sliding over, and plumping them as he kissed me silly.

My heart raced, my body tingled with delicious sensations I'd not felt for such a long time. My hands found his chest before sliding around his shoulders, holding him to me in a passionate embrace as my leg lifted and curled around his. I felt something hard press against my stomach. My face heated on realising exactly what was poking me as he continued his sensual assault on my mouth, his tongue sliding between my lips and dancing erotically with my tongue. I moaned softly as his hands slid up my shoulders to tangle his fingers into my hair. It was pure magic what he was doing to me.

Me.

A blonde, fat-but-not-obese British girl who had become a five-second fool on the internet.

I was being kissed, very passionately, by a rich movie star! This was the kind of stuff which happened in movies, or romance novels, not to below-average girls like me. I was waiting for the spell breaker.

It happened not three seconds later when my front door was flung open.

"Melinda, is that you? Oh. My GOD!" The very un-masculine squeal was courtesy of Zane, who continued squealing like a little girl. He was a big fan of Adam's work, especially when he'd played a gay doctor in *Bedside Manner*. It was also one of Zane's favourite *chick flicks*. Adam pulled away quickly, my face heated with embarrassment, and I looked away.

"Oh, my god, oh, my god, *omigod* it's *you!* Oh, Mr. Jacobs, I'm such a big fan, I *loved* you in *Bedside Manner*. It's like my favourite film of all time. I'm totally fangirling right now." Zane began to fan himself with his hands, hyperventilating with excitement.

I could tell Adam was feeling uncomfortable at being caught out.

"Zane, sweetie, can we, uh, get a minute?" I asked, my heartbeat still pounding in my chest from both the impromptu make-out session, and Zane's terrible timing.

"Huh, what? Oh… *oh!*" he suddenly realised what he'd interrupted. "Of course, I'll uh, be right inside." He slipped back into our apartment, and closed the door. I pressed my fingertips to my lips as Adam turned back to me.

"Sorry," I mumbled, feeling embarrassment wash over me. "I probably should go." He looked at me, his green eyes piercing in their desire.

"I'd like to see you again." He spoke so softly I wasn't sure I'd heard him.

"I… I'd like that."

He smiled, and leaned forward to kiss me again. I still couldn't figure out one thing though: Why me? His lips pressed against mine in a more sedate kiss this time.

"I'm a bit busy with filming this week, but I'll give you a call." He smiled, causing the butterflies which had taken up residence in my stomach, to flutter around madly.

I nodded, unable to speak as I turned, and eased the door to my apartment open.

I felt the puff of his warm breath against my neck before I heard his whispered words, "Goodnight, Melinda."

I watched as he walked down the hall, his hands in his pockets, and a swagger in his step.

"Goodnight, Adam," I whispered back.

I pushed the door open, toppling Zane who had been holding a glass to the door, pressing his ear against it, and trying to eavesdrop on our conversation.

"Zane, what the fuck?" I said while helping him up.

"Oh, my fucking GOD! Melinda was that *Adam Jacobs?*" he asked me, scrambling to his feet.

"Uh, maybe." I said, trying not to look like I was lying and failing miserably.

"No, no, no, no! You do not lie to me missy!" Zane said, putting his hands on his hips and looking all prissy at me. "You tell me right now, young lady who that delectable man was, or all bets are off!" he held up his phone, and I could see the rat bastard had taken a sneaky pic of us canoodling in the hall. The little prick must have silenced the camera click sound

"Adam Jacobs." I mumbled.

"I'm sorry…" Zane said, cupping his hand to his ear. "I didn't hear that."

I scowled at the little bastard. "It was Adam fucking Jacobs, all right?"

Zane squealed with delight. "I knew it! I knew it, knew it, knew it!" he danced around, twirling for a good minute until he stopped and dramatically pointed at me. "Details!"

"No… no, no, no, no, *no!*" I held my hands up and shook my head, I was not wanting to share the intimate details of my day with my gay roomie.

"Oh, yes, yes, yes, yes, yes, YES!" he cried, reaching forward with the speed of a striking snake and snagging my wrist.

I groaned as he tugged me to the sofa and pulled me onto the soft cushions. I was exhausted, emotionally and physically. "Zane," I moaned.

"Uh-uh, cupcake, you are going to spill. Your boyfriend gave me a fangirl attack when I saw him standing there."

"He's not my boyfriend." I reached up and ran my hand through my messy hair.

"Oh really, did I miss something? You know, because the tonsil hockey thing was kinda cute, and a dead giveaway."

"It was one kiss!"

"One that led to a major make-out sesh. And did he kiss you buh-bye? Did he ask to see you again?"

I sighed, knowing Zane wasn't going to let up until he knew the truth. The bugger was a bloodhound when it came to the juiciest of gossip.

"Yes, and yes." I slumped in my seat.

Zane squealed and pressed his fingers over his grinning lips. "Oh, My GOD! Melinda, this is so big, so damned huge, did he rub himself against you, was he hard? Oh my god, I bet he was hung like an elephant."

"Ugh! Zane! Really?" I griped. "I really don't want to think about it."

"But, he did say he wanted to see you again, right?"

I nodded.

"When?" he prodded.

"I don't know, he said he'd call me, and he's busy with filming this week."

"Ooh…" Zane's expression turned from excitement to a scowl.

"What?" I asked, leaning forward, worry gnawing at my stomach.

"That's man-speak honey." He frowned as he shook his head sadly.

"What do you mean?" The worry-ball grew.

"Well, when he says he's busy, that's not a good sign."

I shook my head. "But, he took me out for coffee." I glanced down to find I still had his jacket tied around my waist.

"In a public place?" Zane asked.

"Yeah, and it was going great until we were noticed by the paparazzi, who hounded us."

"Oh sweetie, I think it might have been a publicity thing." Zane said sadly. He pulled me into his arms. "I'll never watch another of his shitty movies again."

"Great, just great," I muttered, getting up off the sofa. It seemed I'd been played for a few extra minutes of fame for Adam Jacobs. Well…

Fuck. My. life.

Chapter Eight.

"Just who is Adam's Jacobs' new mystery woman you might ask? Well, here at Entertainment Insider we have the inside scoop!"

I sat up in bed, the noise from the television bringing me out of my misery-induced slumber.

I pulled the covers off and padded out to the living room where Zane was watching the flickering images. There I was, in all my awkward glory. My high-school photo. Braces, bad, scraggly hair and the horrid curse of acne. The image changed to me working in the bookstore

"Melinda Whittaker is a small-town girl from England, who works in a second-hand bookstore. Her first foray into show business was where she met Hollywood superstar Adam Jacobs after an incident on the set, where she destroyed part of a scene."

The video of my graceless fall played out. "Oh, my god," I whispered, my face flushing hot with shame again.

"The next evening, Entertainment Insider was able to capture the pair on an intimate evening out at a local diner."

The video changed to the diner, where it did indeed look like we were enjoying an intimate moment together, until the waitress appeared.

"The evening took a turn for the worse, however, when Miss Whittaker wore the coffee." The presenter chuckled. *"Maybe someone should tell the Brit how to drink coffee!"*

Chuckles came from the crew in the background of the show. Mortified I walked around, and flopped down on the couch beside Zane. He put his arm around me and kissed my cheek.

"When we asked Adam Jacobs' manager to comment on the blossoming relationship, he returned our emails stating, 'Adam Jacobs is not romantically involved with anyone right now. He is dedicated to his filming commitments.' So, it looks like Adam Jacobs was taking her out on a pity date. Makes sense, she's not his usual type. In the past, Adam has been seen dating models, and other superstar actresses, we doubt he'd ever lower himself to run with the common girls."

"My life is over." I grumbled as Zane changed the channel to a rerun of *The Simpsons*.

"Oh sweetie, it's not over. This will all blow over in a few days, a week, tops." He hugged me tight. "You just gotta roll with the punches, let this make you stronger."

"I need tequila." I pushed myself up off the couch, and headed to the cupboard in the kitchen which held our booze.

"Or, you could drink yourself into a stupor," Zane muttered.

I opened the cupboard to find the bottle gone. "Zane, where's my tequila?"

"You drank it the other night, along with the Vodka, and a third of the bourbon."

"But I hate bourbon," I muttered, while searching for something to drink, and numb the pain.

"Honey, when you're that drunk, you'd drink paint thinner."

I sighed, abandoning my search for alcohol, pain numbing alcohol. I didn't really want the drink, nor did I want to end up like Aunt Maisy, who went through husbands like bottles of cheap liquor, and *then* went through the bottles of cheap liquor after each husband had left her.

"You know what? I have work tomorrow, so I'm going to go curl up in bed and read a trashy book on my Kindle." I strode purposefully back through the living room.

"Good idea, go rest your weary buns, sweetie. Then tomorrow, get all prettied up and look fab-u-lous for work. Don't worry about what anyone says, you are beautiful, you are powerful, and ain't no power in the 'verse can stop you!'"

"Geek!" I called, as I walked down the short hall to my bedroom, rolling my eyes at the *'Firefly'* reference.

"Nerd!" he retorted.

I snuggled in bed, the light from my Kindle illuminating my face as I read a very trashy story until I started to doze off, and the kindle fell back and whacked the small bump where I'd hit the porcelain sink in the diner. Stars flashed before my eyes as the pain throbbed angrily.

"Ah, fuck!" I moaned. "Bollocks, shit, bugger crap, shite!" I let loose the profanity as I rubbed the sore spot. "Bollocks to this." I tossed the Kindle on my nightstand, rolled over and closed my eyes, letting sleep take me away to a safe place.

***

Soft, orchestral music floated around me. I was dancing with someone. My partner towered over me, so my head barely reached the base of his neck. His hands were warm and his scent spicy and masculine. One of his hands firmly clasped mine, and the other pressed against the small of my back. We danced around the parquetry of the dancefloor. I felt soft lips press against the top of my head, and I looked up to be met with a pair of beautiful green eyes. Adam Jacobs' green eyes. His sweet lips curled up at the edges, giving me a delicious smile.

"Melinda." His voice deep, and gravelly caused my body to tremble with lust, and my lady bits melt into a pool of desire at my core. He leaned down and kissed me, his tongue simulating the sinful things, the desire in his eyes promised me he'd do when we were alone. Oh God, I wanted him!

I moaned softly as his hands travelled to the back of my dress, and he pulled the strings binding me to the silky confines. It fell to the ground as we stopped dancing. The music still playing as he artfully undressed me, his mouth seeking soft skin, lips pressing against my neck, before trailing down to my shoulders. His hands slipped over the front of my dress, drawing the bodice down, exposing my naked body. I gasped, as I felt his fingers slide over the heated flesh of my breasts, nipples hardening as he plucked at them. He moved, grinding himself against my ass. I could feel him hard and ready for me through the layers of skirts I wore.

He pulled back with a lustful growl, his powerful hands tearing away the skirts, exposing my nude body to the world.

"Now we can show the world who you are," he said, stepping back and leaving me alone.

The room became dark, but for a single spotlight shining directly over me, and my exposed, naked body. I stood frozen in shock, stretch marks on full display for all to see. Then, the cameras began flashing. I screamed as I tried to cover myself, the flashes faster, brighter, more intense.

***

I woke to the loud rumble of thunder as another flash of lightning blazed across the sky, illuminating my room through the window. I gasped, breathing hard, and fast as the echoes of the nightmare receded from the fog of my mind. I wiped the sweat from my brow and turned to look at the clock. It flashed 12:00. We'd lost power sometime during the night.

I groaned and picked up my phone. There were several texts from friends, and two from my parents asking me if everything was all right. I checked the time on my phone, it was just after two am here, so at home, it would be about eight am. Dad was an early riser, liking to get a head start on the day in the Nursery, and check on his plants. Mum liked to snooze a little longer before she arose and started work in the Nursery's office. I called the home phone, waiting as it rang out, before I tried Dad's phone. It rang twice before he answered.

"Hello Poppet," he said happily. *"It's about time you called your old man. What's happening? Libby said there was something going on with you on the Interweb. You're not doing porn, are you?"*

I couldn't help but chuckle. My father was something of a technophobe, a mobile phone was as far as he'd go, leaving my brother to deal with the computer stuff. "No, Daddy, and it's called the Internet, not the Interweb." I sighed. "Just had a few things happened that haven't been the best."

"You're not pregnant, are you?" That was my father, always jumping to the conclusions that were the worst. *"Because if you are and the father doesn't take care of you…"* I stopped him before he became carried away.

"No Daddy, I'm not pregnant, I had a bit of an accident when Zane took me to be an extra on a movie set. It was videoed and put out on the internet, so, I'm kinda an online celebrity, but I'm hoping it will blow over in a day or two."

"Well, if you're sure. You know we love you, and you can come home any time. We miss you Melinda."

I felt tears prickling at the corners of my eyes. I did miss my family, especially mum's cooking. "I know, Daddy, I love you all too. I'm hoping I can get a few days off so I can come and visit you, not sure when that will be though."

"Well, let me know, and I'll book your tickets."

I smiled, knowing he'd bloody well do it too. "Daddy…"

"Melinda…" he said with a tone I knew would brook no argument.

I sighed again. "Okay, I'll let you know."

"Good. Well, sweetheart, I have to go, got some deliveries to get ready for. I'll tell your mother, and brother you called."

"Give my love to them both, Daddy. I miss you all." I wiped absently at the tears as they fell.

"Miss you too, Poppet, call a little more often, okay?"

"Okay, Daddy." I said goodbye and ended the call.

I sighed, my mind going back to the erotic dream-turned-nightmare. I wondered if Adam Jacobs was telling me the truth, or if I was being delusional about him calling me and arranging another date… if the first one could even be considered a date.

I was more than likely delusional.

Fuck. My. Life.

Chapter Nine.

I was being followed. One guy, who was obviously paparazzi, was walking behind me, lingering a few shops back, taking happy snaps as I hurried to work. I didn't bother with the bus today. My ankle wasn't sore, and apart from a slight bump and bruise on my forehead, I was bright-eyed, and bushy-tailed for a Monday.

I opened the bookshop, and flipped on the lights, ready to begin a hum-drum, *normal* day.

If only.

My first customers were regulars, a little old lady who devoured bodice-rippers like they were going out of fashion, and one of the geeky guys who liked our *Star Trek* and *Star Wars* collections. Today he wore a Mr. Spock T-shirt (A *Leonard Nimoy* one, not one with *Zachary Quinto* from the newer movies) with the caption *Illogical, Captain.* I smiled as I rang up their purchases, the little old lady giving me a sweet smile, and the geek giving me a Vulcan salute as they left. I headed to the store room in back, and picked up a box of second hand books which needed to be sorted, priced, and arranged for sale.

The bell jangled above the door, I sighed and trudged back to the front of the shop, a heavy box of books in my arms. There was a young woman in the shop, she was muttering and pacing in the entry.

"Can I help you?" I asked, with a friendly smile, as I placed the box on the counter.

The woman sneered at me. "Yeah, whore, you can help me. Stay away from him!"

"What are you talking about? Stay away from who?"

"My ADAM!" she screeched so loud, my ears rang. "You stay away from him, you English bitch, he's mine! I love him! We'll always be together!" she screamed before pushing the box of books to the floor. I jumped back, the books scattering as the box tore open on impact with the floorboards. The girl ran out, tears mixing with the mascara on her eyelashes to smear down her pretty face as she slammed the shop door so hard the glass cracked in several places and the bells broke, clattering to the floor. Several pages had come out of some of the older books, and I glanced down at them in dismay. Now I'd have to see if I could repair them, and call someone to replace the glass in the front door.

I picked up the books, trying to keep the scattered pages with the books they belonged to, and wondering about the level of crazy the girl had descended to. I set those to be repaired on the counter, and called Mrs. Phillips to let her know what had happened to her door. She asked me to organise a glazier to repair the door, and have a tea break to calm down. It was sweet, how she worried about me. She even kept a supply of tea in the back room for me, knowing how much I enjoyed it, preferring it to coffee. The television presenter actually got that one thing right, I really was a tea person.

After putting up a 'Back in 5 minutes' sign, and locking the door, I made myself a soothing cup of Earl Grey tea. I sat down on a wonky chair in the back room, and sipped the hot brew while I thought about my life.

Normal… Why the bloody hell couldn't I have normal?

There was a knock at the door, I ignored it, taking another sip of my tea and trying to push everything out of my mind so I could de-stress.

The knocking became persistent. I groaned, downed my tea, and stood. I deposited my empty cup on the table holding tea break supplies, and walked out to the empty store. A man stood at the door, hidden behind a huge bunch of flowers. I unlocked the door and invited him in.

"Delivery for Melinda Whittaker."

Yes, that's me, but I wasn't expecting anything." My eyes perused the beautiful arrangement.

"I just deliver them, lady." The delivery man held out an electronic signing machine. "Sign here." He handed me a small stylus, and I scribbled my signature on the touchscreen.

"Thanks, I guess," I said as he walked out of the store. There was an envelope stuck to the box the arrangement was nestled in. I pulled the envelope away and slid the card out.

Melinda,

I'd love to see you again, I may have some time tonight if you are interested? I'll have a car sent around to your apartment at seven to take you somewhere special. If you're not available, I understand, please let me know.

Looking forward to hearing from you either way.

-AJ.

I almost dropped the card in shock. He'd left his number on the bottom under his signature. I studied the beautiful flowers. My heart thumped hard in my chest, my body tingled. I bit my lip. He wanted to see me again, and it wasn't a fluke!

Then it hit me. He wanted to take me somewhere *special*, I had nothing good enough to wear for a *special* date.

The tight knot of worry settled in my belly again. I placed the card back in the envelope, and began to think over what I should do. I pulled my phone from a pocket, and dialled the number of someone who might be able to help me. If he could keep his fangirling squeal in check.

Twenty minutes later, I had called a glazier, but was told they wouldn't be available to come and measure the glass for another two hours, just before closing time. The door opened, and I looked up from trying to repair the fifth damaged book from the crazy-fan incident.

"Zane," I grinned. He eyed off the flowers.

"Oh girl, I take it all back. He's got it for you. How bad? Hmmm, let's see. Roses, lilacs, tiger lilies, irises, yep... he's got Melinda-itis and it might be incurable." Zane smirked. "So, where is he taking you?"

I sighed, as I slid the next page in, and hoped the light amount of glue would stick. "I don't know, only it's somewhere *special.*" I removed the card from the envelope. I'd already entered his number in my phone, and used a black marker over the number on the card to stop it from getting into the wrong hands. Like Zane's. I loved the guy, but he was dangerous when it came to fangirling over his stars. "So, what should I do?"

"Honey, if it were me, I'd have called him already and said - *Fuck yes, Adam Jacobs. Take me, and bend me over the hood of your Ferrari. Fuck me senseless like the bad girl I am.* But, that might be getting ahead of myself." He grabbed a pile of pamphlets and fanned himself with them.

"I don't know." I was still of two minds. "What if I get hurt? The whole world would be watching me take another catastrophic emotional nosedive, not to mention I'd become a social media pariah, more than I am already." I grabbed my phone, logged on to my Facebook app and turned it toward Zane. "I have seventy message requests from girls who have sent me hate messages, and a Melinda Whittaker hate-group has already cropped up, founded by none-other than Crazy Fangirl."

"Wow, crazy bitch alert." Zane scrolled through the public posts. "You said she did that to the shop door?" He nodded to the cracks.

"Yeah, she was an absolute nutter."

"Do you need a gun sweetie?" Genuine concern showed on his sweet face.

I grinned. "Nope, I have mace, I'll be fine. Besides, no slapper tart is going to take me on, I'd probably weigh more than they do, I'll just sit on them."

Zane laughed. "Honey, you know I love you, but you are far from fat, far, far, *far* from fat." He kissed me on the forehead, avoiding the slight bruise and swelling which had receded since this morning. "I'd say you were prefect, now let's see…" He tapped away on my phone for a few minutes while I worked on another book. "There, done."

"What do you mean, done?" I reached for my phone.

Zane smirked and held it up higher than I could reach even on my tippy-toes, which, like a child I was on in my desperation to grab it.

"I told him you'd be ready by seven."

"WHAT? *Zane!* How could you do that?"

"Quite easily, I found his number on your phone. *AJ* it's cute, I love it! I sent him a message saying you'd be delighted to accompany him tonight, and you'd be ready by seven sharp."

"You bastard, I was going to make a decision."

"Sure sweetheart, and bonny prince Charlie really is my type."

I groaned and buried my face in my hands. "What have you done?"

"I've started you on your path to happiness. Now it's coming up to closing time. I have a few calls to make, and then we'll be ready to get Cinderella off to the ball." He placed my phone back on the counter at the same time it beeped with a message. I peeked through the curtain of my fingers to see it was from AJ.

"Great, I can't wait to see you. There'll be a surprise waiting for you at your apartment." He ended the message with a wink, and an 'x.' It was sweet. I groaned again, feeling like the world was pushing down on me, heavy with dread, but lifted with anticipation of where the night might take us.

"Bloody poof," I mumbled behind my hands. He just had to meddle. And, to make my day, the Glazier texted me with a message that he wouldn't be by that day.

Fuck. My. Life.

Chapter Ten.

Zane and I caught the bus home, at his insistence. When we reached the landing of our apartment, there was indeed a parcel waiting. Several in fact, along with another bunch of flowers.

"Ooh, Pretties." Zane squealed like a little girl on Christmas morning as he dashed towards the boxes. "Here." He shoved the flowers at me before picking up the packages, and nodding to the door handle. "Well come on, these lovelies won't unwrap themselves," he urged.

I rolled my eyes in exasperation before pulling the apartment key from my purse, and opening the door.

Zane bustled in ahead of me, arms full of parcels. He laid them on the kitchen table, and began to unwrap the brown paper packaging. "Oh, oh my god. I've died and gone to heaven."

Inside a tissue-paper lined box was one of the most beautiful sapphire blue dresses I'd ever seen. Zane lifted it out with reverence, holding it aloft. It was backless.

"Uh, Zane, honey, how am I going to keep the girls in order?" I asked, knowing my boobs were not the behaving type without some sort of restraining order in the form of an over-the-shoulder-boulder-holder.

"Titty-tape." He said with a wink.

I swear I must have looked at him like he had grown two heads. "How the fuck do you know about titty-tape?"

"Darling, when you know as many transvestites, and drag queens as I do, you know a lot more than you think you want to know." He hung the dress on one of the knobs of an overhead kitchen cupboard. His phone beeped, and he grinned when he checked it.

"Viola and Perry are on their way to help pretty you up, so I want you in that shower, and scrubbed clean. Viola is bringing her waxing kit to groom the kitty."

"Oh, my god, did you seriously just say that?"

"Honey, I can say a whole lot more, and get away with it than you can, now go, scrub up your pink bits, make yourself squeaky clean for Mr. Sexy-as-Sin." He shoo-ed me away to the bathroom.

I stripped out of my frumpy clothes, and surrendered to the hot spray where I scrubbed my body with a loofah, and washed my hair until I was certain I was squeaky clean. I stepped out of the cubicle, and dried my body, wrapping myself, and my long blonde locks in a towel, before facing an hour and a half of torture in the name of looking sexy.

Viola was waiting for me in my bedroom, the scent of her hot wax crinkling my nose. "Hey hot stuff, ready for my torture techniques?" she winked. Viola was a beautician, and make-up artist who did mostly weddings, debutante balls, anniversaries and the like. She also worked for one of the popular drag shows. I hoped to hell she wasn't going to plaster the make-up on my face with a trowel. She lifted an eyebrow and placed a hand on my arm. "Hey, are you okay? You look a little pale."

"I'm okay, I guess. A little nervous." Yes, the butterflies were galloping around like they were at Royal Ascot. I started to sweat with nerves as Viola ordered me to lay down on a sheet she'd laid over my bedcovers.

"Flat on your tummy, Mel."

I lay down as instructed. It was only the second time I'd had a wax job. Normally I used creams or shaved, but I hated they often left my skin with a rash, and bits of hair still attached to my body.

"Okay, here we go." She spread wax, just this side of burning, over the back of my left leg and then placed a strip of material over it. She pressed down, holding her hand against the material for a second before she stripped away the unsightly hair.

"JESUS FUCK!" I screamed, as the pain of a million hair follicles crying out in the night blasted its way through my nerves. My eyes teared up, and I swear my children and grandchildren cried out in sympathetic pain as the strip was cruelly torn from my skin.

"That's one." Viola showed me the hair-covered strip.

"Bloody hell," I whimpered as she began the process again. There was a knock at the bedroom door.

"Did I feel a disturbance in the force?" Zane asked, trying his best James Earl Jones Darth Vader impersonation – it was so far off the mark, it was actually funny.

"It hurts," I cried.

"Don't be such a baby, how do you think we get through childbirth?" Viola asked, her one-year-old son was waiting at home with his father.

"Drugs, as I recall, you had lots and lots of drugs. Gimme, gimme, gimme," I yelped as she stripped the next one off.

"Jesus, you're such a pussy. If you think that's bad, wait until we get to the front and the pits." She continued to work on my poor legs until they were bare of any fuzz. They were also red raw from the heat and hair stripping. "This should help." She rubbed aloe vera cream into my pain-filled legs.

"I fucking hate you, you know that right?" I asked her as I turned over at her urging. She pushed my arms up over my head and began to apply the heated wax over the hair in my armpits.

"It's okay, I fucking hate you too." Viola leaned down to kiss my cheek. "Now, deep breath, and remember: this is all Zane's fault." She pressed her hand against the linen strips.

"Mother-*FUCKER!*" I cried out as she pulled hard and fast on the strips attached to my armpits.

Viola chuckled. "The things we do for beauty, and to get laid." She grinned as she pulled the next one.

Fifteen minutes later, I literally hobbled back to the bathroom, my blue fluffy-duck dressing gown wrapped tightly around my aching body. Every step I took, I mumbled a mantra. *"You all fucking suck, you all fucking suck."* But secretly, I did really appreciate everything they were doing for me. They were my friends, and everyone knows, your friends hurt you the most because they love you. Right?

I stared at the panties set, and the titty-tape Zane had left out for me. I never even knew I had these panties… *crotch-less panties.*

"Uh, Zane, I think we have a problem here." I called out as I opened the door, the crotch-less panties hanging off my index finger.

"What's wrong sweetcakes?" He rushed toward me with such drama, he could be a soap opera queen.

"I know I don't own a pair of panties without a crotch in them. Where did you get them from? And, please don't tell me they're yours from your drag queen phase."

"Oh, those aren't his, they're mine," Viola called from the kitchen.

"You're having a fucking laugh right now, aren't you?" I called back.

"No, I'm serious. Wear them, Mel, he'll go caveman on you." She came from the kitchen, and stood in the hall, arms crossed as if she wasn't going to argue with me on the subject of crotch-less knickers.

"Viola, I'm not wearing your knickers." I tossed them at her.

"But they're clean, and I've never worn them."

"Dah-ling." Perry, or Miss Periwinkle, as he was known in the Drag Queen circuit, smirked. "You do realise, with a dress like what Mr. Fabulous has sent, you can't exactly wear panties, right? There will be a panty-line, and that simply won't do. I've figured out where he's taking you tonight."

"Oh?" I crossed my arms, and glared daggers from Viola to Zane.

"Yes, He's taking you to a big charity dinner, you lucky minx." Perry grinned knowingly, blue eyes sparkling with merriment.

"Charity for what, exactly?" I asked.

"A children's cancer foundation. It's a thousand bucks a ticket, and all the A-listers will be there." Perry grinned.

I was going to a Children's cancer charity dinner.

With Adam Jacobs.

Without any panties.

Fuck. My. life.

Chapter Eleven.

I didn't recognise the woman in the mirror.

She was beautiful. It couldn't be me, I wasn't beautiful.

The sapphire dress was ankle-length, and looked like it was made for me. A pair of strappy-but-sensible heels were firmly on my feet, and Viola had given me a quick mani-pedi and painted my nails in a soft pink that almost matched the nails themselves.

Diamond and white gold earrings dangled from my ears, and a diamond and white gold necklace adorned my throat, the butterfly pendant settled against the dip in my collarbone.

My eyes sparkled beneath my natural eyelashes after Perry, and Viola, had attacked my face with makeup. They'd both agreed false eyelashes would detract from the natural beauty of my eyes. I'd snorted in laughter at the notion, but they both gave me a look that made me shut right the fuck up… *bastards*.

So now I stood, dressed to the nines, and it was almost time to go. Zane was keeping watch for a car from the kitchen window, which faced the front of the apartment building.

"Oh, my god, it's a fucking limo." He turned, his face alight with excitement. "It's a fucking *limo*, he came to get you in a fucking limo." He ran from the window, and grabbed me around the waist, hoisting me up, and jumping around with me. "Cinderella is going to get her prince tonight."

"Zane! Stop, you'll ruin her make-up," Viola cried. "And her hair!"

Zane stopped, and looked sheepish. "Sorry, sorry. It's just, our little girl is growing up so fast." He let out an unmanly sob.

I rolled my eyes.

"Hey," Viola chastised me. "None of that bullshit. Tonight, you are Madame Sophistication. No cursing, no chugging your drinks, if you gotta pee, make sure there's no toilet paper on your heels." She adjusted my hair slightly.

Perry approached me, holding something in his hands. "Now, the charity function your attending is called Butterfly Wishes. They grant wishes to kids with terminal cancer. So, I thought it appropriate you wear these." He opened his hands, and showed me two beautiful silver Ulysses Butterfly barrettes. Their wings were made of finely crushed glass which shimmered in the light of the kitchen's bare lightbulb. Each wing was attached to two tiny, delicate springs, so they looked like they were quivering, ready to fly. I smiled, they were beautiful.

"There we go, perfect." Perry slid each barrette into my hair, both in the bun.

Zane took a hundred photos, and was about to take another hundred when there was a buzz from the intercom.

"I'll get it," Viola said, as Zane burst into tears and wrapped his arms around me.

"Oh sweetcakes," he sobbed, almost hysterical.

I looked to Perry who smirked.

"It's okay," I chuckled. "I'll be fine."

"If he does anything, or if anything happens, you call us and we'll be right there," Zane sobbed.

Viola cleared her throat, gaining my attention. "Ahem, your date is waiting for you at the front door."

I smiled. "Thank you everyone." I hugged them each again. There was no way in hell I'd be able to look this good on my own, and even though my legs still smarted from the waxing, not to mention other bits hurt like a bitch, and my head stung in places from Viola and Perry's hairstyling escapades, I was grateful I at least looked the part.

"Go on, prince charming is waiting for you." Perry placed a brotherly kiss on my cheek.

I grabbed the black clutch purse which had come with everything else I was wearing tonight, and headed out, my friends waving enthusiastically as I closed the door.

I carefully made my way down the stairs, trying not to rush in my fluttering excitement at going out with Adam Jacobs to a charity dinner. I finally stepped down the last of the stairs, and let my eyes meet his beyond the glass door of my building. His eyes lit up, along with his handsome smile. The butterflies were again galloping around Royal Ascot as I placed my hand on the door handle, and pulled the door open. His hand quickly moved to the door, to hold it open for me. *Such a gentleman.*

"Hi." He smiled as his eyes devoured me.

"Hi," I replied. Yes, we were both very articulate this evening.

"You look absolutely stunning." He leaned in to press his lips against mine. I felt the warmth of his lips as they caressed me, the heat of his desire flowed through me, and was sent straight to my core. I had to be careful, remembering I wasn't wearing any panties tonight. I didn't want any wet patches on my dress.

I inhaled his scent, thank goodness he wasn't the sort to overdo his cologne. It was the perfect mix of perfume, and *him.* I moaned softly, and he pulled away, teeth gently tugging at my bottom lip. I wanted more.

"I wish we could keep going, but one, there's laws against sex in public, and two, we're going to be late."

"Mmm, yes, that would be bad for publicity - being late."

He gathered my hand and kissed it softly. He escorted me, arm-in-arm to the waiting limo, and opened the door, waving away the waiting driver. As he helped me into the seat, he lifted my hand, and kissed it again. From above, a whoop and cheer echoed down to us. A chorus of wolf-whistles reverberated off the old apartment blocks nearby. I looked up, and saw my three friends leaning through the window. Viola giving me double thumbs up, Perry blowing me a kiss, and Zane doing something utterly wrong with a circle of thumb and index finger on one hand, and stabbing through the circle repeatedly with the other index finger.

I shook my head, and blew them all a kiss.

Adam turned and looked up at them, grinning, he closed the door and entered the car from the other side.

"Neighbours of yours?" he asked with a knowing grin.

"I've never seen those people before in my entire life," I laughed.

Adam settled in beside me, and placed his arm around my shoulders. "I'm so happy you came tonight." He leaned in to place soft kisses at my neck, pulled away and gently took my chin between thumb and forefinger, his green eyes gazing deeply into mine "Tonight is a special night. We're going to a charity dinner. This charity is very special to me, and I'm glad I can share it with you."

I nodded, unsure what to say. The only thing coming to mind was probably the most appropriate. "Thank you, I'm honoured you asked me."

He smiled, again pressing his lips to mine in a sweet kiss that didn't lack passion. My body tingled with need, I wondered if I was simply feeling lust for him. After all, he was a gorgeous man, who seemed to be kind and caring, and for whatever strange reason, had decided he wanted to get to know me better. We canoodled all the way into the city, to the five-star hotel where the charity dinner was being held. I checked my makeup, noticing he hadn't smeared too much in our sensual make-out session in the back of a limousine like a pair of horny teenagers going to their high-school formal dance, or prom.

The car stopped and Adam climbed out, quickly moving to my side of the car before the driver. The door opened, and he held out his hand. Nerves caused my hand to tremble, until his fingers wrapped around mine, and he helped me from the car. Cameras flashed, and voices shouted at us as the Paps had their field day. I looked nervously up to Adam's smiling face, his confidence gave me a little boost. "Come on." He pulled me into his side, his arm wrapping around my waist. "I've got you."

Arm in arm, we moved down the red carpet, the limo departing to make way for another.

A shrill voice called out behind us. "Adam!" He stopped, I felt him tense as he turned, a mask of a smile on his face. A smile which didn't quite reach his eyes. He turned and faced the woman.

"Hello, Kira," he said with a saccharine tone that even my teeth found a little too sugary.

"I see you brought a little something extra," she sniggered.

Her date laughed heartily. I recognised him as Sean Milano, a comedy actor whose low-brow antics were favourites of stoners everywhere. You had to be high to understand the humour.

"I'm sure she'll provide ample entertainment for tonight." Kira grinned with a nasty gleam in her eye.

I instantly hated the cow. The paps caught onto the animosity between us, and snapped pictures like they were the last things they'd ever see.

I knew women like Kira. I'd had to deal with pre-pubescent and adolescent versions of her right through school, and the first years of college before I dropped out and came to the States with Asshole Ex. She was going to make tonight a living hell.

Fuck. My. life.

Chapter Twelve.

The dinner was exquisite, though not something I'd eat every day, and I couldn't even pronounce half of the fancy names for the teeny-tiny portions we ate. I'd kill someone for some fish 'n chips right now, Maybe Kira, yeah definitely Kira.

The bitch had been giving me the evil eye all night, and whispering to her cronies, other starlets who had gravitated towards her, and huddled like a football team planning before they got into the scrum. I kept close to Adam after dinner while he hob-nobbed with celebrities, and rich people, most of whom I had no idea of their names, what they did or how they fit into Adam's life.

There were a group of kids there, some looked like they would be better off in bed, tucked up with a movie and a heap of love. Others looked closer to normal, but the start of a hard, long road with, sadly, a literal dead end stretched out before them. I had been told by one of the Foundation's members, all the kids here had some type of terminal cancer, and were here to help promote their wishes in the hopes they came true.

Adam kissed me on the cheek before he stood up. I was chatting to the wife of a congressman, who wanted to visit England for a tour of some of the gardens. I was telling her about my parent's garden, our house was a three-hundred-year-old cottage which had been extended many times through the centuries of its existence, and upgraded to the twenty-first century. The gardens were beautiful, thanks to the devotion of my parents, and we had several trees we believed outdated the house itself. She made a note in her phone to visit when she had the chance, though I highly doubted she'd actually visit.

Adam stepped on stage and the music stopped.

"Ladies and gentlemen, distinguished guests and our special guests." He smiled and indicated the kids off to one side. "Tonight, we are here to raise money for the Butterfly Wishes foundation. A foundation close to my heart, and important to my family. Many of you might not know this, but growing up, I had a twin brother." Pictures were displayed on a white background as the curtain behind him parted.

Two young boys with similar looks and the same green eyes were riding bikes, playing in the mud, swimming at their local pool, and dressed up for Halloween as a cowboy and an astronaut. "My twin developed terminal Leukaemia. Despite the best efforts of medicine at the time, Aaron Jacobs, my twin brother, died six months after his diagnosis." Adam stopped for a moment, taking a breath and settling his emotions. "My father wanted to grant his son a last wish, but was unable to, because we simply couldn't afford it. Aaron wanted to go to NASA, and train to be an astronaut. It was his dream to be one, and go into space. Instead, a kind friend of the family raised enough money so we were able to join a NASA program to launch some of Aaron's ashes into space. A way for him to achieve in death, what he was unable to do in life."

The crowd was quiet as Adam continued. "My brother may not have been able to get his wish, but we have set up the Butterfly Wishes Foundation so others can. Tonight, we have some very special guests who would like to tell you their wishes. I hope we can make them come true." I watched emotion flood his face as he left the stage. I stood up, excusing myself from the table, and our company, and walked towards him. He smiled when he saw me. No sooner had he taken a step to meet me than Kira stepped up to his side, and slid an arm around him. She hugged him tight and said something to him. I was too far away to hear, but I saw the flash of a camera when a Pap snapped a shot of her affectionate kiss to his lips. I felt angry, I saw red, but I kept my cool. I had seen how he reacted to her on the red carpet. But here, he smiled, and nodded as if they were lovers. I huffed a little, then turned my attention to the kids. Tonight wasn't about me, and Adam, tonight was about them.

I stepped over to the kids, and talked to them, noticing that no other 'celebrities' had done anything of the sort.

"Hi guys, I'm Melinda," I said with a smile. The kids responded happily, having someone paying them attention obviously made them feel more important. I sat down, and chatted with them for a while. I learned, Denise wanted to ride a pony across the Rockies, and that she had four good months left before the doctors thought she would deteriorate. Ramone wanted to play one game with the Green Bay Packers, Lucinda wanted to meet Adam, Kieran wanted to dance with Kira Holsworthy, and little Annalise wanted to be a princess for a day at Disneyworld. I smiled as the kids chatted away. Kieran kept looking at me. "Uh, Melinda, were you on YouTube?"

My face heated. "Uh, yeah. I was. I was the extra who fell into a big bowl of punch."

"Wow, that's so cool! Can I get a selfie with you?" He pulled out his phone.

"Sure," I grinned, leaning in beside him. I smiled as he pressed a button and took the selfie.

"Man, it's so cool that I got to meet you!"

I wanted to make this kid's day even better. I scanned the room, and saw Kira still talking to Adam. The moment he broke away from her I pounced.

"I'll be right back," I said to the kids as I rushed after Kira.

I followed her towards the bathroom, losing her in the crowd for a moment, before seeing her bright skimpy red dress enter the ladies room. I entered the sumptuous room, and found her busily checking out her boobs before taking makeup from her purse.

"Ah, Kira, can I ask you something?"

"What do you want?" she snapped, venom dripping from her words.

Woah, bitch alert. "So, you know tonight is about the kids, right? Well, there's a young boy out there who would really like to meet you." I felt slightly nervous.

"Aww, and you want me to make the sick puppy better? It doesn't work like that, *extra*." She rubbed her nose, pinched something between her fingers from a little pill box, and snorted it.

What. The. Fuck?

"I don't go near the sick, I don't want to catch cancer."

I couldn't believe the stupidity of the woman. "Uh, you don't catch cancer, you stupid slag." I snapped. "It's a non-communicable disease which affects not only those afflicted with it, but their entire family."

"Well, why don't *you* go play with the sick children? Maybe you'll get something and die." She snorted with laughter.

I turned, and walked out of the bathroom before I was tempted to slap the bitch into next week, and smoosh the Botox to one side of her face, making her look like a female version of the Elephant Man.

I walked back to the open dining-slash-ballroom area and sought out my next victim, err, I mean conquest. Though I knew he wouldn't take much convincing.

"Excuse me, Adam," I sidled up beside him where he was talking to a stranger. "Might I borrow you for a moment?"

He turned and smiled at me, his eyes lighting up with genuine happiness.

"I'm sorry, Francis, my lady needs me."

I felt a little flutter in my heart when he called me his lady. I let him lead me away from the milling snobs who still ignored the 'special guests' for whom this night was for.

He found a space on the dance floor, pulled me into his arms, and held me close. "I've missed you." He leaned his mouth close to whisper in my ear.

"Really?" I whispered back.

"Mm-hmm"

I felt the warmth of his body against mine through the layers of our formal clothes. I wanted him, but I knew I would have to wait my turn, a young lady who had little time left in this world, needed him more right now.

"I'll tell you what," I whispered. "If you do me a huge favour, I'll do anything you want."

He pulled back, and gazed at me, his eyes sparkling with desire.

"Anything?" he asked, his voice deep and throaty, sending tingles to my core.

"Anything," I promised.

"Okay, deal," he grinned.

I smiled with victory.

"So, what is this favour?"

"There's a young lady at the table behind us who wants nothing more for her wish than to meet some guy named Adam Jacobs. I don't really know who he is, but apparently, he's really famous, like an actor or something." I grinned.

Adam chuckled and leaned his forehead against mine, the tips of our noses touching in an intimate way which sent delightful shivers down my spine.

"I'm so glad you spoke to them. I noticed you with them before, while I was trapped with Kira."

I smiled sadly. "Considering they're supposed to be tonight's special guests, I don't think they've had much attention."

Adam sighed. "It's often the way. Some rich people think they are better than everyone else, and it kinda ruins the night for those who these things are intended for, it annoys me." He gathered my hand and kissed it, then led me back to the table.

Kieran looked up, eyes hopeful. I smiled at him, my heart breaking for the poor kid. He wouldn't get his wish tonight because the one person he idolised, was a pure and total slapper. I stopped in front of Lucinda, whose eyes had become as wide as saucers.

"Lucinda, I'd like to introduce you to someone." I smiled as Adam pulled out a chair beside the little girl. "Lucinda, this is my friend, Adam. Adam, this is Lucinda." I smiled when Lucinda's eyes filled with tears of joy, and she flung her arms around Adam's neck.

He laughed, and hugged the little girl tight. I smiled, my eyes tearing up. Kieran was watching Kira as she swanned around, sipping champagne. I felt my heart breaking for this kid.

I had to tell him, I wasn't able to organise a dance with Kira Holsworthy. I shifted chairs, and sat next to him. "Hey, Kieran." I felt a sad smile on my lips. "I really tried my best to get Kira to meet you, but she…" I didn't want to destroy this kid's teenage fantasy of a friendly starlet whom he obviously had a crush on. "She wasn't able to do it tonight."

"Oh, I see." Kieran sighed, looking downtrodden. "Okay," he sighed, then paused a moment before looking up at me. "Melinda, would you dance with me instead? I'm going to miss my prom because the doctors think I'll be too sick to go, so this was kinda my chance to enjoy what I'll miss out on. A prom."

I looked at the poor kid. "But, what about your school? Won't they bring the dance forward?"

Kieran shook his head. "No, I'm not popular enough. The Prom organisation group is run by the popular kids, I'm not well-liked at school, I'm kinda a geek."

I smiled and placed my hand on his shoulder. "There's nothing wrong with being a geek, some of my best mates are the same." I smiled, stood and held my hand out to him. "Well, shall we dance?" I asked him. He gazed up at me and smiled, a light of happiness shone in his eyes where before there had been dimness and disappointment.

I caught Adam's eye as we walked to the dance floor, and winked. He winked back at me, while still talking to Lucinda. Kieran and I stepped onto the parquetry floor set aside for dancing. He looked down at his shoes, embarrassed.

"Everything okay?" I asked.

"I can't dance." He said sheepishly.

"You can't?"

He lowered his head and shook it.

"That's okay, I can't either, but you know what, let's just wing it!" I smiled as I gathered his hands, placing them on my shoulder and waist. "Okay, you ready?" He appeared nervous but nodded. "Okay, just move with me." I took the lead, and we started to dance in time to the music. I felt his feet step on mine a couple of times as we tried awkwardly to waltz around the dancefloor, his eyes on his feet. "Kieran, keep your eyes on me, you trust me, right?"

He looked up at me. "I'm scared I'll hurt you."

"It's okay, it's how we learn. We have to crawl before we learn to walk."

"And then, when it's time, we fly." Kieran said softly. I knew he was referring to the reality of his mortality.

"Yeah, then we fly." I said softly as we danced.

I noticed Adam and Lucinda had joined us on the dance floor. Lucinda was a slight girl, Adam picked her up and was twirling her around, her dress sweeping the floor as they spun. The music slowed, then stopped, and so did we. Kieran bowed like a perfect gentleman, and I bobbed a curtsey. Hand-in-hand we left the floor, and returned to the table to the applause of the room.

Kira smirked as we passed her. "I'm surprised you didn't fall flat on your face, dumb bitch." She muttered just loud enough for me to hear.

"Trollop." I countered, my good mood plummeting a few notches.

Even a good night could be soured by one nasty arse bitch.

Fuck. My. Life.

Chapter Thirteen.

The night ended as it began, with lot of cameras flashing in my eyes, and Adam ushering me to a waiting car. Once we were secured, the driver sped away. I was tired, but happy, and despite the bitchiness of Kira Holsworthy, I'd had a wonderful evening.

Adam leaned back in the seat of the limo, his arm reaching behind me. He pulled me against the side of his body. I smiled up at him as my body fell against his, my hand accidentally (*I swear!*) falling against his chest. I felt the puff of his breath against my hair before he pressed his lips against the crown of my head, his arm tightening around my shoulders, and holding me close against his body.

I felt warm, tingly, and comfortable against him; even better, his scent enticed me, his nearness thrilled me, and the strong arms around me made me feel like there was no place I'd rather be. I sighed happily, snuggled up this way, I could easily have dropped off to sleep as the car negotiated the streets of LA.

Adam placed a finger under my chin, and tilted my head to look up at him. His eyes were hooded, barely concealing the desire sparkling within.

"I'd like to kiss you, Melinda, but I don't know if I can stop at a kiss," he whispered.

"Then," I swallowed thickly. "Don't stop." I reached up, and pulled his face down to mine. Our lips crashed against each other, my body humming with need as his tongue slid between my lips, I moaned as he tasted me. He lay me gently down on the bench seat of the limo. The leather was soft against the back of my legs as he slowly pushed the hem of my dress up, and over my knees. I felt the hardness of his erection growing, as he kissed me. I nipped, and sucked softly at his lips as they danced with mine

Reaching up, I threaded my hands through his hair, stopping only when he pulled away gently. My heart thudded, and I wondered if I had done something wrong, something he didn't like. The silence was heavy as he looked at me, his eyes gazing over my body as I lay panting with want beneath him.

"You are so beautiful," he murmured. His lips appeared swollen from the passionate kisses, my little nips. He lifted his hand, and caressed the side of my face, resting fingertips against my cheek, thumb sliding over my own swollen lips as jolts of electricity zinged through my body, straight to my core.

His lips replaced his fingertips, which began a slow, torturous journey over my neck, collarbone, the swell of my breasts, and stomach; trailing over my hips, and thighs until he reached the bunched hem of my dress. I moaned softly when his fingers caressed the skin of my thighs, sliding up under the material. I gasped when his hand splayed out, and moved slowly up my thigh, his fingertips massaging the skin beneath them.

"Adam, oh my god," I whimpered as his hand reached the curve of my hip.

"Mmm, no panties?" He whispered against my neck, where he had been kissing seconds before. "That's a bit naughty, attending a children's charity gala without panties. Don't you think so, Miss Melinda?" His voice rumbled against my throat.

"Couldn't be helped, didn't want knickers showing under the dress. It would have been embarrassing." I gasped as his hand slid from my hip to my ass. His fingers squeezed, and kneaded the cheek. I writhed beneath him as he licked, kissed, and sucked my neck, paying attention to my collarbone before he moved up, kissing my jawline and claiming my mouth again.

I whimpered as he pressed himself against me, my body heating to a supernova of lust, and need. The man was driving me bonkers with desire, and I knew I was losing the fight not to shag him right there in the limo. Okay, who the hell was I kidding? I'd shag his bollocks off, then have them surgically re-attached just so I could do it again! It's amazing what modern medicine can do these days.

I felt his fingers slide between the crease of my ass cheeks, his sexy voice breaching the haze of my arousal. "Have you ever been taken here?" He whispered as a finger slid in to touch the pucker of my arse. I yelped, and involuntarily thrust my hips against him, my pelvic bone colliding with his bulging crotch. Adam grunted. I gasped, in embarrassment.

"I'll take that as a no," he said, his voice strained from the pain of the impact.

"Oh god, I'm so sorry, I'm such a clumsy idiot." My voice cracked along with my heart. I didn't mean to hurt him, and I was suddenly crippled with the fear that I'd buggered it all up.

Adam sat back, and studied me, the scowl on his face broke me even more. I fought the tears prickling at the edges of my eyelids. My body trembled with pure mortification, I was about to be rejected by one of the sweetest, handsomest, and kindest guys I had ever had the pleasure of meeting.

Oh god...

No...

NOT THE UGLY CRY!

"I'm really sorry, I-I understand if you want to end the night now, and don't want to see me again. Drop me off here, and I'll find my way home." I wriggled from underneath him.

Adam placed a hand on my shoulder, stopping me as my war with the ugly cry was lost. I felt my sinuses clogging up, the tears falling hot, and hard from my eyes to mess up my carefully applied makeup which had somehow managed to last the entire night, a true miracle. Viola did fantastic work, but no amount of professionally applied blush, lipstick, or mascara, could stand up to the power of the ugly cry.

"I-I," I sniffled, throat choking up as I tried valiantly to compose myself.

Adam continued to gaze at me, his face a mask of *something?* I couldn't see through the tears blurring my vision as they fell. I knew without doubt, I'd seriously buggered up every chance I had with this stunning male before me. I didn't give a shit if he was rich, or famous, he'd seen me as a person after my greatest cock-up on the set of a movie I didn't want to be at. He'd made sure I felt special, and now…

Now I'd ballsed it up completely.

Fuck. My. Life.

Chapter Fourteen.

"Melinda," Adam spoke softly, his voice tearing my heart in two again. Pity. Just what I needed. Not.

"No, it's all right, I understand. Please, just ask the driver to stop." I fumbled for my discarded purse, and one shoe which had fallen off my foot in our limo backseat make-out fest.

A pair of warm hands caressed my cheeks, soothing thumbs wiped away the falling tears, and a pair of deliciously comforting lips pressed against mine, stopping me in my tracks. Adam kissed the fear from me, I lost my fight completely against whatever resistance I was unknowingly holding on to, and surrendered myself to the passion that was Adam-Fucking-Jacobs.

The car pulled up at a kerb, and Adam's driver lowered the dividing window. "We've arrived Mr. Jacobs."

Adam drew back from my mouth, and looked toward the driver. "Thank-you, Phil, you can go home for the night now, I won't be needing your service until tomorrow morning."

"Not a problem, Mr. Jacobs," he said before returning the window to its closed position.

I glanced through the window, wiping my face with the back of my hand as I twisted still half-trapped underneath Adam's body. "Where are we?" I was unfamiliar with this part of LA, even though I figured this had to be his place. I still wanted to be certain.

"My apartment, if that's all right?" Adam gathered my hand, and pulled it away from my face. He pulled a handkerchief from his pocket, and cleaned my cheeks. I suspected I looked like I'd been chewed up, and spat out like a toddler's first sour drop.

Adam didn't seem to care. He finished wiping away my tears, and held the hanky to my nose. "Blow." He spoke sternly, but with a hint of humour.

"But Adam," I started.

"Shh. Just blow your nose, and we'll get you inside."

He seemed to know what I needed, and right now, it was to blow the ugly from my sinuses. I blew, my honking nose-blowing sounded overly loud in the car. Adam chuckled.

"What?" What's so bloody funny?" I snatched the hanky from him, and dabbed at the remnants.

"I had a vision of *Mr. Bean* blowing his nose." His eyes lit up with mirth.

"You what?" I smirked, but tried to look slightly indignant that he'd compare me to *Mr. Bean.* But, inside I was somewhat tickled that he was trying to make me feel better by comparing me to Rowan Atkinson. I pulled my skirts down as Adam moved off me, and opened the car door to get out. "Cheeky bugger," I muttered, trying to give him the stink-eye.

Adam's shoulders jerked up, and down as he struggled to stop his laughter. A chuckle escaped, and soon he was laughing uproariously. I couldn't help it, laughter as they say is infectious, and it certainly is. I giggled, then as he reached for my hand, I chuckled, and was soon joining him in a good old full belly laugh.

He closed the door to the car, and draped an arm around me, pulling me in tight against him as we laughed. Gone were my worries, and woes, as we walked toward two doormen who immediately opened the doors for us. My heart pounded with excitement as I realised he'd actually brought me home. His home!

"Evening Joe, evening Dennis." Adam nodded to the two doormen as he continued to chuckle.

"Evening Mr. Jacobs, Miss, hope you had a pleasant evening," one of the men said as we passed over the threshold.

"Yes, and hopefully it will get better." Adam kissed my temple.

I felt my face heat as we entered the foyer. The place was gorgeous. Fine black and white marble floors, not fake tiles, actual polished marble, led to a bank of two elevators. Adam punched in a code on one, and the doors opened to an art-deco style elevator car.

"Wow," I whispered as Adam pulled out a card, and swiped it through a reader. He pushed a button for the top floor, and pulled me back into his embrace as the elevator rose through the belly of the building. I lay my head against his chest, his hands rested at the bottom of my lower back, fingers gently rubbing over the top of my ass as he hummed a tune I couldn't identify.

The doors to the lift opened, and he guided me from the car, and down a very short hallway to the door of his apartment. He smiled as he swiped his card, and entered a code into a small keypad beside the door. The door's lock clicked, and he held it open for me, allowing me to step inside first.

I was amazed at the simplicity, but homeliness of the apartment. No wait, *it was the bloody penthouse*! Of course it was. Right this very moment, I was standing inside Adam-Fucking-Jacob's penthouse.

The lights of downtown LA glowed in the distance. I was drawn to the wide glass windows that overlooked the city, it was beautiful.

"Not as beautiful as the view I have right now," Adam said. I heard glasses clinking, and liquid being poured into them.

"What?" I asked, turning to see he was bringing over two glasses of something with sparkly bubbles. I glanced behind him to see a chilled bottle of something very expensive-looking sitting in a chiller of ice. Droplets of condensation were forming, and trickling down the frosted stainless-steel ice bucket, and on the two glasses Adam held in his hands.

"You said the view was beautiful." He smiled as he stopped in front of me, and handed me a glass. I hadn't even realised I'd spoken.

I looked up at him, his beautiful face broke out into a grin as he raised his glass, and gently clinked the rim against mine.

"To a wonderful evening, with a beautiful woman. I'm enjoying getting to know you, very much." He whispered the last before pressing his lips against mine, the expensive bubbly ignored for a moment while we savoured the wine of each other's lips. He pulled away, his eyes gazing deeply into mine as he brought his glass to his lips, and sipped. I did the same. The sweetness of the wine incomparable to that of his kisses. The man had such passion, such prowess, I couldn't help but think what he might be like between the sheets. I felt my cheeks heat, and tried to hide behind another sip of the bubbly stuff.

Adam gently turned me back to face the window. I watched the twinkling lights of the city as he moved behind me, and heard the clink of his glass as he placed it on a side table.

His fingertips slid up my arms, fingers going to my hair and unpinning it until it cascaded down over my shoulders, my blonde locks spilling over the fevered skin of my body.

I could feel the arousal building through my body again, the way he kept going, it would peak damn soon, and I wanted this night to last. My hair was brushed aside, and I felt the warmth of his breath as his lips met the skin of my neck, tongue sliding between his parted lips to taste me. I moaned softly when he hit a sweet spot, and licked with strong strokes of his tongue.

My body trembled with the need for his hands to touch me in other places. His fingers pushed gently at the straps of my dress, sliding them down my arms to expose my bare torso. Strips of titty-tape covered the girls. Adam stopped the descent of my dress at my hips, and moved his hands back up my sides. I moaned again as his relentless kissing, and licking of my neck and shoulders turned to erotic nips of his teeth against my skin.

I was starting to pant like a bitch in heat, arousal made my core slick, and throbbing. The stickiness of the tape abraded my nipples in a deliciously torturous way, and they poked against the material like some type of strip-club pastie, offering themselves as sexual sacrifices for Adam's fingers.

I heard him moan softly, his nose sliding up to rub against the shell of my ear, and I felt his erection poking me in the arse.

"Adam," I whispered. The glass in my hand was taken from me, and placed with its friend on the side table. I felt the loss of his warmth instantly, but sighed with happiness when it returned seconds later. His hands slid around the front of my breasts, fingers gently peeling the tape from my skin. I hissed softly as erotic sensations made my body sing with the wanton desire this man evoked from the female population obsessed with his movies.

My breasts now exposed, Adam ran his fingers over the swells, finding the nipples he plucked, and gently twisted them, making me moan, and writhe against his fingers.

"Oh, Adam... oh fuck," I gasped.

Adam chuckled, before he placed a kiss against my shoulder. A travelled south, down, down over my stomach, and under the folded cloth of my dress. I parted my legs, almost instinctually, allowing him to explore my pussy. His nimble fingers slid over the ache which burned along my pussy lips. My moans soft before now became louder, more urgent, as he stroked through the wetness. I slowly ground myself against his fingers, my ass rubbing against his cock, making him moan as much as I was.

"Fuck me, Adam. Please, I need it." I whimpered as his finger slid over my clit. I was ready to combust with the need for him to be inside me. It had been building since he kissed me in the limo when he picked me up from home.

The thought of him taking me tonight was a niggle in the back of my mind which grew stronger, and stronger with each passing hour. Each stolen glance, each kiss, touch, lick, and suck was leading up to what I hoped would be one hell of a memorable fuck.

Adam eased the dress down over my hips, it pooled around my ankles.

"On your hands and knees." His voice sounded hoarse. "This is going to be hard, and fast. I can't hold out much longer."

I heard the desperation in his voice, nodded, and lowered myself to the plush carpet.

"Shoes?" I asked.

"Leave them on, they are sexy as fuck." The nice boy was gone, now the sex god, I suspected he was, had taken over my sweet Adam. I liked them both.

I felt his cock pressing urgently at my bare pussy lips.

"Oh, fuck," he mumbled as he pushed inside me. He placed a hand on my hip, and another at my shoulder and thrust slowly, before he built up a harsh, and fast pace which left my body tingling, my mouth forming an 'O' as I cried out with pleasure at each stroke. Everything bad in my life vanished while he took me on the plush carpet of his penthouse apartment.

My fingernails dug into the carpet as his dug into my hip, his grunts, and groans of pleasure spurring me on as he took me doggy-style. My body burned with his touch, each thrust bringing me ever closer to my climax. I could feel his body, hot and hard above me, as his cock slid between my legs again, and again, to take its pleasure and give me mine. His hand slid from my shoulder to caress, and grope at my swinging breasts.

A few more strokes, and I couldn't hold my orgasm back any longer. I cried out, feeling the bubble burst into a million sparkly unicorns which raced over my skin with hooves dancing pleasurably with each step.

Yes, it was that fucking fantastic an orgasm, but then it *had* been over two years since I'd had a decent one. Adam collapsed to one side, pulling me with him, his body spent as I felt his hot seed slowly pulsing out and down, between my legs as he wrapped his arms around me

"Holy fuck, that was…" He panted, unable to articulate with how spent he was.

"Fucking fantastic," I finished. I stiffened, *his seed was running down my legs!* I wasn't on the pill. He hadn't used a condom. And I knew my body…

Oh shit.

Oh.

Shit.

Shit.

Shit.

Fuck. My. Life.

Chapter Fifteen.

Adam and I moved to his bed soon after. Laying in his arms post-sex was divine, better than a cup of Earl Grey tea with my mum's scones on a grey winter's day. We made love again, and afterward talked about our lives, childhood, favourite things, pets, simple pillow talk. It was something Asshole Ex and I never did after sex. He'd get his jollies off, fart, roll over and be snoring his head off two minutes after he pulled his limp dick out of me.

This was so much better than smelling the aftermath of Asshole Ex's post-coital gas.

Adam sighed, his eyes closing as we lay together in a comfortable silence. I drifted off as well, the light from the living room shining through the open door.

I awoke hours later, my eyes springing open when Adam slipped a hand around my waist, pulling me in tight against his naked body. I glanced at the digital display on his alarm clock, it was after three am. Holy shit, it was after three am, and I had work in less than six hours!

Slowly, so as not to wake Adam, I slipped from the bed, padding on bare feet across the deliciously soft carpet to the living room where my discarded dress, shoes and clutch purse lay. I quietly dressed, before slipping back into his room and kissing his cheek. He mumbled something in his sleep and pulled the pillow I'd slept on close to his chest. My heart warmed and ached for him, but I had to work, I had to go. I found a post-it pad and pen and scribbled a note explaining I had to leave and I couldn't wait to see him again when he was available. I put the note on the bedside table before I turned and prepared myself for what I had to do.

I had to do the walk of shame.

I left the near palatial apartment and stepped into the elevator. I panicked momentarily when I remembered Adam used a card to access the floor, but seeing as I had no problem getting to the elevator *from* the floor, I hoped and prayed I wouldn't need the card to go to the ground floor. I held my breath as I pushed the button. The doors closed and soft elevator music played as I blew out the breath I'd been holding. The elevator descended to ground level as I wondered how the heck I was going to get back to my apartment, I didn't even know where exactly I was.

I stepped out of the elevator and hurried through the grand foyer. The two doormen noticed me coming, one smirked, the other grinned.

"Morning, Miss," one greeted me with a tip of his cap.

"Um, good morning. Can someone call me a cab please? I don't know the address here."

"Of course, one moment," the taller one said, pulling out a cell phone.

I stood under the awning at the front door while the cab was ordered, the two doormen standing guard eyed me. I must have looked a fright, my boobs were sagging, due to the lack of tape, my dress was rumpled, hair and makeup a mess. Thankfully, the cab wasn't long in arriving, and as I slid inside and reached to close the door, I could have sworn I heard the click of a phone camera, but it could have been my imagination.

I gave the cabbie my address and within twenty minutes, I was paying the man the exorbitant fare for my late-night ride home.

I looked up to my apartment's kitchen window, noticing the lights in the kitchen were off, but the blue flickering glow told me the telly was still on in the living area. I shook my head as I walked up to the security door and entered. Adam wasn't far from my mind. I knew he had to be on set today, it wasn't going to be easy for him to find time this week to spend with me, but I was grateful things between us were fine. Hell, they were better than fine. From my point of view, they were fan-fucking-tastic. My heels dangled in my hand as I stepped on tired feet and climbed the three flights of steps which led to my own bed.

And, the Spanish Inquisition.

The minute I stepped through the door, it began. Zane slammed his fists on his hips and smirked at me. "And just where the fuck have you been, young lady? I bet you gave it up all night long for your sweet Adam. Bitch, I'm *so* fucking jealous!" Zane bounced up and down in a very over-the-top gay imitation of Tom Cruise on *Oprah*. Perry sat in one armchair swirling a glass of red wine in his hand, nodding sagely. Viola was curled up on the other armchair. She yawned and stretched. Blinking, she gazed at me.

"Oh. My. God. Girl, you are rocking the "I just got fucked by a Superstar' look!" Viola grinned.

I groaned and rubbed my eyes.

"Come on, bi-yatch tell us all about it. Was he hung, did he treat you good? Was he dynamite in the sack? Don't leave a sister hanging girlfriend!" Zane flopped down on the couch and patted the vacant seat beside him.

I rubbed the back of my neck, I wasn't ready to divulge anything yet, it was too soon, too fresh, too arousing to think about the way he had touched me.

"Ugh, really? How about in the morning when I've had some sleep, or later tonight after work? I'm shagged, literally and figuratively." I dropped my heels to the floor and flopped down beside Zane.

"Oh sweetie, he did you good," Zane grinned. "I can smell the sexual aroma on you from here."

"You're right beside me, you knob-head." I punched him lightly on the arm.

Viola smiled tiredly. "We sat up all night watching his movies waiting for you. You gotta give us something!"

I sighed. "All right, we kissed and made out a bit in the limo."

"Ooh, like a high-school prom date! Sexy!" Viola leaned forward, her elbows resting on knees, and chin resting on her hands. She listened raptly, the boys also leaning in to hear the details of the Gala.

"Wow, that Kira, what a bitch, like seriously. I always thought she was so nice, but damn," Zane scowled.

I yawned, my body finding the wall and hitting it hard. "Okay, I'm done, going to bed." I pushed myself up off the couch and bid everyone goodnight.

Zane stood and threw his arms around me. "Sweetie, I'm so proud of you, you're finally moving on from the asshole. And you got some fine taste too!"

I smiled.

Viola and Perry stood and hugged me, wishing me a good night. I thanked them again for their help in making me look, and feel, like a princess.

"Oh darling, that's because you are a princess." Perry smiled as he air-kissed each cheek.

"I'll never be a queen like you, Perry." I winked.

"That's damn straight, gorgeous." He winked back at me. "But, between you and me," he whispered, "it's more fun being a princess!"

"I'll see you at your next show, have a good day." I blew him a kiss when he moved to wait for Viola to say her goodbyes.

I climbed into bed, exhausted, but woke up refreshed and happy; the post-sex glow still burning brightly as I showered and dressed for work after sending a message to Adam, wishing him a good morning and explaining I had to work, and was sorry I wasn't there to wake up beside him.

I caught the bus, noticing people were looking at me curiously, gazing over their newspapers. Or their phones. I wondered if they were reading the entertainment section, where the Gala had been covered. Surely, I wasn't *that* recognisable?

I stepped off the bus and hurried down the street towards the bookstore. I noticed Mrs. Phillips was standing out front of the shop, crying.

"Mrs. Phillips? What's wrong?" I asked as I ran up to her. She pointed to the shop windows.

'Whore!'

'Slut!'

'Skank!'

'Bitch!'

All those delightful words were graffitied onto the windows. I shook my head in dismay.

"Why would someone think I was a whore?" Mrs. Phillips cried.

I had a sinking feeling the nasty words weren't meant for her… but for me.

Crazy fangirl was my first suspect. I put my hand on my boss' shoulder. "I don't think this was aimed at you, Mrs. Phillips. I think it was aimed at me. Go and open up, and I'll get this cleaned up right away." I headed into the shop to grab something to clean the windows. Worryingly, I still hadn't gotten a response from Adam.

Fuck. My. Life.

Chapter Sixteen.

The windows sparkled thanks to my efforts to scrub the graffiti from the glass panes, and it had been an uneventful day. I looked up as the new bells jingled on the repaired door, signalling the arrival of a customer.

I smiled warmly at the well-dressed man who stopped at the counter. "Good afternoon, sir, can I help you?"

The man smiled, but it was the sort of smile a cartoon shark might give to an unsuspecting surfboarder before he takes a chunk out of their arse, or a leg. It gave me a twisting feeling in my stomach.

"Good afternoon, are you Melinda Whittaker?" he asked. I noticed the newspaper and manila folder he had tucked under his arm.

"Yes… and you are?"

"Douglas Kissinger, Adam Jacobs' agent-slash-manager. I have a few things we need to discuss if you and he are going to be an 'item.'" He used his fingers to make air quotes.

I didn't like him at all from that point. "Okay," I said slowly. "What do we have to talk about?"

"Well, for starters, this." He pulled the paper out from under his arm and opened it to the Goss and Glam section. A picture of me getting into the cab this morning was front and centre, surrounded by smaller pics of me during the Gala, dancing with young Kieran, Adam sneaking in a kiss on the dancefloor, the tension between Adam and Kira on the red carpet when we arrived. "Now, I'm all for publicity." He pointed to the headline. "But this… this is not good for Adam's image."

"Adam Jacob's new girl is all out of sorts!" the headline screamed. It was only a small piece, but it showed me exactly how the media could twist and turn the news to suit them and sell their papers.

Adam Jacobs has been seen with a new girl on his arm. The notorious playboy superstar has hooked up with an extra from the set of his new movie. 'A Duke to Remember.' The same extra who destroyed half the set, cost a half day of filming and became an overnight YouTube sensation with over fifty remixes of her antics being uploaded a day. Jacobs' new fling, a British ex-pat named Melinda Whittaker was seen stumbling out of his apartment building in the early hours of this morning, appearing intoxicated as she did the walk of shame. Jacob's Co-Star, Kira Holsworthy commented, Jacobs was always having flings and one-night stands with extras, and was certain their on-again-off-again relationship would soon go back to being an on-again one, saying she would love and support him no matter what happened. Goss N Glam believes Kira is a very forgiving woman, and can't wait to see their favourite Hollywood power couple back together!"

"What the hell…" I gripped the pages so hard they tore a little at the edges. I sat down on the stool behind the counter as I tortured myself by re-reading the article.

"Now, you see we have some things to discuss." Douglas pulled a few pages from the manila folder and spread them in three neat piles on the counter. "These are standard non-disclosure forms. You will sign them if you want to continue this farce of a relationship."

"Farce?" I glared at him, my body shaking in anger.

"Yes. Surely, there's no way Adam would really be interested in you."

"And why the bloody hell not?" I growled, my blood boiling with anger at this knob-head's insinuation that I wasn't good enough to be wanted by someone like Adam Jacobs.

He sneered. "Well, look at you. You're fat, ugly, and you speak a terribly accented English. I'm amazed anyone can understand you."

"You what, mate? I don't bloody believe this. You think just because you're as American as apple-bloody-pie you can insult me and make me feel like I'm some stupid arse Brit? You're a fucking knob, you are. Adam is a grown man and can see whoever he pleases. If he doesn't want me, then he can tell me himself. He doesn't need some bloody joker telling him what he can and can't do, who he can and can't shag." My accent was becoming more pronounced the angrier I became, I knew it was proving his point, but I was too far gone to give a flying fuck.

"So, are you after his money then? Make him fall for you, get him to marry you, then divorce him for his millions? If you want, I can slip in a hidden clause where you will get a sum of money for the duration of your 'relationship' as long as everything you do is positive towards his image. If you're going to continue, I need to protect my interests, and my interests involve Adam."

I glared at him as if he had sprouted two horns, goat legs, a tail and was brandishing a pitchfork. "You're a right prick, you are. I'm not signing shit and if you think I'm after money, you're dead wrong. So, pack your 'non-disclosure agreement', shove it up your arse, get on your bike and fuck right off." My voice was low and angry.

"If you don't sign these forms, I'm going to recommend Adam ceases this relationship."

That did it, my temper skyrocketed. "Anything Adam and I do is our own private business, nothing you say or do can stop him from seeing me if he wants."

He smirked, something which didn't sit well with me.

"Listen to me little girl. Adam's star is rising, and I'm not going to allow some London whore ruin his and my career." He snatched the pages from the counter. "I think our business is concluded." He settled the pages back in the folder. "You can keep the paper, there's plenty of them around." He turned and swaggered from the store.

I flopped back onto the stool, my heart racing, pounding hard in my chest as I felt the anger dissipate, but the fear of losing someone I was just getting to know began to gnaw at me.

I sent Adam a text, *Please, call me, I just had a visit from your manager.*

I waited all day, but received no reply.

Fuck. My. Life.

Chapter Seventeen

After the day was done, All I wanted was three things:

A soak in the tub surrounded by bubbles,
A large glass of alcohol, and
A call, text, even a bloody carrier pigeon from Adam to tell me either way where we stood.

I got the bath and the alcohol, but not the third thing on my wish list. In fact, with each passing day of that long-arse week, I pushed my way through paps and angry fans of Adam's who hung around the store, and began to doubt there really was anything between us.

Was I really stupid enough to think some rich, famous, and bloody good-looking actor could be interested in frumpty-dumpty me? The man could have supermodels and actresses hanging off him on command, what was it about me he could possibly want?

The afternoon edition of the newspaper had my answers.

It was all over the front of the Goss and Glam section.

The pictures spoke a thousand words, even though I only needed two to confirm my fears.

Kira Holsworthy.

The photographs were recent, within the last week. Adam and Kira were sitting in an upscale café, laughing, smiling, holding hands, then my eyes settled on the worst picture of all… Adam was kissing her. My throat closed up as I felt my heart break. Shattering in a million pieces. I felt the tingle of an ugly cry beginning to burn in the corners of my eyes and deep within my sinuses, but this time… This time there was no handsome man to hand me his hanky, to soothe my fears and tell me he was there for me, that he wanted to be there for me. The proof was right there in newsprint colour.

I sat feeling numb for the next ten minutes, serving customers as they came and went. The store had been busier than ever and I'm certain Mrs. Phillips was happy for the business. I couldn't figure out how I had been so stupid to fall for him. There was a nagging doubt in the back of my mind which said all the things in the paper weren't true, that there was a perfectly good reason he was with her, enjoying her company, *kissing her*.

The bells jingled and I looked up to see Zane.

"Hey," I said despondently.

"Oh sweetheart." He turned and flipped the sign on the door from open to closed, and locked the door. Thankfully the shop was empty. Zane slid behind the counter and helped me off my perch. He guided me to the back room and flipped on the kettle to make a cup of tea.

"I'm sorry honey, I don't know why he'd do something like this." Zane stirred sugar into his black coffee before he handed me a cup of Earl Grey. I held the cup in my hands and inhaled the scent. It soothed me a little, but I felt empty inside. I pulled my phone from my pocket; still no calls, no messages from him, but there was one from my mother, and another from my brother asking me to call them as soon as possible. For both to message me, it had to be serious. Surely, they didn't know about all the crap going on in my life? I knew I needed to hear the voices of my family, even if I couldn't be there to take comfort in my mum's arms, or my brother being an arse, a loving arse, but an arse all the same.

"That's odd, I have messages from home."

"Maybe they want to make sure you're okay? Did you talk to them about your new…? I mean…" Zane stopped, trying to figure out what to say.

"No, and it's okay. I did tell Dad about my day as a clumsy extra, but nothing about Adam. I guess it was for the best. My brother did ask me about Adam when we last Skyped a couple of days ago. He'd seen some news report on the telly and wanted my side of things." Zane gave me a sympathetic look as I dialled mum's number. It rang twice before she answered.

"Melinda! Oh honey, you need to come home right away." Her voice sounded strained, stressed, as if she had been crying.

I could hear the sound of wind as if they were in the car. Mum could never stand to have the car windows all the way up, she felt too claustrophobic. My gut clenched, something was terribly wrong. "Mum, what's wrong?"

"Your father's been taken to hospital, he collapsed half an hour ago, Robbie and Leo were doing CPR, he wasn't breathing on his own and then the ambulance came and got him…" Mum's words tumbled out on top of each other before she broke down in a sob.

"Mum, wait, what? Slow down. Dad's in hospital?"

"Yes darling, we're on the way now, your brother is driving. We don't know if… if…"

I'd heard enough. I jumped to my feet and grabbed my purse, my tea forgotten.

"I'm on the way to the airport now Mum. I'll catch the first flight I can."

Zane stood up and followed me out to the store.

"I'll let you know as soon as I can, which flight I'll be on, Mum."

"Thank you, baby, just get here as soon as you can, we love you."

"I love you guys too, and Mum, Dad will be okay." I knew I had no right to make such a promise, but I wanted to do everything to keep Mum's hope alive, she needed it to keep her strong.

I said my goodbyes, hung up and swung toward Zane.

"My Dad collapsed, he's been taken to hospital, I have to go home." I closed the shop and sent a message to Mrs. Phillips who was at the salon having her hair done.

I didn't think my life could get any worse, but it just did. What was it about Murphy's law?

Anything that can go wrong, will go wrong?

Fuck. My. Life.

Chapter Eighteen.

Zane dropped me off at LAX, I'd booked a last-minute flight at the cost of the last of my carefully saved funds and hurried through the departures section to find my gate.

"Good luck, and let me know when you get there, and when you're coming home," Zane begged as he hugged me tight.

"I will, and Zane?" I pulled away so I could look at him.

"Thanks for everything," I said softly.

"Why do I get the feeling you might not be coming back?" Zane frowned.

I hadn't even considered the possibility that I wouldn't be coming back. "I might, I just don't know yet. It depends on how things go with Dad, and… other factors." I tried not to think about my broken heart which had been torn to shreds.

Zane nodded. "I know sweetie, I know. Just, look, call me when you get there, I don't care what time it is over here, just do it, okay?"

I nodded and headed for the gate as the call for boarding the flight to London was announced. I boarded the plane, getting ready to settle in for a twelve-hour flight in cramped conditions, smooshed between a large woman and an already screaming child in the middle row. I waited until we'd taken off, put the headphones on and watched an in-inflight movie. And, yeah, of course, fate had to be a bitch and tease me, break my heart even more. *Modern Art* was playing. One of Adam's breakout movies in which he had naked scenes. Tastefully done though, all the good bits I'd gotten an eyeful of and other-parts-full, in the privacy of his penthouse apartment, were not shown.

I turned the movie off as he began to strip for the female actress portraying the artist love-interest. Unfortunately, the fat lady beside me was watching it on her screen and had her headphones up so loud I could hear every word of the film.

It was going to be a long-arse flight. I pulled my sleep-mask out and slid it over my eyes. My emotionally drained body was exhausted and I slipped into an uneasy sleep. My dreams were filled with the beautiful body, and gorgeous smile, which had broken my heart.

I awoke almost eight hours later to find the flight crew were serving dinner. My stomach grumbled right on cue. The hostess handed me a sealed plate of crap-looking pasta, but I was so hungry, I didn't care. I devoured it and the cup of weak tea they'd handed me. I was going to need my strength for Mum when I arrived home. My head hurt with worry for Dad. I hadn't heard anything after I texted Robbie and Mum to let them know which flight I was on. When boarding was called, my phone had been switched onto airplane mode. I didn't know if there had been any contact since. The continued silence from Adam pushed the jagged knife deeper.

I turned on another movie, an Adam Sandler comedy, without really watching or following the film. My mind was elsewhere, on my Dad, on Adam's actions and behaviour, on the visit I'd received from his agent. I didn't know what else I could have done. We were both interested in each other, both attracted to each other in a magnetic way, so where did we all go wrong?

I had to stop dwelling on this, it wasn't helping. I wanted to ugly cry again, and I hated it. I sucked in a deep, calming breath and focused on positives, even though the nature of my visit was to support my family, and to be with my Dad during his illness. I sat through the rest of the flight restlessly watching the film, until the airline hostess prepared for our descent.

The plane landed with a crunch and squeal of tires. We taxied to the arrivals gate and I stood. Along with other passengers, I stretched my weary muscles. The baby next to me woke up in his mother's arms and began screaming again. The mother put him up on her shoulder and cooed to the tyke as she gently patted his back. I smiled at the poor baby, he'd had a bad time, and had only really gotten to sleep in the last hour before we landed.

While we waited to depart, the baby burped, and projectile vomited all over the front of my shirt and in the ends of my hair. The stink of sour milk and vomit assailed my nose. My stomach turned and I tried not to retch. The mother was completely oblivious to what had happened as the line of passengers moved forward and she joined the flow. I looked down to the splattering of puke soaking into my shirt. Other passengers noticed and gave me equal looks of disgust and sympathy as they held hands over their noses and tried not to retch themselves. I sighed. This was turning out to be a wonderful, fantastic week. One I couldn't wait to see the arse end of.

I disembarked the plane and waited by the carousel for my luggage to arrive. There was a large area surrounding me, devoid of people as they waited for their luggage on the other side of the carousel. Yep. I was the reason for the isolation. I was Puke Girl. Able to keep a crowd at bay with a single baby's spit-up.

The carousel stopped as the last bag was claimed.

My luggage hadn't come through. I had no carry-on other than my purse with my passport and travel documents in it, and that was on me. I looked again at the empty carousel.

Great, just great. My love life was in the shitter, my Dad was in hospital after collapsing, I'd been humiliated by crudely written graffiti on the windows at work, a baby spat up on me, and now…. my luggage was missing.

Fuck. My. Life.

Chapter Nineteen.

Robbie held his arms out to hug me when we finally caught up. I held a hand up to stop him, pointing at the drying vomit attached to my shirt.

"Oh, wow, sis that's gross."

"Yeah, try wearing it," I mumbled. "The fucking airline lost my fucking luggage. Apparently, it's on a fucking flight to fucking Australia which left at the same time and from the gate beside my flight." I pulled out the slip of information the lost and found luggage department had given me after I reported my bag missing.

"Oh, bugger me." Robbie's fingers lifted to hold his nose. "That's some bad luck, ol' girl." He walked beside me, but a few steps away. "Look, let's get you a clean shirt before we get in the car." He veered towards one of the souvenir shops where they sold cheap I ♥ London t-shirts. I hurriedly changed and handed the tag to the store clerk where she scanned the bar code, Robbie paid for the shirt. My old one was dumped in the first rubbish bin we came across.

"Well, Dad's alive, but the Doctors say he might have slight brain damage, affecting his speech and movement. Despite us trying CPR, he was without oxygen for a couple of minutes." Robbie explained as we climbed into the van Robbie did the nursery deliveries in. "He hasn't woken up yet. Mum's been beside herself, and I've been barely able to hold it together."

"What's Gary doing? Hasn't he been there for you?"

"Gary decided he wasn't gay after all." Robbie sighed as he indicated to pass a slow-moving car.

"Oh sweetie, I'm sorry."

"Well, we can't all find the love of our lives, unlike some. How's that actor bloke you were telling me about, he treating you right?" He turned onto the road leading towards home.

"Oh God, no. Everything went bollocks-up." As we left London and headed towards the little village of Miltonford, towards my childhood home, I told Robbie everything.

I watched as his face turned from disbelief to anger, steering-wheel-white-knuckle-grip anger. "I'm going to friggin' kill the prick."

My brother, normally a pacifist who would never hurt a fly, wanted to kill a movie star for breaking his sister's heart. He's such a sweetie.

"It's okay, really, I'll get over it. Right now, I want us to focus on Dad." I changed the subject as the exit signs for our village came into view and he merged off the motorway.

"Mum's been sitting by his side since they moved him to critical care. Let's get you home, you can clean up a bit, you still smell like puke, then I'll take you in to see him."

I sighed. "Okay, but I need to stop by a shop first, get some essentials to tide me over until my luggage gets here."

Robbie nodded and pulled into the village's small shopping centre where I quickly stocked up on knickers, socks, and a new bra before grabbing a couple of pairs of jeans, shirts and a sundress. It wasn't fancy, but I wasn't here to impress anyone.

With my purchases in hand, Robbie led me back to the car. I headed for the driver's side, before remembering, the passenger side was on the left, drivers on the right.

Blonde moment - Achievement Unlocked.

Robbie stopped behind me. "Miss driving that much?" he chuckled.

I snorted, "You know you'd probably be right next to Dad in the hospital if I drove." I grinned. Yes, my driving was terrible, it was one of the reasons why I walked, or caught public transport.

Robbie laughed. "You tit," he teased.

I smirked and flipped him the bird. "Get in the bloody car." We continued our journey towards home.

I smiled sadly upon seeing the heather row hedge bordering the house lot. Beside it was the large field which housed the nursery and greenhouses, including a parking lot for customers, and a small office with tea-room for the few part-time sales staff who worked there. Mum and Dad had built it up from a back garden shed operation, with a few seeds and seed-planters, to the business it was now. Towards the back, in specialised greenhouses, Dad had a flower nursery, from which he provided local florists with beautiful blooms, including hard-to-grow orchid and tulip species. Some of the best florists in London sought out my father's flowers, and I wondered how badly this current health emergency would affect the business.

It was everything my parents and brother had. They worked hard to keep their pantry full of food and their business profitable. I sighed as Robbie eased the car into the drive.

"Robbie, what are we going to do?"

He killed the van's engine and sighed. I could see the worry in his eyes.

Who was going to take care of the nursery? Robbie and Mum didn't have a green thumb between them, and me? I unintentionally killed plastic plants on a regular basis!

"I don't know, Mel." He shook his head. "I just don't know." I knew he was thinking the same thing.

One of us would have to care for Dad's plants in the nursery while he was poorly.

I had a feeling the responsibility would fall to me.

Fuck. My. Life.

Chapter Twenty.

I'd showered, scrubbing the stench of baby puke off my body and out of my hair using Mum's top-shelf shampoo, hopefully she wouldn't pitch a fit, like when I was in high school and ended up stealing it, swapping it out for a cheap no-name brand which left her hair fuzzy - as if she'd stuck a fork in an electrical socket. Robbie was waiting patiently when I re-emerged, a cup of tea in his hand. He passed the remains to me, and I took it gratefully. It was so much better than the tea back home in the States.

Home? Was it really my home now?

I had Zane, Viola and Perry, my job, the apartment I shared with Zane. But what else did I have? If things had worked out better with Adam, then maybe I could have felt like it was still home. I sighed, my thoughts wandering back to him.

"You okay there, Mel?" Robbie asked. "You looked like you were deep in thought?"

I broke out of my reverie and stared at my brother. "Yeah, just got a few things to think about."

Robbie took the cup from my hands and pulled me against his chest, his arms wrapping around me in a brotherly embrace. He was hurting too, I could tell. Both our lives had taken twists, but through family, we would stick together.

"Yeah, I know the feeling." He held me close for a few moments. "Okay, enough bonding, let's go see the old man."

The drive to the hospital was quiet, both lost in our own contemplative worlds.

"Dorian was asking about you the other day," Robbie said softly.

"Dorian? Dorian Arnold?" I asked with surprise, recalling the high-school boy who had been sweet on me. He hadn't been so kind in his earlier years, pulling my hair and flipping my school skirt up to flash my knickers to the rest of the school.

"Yeah, Dorian, from school. He saw you on YouTube, said it was awful how people were making fun of you."

"Well, that's a change from calling me 'Smelly Melly' in front of the whole school," I huffed.

Robbie chuckled. "Yeah high school was terrible, but he's changed a bit I guess."

"He was a right royal pillock back then." I sighed, as I stared out the window at the clouded dreariness seeping into the blue sky.

"Yeah, well I like to think he's changed. His ex-girlfriend got hard into drugs, heroin or something, and lost their baby because of it." Robbie pulled up at an intersection, the clicking of the indicator timing in syncopation with the windscreen wipers on the van as a soft misting rain fell.

I looked up, there were small patches of vibrant blue, but the clouds had boldly begun to cover the rest of the sky with their greyness. A perfect fit to my mood. Robbie pulled out onto the main road leading into the village, past the old castle where we used to go hunting for brightly painted Easter eggs as children.

The great stone castle was hundreds of years old, older than our little cottage, but a testament to builders of the time. Weddings were often held in the castle ballroom, and once a month they had a farmer's market in the field in front of the castle.

The bloodlines which had once laid claim to the castle, had long since gone from the world, relegated to history, and now the local historical society took care of the grand structure. There was always some sort of restoration work going on, and I knew tours of the place were held every Saturday.

As a child, I had often let my imagination run wild, thinking that when I was older, one of the castle lords would sweep me off my feet and make me his wife, a fantasy I'd played out with my dolls in the sanctuary of mum's garden. That was years before I knew that there were no longer any lords, or pretty ladies, for this castle. Only restoration workers and volunteer tour guides, who were bored housewives. An hour's worth of orientation and history on the castle would get them through their tours.

Yet another dream shattered.

The village was quiet, almost sleepy. Except for the pub, where a football game was in progress on the large screen. The doors to the pub were wide open, and as we passed, I could hear the shouts and jeers of the local boys as they watched their teams go at it like rabid dogs over a round ball.

Robbie turned at the nursing home, and drove a hundred meters until we reached the hospital car park.

"Well, this is us," he muttered softly.

I felt trepidation at seeing my father, who was always so vibrant and full of life. Now he was at the mercy of medical machines which kept him breathing until the doctors were sure he was able to do it on his own.

"Ready?" Robbie asked me.

I studied his face, trying to see how much I needed to prepare myself before coming face to face with our father's mortality. I thinned my lips in a tight smile and nodded.

"As I'll ever be, I guess." I unbuckled my seat belt and slid out of the passenger side of the van into the suddenly chilled and damp air. Robbie clicked the lock on the key fob and the van's doors locked behind us as we walked towards the hospital doors.

The hospital was as I remembered it, cold, sterile and unwelcoming. Would it kill them to have a bit of sunny yellow? Maybe a cheery green instead of stark white and a poor approximation of robin's egg blue? The colour scheme itself was enough to make one sick enough to be admitted. The stern looking faces of hospital patrons and administrators glared down at us as we passed. A portrait of the Queen smiled regally at us, flanked by the Union Jack and another flag bearing the village's coat of arms, borrowed from the castle and claimed as its' own. The Queen's visage was a much friendlier and warmer greeting than the cold stares of old men in the portraits. Their soulless stares gave me the willies every time I had to come into this sterile place.

Robbie stopped at a nurse's station, and checked in. I rolled my eyes as the clueless nurse flirted with him. Yes, even I could admit my brother was a looker, but he was also very much gay.

Robbie nodded down the corridor, before he walked off. I almost tripped over my feet trying to catch up to him. We pushed through a set of double doors leading to critical care.

"They're only letting two people in at a time to see him. Mum hasn't left his side since they brought him down here." Robbie stopped by a door. On a small whiteboard beside the door *Mr. Whittaker* was scrawled in black marker, below was written a whole heap of medical mumbo-jumbo I wouldn't have a snowflake's chance in hell of deciphering.

Robbie knocked on the door and opened it for me.

My mother looked up from where she sat holding Dad's pale hand. I watched as she flew to her feet, her face scrunching up as if she had sucked on a very sour lemon drop as I stepped in to Dad's room. The beeping machines became background noise as I rushed into my mum's embrace. I dared to glimpse my Dad's comatose body as I held my mum tight.

"Oh, Melinda, you look terrible!" were the first words out of my mother's sobbing mouth.

Terrible? Really? You think?

Fuck. My. life.

Chapter Twenty-One.

Mum explained Dad's condition, which had remained unchanged since they'd brought him out of emergency and the small procedure they'd done to prevent any more clots. I all but ordered her to get something to eat and go home to shower and change. I settled in the chair beside Dad's bed, taking his hand and, as Mum had encouraged me to, started to talk to him.

"Hey, Daddy," I whispered, my voice choking up as emotions battled their way through my body. Fear, grief, sorrow, anger, disbelief, all those and more ran the gamut of my emotions.

"You silly old bugger, why did you have to go and have a heart attack, and then a stroke for? You wanted me home that badly you ol' duffer? You should have just asked me, I would have come." I sniffled as the first tears pricked my eyes and broke free.

"You're going to make me ugly cry aren't you, you old sod?" I shook my head. "I only ever did that for one other bloke, you know that? He's… he *was* worth it too." I sniffled, my hand holding his tight.

"I really thought he might be the one. Kind, generous, the sort of bloke I think you'd get on well with. Even though he's a big celebrity, he's real, you know? Happy to be around real people." I shook my head, as I sat there, before I noticed the tissues on the side table by his bed. I plucked a couple from the box before I blew a honking round of ugly into the tissue. The memory of my *Mr. Bean* impersonation in Adam's limo came unbidden, bringing a fresh round of ugly cry.

"Fuck," I muttered, tossing the tissue into the waste bin. "I got sucked in again, Dad. I don't know why it keeps happening. I

mean, am I really so dammed gullible that men walk all over me?"
I sighed. "Anyway, I'm thinking of coming home for good, there's
really nothing left for me in the States. Adam's not returning my
messages, nor has he called, or contacted me, in over a week.
Maybe it was all just a bit of fun for him, you know?" I pulled
more tissues from the box to wipe my eyes and blow my nose
again. "I thought it was more, the way he looked at me, the way
we spoke together after…" I shut up, even though he was
comatose, and probably couldn't hear me, I didn't want my Dad to
know what I got up to in the sack, or after being in the sack. "I just
don't…" My phone vibrated with a text message. I'd put it on
silent, though knowing hospitals didn't like people to have their
phones on them, didn't deter me from leaving mine on. You know,
just in case *someone* called. Yes, my broken heart was stupidly
holding on to a candle of hope.

I pulled my phone out and checked the screen, it was from
Zane.

"ARE U ALIVE?"

I cursed, realising I'd forgotten to call or send him a text
when I'd arrived. I stood and headed to the bathroom, my bladder
deciding then and there to declare it's requirement for relief.
Holding my phone in one hand, I shimmied my jeans down and sat
my arse on the cold porcelain rim. I squealed, my arse shooting up
off the porcelain faster than a Saturn V Rocket. "Bloody males,
who the bloody hell leaves the toilet seat up?" I dropped the old
plastic seat down over the rim of the bowl to protect my arse from
the chills.

I settled back down on the toilet and returned my attention
to the matter at hand – allaying Zane's fears.

"I'm ok, got in after baby puke incident, then had my luggage go on a flight to Australia, made it home ok though." I typed hitting the send button.

"Thank fuck 4 that, what u mean baby puke? And what happened 2 ur luggage?

I rolled my eyes, Zane was a serial texter, if he could shorten it for speed, he would.

I typed again.

Getting off plane, baby puked all over me, got to luggage collection, no luggage, it's on the way to Australia, hoping to get it back this week. Am in hospital with Dad."

"You're in hospital? R U OK? WTF happened?" The reply came back faster than I had imagined Zane could type.

I shook my head and chuckled. *"No, you wanker, VISITING Dad in hospital. No change, still comatose. Hoping he'll wake up soon though."*

"O FFS bitch U gave me a heart attack 4 a sec there. Important news! AH X got married 2 slut #2 and U had a visitor, AJ came over."

My hands shook so much, I dropped the phone. I watched it in slow motion as it turned lazily in the air, as if it were in an aerial ballet, before it hit the front of the bowl not covered by the old-style toilet seat. I swear I saw the screen crack as it struck. I tried to mount a mid-air rescue mission with my thighs as it bounced, but alas, the phone was in cahoots with fate, gravity, and whatever other forces in the world wanted to fuck me over, as it splashed into the toilet water… that I had just added to. I stared at the phone as the screen flickered in the mixture of water and my own piss.

"Oh fuck, fucketty fuck, fuck, FUCK!" I stood and turned to retrieve my phone. But the damage was done. The phone was dead the screen cracked and it had sunk to the bottom of the bowl.

"Oh gross, crap, this is so disgusting!" I gingerly dipped my hand into the toilet and plucked my phone from the uriney depths. Grabbing a handful of paper towels from the dispenser, I dried the phone, my jeans around my ankles as I attempted to turn the phone back on, hoping it would have survived the toilet drowning. The screen remained black. Nothing. Nada. Zilch!

I couldn't retrieve Zane's number, or remember his email address. I'd never put my contacts on the SIM card, I didn't know how to. I had closed my Facebook and email accounts due to the amount of hate mail and bitchy messages I'd received during my time with Adam.

Somehow, I didn't think a bowl of dry rice would fix this one.

Fuck. My. Life.

Chapter Twenty-Two.

After washing my hands and phone (which probably made it worse) thoroughly, I headed back to sit with Dad. Flopping into the uncomfortable chair my mother had so valiantly occupied since he was placed into critical care. I closed my eyes and rubbed the bridge of my nose in agitation

"Fuck,." I muttered in frustration. "Fuck, fuck fuck…"

"P-p-p-pop…pet, l-an…la-…" The whispers of Dad's voice floated to my ears. I closed my eyes, great, now I was imagining things. I placed my hand over his and gently squeezed his fingers. He squeezed them back. Wait! *He squeezed my fingers back!* My eyes flew open to stare into his.

"Dad…?" Hot tears flowed free and fell as I broke down by his bedside. I buried my head against the starched white linen of his hospital bed, his hand shifting and patting me gently on my tousled hair. I could feel the serious tremor in his hand as he gently soothed me, his voice shaking as he calmed me.

I didn't hear the door to his room open, but suddenly Robbie and Mum were there beside me, crying with happiness to see Dad was awake. We were shortly bustled out by the doctors and nurses who came in after Robbie pressed the call button.

"Oh, thank God." Mum pulled both Robbie and me in for a hug which threatened to break a rib or two.

We waited anxiously for the doctors to finish with Dad's check-up before his doctor allowed us back in to the room, ignoring the two people per visit policy.

"Mr. Whittaker is extremely lucky, most people his age who suffer what he has, don't make it. You said, before this happened, he was strong as an Ox, now he'll be as weak as a day-old kitten for some time. His motor functions should come back in time, but he won't be as able, or as strong, as he was before his stroke. The minor paralysis down the side of his face is typical, and will impede his speech, though we are hoping it will resolve with time." Doctor Foster looked over our little family, Mum was perched on Dad's bed, her hands holding his tightly

"Wo…r…k…." Dad mumbled, the right side of his face drooping like one of the bloodhounds they used for hunts at the local hunting club.

The Doctor stepped closer to Dad. "Oh no, Mr. Whittaker. I'm sorry, but you won't be returning to work any time soon. You have a lot of physical therapy ahead of you."

I glanced at Dad and saw his face drop in disappointment. I knew it would be hard for him after being so active.

"Don't worry about the nursery, Dad." I soothed.

"Yeah, Mel and I have it covered. We've got it sorted." Robbie smiled at Dad, and then me. "You need to concentrate on getting better, when you're back on your feet, you can take over again." He grinned as Dad reached over with trembling fingers and patted him on the knee.

"Goo…d…" It seemed like he wanted to say more, but his lips didn't want to co-operate. He sighed in frustration.

It was worrying, I'd never seen dad frustrated before. He was always so composed, even when deliveries went awry, or a staff member had to quit, putting a strain on the nursery's day-to-day running until the staff member could be replaced.

Mum smiled at us. "Everything will be fine, Gil," she promised Dad.

The Doctor took one look at Dad's face and frowned. "I think Mr. Whittaker needs some rest, folks. We've got a big day tomorrow, planning his therapy regimen. We want him to be ready to go home as soon as possible, we've found patients recover faster in familiar surroundings."

"When can we get him home, Doc?" Robbie asked.

"Well, depending on how he responds to his treatments and therapy, two, possibly three weeks, could be more though. It's all dependent on Mr. Whittaker's recovery, and we need to make sure he doesn't undertake anything which will cause too much stress."

Mum nodded, her hand clasping Dad's tightly. Robbie and I shared a glance, we knew she wasn't taking this in, she was off with the fairies, just glad Dad was awake. I noticed Robbie was tapping away at his phone, hopefully taking down notes. The Doctor removed a pamphlet from his clipboard and handed it to Mum.

"This pamphlet tells you what you might expect, though every case is very different. After the primary recovery period, Mr. Whittaker could have recurring problems with motor functions and speech, when he is upset or stressed. CT scans did indicate slight damage to those particular regions of his brain due to the lack of oxygen during his episode."

"Ok, so what do we need to do when we get him home, Doc?" I asked.

"That's a while away yet, but make sure he's comfortable and has familiar things around him. There appears to be little to no memory loss, as he did recognise you as soon as you woke, but further tests and time will reveal further information."

Mum smiled at me and gripped my hand, her thumb caressing my knuckles. I returned her smile and patted her hand with mine.

"As I've said, patients always seem to recover faster when they are in a familiar environment, people they know, routine." He smiled and rose from his seat. "I'll leave you all to visit, but I'll have to ask you to leave in about a half hour, Mr. Whittaker needs to rest."

"Doctor, I'd like to stay with my husband, if that's all right?" Mum gave the doctor a look which brooked no argument and the doctor smiled.

"Of course, Mrs. Whittaker, but please be aware of any stress."

"N...no...st….r...ess" Dad rasped out brokenly, he smiled lopsidedly at Mum.

Mum's eyes filled with tears, she leaned down and kissed Dad's hand.

"Okay, looks like it's time for us to go." Robbie pulled me up beside him and wrapped an arm around my shoulder. "Come on, Mel, let's go to the Pub, we have some catching up to do." He leaned in and kissed my temple.

I nodded. "I'll come by in the morning, dad. Okay?" Dad blinked slowly, one eyelid slower to respond than the other with the semi-paralysis to one side of his face. He grinned, but it was more of a one-sided lifting of the corner of his lips. I pulled away from Robbie, who followed me to Dad's side, and we each kissed him on the cheek in turn, while Mum lay her head in his lap. Dad's hand rested on her head, fingers trembling as he stroked her greying hair.

We left the hospital, my thoughts on my parents and their love for each other drifting to my own devastatingly screwed up love life. Why couldn't I be happy like them? Why couldn't I have a normal, loving relationship with a man?

Fuck. My. Life.

Chapter Twenty-Three.

The Pheasant's Nest and Hound Pub was bustling with the post-football crowd celebrating their win. Finding a seat to enjoy a quiet beer amongst a jostling, screaming, drunken crowd of smelly arseholes who were near-rioting with joy over their win against the competition from the next town over, was impossible. More than once I had been jostled, and three times my arse had been groped and pinched, so it now felt like a whole bloody army of over-enthusiastic grannies had come across me and mistaken my arse cheeks for my face.

We finally found a small high-top table and settled in with our pints. I savoured my first good swallow of beer. So much better than the American rubbish they passed off as ale. Like the *Monty Python* boys said, American Beer was like making love in a canoe… 'Fucking close to water'.

"Oh, bloody hell, that's good," I sighed and wiped the foam from my lips with the back of my hand. I know, real dignified, but whatever.

Robbie smirked, back on his phone.

"Ah, shite, you just reminded me, my phone died" I pulled out the dead phone, all it needed now was a proper Viking burial.

"What's wrong with it?" Robbie took the phone from my hand.

"I dropped it in the loo, *after* I went." I smirked over the foamy rim of my pint and waited for the reaction I knew was to come. Beer liberally sprayed the tabletop as Robbie spluttered.

"Robbie!" I chided him, holding my precious glass high in the air to avoid the overspray.

"Oh fuck, you are so gross!" Robbie dropped the phone as if it had burned his fingertips. He wiped his hands on his jeans. "My god woman, and you claim to be my sister? You're going to buy me a beer after that terrible shock I endured, and some new pants too." He took a stubby pencil from one of the gambling displays set in the middle of the high top and poked at the offensive phone which now sat in a puddle of spat-out beer.

"So, it's fucked?" he asked, poking again.

"Yep, royally fucked."

"How the bloody hell did you manage to drop it into the toilet, you twit?" He laughed at me.

"Zane delivered some news via text, and I got a shock."

"What?"

"Well, Asshole Ex is marrying slut number two."

Robbie's face softened and he placed his hand over mine.

"Oh Mel, please don't worry about that tosser prick. I'm glad you found out he wasn't right for you, I had a bad feeling about him from the start, love."

"Yeah, well I loved him, Robbie, and I thought he loved me too. It hurt, you know? I followed him to the US, thinking it was right and we would be fine." I shrugged as I felt tears prick my eyes. Tears for the asshole? "But no, he had to chase as much skirt as he could while he was working, I heard later, he was even shagging his secretary in his office when I came to take him out for lunch. Her friend covered for them both by telling me he was in an important meeting! Yeah - a meeting of his dick with her snatch!" I downed the last gulp of my beer. "Another?" I asked Robbie who was only half-way through his own.

He nodded. "Yeah, but this will be the last one. I gotta get you home tonight, and we've got work to do tomorrow, there's orders waiting and deliveries to make."

"Yeah, yeah." I pushed myself up from the seat and zig-zagged through drunken bodies to the bar, trying to avoid grabby hands, and leering lads drunk on piss, and high on celebrating their team's victory.

"Melinda Whittaker! Holy shit, is that you Smelly Melly?"

I cringed at the hated high-school nickname I had been stuck with for most of my formative years. I was suddenly grasped about the waist and swung around, I shrieked in fright until my feet were back on the ground. My 'attacker', Dorian Arnold, turned me to face him. He wasn't as ugly as I remembered, having lost the greasy look to his face, the pimples which came with growth spurts, and broken voices from the descent of male genitalia in adolescence. His breath reeked of garlic and beer, making my stomach churn a little as he leaned in a tad too close.

"Bloody hell, you scrub up well!" There was a slight slur to his speech.

"Dorian?" I asked, though I knew full bloody well who he was.

"Yes, she remembers me!" He pulled me in for a hug, squishing my tits against his chest. He held me tight against him for a moment too long, I felt the tell-tale sign of arousal, and it wasn't impressive.

"I'd heard from your fag brother you were coming back in to see your poorly old man." He leered at me, his eyes roving downward to my dishevelled shirt now showing far too much cleavage for my liking. I tugged at the neckline, trying to hide the lacy bra I had bought. Unfortunately, the movement drew his piggy eyes to my chest again.

"So, what you doing here anyway? Not with that American guy anymore, I heard?" He draped an arm around me and tugged me in close.

I tried to pull away, but his arm was tightening around me. I swear I felt the bones in my shoulders creak and shift.

"No, and I'm not looking for anyone else. Now sod off," I said through gritted teeth.

"You heard Mel. Sod off." Robbie's angry voice quietened the bar.

Dorian turned, dragging me with him. "Or what? The fag will go all fairy twinkle toes on me and kick my arse?" he sneered.

"You're damned right, asshole," Robbie spat.

Robbie moved lightning fast, a tribute to hours spent in our uncle's boxing gym two towns over when he was having trouble at school with bullies. It boosted his confidence and gave him self-defence knowledge. Or in my case, sisterly defence. In my opinion, bloody handy to have. Unfortunately, Dorian was also a boxer, something I think Robbie had forgotten. I know I bloody well had. And though Dorian was drunk, he was still sober enough to dodge and counterstrike, laying Robbie down on the sticky bar floor. I rushed to my brother's aid, my anger boiling over as I helped him to his feet.

"Dorian, you're a stupid fuck. You're a right pillock you are! Seriously, what is your problem? I said I wasn't interested, and you still pushed. You're a wanker, and you always were a wanker. Robbie said you'd changed, but you haven't." I helped

Robbie out towards the pub's entrance as the innkeeper came from behind the bar to break up the fight that never eventuated.

"Cyril, sorry for the disturbance." I handed him a twenty from my meagre savings, I'd exchanged US currency to Pounds. I hoped it covered the price of our drinks

We left the pub and I helped an unsteady Robbie to the Van. "You alright?" I asked my brother.

"Nope, I can't see straight and my head is killing me." He fished in his pocket for the keys. "You're going to have to drive."

He dangled the keys in front of me. "Great." I snagged the keys from his fingers and helped him into the van. "Just bloody great. Don't you go to sleep on me, you might have a concussion."

I hated driving, and now I also had to make sure Robbie didn't fall asleep for at least an hour after his headshot. Already I could see his eye puffing up, and I knew he'd have a shiner in the morning.

Fuck. My. Life.

Chapter Twenty-Four.

The van rumbled over the bitumen, the headlights revealing the eyes of a lone fox as it glanced up at us in the middle of the road before it hurried away, out of sight and danger. I smiled at seeing one of our most beautiful, and cunning, creatures in the wild. Robbie held a hand to his swelling and slowly bruising face. A thought caused me to frown as I drove, my body tense, senses on high alert despite the pint of alcohol in my system.

"Robbie, do they always treat you like shit in the pub?"

He chuckled, it sounded strained. "No, Mel, just a few of the lads, it's nothing."

I turned to look at him, the lights of the dash shining in my face.

"It's not nothing, Robbie. They shouldn't treat you like that, you're a person, not some 'thing' to be abused and treated like shit..."

"Road..." Robbie spoke sternly.

I continued on. "I mean, what, they don't think that you've gone through enough in your youth, trying to figure out who you are?"

"Road, Mel..." Robbie spoke a little louder, his voice holding a note of warning I barely noticed.

"They're nothing but pillocks, Robbie, you're so much better than them." I turned to look into his eyes.

He sat tensed, eyes glued to the road as he grabbed onto the handle at the top of the van's passenger door frame.

"*Jesus fucking Christ Mel, get your eyes on the fucking road*!" he shouted and his eyes widened.

I turned back to look at where the van was travelling. We were on the right-hand side of the road, approaching a corner which curved around one of the small hills leading to the river.

"Oh, bollocks!" I shouted as I hit the brakes. The tires squealed against the friction of the bitumen and we came to a shuddering stop just shy of the steel barrier we would have broken through. "Shite, sorry, sorry. Bugger, shit, fuck shit, shit, shit." I muttered agitatedly as I crunched and ground the gears until I found reverse and managed to get us back on the road, and on the correct side to boot.

"You never could chat and drive." Robbie mused.

"Sorry." I apologised again, and started back down the road towards the turn-off to our home road.

"Just get us home in one piece will you Mel? I need an ice pack, and something for this headache, maybe some scotch. Dad's secret stash will do nicely."

I bit my bottom lip, and focused on getting us home.

Twenty minutes later, after getting lost on the dark roads which once were so familiar to me, I pulled onto our gravel driveway and parked the van in its spot next to Dad's Range Rover. Mum's little hatchback was at the hospital with her. I turned off the van's engine and checked on Robbie. He grinned. "Well, we made it, but like hell you're ever driving again."

I grimaced and punched him playfully on the arm. "Dick."

"Yes, I like those." he grinned.

"Yeah, me too." I chuckled.

"Ew, gross, you're my sister, you can't like the same things I do." Robbie unbuckled his seatbelt and climbed from the van. He was steadier than he'd been when we left the pub, which was a good thing.

"Oh, yes I can too like the same things you do, Robbie Whittaker." I poked my tongue out at him as I too left the van.

Robbie flipped me the bird and held out an open hand for the keys. I tossed them to him, and his hand closed around them mid-air with a slight, meaty thump and jangle of metal. The cottage was dark, but soon light shone as Robbie walked through and turned on every light in the kitchen, dining and living rooms.

"Be a love and grab me the frozen peas?" Robbie settled down at the kitchen table.

I grabbed the peas from the freezer side of the fridge. After I wrapped them in one of Mum's tea-towels, I pulled up a chair beside him and held it to the swelling side of his face. He was deathly pale.

"He copped a good one on you, Robbie old boy." I watched him wince with the pain of the chilled peas against his injured skull.

"Yeah, I thought he'd changed, bastard was faster than I remember. Uncle David used to put us together in the ring on school holidays, sometimes I got him, but more often than not I ended up bruised and battered. He went semi-pro for a bit until his girlfriend hooked him on drugs. He failed a drug test and was ejected from the circuit. Sad really. I thought he'd really changed after all he'd been through. Now, I guess he's just bitter with life."

I sighed as I held the tea-towel-wrapped bag of peas against his head. "That's easy to be, these days."

Robbie smiled at my words. "Yeah, well, don't you get too far down dreary lane, old duck. We got plans to make. Dad's going to be out of commission for a while. Are you going to stay here and lend a hand?"

I grinned, my mind wandering back to American soil, where Zane, my meagre possessions in our two-bedroom apartment, and nothing else really waited for me. "I might as well. All my stuff back in the states could fit into two and a half packing boxes and a large suitcase. I told my boss I didn't know if I was coming back, or when, so I probably don't have a job to go back to, nor do I have anyone waiting for me there. I saw in the papers that the guy I was seeing? The actor? He was with another actress, very intimately."

Robbie took the peas from my hand and laid them down on the old, scuffed wooden table.

"Mel, you don't think you could have been mistaken at all do you? I mean could he have been rehearsing a scene or something?"

I shook my head, remembering the photos. "No, he was in a well-known café wearing casual clothes. The only film I know he's doing is regency." I sighed, my finger tracing along the smooth worn woodgrain of the table. "I thought it was something special, he made me feel special, took care of me when we were…" I bobbed my head, feeling my cheeks flush.

"Bonking?"

"Crudely spoken, Robbie. But it wasn't bonking, this was tender, nice, made me feel like I was important in the equation, you know?"

"Oh… Oh my God. He made love to you?" Robbie's eyes widened.

"Yeah, I think so. And now, I've lost the one chance I hoped to have for happiness."

"Did you do the ice-cream thing?" Robbie asked, knowing my penchant for ice cream when things got bad, like really, really dead-kitten bad.

"Yep, and the ugly cry."

"Ouch, it was bad then."

"Yep." I stifled a yawn.

"Go to bed, Mel, I'll write out some plans for the nursery, and we'll go over them in the morning. First off, we need to get Dad's greenhouse cleaned up where he was working, he knocked over a few pots when he collapsed."

I nodded and stood up.

"Thanks Robbie." I draped my arms around him, hugging him tightly.

"For what?"

"For being the brother who wants to punch people for being assholes to his sister, for being there for Mum and Dad when I bailed on them, and when they needed you."

"You never bailed on them Mel. You had to go live your life, spread your little wings and fly like a bird."

I sniffled, feeling tears prickle at my eyes. "Yeah, and look where that's gotten me."

"Experience, Mel, you chalk it up to experience. Then, you tell the world to sod off. You hold your head up high, shoulders back, titties out and you walk over those twats who caused you grief by showing them you are stronger than they are." He smiled, putting a hand against my cheek. "Bloody well worked for me."

"You don't have titties, Robbie." I chuckled.

"You never saw me in my Drag stage," he grinned.

My brother in Drag? The vision would be forever burned into my mind.

"Pillock." I muttered slapping him lightly on the shoulder. "I'm going to bed, *Priscilla*."

"Oh, Mel, you didn't see me in sequins and a gown. I borrowed your High School Formal dress for the occasion! Fit me like a glove!" he shouted to me as I walked down the hallway to my old room.

"I'm burning that dress as soon as I find it!" I shouted back.

"I'll tell Mum! She loves that dress!"

I shut my bedroom door, turned and looked at my old room.

The memories flooded back. Good, bad, ugly and cherished I let a few tears roll down my cheeks before I wiped them away and forced them back. I changed into a pair or sleep shorts and a tank top, pulled back the sheets and flopped onto the single-size spring mattress.

Only to spring back up with a yelp as one of the old springs broke and poked me in the arse.

I looked at the offending spring sticking out of the mattress and the newly torn sheet.

"Bollocks."

Fuck. My. Life.

Chapter Twenty-Five.

Birdsong greeted me, along with a near-blinding ray of morning sunlight across my closed eyelids. I groaned, rolled over and was instantly wakened with the sharp reminder that my old spring mattress was no longer suitable for its original purpose. I had been so exhausted and overwrought last night, I didn't bother to flip the mattress, or switch it for the one under my bed in the old trundle. Wide awake, my stomach grumbled, the smell of freshly cooked toast and tea wafted from the kitchen.

I rolled out of bed and slipped socks on my feet to avoid the cold wooden floor, which had been the bane of my morning existence from when I was a teen, and joined Mum and Robbie in the kitchen. Mum glanced up from preparing the teapot in the 'proper' English manner, or at least her version of it - warm the pot with boiling water, drain it out, add one tea bag for each person and one for the pot, add the water to steep the tea for a minute or two, and serve in fine china teacups.

I padded to her side, put my arm around her shoulders and drew her close in a one-armed hug. "Morning, Mum." She'd had a shower and had that clean, fresh *mum* scent that I love. "How's Dad?" She smiled at me.

"Much better, he's had some liquids, and very soft foods, though he can't wait for my corned beef when he gets home." She poured herself a cup of tea.

I reached to grab one of the sturdy mugs from their hooks and reached for the teapot. The minute I did it, I knew it was wrong!

"Melinda Louise Whittaker, don't you dare!" she warned me.

I cringed at the use of my full name, put the mug back in its place and reached into the china cup cupboard. Tea, in my mother's opinion, was sacred and must be served in a proper cup. It didn't matter how much you might think you needed for your first one of the morning. I glanced at the clock hanging above the lace curtained kitchen window. It was already ten-thirty.

"Where's Robbie?" I asked Mum as she finished making my tea and handed me cup and saucer.

"Out loading the van for the next round of deliveries." Mum sipped at her tea. "We can't afford to fall behind on the work contracts we have in London, they keep the staff paid and the business running."

"I don't know what I'll do until your father is back on his feet. Lord knows I can't keep his nursery plants going, much less the ones in the flower greenhouse."

I slurped my tea, earning a scathing glare from my mum. "Don't worry, Mum. I'll sort it out." I tried to sound reassuring, yet I had a sneaking suspicion I was failing miserably. I downed the rest of my tea, remembering to gently set Mum's china teacup in the kitchen sink, lest I be forever cursed for eternity, more than I already suspected I might be. "I'm going to see if I can find Robbie before he heads off." I headed towards the back door.

"Melinda, you might want to put some clothes on."

"Clothes, right." I turned on my heel and dashed back to my room, pulled on a new pair of jeans, and a shirt, before dragging a pullover on.

I hurried back to the kitchen and through the back door to the mud room where I located a pair of Mum's old wellies. Thankfully, they fit me, as we're a similar size. As my right foot slipped in, something small and furry, shifted and squeaked.

I shrieked, hopping on one foot away from the cursed wellie. As I retreated, a mouse scampered out of the fallen boot, and I stumbled backwards, falling on my arse, with one booted foot in the air, and the other rapidly joining it. Codsworth, the family's ginger cat, who was laying on one of the chairs in the sunroom opened one eye and looked at me like I was crazy.

"Coddie! Get the bloody mouse!" I shouted at the old ginger. He yawned, displaying rows of uselessly sharp teeth before laying his head back down on his paws, flicked an ear and began purring in his sleep.

Mum rushed into the mud room and skidded to a stop. "What happened? Whatever are you doing on the floor?" She offered me a hand up.

"There was a mouse in the wellington, Mum, and that bloody useless cat did nothing."

Mum laughed. "Oh sweetheart, his mousing days are long past. Just remember to give your boots a shake next time, dislodge any unwanted visitors before you put them on." We heard the van starting up. Mum grabbed the now mouse-free boot and handed it to me. "Hurry up or he'll leave and you'll have to wait for him to get back after three in the afternoon. He's got a few deliveries in London today."

"Bugger." I turned and ran awkwardly in my wellies to where Robbie was reversing the van in order to turn around and drive out of the yard.

"Robbie!" I shouted over the noise of the van revving as he accelerated. He heard me and hit the brakes, the van skidding in the gravel and leaving two patches gouged out in the tiny rocks. He rolled down the driver's side window and grinned.

"Mornin' Mel, need a lift somewhere? I'm going to be out most of the afternoon."

I grimaced when I noticed the purplish-black bruise under his eye where Dorian had punched him. "No, just wanted to know what I can do to help today?" I wanted to feel useful, I knew Mum was going back to the hospital shortly to sit with Dad, and I felt really guilty about Robbie getting hurt at the pub.

"Well, Dad's greenhouse, where we found him, needs to be cleaned up; think you can handle that?" I bit my lip and thought for less than a second.

"Yeah, I guess so."

"Great, and if you want to do some garden tending, Dad's plants could probably do with some positive energy right now. You remember where his notebooks are, right?"

I nodded. "Yeah, in the tool shed at the side of the greenhouse."

"If you get stuck, or lost, just follow Dad's notes. Oh, and I almost forgot." He reached over to the passenger side and grabbed a bag. "Don't drop this one in the loo okay?" He handed me the plastic bag and I peeked inside. There was a new phone to replace my old one.

"Thanks Robbie." Did I say, I have the best brother?

"Send me a text so I have your new number, I wrote Mum's and my numbers on the box. I gotta go do these deliveries, see you later." He pulled out of the cottage's driveway, leaving me holding my new phone. I dropped the bag in my room, before heading back out to the gate in the hedge leading to the Nursery and Dad's greenhouses. My boots crunched over the finer grade gravel paths running between the structures. I could hear the soft murmuring of customers and Dad's nursery staff as they selected young, healthy plants for their own gardens.

I entered Dad's special greenhouse with trepidation, it was where he worked on his pet projects, his 'non-biological babies.' I was wrapped in the warmth of the greenhouse and it didn't take long to see where he had fallen. The gravel had been disturbed, leaving a body-sized shift in the gravel. A large area had parted to the packed earth below where it looked like someone had come skidding to a stop. Several clay pots lay broken, their rich soil and new flower bulbs scattered on the gravel and wooden workbenches.

A broken Orchid lay wilting on the ground under the workbench. I leaned down and picked it up. The flower was gorgeous, tinged pink on the outside edges of its pure white petals and sepals, but with a light green and white lip. The throat was a dusky purple. It was one of the most beautiful Orchids I'd ever seen. I noticed the white plastic strip Dad had cut from a butter container. *The Melinda Orchid – Orchidaceae Melinda.* I swallowed around the lump in my throat, my father was breeding a hybrid orchid for me.

I held the delicate flower in my fingers and studied it, my lip trembled as I was overcome with emotion. My dad had created, and named, a flower after me, and I had very nearly lost him before he could give me his beautiful gift.

I dropped to the floor of the greenhouse, my body heaving with sobs, big, runny-nose-that-turned-into-clogged-up-nose sobs.

Ugly Cry: 3 – Mel: Big fat zero.

Fuck. My. Life.

Chapter Twenty-Six.

A pair of strong, work-worn hands embraced me, boots scraping more of the gravel away as the hulking body settled behind me and made soothing hushing noises.

"Shh, there lass, don't ye cry now. All be right. Yer Da be alive, and he'll be back on his feet in no time." The strong Scottish brogue of Uncle Leo greeted me as he gently rocked me in his arms. I sniffled. Leo is Dad's best friend, and my godfather; though no relation, Robbie and I still call him Uncle and he loves the title, and us as if we were his own niece and nephew.

"I was so frightened I'd lost him, Uncle Leo," I sobbed against his chest. "I had the worst week after one of the best few days, and it all went to shite."

"Aye, Lass, tis the way of things." He pressed a kiss to my hair and raised a hand to caress the edges of the wilting orchid. "He was so eager to see this bloom, ye should make up a bunch for him and take it to his bedside, I think he be mighty pleased with it." Leo's finger traced the bright pink edges of the delicate flower. "I remember when ye were just a wee babe, ye'd have trouble sleeping in yer cot, so yer Da would bring ye out here and ye'd stare at the flowers and babble on like a magpie until ye were too tired to babble and fell asleep. Yer Ma would come in and try to take ye back to yer cot, but yer Da wouldn't let her. Now, ye brother, ha, he was a different nut that's for sure. Mama's boy." He chuckled; I couldn't help but join in. Robbie *had* been a mama's boy, and I remembered when I would get him into trouble, Mum wouldn't believe he'd done it on his own. She always said, I must have been behind it in some way.

Uncle Leo sighed. "Ye be right now, Lass?"

I nodded. "Yeah." I pushed myself up from the gravel, brushing my jeans free of the tiny sharp stones. Uncle Leo got to his feet, the large Scot towered a head over me.

"Good lass, now give me a proper hug." He smiled brightly as I moved into the security of his arms, feeling them wrap around me like a big hairy bear.

"What are ye doing in here anyways?"

"Robbie asked if I could come and clean up in here, make sure Dad's plants were looked after." I nodded to indicate the disarray before us.

"Aye, I was going to do that after I got Mr. Cutter's usual order for him, but I heard crying as I was heading to the fields, so I came in to see who was in here."

"Old man Cutter is still alive?" John Cutter was a retired high school teacher. He'd taught Dad, me, Robbie and countless other local kids before he retired. He always gave his wife, Dulcie, a bunch of fresh cut flowers on a Saturday. Every week, without fail he would come by the nursery.

"Aye, as is Mrs. Cutter, though she's been moved to the hospital where they've got palliative care, she's not long for this world, Doctors think a week, maybe two." Leo shook his head. "I doubt he'll be long for the world after she goes." Leo looked around at the blooms in large pots. "Now, let's see here, he wanted some lavender, which we've got outside, and a few roses… oh and a tiger lily or two, care to come with me and help gather the flowers? I'll help ye in here when we're done."

"Sure." That seemed to be what I needed, mindless work for a few minutes before I came to do the hard, emotional crap which needed to be done.

I followed Leo outside into the sunshine and down the muddy track to the flower beds. A variety of roses in magnificent colours awaited us in the fields, standing at attention like multi-coloured soldiers in neat rows. A softly blowing wind gave the heads of the roses a light nodding motion as if to approve my return.

Leo and I clipped a few long-stemmed blood red and pure white roses, searching for the perfect ones. We trimmed those that were marred slightly, or had a small nibble taken from their delicate petals by a pest and dropped them into a tub for drying and making potpourri. Marigolds sat gaily beneath the flowers, a co-planting deterrent against most of the nasty bugs which liked to nibble at the floral crops.

Next, we moved to the Lavender which grew in abundance. A long but short in height hedge-like row of the purple flowers greeted us as we carefully cut their long stems. The strong scent of the herb-flower pleasant to the nose. Leo led me to the Tiger Lily, which stood proud amongst other varieties my father carefully cultivated and sold as part of the floristry supplier part of his business. I watched Leo as he selected a perfect bloom and trimmed it from the mother plant, wrapping the stem in tissue paper as he had done with the roses and the thick bunch of lavender flowers I cradled in my arms like a precious newborn.

"All right, let's go and put this all together." Leo turned from the fields to return to the Nursery proper.

He led me to the grey brick building housing the main shop, florist, offices and tea room. Mr. Cutter was sitting at a small table with Maisy, one of the shop girls who had been with us for as long as I could remember, enjoying a cup of tea. I smiled at him and waved. He looked at me in surprise, his bushy white eyebrows almost launching to the top of his forehead as he recognised me.

"Melinda!" he croaked, his voice raspy with age. He struggled to his feet, leaning heavily on a gnarled old cane as he got to his feet. "I heard you had come home, and about time too girl, you've been missed by your family; sorely, sorely missed." He placed a hand which shook slightly on my shoulder.

"It's lovely to see you as well, Mr. Cutter. We've been out collecting Dulcie's flowers for you," I smiled.

His face clouded for a moment. "Ah, my beautiful Dulcie. She doesn't remember me most days now. The Alzheimer's and the cancer will take her soon. Though she has her good days and bad, I still visit her every day in the hospital. No doubt I'll be joining her soon enough. I'm in an assisted living cottage on my own, but when she leaves me, I think it will be my time soon after."

"But Mr. Cutter, you are still so strong."

"Bah, not as strong as I used to be, Melinda. I'm an old man in my nineties, I've lived, loved and lost. I only wish for a young person such as yourself to enjoy the love I've had with my Dulcie for yourself."

I nodded. "Is it worth it, Mr. Cutter?" My thoughts drifted back to Adam.

The old man looked up at me from his hunched over stance. He paused a moment, wisdom of his age staring back at me. "Yes, it is."

I saw the indisputable truth in his eyes - the love, the joy, and even the pain, was worth it to be with the person you loved.

I wasn't a believer in love at first sight, But, in the short time I'd known him, I'd fallen hard for Adam Jacobs, even though he didn't feel the same way about me.

I wondered if, in time, I could let him go.

I had no choice.

Fuck. My. Life.

Chapter Twenty-Seven.

Leo brought out the flowers for Mr. Cutter to take to Dulcie, the arrangement was beautiful, with the Tiger Lily bloom taking centre stage in the arrangement.

We headed back to the greenhouse and spent the next few hours returning the chaos to some semblance of order. I re-potted the Orchid, my namesake and fed and watered the poor plant in the dire hope it might survive.

Leo put on some soft jazz, which he claimed my father played to soothe the plants. It seemed to work on humans, too. I made myself busy with tidying work, and blocked all thoughts from my mind as I worked.

Robbie came to check on us just as we'd finished and grinned. "Well, I didn't think it was *that* bad, but it looks so much better now. Come on, Mum is at the hospital and wants us to go there to see Dad, they're going to move him out of critical care and onto a ward."

Leo nodded for me to go with my brother. "Tell yer Da I'll be there in a few days to visit with him," he said as we left the greenhouse and headed in separate directions.

I headed back to the cottage for a shower, while Robbie took a phone call in the office. I showered, changed my clothes, and sat on the bed to open the box which held my new phone. I quickly set it up with the basics; being a pre-paid would be fine for me until I could get hold of the telecommunications carrier I used in the states and cancelled my old phone service. It would be another, semi-conscious, step towards never going back. I studied my new, but cheap, smartphone. It wasn't top of the line but it still had the usual features including Facebook, Twitter and the rest.

I tried to fight the urge, I really did, but I lost. I jumped on Facebook without logging in, I had deleted my old account and toyed with the idea of having a new one, but scrapped it. I didn't want anyone to stalk, or abuse me, on social media. I found Zane's Facebook profile and hit the *send message* button. Of course, in my excitement at finding Zane's profile, the login screen popped up. Damn. I sighed, then did the stupidest thing I could have done; I google searched Adam Jacobs.

The first hit in the search was a wedding proposal story. *Adam Jacobs Proposes to Kira Holsworthy! Stars to wed! Wedding of the Century!* I felt a huge lump swell in my throat as I looked at the pictures through tears. Adam was holding Kira, both had smiles on their faces. Both looked so happy.

"Don't cry, don't cry, don't cry," I chanted while holding my phone in such a death grip I was certain I'd have to get a new one or replace a screen. I closed the browser when Robbie entered with a grin on his face.

"You'll never guess what!" His excitement was palpable in the air.

"What?" I asked, perhaps a little too brusquely, yet he didn't seem to notice.

"I may have just landed us a pretty damned big contract for floral arrangements!"

"How damned big?"

"So damned big, people will be wanting our business for years to come if we can pull it off!" Robbie pumped his fists in the air.

"Robbie, how are we going to do this without Dad?" Yeah, that's me, the realist putting a dampener on Robbie's excitement.

"If we get it, the contract won't start until next month, just before your birthday, actually." Robbie nodded his head back down the hall. "Come on, ol' girl, let's go see Dad and tell him the good news. This will get him back on his feet."

I pushed myself off the bed and slid the phone into my purse. "It's only good news if we get it, but good job Robbie." I followed him out of the cottage.

The drive to the hospital was quiet, but for the radio station which was running a competition for people to win a VIP pass to some movie set nearby. The people who called in had to guess the title of the movie. Robbie pulled up to the hospital and turned off the ignition, killing the radio just as the next contestant was going to guess the movie's title.

Once out of the van, I stretched. My back popping slightly from the manual labour of cleaning up Dad's greenhouse and picking flowers. I wasn't used to it, back in the States, it was mainly sitting at the counter, repairing second hand books then stacking them on shelves. None of this raking, potting, planting, cutting, watering, feeding type stuff. And, bending, constant bending.

I followed Robbie through to the nurses station to find out where Dad was now located. We negotiated the hall as directed by the nurse, and I realised we'd pass by the palliative care unit. As we rounded the corner into another section of the corridor, I noticed a bunch of flowers laying abandoned in the hall, outside the door to the palliative care unit. They were familiar. Roses, Lavender and a Tiger Lily which had separated from the arrangement.

"Oh no," I whispered.

Robbie stopped and turned to me. "What's wrong?" Concern masked his face.

"Mrs. Cutter…" I pointed to the flowers on the floor. "Those flowers were for Mrs. Cutter." I picked them up and placed the Tiger Lily back in its position, before I looked to Robbie. "I have to see."

Robbie nodded, we pushed through the closed double doors of the unit and approached a nurse at the desk. "Hi, I'm looking for Mrs. Dulcie Cutter, is she still here? We're friends of the family."

The woman smiled warmly. "Certainly, I'll take you to her room. Usually her husband is here around this time of day, but he's late which is quite unusual." She stepped from behind the desk and led us down the corridor to the private rooms.

I glanced at Robbie, concern prickling my spine. Dulcie was still alive, so something must have happened to Mr. Cutter. "He came to our nursery and floristry this morning as usual to buy these flowers for his wife, I found them on the floor in the corridor."

"Oh, dear. I did hear an older gentleman had collapsed in the corridor, but I was on my break when it happened a few moments ago. Let me contact the Emergency Department. Just a moment." Returning to the nurse's station, she reached behind the desk, picked up a cordless phone and dialled a number.

"Hello, Nancy? It's Estelle in Palliative, do you have the gentleman there who collapsed in the West Main corridor?" She paused for the reply, "Okay, and did you get a name?" She frowned deeply at the reply. "Oh dear, he was the husband of one of our final stage patients here in Palliative. Thank you, Nancy." The nurse, Estelle looked at us sadly as she hung up the phone.

"I'm so very sorry, but Mr. Cutter passed away, the doctors suspect it was a brain aneurysm, very sudden. I doubt Dulcie will understand, although she is having a good day today, very lucid. She is fading fast poor dear." Estelle led us to the room where Dulcie Cutter lay covered by the starched white sheets of her hospital bed. A blue coverlet over much of her body. The room was stark, but for a vase of week-old flowers which needed to be replaced.

"Dulcie, you have visitors," Estelle said cheerily.

Dulcie looked up.

"Gilbert Whittaker! My goodness, look at you. This must be your lovely bride-to-be, Angie." She struggled to sit a little higher up in the bed. "Have you come to see my baby? He's a lovely little lad, John is so pleased to have a son. He'll be here soon, and he always brings such lovely flowers, every week, such a good husband. That's true love dearies, like I can see you have for each other, hold on to it." She drifted off and was quiet for a moment.

"I'll pop these in water for you Dulcie." I gathered the vase and used the adjoining ensuite to clean out the old dead blooms and replace them with the new ones. I placed them by her bedside table where she could enjoy them.

"Oh, thank you, Angie." She had obviously mistaken Robbie and me for our parents at our ages. "Where's that nurse with my baby?" Her sunken eyes scanned the room. Her thoughts were in the hospital after giving birth to her firstborn son. Tragically, the child had died suddenly in the hospital not a day after he was born.

"My baby, nurse, bring me my baby!" Dulcie shouted frantically. "Where's my boy?"

Robbie looked at me, my heart broke for the old woman. Her body frail, she had lost so much; her memories, her family, the love of her life. I sat beside her and gathered her hand into mine.

"I'm certain the nurses are making sure he's okay, Dulcie." I attempted to calm her.

"Who? Who the devil are you? Are you my John's whore? He'll never love you, you tart!" The old woman puckered her lips and spat at me.

I gasped, as a glob of saliva dribbled warm and wet down my cheek. I moved to stand, but Dulcie grabbed my wrist with lightning reflexes; her bony old hand held more strength in her fear and anger than I realised.

"Help! Help, John! This whore is trying to take you away from me!" she screamed.

The nurses ran in to her room, Estelle gazing at me apologetically as they moved closer to calm Dulcie down.

The poor, confused old woman smiled at us when she noticed the flowers.

"Oh, what lovely flowers they are, just like my John brings on a Saturday." All thoughts of whores and missing babies forgotten.

"Well," Robbie said.

The nurses had stepped back, but kept close watch on Dulcie as the medicine they'd injected into the cannula in her arm began to take effect. Her head bobbed, her eyes losing their lustre of wakefulness.

"We'd best be off then. It was lovely to see you, Dulcie." He slipped his arm around my waist as I wiped my face clean of Dulcie's slobbery missile.

"That could have gone better," Robbie murmured as we left the unit.

I nodded, grief in my heart. I knew we'd have to tell Dad what had happened to Mr. Cutter and he'd be devastated.

Fuck. My. life.

Chapter Twenty-Eight.

Dad's eyes reflected his sadness at the news of Mr. Cutter's passing. Mum sniffled in an attempt to hold back the tears which threatened to fall. "Poor Dulcie, she won't even realise he's not going to be there tomorrow." She dabbed at her eyes with a tissue and gripped Dad's hand a bit tighter, unwilling to let him go. "I'll call Montrose Funeral Home in the morning, no doubt they'll be taking care of the arrangements for his service, we'll offer to do the floral arrangements for free." She sighed and turned toward Robbie and me.

Mum reached out and gathered my hand. "I'm glad you got to see Mr. Cutter before he passed, darling. This news must be quite a shock, especially after everything you've been through."

Dad sat silently, though his speech was very limited, mainly grunts and broken syllables, he was alert and aware, which was more than we could have initially expected. I noticed his eyes studying the pitcher of water and glass on his side table.

"R…b…ie…" he grunted, trying to speak. "Wat…wat… rrr.." He dribbled a little from the palsied side of his mouth.

"What, dad?" Robbie followed dad's line of sight. "Oh, I see! Hang on, old chap." Robbie picked up the pitcher and poured the iced water into the glass for Dad. He put a fresh straw in the cup and helped Dad to drink it, holding the straw to his mouth for him.

"Robbie," Mum said. "Tell us about this new contract?"

"I got a call this morning from a lady in the US, she wants to set up a meeting. Apparently, she works for some film company, and they are doing some shooting for an upcoming feature film at the Castle in the next few months."

"Oh, how exciting!" Mum exclaimed.

My new phone buzzed before ringing. Odd, the phone was brand new, who could possibly have my number? "Excuse me, I'll be just a sec." I stood and pulled the phone from my purse. Not surprisingly, I didn't recognise the number. I hadn't yet had the chance to add any contacts apart from Robbie, mum, the house and business numbers.

"Uh, Hello?" I answered cautiously.

"You bloody tart! All this time you've been home and you never once thought to call me!" The indignant voice of my friend Libby blasted me through the tiny speaker on my phone.

"Libby, oh, my gosh! It's so good to hear your voice, you cow. How did you get this number, it's brand new!" I laughed, happy to hear a friendly voice, even if she was snapping at me like a Yorkshire terrier on her rags.

"Yeah, yeah, you bloody trollop! When I heard you were here, I had a friend track it down. The first number he gave me rang out, he called me a while ago with this one. You owe me a catch-up sesh! I have a photoshoot at the Castle later today for someone's wedding, then I'm free for the rest of the afternoon. Danny is taking over the photography duties. When will you be home?"

"Once we're done here at the hospital, I think Robbie will be taking us home, or I could meet you at the Castle?"

"Yeah, probably best to meet me at the Castle, I'll have my own ride. I'll be finished at about two, then we'll go into town for a coffee, or hmmm, something." I could almost hear the grin in her voice.

"That would be fantastic, it's been hell these last few weeks."

"I'll bet it has, I've seen the crap. But honey, just remember, don't believe everything you read in the papers, okay? Ahh hell, I gotta go, I'm getting a call from work, bloody slave drivers."

"Okay, I'll see you after two." I hung up after saying goodbye. I needed girl time desperately. It kinda worked with Zane back in the states, he was close enough, being an effeminate gay guy, but nothing really kicks depression's arse like a good whinge, bitch and moan session with friends who are also girls.

I headed back to Dad's room and settled on a chair next to my brother. Mum was busy wiping dad's face clean of drool and dribbles of water. I could see in his eyes, it was embarrassing him, having Mum wipe his chin like a baby. Before his stroke, he was such a strong, vibrant man. To see my father, a man who was able to carry me on his shoulders when I was a little girl, reduced to a shaking, weak man, stuck in a bed with his wife attending to his uncontrollable drooling, broke my heart even more.

I sucked in a deep breath. "That was Libby on the phone." As I spoke, I remembered I had to save her number in the contacts list, or she'd have a huge bitch at me about it. I quickly updated the phone to include her number. "I'm going to meet her at the Castle after two this afternoon." I glanced at the time on my phone, it was just after midday. A knock on the door of the room heralded the arrival of an orderly with the lunch cart.

"Afternoon Mr. Whittaker," the overly cheery orderly called from the doorway. "Lunch time." He carried in a tray with plastic covered platters which tried, but failed, to make people forget they were in a hospital. They even smelled like hospital, the scent overpowering the aroma of soup and fresh bread. Green jelly sat in a plastic cup, it obviously wasn't one of those home-made jellies. A carton of orange juice accompanied the meagre fare. The orderly placed it on the tray table for Mum to serve Dad when he was ready and the soup had cooled down a bit.

Robbie and I exchanged a glance.

"I think It's time for us to go, Mum. I've got some orders to fill out back at the Nursery for tomorrow, and then I'll drop you at the Castle, Sis." He smiled at me.

I understood what he was doing, giving Mum and Dad some privacy so she could spoon feed him. He was still too weak to lift the spoon to his own mouth. I stood up, slid the phone back into my purse and sidled up to his bedside. I kissed Dad on the temple. "Be back later, might even be tomorrow, okay, Dad?" I draped an arm across his shoulders and chest, hugging him as well as his position would allow. I felt his right arm move slowly around me, the hand curling around my shoulder as he hugged me.

"Lo…love… you popp...et." Each word and syllable struggled to break free of his lips and tongue which were struggling to remember what they were supposed to do.

"Love you too Dad." I stepped away so Robbie could take my place. I shifted back to Mum and hugged her tight. "See you later, Mum."

"Don't be too late in tonight. I'll call the funeral home to organise flowers for Mr. Cutter. Hopefully, we'll know what they want for the arrangements by tomorrow."

"Sounds good, Mum."

Robbie stood beside me. "Come on, brat, let's go." He playfully punched me on the arm.

I scowled and punched him back.

He yelped and rubbed his arm. "Mum, Mel hit me!"

"Melinda, don't hit your brother."

I stared at my mother in shock, then glared at my little shit of a brother.

Fuck. My. Life.

Chapter Twenty-Nine.

The grounds of the Castle were the same as I remembered, though there were a few new rose varieties in the main gardens which I noticed. A vintage Rolls Royce stood proudly in the circular gravel drive in front of the Castle's main doors. The fountain with its piddling cherubs burbled merrily in the afternoon sun.

"Okay, that's lovely, just another one and I think we'll be done." The voice of Danny, the photographer echoed across the ancient stone walls looming high behind the happy couple as they snuggled beside each other.

"Fucking weddings, you know those two will be at it like rabbits before the night is out." Libby lit up a cigarette, dragging on the white stick of tobacco before exhaling, blowing a perfect smoke ring before blasting a thin column of smoke through the expanding circle of smoke.

Yeah, that wasn't sexual innuendo on her part at all. "Love stinks," I agreed.

"Yeah, yeah. I know. But seriously, if he hasn't been able to find out where you live, contact you, or whatever, then that's his fault, not yours, love." Libby inhaled another long drag on her smoke before sliding her handbag over her shoulder and walking towards her car. I jumped off the low stone wall I'd been sitting on and followed her, my trainers crunching over the gravel driveway as we headed to the visitor's carpark.

"So, let me get this straight. After all the hoo-ha on the film set, where you embarrassed yourself completely, he invited you out to a charity thing. You did the beast with the two backs, he gave you all these pretty things, even said he wanted to see you again after he was finished with a big arse workload, then goes and snogs some uppity starlet slut for the paps to capture in full? What a bastard. You're better off without him." She inhaled one last drag on her cigarette before dropping the butt to the ground and crushing it into the gravel with a boot heel.

"That about sums it up." I waited for her to push the unlocking button on her key fob.

The car doors clicked, I opened the passenger side and slid in. Libby threw herself into the driver's side and slammed the door. She was always rough and ready, how the hell she managed to work with such delicate photography equipment, I'll never know.

"Well, I'd say fuck him, but you already did. And what was with that arsehole manager of his?" She turned the key in the ignition.

My reply was broken off by the loud death metal thundering through the sound system.

"Can you turn that down?" I shouted over the blare of some guy singing heavy falsetto about death and fucking, and a base drum beat which seemed to be impossible for a human to play.

"Nope, sorry. Damned volume and on/off button is broken, plus the CD won't come out, fucking player is fucked!" Libby shouted back as she reversed the car out of its parking space and shifted it into drive. She took off like a bat out of hell, gravel spraying up everywhere behind us.

"Fuck I need a coffee. You okay to go to Rosie's?" she shouted.

I nodded, even though I'd barely heard what she was saying over the screaming voice of the band's lead singer. My head was pounding by the time we arrived at the Village Square where most of the cafes and eateries were located. Libby pulled the car into a parking spot and mercifully, she turned off the car. I swear my ears were about to start bleeding.

"Oh, thank fuck for that. You gotta get that thing fixed." I unbuckled my seatbelt and stepped from the car.

"Yeah, but I have to finish paying for school first, then I'll worry about my baby." She patted the car affectionately. "Besides. I love that band, and that's like, their break-out album."

"Break-out album? What, they broke out of prison by torturing the prison guards with their music?"

Libby chuckled as I stepped up onto the kerb and headed towards Rosie's. "Ha-ha, very funny." Libby's sarcasm meter was off the scale. "You do stand-up comedy, or is it just fall-down?"

"Mostly fall down." I poked my tongue out at her. She draped an arm around me and hugged me tight as we pushed through the doors of Rosie's Café. Fond memories of my younger years came rushing back to me as soon as I smelled Rosie's scones, I'd know that scent anywhere. We sat down at a small booth where the morning sun had bleached the once dark-green vinyl to a few shades lighter. The vinyl covered cushions at the back of the booth cracked and broken. Ollie, a kid from Year 10 at school, had coloured in the cracks with a marker and drawn a couple of cocks on the seat. It was before he'd been killed in a car accident. Of course, I had to sit right on one of the crude drawings.

"Libby, I see the cocks are still here. I know they were kept to honour Ollie after he was killed, but I didn't expect to still see them."

"Yep, Rosie can't bring herself to recover the seats and get rid of them."

A waitress approached and asked for our orders, after she left I looked back down at the cocks. I remembered Ollie as a red-haired boy who had a heavy mixture of freckles and acne.

"He asked me out once, but I turned him down, then the next week he was gone." I spoke softly.

"Yeah, I know, right? You never know when your time is up." Libby absentmindedly plucked up a sugar packet from a container on the table and fiddled with it in her idle fingers. "So, when's your dad coming home?"

"Hopefully in a few weeks. The doctors have given a good prognosis for an almost full recovery Until then I'm home, then after he's back on his feet… I don't know what I'm going to do."

"Well, you'll still be here for your birthday, won't you? That's like next month or something, right?"

I nodded. "Yeah, end of next month." I replied.

"What have you got planned?" Libby's eyes caught mine, I knew that look.

"Oh no. No, you bloody-well don't!"

"Oh yeah," she nodded. "Fucking PUB CRAWL!" she shouted, clapping her hands with an explosive crack which startled two little old ladies enjoying tea and cake on the other side of the café.

I groaned and dropped my face into my hands.

Libby's pub crawls were legendary.

Legendary for shenanigans, hang overs and life-long regrets.

And the worst part?

Once she'd decided on a pub crawl, there was no way out of it.

Fuck. My. Life.

Chapter Thirty.

The following weekend was the funeral of Mr. Cutter. Sadly, as expected, Mrs. Cutter had also passed in the week. So, the Funeral home had worked swiftly to have a double funeral for the well-known couple. It was what they both would have wanted.

On Saturday, I worked with Robbie and Leo to create the floral arrangements for the church, cemetery services and the wake. Mum had managed to wrangle a day release from the hospital for Dad so he could attend the funeral. I was working when Mum wheeled him through the nursery, and I watched as a smile lit up his face when he saw the beautiful orchid he had cultivated for my birthday.

Somehow, I had managed to keep it alive. The nursery staff flocked around him and welcomed him back, as if welcoming a hero back from the war. Mum explained it was only a day release and he'd be starting his rehabilitation therapy the following week. Robbie and I were confident we could hold down the fort during the time it would take Dad to rebuild his motor skills enough to be able to return to work. Even if it was part-time with Uncle Leo helping him.

I wiped my hands dry after spraying the floral arrangements with water and headed to the house to dress while two of the staff loaded the arrangements into the van. Robbie was almost ready and would deliver them to the locations where they were required.

I showered, changed and checked to make sure Mum and Dad were ready. I knocked softly on their bedroom door, and from beyond, I heard the squeaking of springs along with mum and dad's grunting.

Oh... my... fucking... god!

"They're not, are they?" I whispered as I leaned against the door, straining to listen. The plain walnut door opened and stumbled against Mum.

"Melinda, thank goodness. I'm having trouble getting your father's trousers on him, can you give me a hand please?"

I looked up at Mum, guilt causing my cheeks to burn. Mum smirked, she knew I was eavesdropping and what I'd thought. I looked abashed and entered the bedroom to find Dad lying on the bed, panting with exertion. His pants were around his ankles. I instantly noted the problem, the pants were still zipped.

"Mum, didn't you unzip Dad's pants before you tried to pull them up?"

"No, I guess I didn't." Mum scratched her head in wonderment.

"Okay, let's get this done." I stepped closer to Dad, flicked open the button and drew the zipper down so the pants would fit over his arse and hips. "Dad, I'm going to help you to stand and then Mum is going to pull your pants up, okay?" Dad nodded a twinkle in his eyes, he was finding this funny, the cheeky bastard.

Mum helped Dad to sit up, I slid my arms under his armpits and wrapped my hands around his back. I groaned and grunted, Dad's weight against mine, as I managed to stand, lifting Dad with me. "Okay, mum, go!" My voice sounded strained as Mum grabbed Dad's pants from around his ankles and yanked them, up, zipping them and buttoning the top.

"Okay, you can put him down now."

Oh, thank fuck!

I moved Dad back towards the bed, my foot caught up with one of his and we both toppled onto the mattress.

I could feel dad's chest jerking, and shot back onto my feet with lightning speed. My heart thundered in fright, I was terrified he was having a fit. It was something the doctors had warned us could happen as they weren't sure of the extent of his brain damage. The unaffected side of his face was curled into a smile and he was laughing silently.

"Cheeky bugger." I playfully slapped him on the shoulder and my heart rate returned to normal.

"Right, you two, no more arsing about or hanky-panky. We have to get going soon."

I grinned as straightened my skirt and left Mum and Dad in their room. I was waiting in the kitchen when Mum wheeled Dad into the room. She smiled at me. "Ready, Poppet?"

I smiled at her use of Dad's pet name for me. I nodded and stood, we moved to the front door and I held it open for Mum to wheel Dad through. She loaded him into the wheelchair-accessible taxi which had arrived and we headed into town.

Throughout the service for the Cutters, my mind wandered back to Adam. I wondered if things were different, would this be us in sixty-to-eighty years? Would we have lived a wonderful life together, in sickness and in health? Would we have had beautiful kids to dote on, cry over, and love unconditionally?

I glanced beside me to my parents. Mum sat at the end of the pew, holding Dad's hands while he sat in the wheelchair in the aisle. Mum dabbed at Dad's eyes as he wept for the man who had helped him so much in school, and even more in life. Occasionally, she dabbed at the corner of his mouth. We stood for the first hymns, sat down again, stood for another hymn. Recited the Lord's Prayer, and nodded solemnly when the vicar publicly thanked our family for the donation of the floral arrangements.

Mum squeezed Dad's hands tightly at the conclusion of the church service. The two coffins were carried out by friends, as the Cutters had no living relatives to honour them. Their children had both died within years of each other when they were young.

I felt the tears prickling the corners of my eyes when I thought about it, watching my own children die from a disease, or an accident would destroy me. Even worse, would be never having children with someone I loved in the first place.

I sniffled again, thinking of Adam Fucking Jacobs. Why couldn't I get him out of my head? Or my heart.

"You all right, sweetheart?" a little old lady, I didn't recognise asked as I sobbed softly into my handkerchief.

"Yes, I'm okay. Funerals get to me, you know? The Cutters were such a lovely couple, I can't believe they're both gone."

"Oh, I know, dearie. I would like to see everyone as happy in life as they were, despite the things life threw at them, they endured together. As it should be." The old lady shuffled out of the pew, following the caskets outside to the hearses.

As I watched them load the wooden caskets into the backs of the vehicles, I wondered if I'd ever find someone I could spend the rest of my life with. Of course, my brain gave me the image of the man who haunted my dreams.

Adam. Fucking. Jacobs.

Why did I torment myself with constant thoughts of him?

Fuck. My. Life.

Chapter Thirty-One.

It was a few days later, I awoke to the sound of my brother retching in the bathroom. I shot out of bed and hurried to the bathroom door, knocking on the wood. "Robbie?"

Mum had left early for the hospital to spend the day with Dad and to help him get a head start on his rehab exercises.

Robbie groaned before he puked again.

"That's it, I'm coming in," I said determinedly. I pushed the door open and found my sickly brother kneeling, pale, on the cold tiles of the bathroom. The stink of his vomit churned my stomach. "Are you all right?"

He groaned and turned his head back to the bowl, his body shivering before it tensed with the need to be sick again.

I grabbed a washcloth from the basin, wet it, wrung it out, and placed it against the back of his neck. I barely held my own stomach in check with the sight and smell of my brother being sick.

"Ugh…" he groaned as he lifted his weary head up. "I think I ate something bad at the pub last night." He heaved again, what little was left in his stomach splashing in to the bowl of the loo.

I grimaced as I leaned over and pulled the old chain to flush the toilet. "Come on, let's get you back to bed. I'll make you a cup of tea and some dry toast." I helped him to his feet and we shuffled back to his room. I tucked him into bed and grabbed a bucket from the laundry to put beside his bed in case he needed to puke again.

"Oh shit," he moaned when I returned with tea and toast. "The meeting with the client for that big contract, it's this afternoon!"

"Well, bugger. You're not going to be well enough for that." I sat next to him on the bed.

Robbie reached out and weakly grabbed my wrist. "Sis, you're going to have to do this." His eyes pleaded with me to say yes.

"What? No!" I was shocked. "Can't you cancel it? I'm sure the client will understand. I mean you're definitely not well enough to negotiate a contract, and I'm no good with people, I think we've fully established that."

"That's a load of toff and you know it." Robbie flopped back against the pillows. "You'll do fine. Mum even made up some scone dough to have at the meeting. All you have to do is bake the scones, and give them a real proper afternoon tea. Take them for a tour of the place and you'll have it in the bag."

"Your confidence in me is amazing, Robbie, I don't really have a choice in this, do I?"

"Nope." He shook his head and turned deathly white. I reached for the bucket just as he power-puked all over the bedsheets and my lap.

"Oh, my god. Robbie, are you sure you're okay?" I remained still so as not to add to the hot, wet puddle of gross spreading over the covers and soaking into my PJ's.

"Sorry, couldn't stop it." His body shook.

"It's okay, can you manage a shower?" He nodded. "I'll change and make your bed then I'll jump into the shower and get ready for this client. Who is it by the way?"

"All the information is in the office." Robbie threw back the bedcovers from his shaky body. I helped him to the bathroom, and left him to deal with his shower while I dealt with the covers and my puke-covered PJs.

I hurried to Mum's office and found the appointment book. Within the pages were sheafs of paper with the requirements of the contract and the client's name - Alison De Rosa. It sounded familiar, but I couldn't figure out where I knew it from. The appointment book showed we were expecting her at two o'clock. I knew Mum would be out for the whole day, so it was up to me to get the place ready for our visitor.

As soon as Robbie was tucked back in bed, with a large glass of water and something I hoped would help settle his stomach, I showered and set about cleaning the house. By the time midday had arrived, I was already exhausted, but the house was spotless.

I looked around the living room where I would be serving tea and scones. A loud crash from the kitchen had me running to see what the fuss was. On the floor, I had swept and mopped not twenty minutes before, was the broken bowl containing the scone dough Mum had prepared earlier. A trail of powdery white cat paw prints led from the kitchen to the back room.

The culprit had made his escape.

"Bloody hell. This is just what I need." I crouched down to clean up the mess the cat had made. As I dumped the broken glass and dough into the bin, I heard knocking at the front door. *Who could that be?* I dusted the flour from the front of my dark blue blouse as I headed to the front door

I opened the door and came face to face with a woman, who was vaguely familiar to me. "Hello, I'm sorry if I'm a little late." Her American accent instantly threw my memory into overdrive. I was hurtled back to the charity ball Adam had taken me to. This woman, was the wife of a congressman I'd had a conversation with about gardens at the gala Adam had taken me to on our first date.

"It's so nice to see you again, Melinda," she beamed.

She shook my hand enthusiastically, I hadn't even realised I'd extended it to her. I was shocked to see her standing at my front door. I gabbled nonsensically for a moment before I found my tongue.

"Mrs. Del Rosa, I'm sorry. I didn't know it was you, and you're not late, you're early." I stepped back to allow her inside. "The meeting was for two o'clock."

"Oh? I thought it was for twelve, I often confuse times." Mrs. Del Rosa chuckled as she stepped into the entry. I took her elegant coat, and hung it on the coat-rack. I flinched slightly when I saw I had left a white hand print on the dark grey material.

"I was just cleaning up a mess the cat made, my mother had left some scone dough for me to fix for afternoon tea." I indicated the kitchen where I had come from. "The cheeky sod knocked the bowl off the bench, so I do apologise, but I can only offer you biscuits with your tea."

Mrs. Del Rosa shook her head and *tsked* "Not good enough. I was promised a proper English tea, and I'd love to experience one. You have flour?"

I nodded, Mum always had two large canisters of cake flour for baking. She would often take a selection of cakes or slices to the local nursing home, along with any of the cut flowers not used in the nursery shop. Saturday mornings were often filled with the scent of cinnamon sugar and vanilla goodies baking in the oven. I smiled at the memory before Mrs. Del Rosa breezed past me and into the kitchen. I hurried after her. "Ah, yes, she does."

"Excellent, and do you have lemonade? Plain, clear lemonade?" I nodded before pulling a bottle from the fridge and showing her. She took it from me and placed it on the bench before unbuttoning her designer jacket. She strode with purpose to the wall beside the kitchen's back door, where she swapped one of mum's aprons for her jacket. She grabbed another one with *kiss the cook* emblazoned on it, for me.

"Now, let's make some lemonade scones." Her smile lit up her face.

The client had to be happy, and my mum's baking skills certainly hadn't been passed down to me. This was going to be a disaster…

Fuck. My Life!

Chapter Thirty-Two.

The aroma of freshly baked scones filled the kitchen. Mrs. Del Rosa whipped up another bowl of cream when I readily agreed to her suggestion of taking a batch of scones for afternoon tea to the nursery staff. I spooned mum's home-made strawberry jam into a bowl and placed it on a tray by the plate of hot scones covered by a check patterned tea towel.

We'd chatted easily while we worked, about little things in life which gave us pleasure. Friends, family, lost loves… I felt my chest tighten and my eyes prickle with tears when we spoke of the last. Bugger that Adam Jacobs arsehole. I noticed her eyes misted over when we spoke of love. I wanted to question her on it, but thought better than to pry. Besides, her love life was about as much my business as my love life was hers. Plus, she was a client. One whose business would help to keep us afloat while Dad was recovering.

"I think this is about as whipped as it's going to get before it turns into butter," she chuckled.

"They have tea and coffee making facilities in the staff room, so we can drop these in there for them."

Mrs. Del Rosa placed the bowl of whipped cream on the tray. I lifted it very carefully, not wanting all our hard work to be wasted by my clumsiness.

Robbie was still resting, I'd checked on him while the scones were baking. He lay pale against his *Batman* pillowcase as he slept, open mouthed and snoring slightly.

I led Mrs. Del Rosa through the small gate to the nursery, and heard her gasp when she saw how big the place was. "Mum and Dad had plans to expand, build a café and a small hedge maze and playground for kids over there in the vacant field." I explained as we moved through the potted saplings and young flowers lined up on metal shelves for sale. "We do a bit of business with local florists, and a small group of florists in London itself." I entered the nursery building where the staff were taking care of customers.

"Och, what d'ye have here lass?" Uncle Leo's Scottish brogue broke through the voices of staff and customers.

"Afternoon tea," Mrs. Del Rosa smiled.

Uncle Leo stopped dead in his tracks when he noticed the American woman before him.

"Well, aren't ye a bonny lass?" He grinned like a bear who had gotten into the honey pot.

Mrs. Del Rosa blushed when Uncle Leo lifted her hand to his lips and kissed it.

"Leon McLeod, at ye service." He peered up at her from over her hand.

"Alison Del Rosa," she replied, her face radiant with the delighted blush blaringly obvious for all to see.

"And what brings ye to the Whittaker's fine nursery today?" Uncle Leo asked.

"I'm about to give Mrs. Del Rosa a tour of the nursery, she might be contracting us to provide floral arrangements for…" Oh crap, I'd forgotten what the actual job was! I'd flicked through the paperwork so quickly. Between maniacally scrubbing the house with disinfectant, in case Robbie's food poisoning wasn't food poisoning, but some ugly little stomach bug capable of taking down humanity with one single microscopic germ, and checking on the *dying* man, nothing had registered about what the flowers were for.

"I'm a producer for an upcoming movie we're going to be filming at your local castle. A regency piece. We're hoping for good reviews when it comes out. Honestly we think it's going to be a box office smash."

Uncle Leo grinned, without taking his hand from hers, Mrs. Del Rosa didn't seem to mind. "And who is in this film? Any big names?"

Before she could answer, my mobile phone rang. "Excuse me, I have to get this." I turned away and headed to the office while Uncle Leo continued charming Mrs. Del Rosa in his Scottish way.

"Hello?" I answered.

"Melinda, sweetheart, how's everything going?" Mum's voice sounded stressed.

"Fine Mum, everything's fine. Or, at least it will be when I can pry Mrs. Del Rosa away from Uncle Leo's grip."

"Who is Mrs Del Rosa?"

"The client, Mum."

"Oh, well in that case, yes, do get her away from Leo's charms. Why isn't Robbie looking after her?"

"Robbie's sick in bed, he couldn't stop puking this morning,"

"I told him not to eat at the pub on a Sunday night. The cook there is useless, silly boy won't listen to his mother." She launched into a tirade about ungrateful boys who didn't eat their mother's cooking, I had to stop her before she got too far into it and I would have a hard time shutting her up and getting back to Mrs. Del Rosa.

"How's Dad doing?" I interrupted.

"Slowly getting there, dear, he's getting stronger every day. The doctor is having him transferred to a rehabilitation ward where he'll be able to make use of their facilities without hauling him from one end of the hospital to the other. He can at least hold a spoon now."

"That's good news." I turned towards Uncle Leo who had settled Mrs. Del Rosa on one of the old-style park benches set against the corrugated wall of the office. His attention on Mrs. Del Rosa, and her attention firmly on him. I felt my cheeks heat when Uncle Leo reached over to one of the display bouquets, plucked a white rose with red tips on its petals and handed it to her.

"Mum, I gotta go, or we'll be attending uncle Leo's wedding." I hung up as Mum was about to start on a tirade about the flirty nurse, who I knew was a genuinely friendly woman.

Nervously, I approached the smitten couple. "Mrs. Del Rosa, sorry to interrupt, but would you like to see the flower fields?"

"I'd love to." She turned back to uncle Leo and smiled charmingly at him. "I'd better go, Leon, but we will definitely be catching up for a drink." She smiled, reached into her clutch purse, removed a business card and handed it to him. "This has my personal number on it." Her fingers trailed over his as he took the card form her manicured fingers. "Call me, anytime," she winked.

My mind instantly zoomed to thoughts of Uncle Leo and Mrs. Del Rosa entwined in each other's arms, their bedsheets tangled around naked, sweaty bodies. Suddenly, it wasn't the naked arse of the man I called Uncle and my client who were in the moaning, writhing mess, it was another man… one who haunted my dreams, both waking and sleeping.

"Melinda?" A voice broke into my daydream.

"Oh, sorry, shall we continue?" I asked Mrs. Del Rosa.

"Of course. I can't wait to see the fields and the workshop where you'll put everything together."

For the rest of the tour, I couldn't get my mind off the image of my body flush with desire, and the beautiful body of Adam Fucking Jacobs.

The bastard had his claws deep inside me.

Fuck. My. Life.

Chapter Thirty-Three

Mrs. Del Rosa was incredibly happy with the tour, and before she left, she assured me we had the contract. I sighed happily, as I leaned against the closed front door. At least something was going the Whittaker's way for once.

My respite was short lived when I heard Robbie's pitiful moan. Maybe he was feeling hungry, I headed to the kitchen and put together a tray with dry toast and black tea.

"Knock, knock, it's Nurse Ratched," I chuckled.

"Bugger off, I'm dying in here," Robbie bemoaned.

"Yeah, yeah, I know. I've heard it all before." I pushed the door open with my foot. The room was dark with curtains drawn and windows closed. The stench of sick and *male things* filled the air. I hadn't noticed before just how dirty his room actually was. "Robbie, what's going on? Usually you're the neat freak and I'm the slob." I set the tray down on his nightstand and moved the bucket, which was where the sick smell was wafting from. I crinkled my nose, trying to ignore the churning of my stomach contents. The mixture of jam and cream scones, and tea swirled in my stomach and began a valiant attempt to return to the light.

"I'll ugh… just go take care of this, shall I?" I swallowed hard, trying not to choke on the bile which had seared its way to the top of my throat. I swallowed thickly again, and with the bucket clutched firmly in my grip, I dashed to the bathroom to spill my guts over the porcelain throne.

How I'd ever be a good mother, I'd never know. I hated the sight of vomit, the smell… even worse.

I finished purging, and I can tell you, cream is not as nice coming back up as it is going down. I took a deep breath, and tipped the bucket's contents into the toilet to join my own grandiose effort before flushing the evidence away. The toilet was scrubbed within an inch of its porcelain life with disinfectant and I grabbed Robbie some clean towels in case he needed another shower.

I brushed my teeth, revelling in the clean, minty goodness. I headed back to Robbie's room with the freshly cleaned bucket and clean towels.

"Sympathy puke, sis?" Robbie asked as he sat up and chewed on his dry toast. "I knew you loved me."

"A sympathy puke doesn't mean I care, or love you, you bastard. How dare you get food poisoning and throw me to the wolves like this. Did you know I actually *knew* the client from America?" I sat down on the side of his bed. "You owe me big time, buster!" I poked him in the chest.

Robbie grinned. "I'll make it up to you, I promise. I've organised something fantastic for your birthday too, by the way."

"What is it?"

"It's a surprise.

"I hate surprises."

"I know, but you'll love this one."

"I bet I won't."

"You'll be surprised." Robbie grinned as he picked up his cooling tea with both hands and slurped noisily.

"Just tell me, would you?"

"Nope." He shook his head, taking another noisy slurp.

"Pig, after all I've done for you today."

"Mel, I'm not going to ruin your birthday surprise, okay? I've put a lot of effort into the planning and preparation for this, so back the fuck off."

"Robbie Whittaker! Watch your tongue." Mum's voice made us both jump and turn towards the door.

"Sorry Mum," Robbie said with a cheeky grin.

Mum looked tired when she entered the room. She stepped close to Robbie's bed and began to fuss, placing a hand to his head and checking his temperature, before pinching his cheeks gently to ensure he wasn't dehydrated.

"Mum!" he protested.

I chuckled at his discomfort.

"Mel took good care of you, did she?" Mum asked.

"Yeah, she even got the contract," Robbie smirked.

Mum looked incredulous. "Did you? Did you really?"

I scowled before answering. "Yes, Mum *I* got the contract. Mrs. Del Rosa said it was ours. I'm just waiting on the paperwork to come in so you can sign it, then we can get started on planning and whatnot with their props department."

"Oh darling, that's excellent, your father will be so proud." Mum moved to the other side of the bed where I was seated and gave me a big hug.

"How is the old man?" Robbie asked.

"Better today. He fed himself some porridge and his speech is improving. He still has a stutter, but he's putting together simple sentences." Mum smiled. "It's all small steps right now, but hopefully, given how healthy he was before the stroke, the doctor thinks he should be at least ninety percent recovered. He might have some days when he's a bit weaker than he should be, or he might forget words and become easily frustrated, but the doctor said the prognosis was very good."

"That's great, Mum." I hugged her back.

"Well, we also have to prepare for the fact that he's not going to be able to do as much around the nursery as he used to, so we're both going to have to ask you kids to help out."

"I thought we were already." Robbie said.

"Well, more so Melinda. Your father hasn't changed much in the way things work, but we are in the process of getting council permission to expand from the nursery to Mark's field next door. It all came through the day before your father had his stroke." She coughed, her voice tightening with the memory.

"So, you're definitely going ahead with the hedge maze and the café?"

"Oh yes, darling." Mum replied. "It's your father's dream to have the nursery expand. When you were both little, we used to hire out the cottage garden for wedding photography. I think your father would like to do it again, or at least he did before his turn."

"Mum…." Robbie leaned forward and placed a hand over Mum's. I joined in, placing one of my hands over theirs. "We're here for you and Dad, we'll happily support you in every way we can."

I made a decision, then and there. There was nothing left for me in the states. My family, my future was here in England. It was where I needed to be. "I'll be here for you, mum. I'm going to move back home so I can help you and Dad run the business."

"Darling, thank you." Mum drew me into her motherly embrace. I hugged her back, but my mind was on everything I'd have to do now. I had to somehow contact Zane, which would probably mean finding him on Facebook. It was not going to be easy, he had high security settings on his profile which made it near impossible to contact him. I needed to let him know I was moving back home to England. I'd also have to call my boss and let her know not to hold onto my job for me.

And, I'd have to give up any hope of finding out whatever happened to my chances with Adam Fucking Jacobs.

My heart broke a little bit more. Though, really, it had never been healed in the first place.

Fuck. My. Life.

Chapter Thirty-Four.

A week later, it was all systems go. Dad had taken his first tentative steps in rehab, but then caught a cold from someone at the rehab facility and was laid up in hospital again. A lot of his progress had gone downhill while he was sick, and the doctors were watching him closely, making sure he was getting better.

I'd managed to get onto my old boss, Mrs. Phillips, who started crying as soon as I told her I wasn't coming back because my family needed me at home. Though upset, she understood, and assured me there'd be a place for me at the store if I ever returned. She started to say something about a man coming to see me, but I heard the 'call waiting' signal, and as I was using the office phone, I had to end the call with a profuse apology.

The incoming business call was from the props department, letting me know they'd sent an email with their requirements for the filming schedule and what they needed on what day. Etc. etc. blah-blah-blah. I had kinda stopped listening because Robbie appeared at the door and was trying to distract me.

"All right, thank you, we'll get started right away on preparations." I said good-bye and ended the call.

"You're such a pillock." I flipped my brother the bird as I hung up.

He grinned and flipped me off right back. "So, who was that? Your boyfriend?"

"Nope, yours." I poked my tongue out, I know childish, but it felt good. "Actually, it was the new clients. They've emailed some stuff for the filming schedule, so you might want to get onto that, I don't have the passwords for the email." I pushed past him.

"Got it. Oh, and Libby called, looking for you."

He held up my mobile. "Something about a pub crawl for your birthday this weekend? I told her my plans and we're joining forces."

I groaned. My life was going to become an even greater living nightmare next weekend. I turned and snatched my phone from his hands

"She wants to take you out shopping later today to get you all tarted up, so she said she'll be here in ten. I told her you're already a tart and not to bother!" Robbie called after me as I stormed down the hallway to the kitchen.

"Pillock!" I shouted over my shoulder.

"Slag!"

"Slapper!"

"Takes one to know one!" he laughed.

"I swear you two are worse than teenagers. It's like having my adolescent babies in the house all over again," Mum huffed while scrubbing the dishes.

I picked up a tea towel and rubbed them dry as she placed them in the draining racks.

"It's all in loving fun, Mum."

"Oh yes, I know, darling, but you shouldn't swear, it's unladylike." Mum placed a glass on the rack, and scrubbed at another. A soft rhythmic thumping sounded in the distance, growing steadily louder as we worked. Soon the windows started to pulse and rattle in their frames in time to the heavy bass beat.

"What on earth is that noise? An earthquake?"

"Libby's here."

"How do you know?" Mum asked.

"The noise, the vibrations? Her stereo is busted. She can't turn it off, turn it down, or get the heavy death metal CD out of the player, so it plays nothing but that CD at full volume."

"Good lord." Mum shook her head as the music stopped followed by the sound of a car door being slammed shut, then again, and again. And of course, then came the obligatory string of curses, before the door was slammed one last time. "Go and let her in, I'll put on a pot of tea." Mum tugged off the bright canary-yellow rubber gloves adorning her hands while she washed the dishes and put the kettle on.

I headed to the entry and opened the door to greet Libby.

"Hey slag." She grinned.

"Hey trollop." I laughed as we hugged. "Come in, Mum's put on the kettle. I just need to change and we can go after a cup of tea."

Libby rolled her eyes. "Yeah, okay. Fine." She plastered a smile on her face as she headed for the kitchen where the sounds of mum putting the kettle on were heard.

"Hello Elizabeth, how are you darling?" Mum asked as Libby strolled into the kitchen as if she owned the place.

In truth, she kinda had laid claim to our family a long time ago. Her own family were the sort who often had children's services or the local council visiting them over complaints. How Libby could stay in her home with her parents, I'll never know.

"I'm great, thanks Mrs. W. How's Mr. W doing?"

"Oh, poor darling, has a cold right now. It's stopping him from getting back on his feet, but the doctors say it shouldn't be too much longer before he's recovered." Mum poured tea for all of us. I recognised the effort she'd gone to, and realised how long it had been since she'd had any of her friends to afternoon tea, or a good whinge, bitch and moan session.

"So, Mrs. W, I'm going to steal your daughter away for a few hours, so we can go find the perfect outfit for her birthday surprise."

"That sounds lovely, Elizabeth." Mum smiled over her teacup.

Libby grimaced slightly at the use of her full name, which she hated with a vengeance.

"I'll go and get changed." I glanced down at my pyjamas before slipping away, leaving mum and best girlfriend chatting about inane things.

I pulled on a long-sleeved shirt and pair of jeans. My luggage had yet to be returned to me, though I'd received a letter saying they had finally located it, and it was making its way home from Australia. I couldn't wait to get it back, there were clothes in there I missed. And, *comfort things* like my vibrator.

Yeah, I was starting to get the *edge* which needed to be worn down by a good battery-powered orgasm. Some good old-fashioned, stress-relieving, *private* time would be just what the doctor ordered.

I returned to the kitchen to find Mum on the phone.

"Come on, slag, let's go get you something jaw-droppingly sexy to wear this weekend." Libby grabbed my hand, only slowing so I could snag my bag, keys and phone before she led me to the little car of death metal, doom and premature hearing loss.

Fuck. My. Life.

Chapter Thirty-Five.

I was working on a floral arrangement for an upcoming wedding when Robbie sauntered into the workshop. "Ah Mel, thank god. I need your help."

I looked up from the bunch of deep purple roses I was using to form the bridesmaid's bouquet. "What's up?

"Andy called in sick, so I'm down a pair of hands to deliver these arrangements to the castle for the movie. Can you come with me, please? I'd ask Uncle Leo but he's visiting Dad."

"Yeah, sure I can." I pulled the dark green apron off and packed the flowers away in the cool room to keep them fresh until I could return to finish the job. I followed Robbie out to the van and climbed in the passenger side.

It was a quiet drive to the castle. Robbie had to stop at the gate and show ID before we were checked off a list and allowed through the gates with some guy on a four-wheeler motorbike to escort us to where we needed to be.

The grounds of the castle had been transformed. Horse drawn carriages were being worked on, along with a small herd of horses, who were being tended to by grooms and farriers. A group of large caravans were lined up, each with a gold star on the aluminium door with black writing declaring who was in which trailer. Men and women hurried about with various pieces of film equipment in their hands or on hand carts.

We passed by too quickly and the words were too far away for me to figure out who was in this movie.

Robbie pulled up near the double doors to the castle's ballroom, the guy on the four-wheeler bike turned, waved, and headed back.

"Okay, we gotta find someone named Maddison, she's one of the prop people, who will tell us where all this needs to go." Robbie nodded to the back of the van and the carefully prepared floral arrangements.

I slid from my side of the van. The sun beat down on us, warming through the thin black material of the *Whittaker's Nursery and Floral supplies* work shirt I wore. I squinted as the glare of the sun tortured my retinas, searing them with the cheery brightness trying to find its way into the darkened parts of my heart.

"You okay?" Robbie asked.

"Yeah, I left my sunglasses at home.

"Hang on… here," Robbie leaned back into the van and pulled out a Whittaker's hat.

"Thanks." I gratefully pulled it onto my head, ignoring the fact my hair would be a total mess, but at least my eyes were sheltered from the worst of the glaring sun. "Right, let's go."

We entered the cool ballroom and I glanced around. The last time I had been here was for my high school formal, and I'd managed to make an arse of myself by falling on it. Was there any part of my life which didn't suck or plagued with bad luck and poor judgement?

"Do you mind waiting here?" Robbie asked, reaching into his back pocket and pulling out the paperwork for the job.

"No problem." I watched as my brother walked away, past a group of men who were setting up a table.

The setting looked eerily familiar, and then I realised! The feckin ballroom was decorated the same as the one on the set of the damned movie where my life took one hell of an unexpected turn. The set here was replicated to look exactly like the ballroom back in LA.

Something in my gut insisted it was a bad idea to be here. It got even worse when I heard a familiar voice.

"I don't care if she's got ten years of experience, I want my own dammed nail technician. Fly her in right now. I swear this broken nail will stop the film if I don't get it fixed right! It will look absolutely horrific!" The high-pitched voice of the world's hottest actress had me cringing.

Kira Holsworthy breezed past me, ignoring me like the insignificant person I was. Her trailing group of assistants nodding like the yes-men and - women they were.

My heart plummeted to the centre of the earth, where it was burned to a crisp. If she was here… and the film was about a regency romance…

Oh… My… Fucking GOD!

My heart beat faster and faster, out of control. If she was here, then….

Someone called to another faceless person in the room, and my world spun out of control. "Sarah, we need to get Mr. Jacobs in here for some test shots once the florists are done."

The voice of a woman replied, "Of course, sir. I'll fetch him right away."

I began to breathe heavily, hyperventilating in the cool ballroom which suddenly felt far too hot and claustrophobic.

The sound of switches being clicked, and the instant buzzing of studio lights as they hummed with electricity, filled my ears like an angry crowd of bees. My mouth dried and I felt the nervous nausea creeping up like an unwelcome result of a night of drinking to excess. The room closed in on me even more. I couldn't move.

"Mel?" Robbie's voice drifted in through the haze. "Are you okay?" I nodded.

"Okay, let's get these arrangements out and in place," he said.

I hadn't noticed he was talking to a couple of men who had come to help with the flowers.

I followed him out on autopilot and helped to unload the flowers from the van. My body moved robotically, while my mind was blank with one of those old television station *Please stand by* screens emblazoned over it.

Station closed.

We are experiencing technical difficulties.

Then I heard the most beautifully devastating voice.

His.

Adam Fucking Jacobs.

"Yeah, okay. I can do that. Let's see where this goes first, I'm still trying to find her."

I peered up from under the peak of my cap to sneak a look. He looked a little rough. There were dark circles under his eyes and he looked stressed.

"We're going to have to get you in for some make-up soon, Mr. Jacobs," one of the assistants surrounding him commented. He grunted as he handed his phone to another assistant.

I kept my head down as I followed Robbie, who opened the back of the truck and handed me the smallest of the arrangements. I followed the others back into the coolness of the ballroom. The props director indicated where the arrangements were to go. Of course, mine had to be placed about three feet away from where Adam Jacobs was standing.

I moved quickly, keeping the flowers at face height so I didn't see him, nor could he see me, before setting down the arrangement and finding myself without a way to hide myself other than to make myself seem as insignificant as I really was.

I hunched my shoulders a little, and kept my head down, the peak of my cap was low over my face as I passed Adam. I couldn't help but inhale as I passed him, his scent tortured me with memories of being wrapped in his arms, the sheets of his bed infused with his masculine scent which sent warm, fuzzy tingles to my traitorous body as it remembered every touch, caress, lick, kiss and stroke of the various parts of his body over and inside me.

I bit my bottom lip, I couldn't approach him to ask why he hadn't tried to contact me to at least let me know he was really with someone else – *that bitch, Kira-* and I was just his *bit on the side* as the papers had declared me.

I scurried past Adam and back to the van where the last of the arrangements were being unloaded. There were also a couple of bouquets for the trailers. One for Kira, and one for Adam. Thankfully, Robbie offered to deliver those.

"You look a little pale, why don't you go sit in the van?" he offered.

I nodded gratefully. I did feel flushed, and sick to my stomach, after seeing Adam fucking Jacobs. I climbed into the van, removed the hat and leaned my head against the passenger side window. I closed my eyes and wished the world would go away for five minutes while I pushed the reset button and got a grip on myself.

Robbie hopped into the van, closed the door and clicked on his seatbelt "You okay? Here, let me put the window down for you." He started the van and pressed the button to lower the window. I jolted away from the downward moving glass and looked across to the ballroom.

My eyes met those of a certain famous, and extremely gorgeous, Hollywood actor.

"Melinda." His mouth said the words, but I couldn't hear them over the revving of the van as Robbie shifted into gear. Adam's eyes widened when he realised I was about to get away. "Melinda!"

Robbie had started to accelerate away, and I watched as Adam ran towards us, chasing us in the light dust trail the van kicked up, his period costume's coat-tails flapping in the wind. It was like a scene out of *Terminator 2: Judgement day.* – if the T-1000 was wearing a period-costume with coat-tails instead of a police uniform.

Beneath the white leggings, his muscles bunched and released, giving him more speed, but Robbie accelerated down the gravel road. I could see the desperation in his eyes as he chased us down the gravel road to the exit. Robbie didn't realise we were being chased, and I, like a fool said nothing.

As we left the castle grounds, and turned onto the bitumen road, I saw the look of defeat on Adam's face in the side mirror when he realised we weren't stopping. He panted, stopped at the gate and stood forlornly on the bitumen road as he watched us drive away.

Something tore within my heart. Could I have been wrong about him?

Should I have believed the newspapers?

Should I have asked Robbie to stop?

My crispified heart hardened into a diamond.

I fought the one tear threatening to break free, and failed. It was blown across my cheeks and into my hairline by the wind.

Robbie glanced over at me. "You okay?"

I nodded and reached over to roll up the window.

"I'm fine."

Liar.

Fuck. My. Life.

Chapter Thirty-Six

The darkness of the blindfold wrapped around my eyes kept me from figuring out where we were going. Fortunately, I was safe, or at least as safe as I could be considering it was Libby and Robbie delivering me to the first stop on my 'Grand Birthday Adventure.'

After the disastrous day at the castle, where I was literally chased by a man in tights; I had mentally shut down to try – unsuccessfully- to sort my feelings out, I needed this. Going out, getting totally drunk off my tits, and maybe picking up some hot guy to shag until dawn broke. Then, to do the traditional *walk of shame* before heading home via a cab, or Robbie who was the designated driver. We'd had a small birthday celebration at the hospital rehab centre. Dad had recovered from his cold and was barely walking with the aid of a walking frame and rehab nurse.

The staff had allowed Mum to bring in a birthday cake and we had a small party in the rehab gardens while other patients strolled along the paths

Our first stop after we left Mum and Dad, however was to be one hell of a surprise. Robbie drove us to London, while Libby and I sipped on mixed vodka drinks and bitched about all things, men, work, life in general, before singing to top-forty hits on the radio Thankfully we took Robbie's car, and not Libby's, so my hearing was safe… for now.

I felt the car draw to a stop, and Libby helped me out. The noise and smell of London assailed me immediately. The cacophony of sound hit me like running into a brick wall. Libby guided me past what I assumed was a long line of people, waiting in line, if their indignation-filled curses directed towards us was any indication.

"Fuck off wankers, we're on the guest list." Libby shouted back at the disgruntled voices as she undoubtedly flipped them all the bird with a smirk.

I was dragged up a step, almost tripping as Libby pulled at my arm. The scent of bodies, alcohol and stale smoke, both tobacco and the greener variety, tickled my nose. The heat of many bodies filled the place. I assumed it was a night club of some sort, even though the music playing was low, and the throb of the bass notes was muffled by so many bodies.

Libby set me down in a seat and I felt her sit down beside me. "Can I take this off yet?" I asked.

"Nope, you just gotta wait." I heard Libby rummage through her purse for something, and I settled back to wait.

I smelled my brother's aftershave before I felt him settle down beside me. "You ready?"

"Yeah, I am, ready to take this fucking blindfold off. Where are we exactly?" I asked.

"Shh, show's starting." I heard the smile in Libby's voice.

"Ladies and gentlemen, welcome to the Ruby Slipper, I'm your hostess with the mostest, Miss Teak! Tonight, we have a very special show for you, for one night only. We at the Ruby Slipper are so very proud to present, our sisters, all the way from the United States of America, the Queens of L.A!"

The blindfold was whipped from my eyes and I looked around. Up on stage was a drag queen wearing a full green ball gown, her hair was piled up high in a bright red beehive style, complete with three bees.

"You brought me to a drag club?" I laughed, punching Robbie in the shoulder.

"Just wait till you see *who* is in this show," he winked.

I frowned, and glanced from him to Libby. "What? Who?"

Libby grinned and nodded to the stage where the overly done-up drag queen was introducing the stars of the show.

"Miss Jen. U. Wine!" An African-American drag queen stepped out onto stage, sequins shimmering as she (*he?)* blew kisses and threw glitter over the front row.

"Hellooo darlings!" she crooned and sashayed across the stage before waiting for the next Queen of L.A. to be introduced.

"Madam V. Vacious!" Another drag queen swanned on stage.

I kept watching the stage and glancing back to Robbie and Libbie, waiting for the big reveal.

"Miss Periwinkle!

"Oh, my god, Perry!" I gasped and cheered with the crowd. Perry swanned onstage winking overly-long and glittered fake eyelashes at the crowd.

"And introducing… a Drag Queen in training… Princess Z!"

I swear I almost fell out of my chair.

Zane, in full drag pranced onto the stage. He lifted his arms up and cocked a hip to the side. He was dressed like Liza Minnelli in *Cabaret.* His outfit shimmered with countless sequins, his bowler hat had a band of sparkly white diamantes, and he wore a pair of impossibly high stiletto heels.

"You're fucking kidding me!" I laughed with delight, clapping my hands and cheering the loudest I could.

Robbie laughed beside me. "I thought you might like this."

"How did you know?" I turned and threw my arms around him.

"I'll tell you later," he shouted over the noise, nodding to the stage where a chair had been set up.

Zane, or *Princess Z,* took up a position on stage as the lights dimmed and the other queens left the stage.

The music began softly, before building to the opening notes of *Cabaret*. Liza's voice drifted over the hushed crowd, Zane lip-synched and began a routine which included high kicks and fancy spins. I was completely bedazzled for two reasons: 1. He could kick and spin on those heels, and 2. He didn't bust a nut, or have an embarrassing wardrobe malfunction in the teeny-tiny shorts he was wearing for the routine.

I watched and sang along to the musical numbers the queens performed, enjoying every moment of watching my friends as they got their Drag on. As the show was wrapping up, Perry stepped to the front of the stage, a stage hand passed a microphone up to him.

"Now, darlings, we have a very, very special friend in the audience tonight." Perry held a hand bedecked with jangly fake bangles and long fake fingernails up above his brow, as if scanning the crowd. "Where's Miss Melinda?"

"Oh no," I moaned.

Robbie grinned when Libby stood up and waved her arms in the air. "Here, over here!" she cried. The spotlight lit us up like one of those old World War 2 spotlights they used to sight enemy bombers during the Blitz. I hunched my shoulders, and covered my face, trying to hide.

"There she is! Melinda, come on sweetheart, do you know how long we've spent trying to find you?"

Robbie and Libby's hands pulled mine from my face, burning hot with embarrassment.

"You two, are a pair of sodding pricks," I mumbled behind a smile.

"Good thing you love us," Robbie planted a kiss on my cheek.

I turned to Libby. "How long do you think I'd get for fratricide?"

Libby laughed as they dragged me up on stage and planted my arse on a chair in the middle of the stage

"Now, we know it's your birthday today, so, we would like to sing you a little song," Perry crooned.

The intro music from *Sister Sledge's 'We are Family'* blared through the speakers as a curtain of bubbles descended from the top of the stage's rigging. To my surprise, Robbie and Libby joined the drag queens as they sang the song.

Something told me they needed to stick with lip synching, but I was so moved, I started to cry. I felt warm arms surround me as Zane hugged me tight. "Missed you, bitch," he whispered in my ear as the song ended. I wiped my eyes, Realising I'd smeared mascara over my cheeks when I noticed my fingertips were black.

The crowd cheered when the lights faded, plunging the stage into semi-darkness and I was ushered to my feet. However, this is me, Miss Clumsy. I tripped, the first thing I reached out for, and grabbed, were the bodices of the nearest two drag queens. They shrieked along with me as the fronts of their dresses tore free. Fake tits and sequins bounced across the stage as the stage lights came back up for the encore bow.

It was a Drag-Queen disaster.

Of my creation.

The entire club was quiet for three seconds, before I dashed off stage and into the crowd, hot tears probably ruining the rest of my makeup, just as my night had been ruined with my epic clumsiness. Again!

Somehow, I managed to find my way to the ladies' toilets. It's strange how women always seem to know where they are in an emotional emergency.

I locked myself in a stall.

My entire life was a disaster I felt like I had no control over. No matter what I did, or how careful I was, something always went wrong.

Forget Murphy's Law, this was Melinda's fucking Law.

Fuck. My. Life.

Chapter Thirty-Seven.

About twenty minutes later, I was coaxed out of the toilets with promises of alcohol, copious amounts of alcohol, and moving to another club. One where no amount of my clumsiness was going to embarrass me and everyone would be dancing around like they were having a synchronised epileptic fit with no concern for how they looked.

Zane joined us and gave me a sympathetic hug.

"That's my Mel," he smiled.

I'd missed his effeminate American accent. He wiped away my makeup and applied a light coating of foundation to cover the red, streaky tear lines which I'd seen in the bathroom mirror adorning my face like dried up river beds on the surface of planet Mars. I almost felt human again.

"How did you know Zane was coming here, Robbie?" I asked my brother as he drove.

"I've been chatting to Zane on a dating site for a while now, but hadn't realised who he was to you until I told him my last name. Then, he explained how he knew you."

"Dating site?" I glanced from Zane to Robbie, eyebrows raised in question.

"Friends only," they both said suspiciously quickly and in near-perfect sync.

"O-kay then." I left the matter of sleeping dogs to lie as we drove to the next stop.

The line was longer here than at the Drag club.

"Isn't this…?" I gazed at the sign above the door. *Liquid Drive* was the name of the nightclub, one of the most exclusive in London. Socialites and famous people flocked to it. I had no idea how we were going to get in here, but I'd wait and see. Robbie parked and led the way to the front doors.

"Whittaker, party of four." He spoke smoothly to the big, burly bouncer who looked like he'd just finished a tour of the WWE.

Mr. Muscles checked over the list attached to a clipboard in his hands. "Of course, you're in the VIP section, Mr. Whittaker. One of the hostesses will direct you to your booth."

I stared at Libby, frowning in confusion. *"VIP?"* I mouthed at her.

I could have sworn I heard her say *"Squee!"* under her breath. She grinned and clutched my arm, jumping up and down in excitement like a kid going to a carnival for the first time.

We followed the hostess, who had arrived within seconds to lead us through the throng of partygoers to the VIP section upstairs. There were several sectioned off areas where dark red velvet curtains hid those within. Our section overlooked the dance floor through, what the hostess informed us, was a one-way panel of glass. It enabled us to watch, without being seen, the throbbing mass of people on the floor below as they moved to the heavy bass beat vibrating through the plush carpet beneath our feet.

"Drinks? Robbie asked when a waitress appeared at our curtain.

"Fuck yes." I flopped into one of the deliciously luxurious seats.

"What would you like, birthday girl?" Zane asked.

"Anything, as long as there's alcohol in it!" I stared out at the bright coloured lights as they swirled and shifted in time to the blaring bass of the club music.

Drinks were brought around in short order and I enjoyed the Sex on the Beach Zane had ordered me. I almost felt the alcohol surging through my bloodstream. My inhibitions washed away in a flood of liquid courage.

Zane flopped into the chair beside me. "Oh, my god Mel, that shit was too funny back at the drag club," he laughed.

I gave him the foulest stink-eye I could manage. The bastard laughed even harder, snorting and coughing when his daquiri slid down the wrong hole.

My glass was empty, and another round was placed onto the table. "I'm sorry I didn't try harder to get back in contact with you, Zane." I felt melancholy slip in with the alcohol.

"It's okay sweets, you haven't been yourself lately, what with all this shit going on with your dad, and *he-who-shall-not-be-named* being in all the papers and tabloids with that bitch." He sipped at his drink. "How are you coping with that, by the way?"

"Ugh, terrible. I saw him at the Castle the other day."

"Omigod, what happened?" Zane gasped dramatically and leaned forward, trying to get as close to the gossip as physically possible.

No sips for me, I gulped at my drink. "After he spotted me, he chased the van down the drive to the road. Robbie didn't notice he was behind us, and I didn't tell him. Needless to say, I won't be doing any more deliveries to the Castle unless there is no way I can avoid it, until the filming is done and he's gone back to the States.

"Ouch, damn sweetheart. Did you know he came to our apartment looking for you?"

"No." I paused, trying to think thinking back to the last phone conversation I had with Zane before losing my phone. "Wait, was that what you were trying to tell me when I dropped my phone in the loo?"

"You what?"

"Oh yeah. *After* I'd relieved myself." I shook my head and continued. "Of course, I had to try to rescue it, but it was a lost cause. It died then and there."

"Oh honey, that's just wrong." Zane placed a hand on my shoulder. "But, honey, he is really into you."

"Sure, uh huh. That's why I saw pictures of him with Kira Holsworthy making out at a very public café." I downed the contents of my glass and put it on the table beside my chair. I was over conversations about the man who'd broken my heart

"Okay Libby, you got moves?" My voice sounded slightly slurred. "Let's see them, twat-waffle!" I grabbed her by the hand and led her down the stairs – very carefully, to the dance floor where we joined the throng of people already pounding out their moves.

The heat and press of the dancing bodies warmed me to a point I felt comfortable in my inebriated state. My hand clutched at Libby's as we moved deeper into the throng and let the music take control of our bodies. My eyes closed and I lifted my arms to the sky, reaching for the unreachable.

Hips and arse bumped against mine as I was moved slowly through the press of bodies, Libby vanished behind a wall of bodies. I glimpsed her being dry humped by two guys who probably thought they were pulling some sweet moves on the little firecracker who was one of my best friends. From the looks she threw my way, as I moved with the current created by dancing bodies, she didn't mind one bit. I smiled, and swayed my body to the beat. I lost track of time, but became aware of a pair of warm hands on my hips, a strong, muscular body pressing against me, and a slight bulge pressing against my arse.

Warm breath caressed the skin at my neck and shoulder, causing strands of hair which had come loose from my ponytail to drift and catch on my dry lips. I pulled the strands clear and licked at my lips, moistening them and tasting the salt of my sweat and the remaining oily flavour of the lip gloss Zane had carefully applied in the car for me.

I reached behind me and put my arms around the back of my dance partner's neck. Short hair tickled my fingertips, long enough for me to run my fingers through the strands. I imagined what it would be like to gently grip the fine strands as I rode him, the bulge in his pants rubbing against my ass was a good indicator of how well-endowed he was.

The guy's scent seemed familiar. I ignored it, my drunken brain playing tricks on me.

Then his voice whispered against my earlobe before he gently took it between his lips and sucked.

"I've missed you, Mel."

It was then my alcoholically dazed state dropped away and I returned to full sobriety at the speed of light. I turned, shivering with delight when his teeth gently scraped my earlobe with the movement. I stared into *those* eyes. Eyes that haunted my dreams, both sleeping and waking.

Those eyes which broke my heart a million times every night.

His arms held me close to him.

His gaze held mine.

His heart beat hard against my chest, recapturing my own.

Adam.

Fucking.

Jacobs.

This time, I couldn't run.

Fuck. My. Life.

Chapter Thirty-Eight.

Adam gathered my hand, led my stunned body from the dance floor and up a flight of stairs to another VIP area. This one had closed off rooms guarded by four burly security men who stood at the entrance to discourage any uninvited people from entering.

They nodded at Adam as he guided me through the entry.

"Adam, wait," I called as he tugged me through an open door. As soon as I was through, he turned and shut the door, pressing me back against it.

"Mel," he whispered, before his lips took mine in a kiss screaming of sheer desperation.

My heart pounded, blood pulsed hard and fast through my body when I felt his hands slide up along my arms, over my shoulders and along my neck. He cupped my face gently, tenderly, and his lips and tongue tasted, teased and explored my mouth.

I moaned, I couldn't help it. I submitted to him, melting into a gooey puddle of Melinda. His body heat warmed me through the slip of material which passed for a dress (*thank-you, Libby*). I felt his body's response to being so close to me, he moaned into my mouth deeply, softly, almost a growl.

My body pulsed with the need to have him again, and again, and again. Until we were either passed out exhausted, or the club closed and we were kicked onto the streets amid a frenzy of cameras flashing and uncomfortable questions being yelled.

Those thoughts snapped me from the Adam-induced haze which had taken over my mental capabilities. I pushed him away.

"Adam, stop, we can't do this, you're getting married."

He pulled back, looking at me as if I was totally daft.

I folded my arms across my chest, trying to prevent my tight nipples from poking through the thin material and showing him how aroused I was. I only succeeding in pushing the cleavage up. "You never told me you were with Kira," I said crossly.

He chuckled at me! Actually, laughed which made me even more cross. I turned to leave but he caught me by the arm. "Mel, I'm not getting married, and I'm certainly not with Kira. What's this all about?"

I looked at him, my eyes glowering as I pulled my phone from inside my bra, where it was hidden. His eyes followed my fingers as they dove into my cleavage.

"You know, I could have gotten that for you." He grinned cheekily.

I unlocked the phone and quickly typed my search into Google. Instantly pictures of Adam and Kira filled the screen, along with an article announcing their engagement.

I shoved the phone under his nose. He took it and lowered himself into one of the armchairs.

Yeah, that's right you sodding prick, I'm onto you. I watched his face go from surprised to shock to raging anger.

"Fucking assholes." His face had paled, then reddened as his anger grew. "Motherfucking son-of-a-bitch." He pulled his phone out and punched in a number. Yeah, he was too angry to dial like a normal person. I'm telling you, he *punched* the number in. I had no idea what I'd unleashed.

"Doug, it's Adam. Yeah, I don't know what's happening, but fuck man, what's this shit about Kira and me getting engaged?"

I watched and waited as Adam listened, by now I knew I'd thought wrongly about him and Kira.

"So, why didn't you put out a rebuttal, put a stop to this shit? You know as well as I do, none of it's true."

I sidestepped warily to the seat opposite him, the vein in his forehead pulsed and a tick was evident in his jaw. I had never seen the man so angry. I stood behind the back of the chair, subconsciously using it as a shield, my fingers digging into the plush leather back as Adam listened to his manager.

"For exposure and publicity? Are you fucking kidding me? Fucking seriously? I find someone I want to get to know as a person and you let this crap out? You knew I was interested in Melinda, I mean come on dude, what you've done is all kinds of fucking wrong."

Silence.

"Not happy about this? Ya think? I'm fucking furious right now!" Adam gazed at me, his eyes turning from fury to apology. I stepped around the chair and sat down opposite him, my hands settled nervously in my lap. For all the alcohol I'd had, it seemed to have evaporated in the heat of the moment and the sobering of the current situation.

Adam reached out and gathered one of my hands in his, thumb running slowly back and forth over my knuckles as he kept his eyes on me and listened to his manager speak.

"Doug, I told you, I made it crystal fucking clear, I was in a blossoming relationship with a woman, not a starlet. I don't want the diva bullshit. I want normal, why the fuck can't I have normal?"

I couldn't help but smile at those words. Adam Jacobs was about as far from normal as one could get.

"I'll talk to you later. In the meantime, sort this fucking mess out!" He ended the call, tossed the phone onto the coffee table, and rubbed his hands over his face in exasperation.

"I'm not normal," I said softly.

He looked at me over the tops of his fingertips, his eyes shining with something I couldn't quite put my finger on.

"No, you're better than normal." Adam gathered my other hand, clasping both in his before he leaned forward and, lifting them to his lips, kissed my palms. Fucking manager.

"I met your manager a while back." My eyes dropped to my knees, peeking out from the scrap of material Libby had insisted was a dress.

He frowned. "When?"

"After the gala. You hadn't called or messaged me, which is okay, but I got into my head we had something special. I couldn't believe I was nothing more than a one-night stand. He showed me pictures of when I was getting into the cab at your place, doing the whole 'walk of shame' thing. He wanted me to sign a non-disclosure statement, saying the whole relationship was a farce, but he still had to protect you."

Adam's scowled, and that same nerve in his jaw started to tick. "What did you say?"

"Told him to shove it up his arse, anything that happens between us is our own private business."

"That's my girl." Adam reached over to caress my cheek.

I looked at him, my eyes gazing into his. "So, you're not getting married to Kira?"

"No fucking way, if she were the last fucking woman on Earth, I'd stay a bachelor. The pictures were from two years ago, when I was with her. She's too much of a diva, clingy, demanding, I don't want that. My life is hectic enough as it is. I need someone to calm me, soothe me when I've had a rough day. Someone I can share the highs and lows with, someone I can protect and take care of. Someone who wants the simple things out of life, who can ground me."

"And you think I'm that someone?" I snorted a laugh. "My life is one disaster after another. I ugly cry at least three times a month, and that doesn't include when I'm on my period. Right now, my dad is in hospital after suffering both a heart attack and a stroke. At first they thought he'd be brain damaged from lack of oxygen during the heart attack, but it's the stroke stopping him from doing a lot of the things he could before." I glanced down at our joined hands. "I destroy movie sets, topple drag queens from the stage, get into punch-ups, and I can't drive for shit."

Adam stopped me with a finger pressed gently to my lips. "You're also kind, considerate, caring and loving. You dance with kids who have terminal cancer and try to get their wishes to come true. You aren't afraid to ask someone you don't like if they can help, then take their place when they refuse." Adam released my hands to cup my face. "You are perfect. Everything about you is perfect." He leaned forward until his lips touched mine. "I want to make this work. I want this, I want *you*, more than I've ever wanted anything."

The realisation hit with the force of a baseball bat upside the head.

He did want to be with me.

I'd been wrong about Adam Jacobs.

Fuck. My. Life.

Chapter Thirty-Nine.

"Really?" I asked, my voice shaky against his finger. He smiled and shifted his hand to my cheek, fingers curling around the back of my head.

"Yes, really." He drew me to him, lips brushing gently against mine.

I could smell the cologne he wore, deep, sweet and musky, and so panty-meltingly masculine. He took me with him as he leaned against the back of his chair, strong hands pulled me into his lap and I sat with my legs across his lap, bridal style.

"So beautiful," Adam whispered before he leaned forward to kiss me again.

His lips caressing mine, tongue sliding through his lips to trace over mine. I melted into a Melinda puddle right there in his lap. It was better than the best chocolate, champagne, cute fluffy kittens, mum's homemade hot chocolate with five marshmallows bobbing in the cup on a winter's day, and sipped in front of the fireplace while the snow drifted down.

The world dropped away, and all there was before me, all that mattered in this very moment, was Adam Fucking Wonderful Jacobs. Movie star, rich guy, charity man, and a guy who wanted to make *us* work.

Adam's kisses were tender, soft, loving. Each time he pressed his lips to my face, or neck, he paused as if trying to figure out where the best place for his lips was in order to give me the most sensual sensation. His hands slowly explored my body, finding sensitive areas which caused me to moan softly in his embrace, against his lips. He shifted me, so my legs hung over the armrest of the chair we were sitting in, a hand sliding between both legs to my thighs, fingers trailing under my dress in search of the hidden treasure he sought.

I giggled when he touched on a ticklish spot.

He leaned back, a cheeky grin on his face. "You're ticklish, hmmm, I'll file that away for later reference?"

"Uh… no… no, definitely not…" I tried hard to hold in the giggles by biting down on my bottom lip.

"Oh, I think you are." His eyes sparkled with a devilish glint.

"No, no, no, no, nooo!" I squealed as his fingers slid up my side and he began to tickle me.

My inner pig/mule/Melinda came into being as I giggled, snorted and kicked against his tickling fingers. I arched my back in an attempt to squirm away from him, I tossed my head back and connected with the edge of the coffee table.

I saw stars, and they weren't like little Adam Jacobs' swirling around my head like cartoon birdies.

"Ow! Shite! Bollocks, fuck, crap, fucketty fuck, fuck, fuck!" I reached for the back of my head as tears filled my eyes.

"Oh shit!" Adam sat me upright, his nimble fingers slipping from their devilish position to check the back of my head.

"Ow!" I moaned as his hand slipped over the already forming egg at the back of my skull.

"Are you okay?" Adam held me hard against his chest, wrapping his arms around me in a protective gesture.

"Is there blood?"

"Doesn't look like it, but there's the beginnings of a huge lump forming back there."

"Yeah, I can feel it."

"I'm sorry baby." Adam kissed me on the temple.

Baby... he called me baby! I swooned.

"I think we need to get you checked out, you're looking flushed and glassy-eyed." Adam reached behind me and picked up his phone from the coffee table.

"I'm okay."

"Are you sleepy, nauseous, do you have a headache, are there flickering lights in front of your eyes?"

"Adam, I just whacked my head on a coffee table, do you know how many times I've done something similar? I'll be fine."

"You could have concussion, I just want to make sure you're okay."

I sighed, who could argue with those eyes? "Okay, fine, let me text my brother and friend, they brought me here and will panic if I disappear. I grabbed my phone, there were already three texts from Libbie, two picture texts showed she was about to have the time of her life with two guys, the two she'd been dancing with.

OMG! It's Lars and Jorgen from the Dead Sinners Society! That band I have playing in my car. It's THEM! I'm gonna get shagged by DSS! BEST NIGHT EVA! Sorry to bail on ya babes, catch up tomorrow and I'll spill ALL! ♥♥♥ I sighed, so much for Libby panicking and wondering where I was.

"Well Libby's good, she's got some action tonight." I opened my brother's texts.

Where r you, sis? Libby said you went off with some hot guy? Are you ok? U need me to kick his ass? Call me!

I chuckled, then winced, as pain sheared through my head.

"I just have to call my brother, let him know what's going on."

Adam nodded and kissed my cheek, before he reached up, took my chin in his fingertips and turned my face to kiss me on the lips.

I heard my brother answer and reluctantly broke free of Adam's kiss. "Hi, Robbie." I tilted my head so Adam could continue to assail me with kisses.

"Bloody hell Mel! Where are you? Libby said you left with some bloke?"

"Yeah, but I'm okay. I hit my head so we're heading to the hospital to get me checked out at his insistence."

"You knocked your head and he still wants to spend time with you? Is he aware of your clumsiness?" Robbie laughed.

"Yes, you git. Anyways, I'll be able to find my own way home, so don't worry about me okay?"

"If you're sure? I don't want Mum to end up in hospital alongside Dad if I have to tell them you went away with a stranger and didn't come home last night."

"Don't stress, I'll be home tonight."

"Okay, but at the first sign of trouble, call, okay? Even if you let it ring once and have to hang up, I'll come find you."

"Yeah, I know you would, but honestly, I'm fine. Go pick up someone nice."

"Oh, I think I already have." Robbie sounded pleased.

"Have fun!"

"Oh, I will! See ya, and remember, call if you need an escape."

"I'll be fine," I said, ending the call.

While I was on the phone, Adam was on his. "Yes, that'd be great, bring the car around to the service door. Thanks Mick." He ended his call and turned to me. "Looks like someone tipped off the paps. Apparently, there's a group of them outside the main entrance, waiting for me to make an appearance." He kissed my neck. "We're going to have to make a sneaky exit. I have a couple of security guys waiting for us to leave through the service door, and my driver will meet us there." He helped me to my feet before grabbing his jacket.

"Oh wait, my purse!" I looked around before remembering I had left it in the other VIP booth.

"Already taken care of, one of the security guys has it, and will bring it to us when we leave." Adam placed the jacket around my shoulders. I felt comforted by the closeness of it, and his scent, even more so, I felt aroused. The things that man's cologne did to me.

Adam ushered me into the corridor, where a security guy was waiting. "Your purse, miss." He handed me my clutch.

"Thanks." I smiled as I curled my fingers around the bottom of the purse, clutching it like an eagle with its prey. A slow, but hard and painful pounding had begun in my head, and I knew I'd be waking up with a monster headache in the morning.

Adam held my free hand and led me down the corridor, through to the service area of the nightclub. The pounding beat of the bass heavy music added to the pounding in my head and I felt tired, a little dizzy. "Hang on a sec." I leaned against the wall as the alcohol and head injury worked against my consciousness. Adam was talking to me, but I couldn't make out what he was saying. It took a few seconds for everything to come clear again.

Adam studied my face, his concern evident.

"I'm okay, sorry, I think I had too much to drink as well as the bump on the head. Not a great combination."

"I'm definitely taking you to a hospital right now." Adam leaned forward, slipped an arm under my legs, and swept me into his arms.

He carried me outside, I leaned my head against the warmth of his shoulder and sighed. I was more than happy to be transported this way for the rest of my life.

As soon as the door opened, and we stepped outside, we were almost blinded by the flashing of cameras and shouted questions. Adam moved quickly to the waiting car, while security guys, who looked like they could be rugby players, pushed back the crowd of paparazzi.

The noise of their shouting reverberated in my head until Adam settled me in the car, slid in beside me, and closed the door, blocking out most of the noise before the driver sped off.

"Nearest hospital please, Mike. My girlfriend has hit her head." Adam clipped my seatbelt on before he took care of his own. He carefully checked over my bump, again. "Hmm, I think you hit your head harder than we thought. There's blood after all." Adam showed me the blood on his finger.

That was it, I was gone. Done. Did I mention I can't handle the sight of blood?

I felt the rush of bile screaming up my throat, burning my oesophagus as it thundered through my system and powered from my mouth, all over Adam's nice, clean car.

All over myself.

All over Adam.

But the one thing which had shocked me the most and knocked me for six?

Adam had called me his girlfriend.

His *GIRLFRIEND*.

Oh… My… Fucking…

GOD!

Fuck. My. Life.

Chapter Forty.

I winced again as the doctor poked and prodded at the back of my head. The nurse beside him preened, and flirted, shamelessly with Adam, but he politely ignored her after signing an autograph. I sat in a hospital gown, while Adam stood handsome in a set of nurse's scrubs. Our stinking clothes were sealed in a bag. I felt so embarrassed, but there was nothing I could do, but sit and listen to the doctor as he examined me.

"It looks like a small abrasion, and the lump should go down within a day or two. The vomiting, I would attribute to the alcohol consumption as your reaction times are normal. Your pupils are also responsive so, it's unlikely you have a concussion."

"So, she's okay to be released, Doc? I can take her home?" Adam asked as he slipped an arm around my shoulders and kissed my temple.

I swear I heard the nurses, who were peeking out from behind the exam room door, sigh with jealousy. I snuggled up against Adam, and felt his thumb rubbing up and down over my shoulder in a comforting gesture.

"I don't see why not. She'll be fine, though she'll have a headache in the morning. I'm not recommending she takes any painkillers for a few hours yet, let her body clear out the alcohol in her system first, then in the morning she can have something to help with the pain." The doctor stepped away, peeled the gloves off his hands and tossed them into a nearby bin.

"Thanks again, Doc. If there's anything I can do to repay you for seeing us so quickly, let me know." Adam smiled and this time I know I heard the nurses sigh.

"Well, actually Mr. Jacobs, my daughter would love an autograph, and if I could get a picture with you?" The doctor held out a pen and a notepad.

"Sure thing, what's her name?" Adam accepted the pen and paper while I slid down from the examination table. My man, hmmm, I love the sound of that, *my man* was suddenly inundated with staff members begging him to sign everything from bits of paper to scrubs. One male nurse wanted him to sign his chest!

Once done, we hurried from the hospital, trying to avoid being accosted by more fans for autographs. Adam's car and driver were waiting for us.

"Okay, let's get you home." Adam bundled me into the car and slid in beside me. He dumped the bag with our soiled clothes on the floor, thankfully it was sealed, and the driver had managed to clean the car, though it still smelled a bit sour, he'd done a stellar job.

"What's the address, Miss?" Mike, the driver asked from the front.

"Henley's Road, south of Grantley Village. It's a large nursery, you can't miss it. My parent's cottage is behind it."

The driver nodded and tapped on the GPS system attached to the windscreen. "Henley's Road, got it."

"Mike," I said sheepishly.

"Yes, Miss?"

"I'm so sorry for throwing up in the car."

"Not a problem, Miss, happens more than you think."

I smiled abashedly and leaned back, the surgical gown sliding up over my legs. Adam took the opportunity to slide his hand down my bare back and his thumb slid inside the waistband of my panties. I snuggled up against him as Mike drove us out of the city. We spoke softly, canoodling in the back seat of the car, ignoring the world as it slipped by.

Mike slowed as we drove past the nursery, turned off the road and onto the gravel drive leading to the cottage.

The inside lights were off, but the front light shone brightly, illuminating the front steps. Mum's car was parked in its usual space, it appeared Robbie had yet to return from the city. Adam stepped out, and helped me from the car.

"I don't want to leave you after your injury." He caressed my cheek. I leaned into his palm almost purring like a contented kitten. "Do you mind if I stay the night so I can watch over you?"

"You want to stay the night?"

"Yes."

"With me?"

"With you."

"In my cottage?"

"Well, I'm not really looking forward to staying in the tool shed, but if that's where you want me. It won't be easy to watch over you from there though."

I playfully slapped his chest. He smirked, kissed me on the nose and n turned back to the car, retrieving the bag of barf-soiled clothes.

I thought about it for a second. Adam Jacobs wanted to stay with me tonight! In my parents' house. Not in some posh hotel which he undoubtedly could afford. No, he wanted to stay in my home, where I grew up. With my mother sleeping not two rooms away from my own. He wanted me to be comfortable, to feel safe, secure. Damn, I must have won the boyfriend lottery.

"Okay, but we have to be quiet. Mum's probably sleeping after helping Dad with his rehab all day. She'll be exhausted."

Adam nodded, leaned in through the open back door and spoke softly. He closed the door and Mike drove away, leaving us alone in the cool evening air in front of my family home.

I held Adam's hand and led him to the front door, slipping my keys in and opening it for him. His hands slid around my waist, pushing aside the split material of the surgical gown. His hands were warm against my skin and his lips met the curve of my neck where it met my shoulder. I turned and softly closed the door, locking it again.

"Where's your room?" he asked.

"Down the hall, first on the right." I spoke quietly. "Bathroom is next to it, if you want to have a shower or use the loo."

"Only if you come in too," he winked cheekily.

"I just have to take care of the clothes, and I'll be right in."

"Okay, I'll meet you in bed." He winked again in the dim light of the entry.

I giggled as his fingers trailed down my sides causing little bumps to break. He pulled away from me and padded quietly down the hall as I headed through the kitchen to the laundry. I rinsed the vomit from the clothes, and set them to soak in the laundry tub with some eucalyptus wash Mum kept for emergencies such as this.

I crept back to my room, after slipping my shoes off so I could move with more stealth through the house. I didn't want to wake up Mum with my heels clip-clopping on the floorboards in the hall. I opened the door to my room to find a trail of clothing. Men's clothing. Socks, surgical scrubs and a pair of boxers led towards my bed, where a very manly lump was laying beneath my pink comforter.

"Good evening, grandma. My what big eyes you have," I said jokingly.

"That's not all that's *big* on me, my dear, won't you come closer?" Adam flung aside the blankets and invited me into the single bed.

I stripped slowly, his eyes devouring me as I tried to be as sexy as possible in the dim light of my bedside table lamp. My stuffed animal collection was getting a good show along with Adam. He grinned and beckoned me closer. I sashayed, step by tiny step, stopping when one of my stray stuffed toys squeaked beneath my foot. I kicked it aside to join the others in the pile before moving closer to the bed.

I slid in beside Adam, there was very little room for us both, and he pulled me on top of him. I could feel something very large indeed pressing against my hip. I snuggled close, his body moving beneath mine as his hands slid over my ass, and his lips pressed hard against mine. I moaned as his tongue pushed between my lips and caressed mine, his hands sliding up higher over my back. I ground myself against him, only to have him grunt at the sound of a spring giving away. I pressed myself harder against him, showing him how much I wanted him, despite the slight pounding in my head, which was getting better with the flush of endorphins from our activities.

"Babe," Adam whispered.

"Yeah?" I leaned down to kiss his stubbly chin, and along the jawline to his throat.

"I think I've got a spring in my ass."

"What?" I pushed up.

"I think I've got a spring in my ass."

"Oh, my God! I'm so sorry, I need a new mattress, badly."

My bed had attacked my lover!

Way to go Mel.

Fuck. My. Life.

Chapter Forty-One

I scooted off his heavenly body. "Let me see."

Adam swung his feet over the side of the bed, and as he stood, I couldn't help but get a good look at his assets, both front and back. And surely, on his magnificent posterior, there was a small, red mark.

I giggled. "It's just a little prick."

He spun around, almost turkey slapping me. His expression was aghast. "It's not, it's huge!"

"It's just a little spot, I promise." I turned to look at the bed. "But, we can't lay on the bed like that." The offending spring, which I thought I'd managed to push back under the mattress, was now sticking up through the top.

Adam grinned cheekily. "I have an idea."

He moved to the side wall, where my collection of stuffed animals lay in wait.

He picked up as many as his muscular arms could carry, then arranged them on the floor. "Grab a sheet and the covers." Adam nodded to the abandoned bed.

I pulled the covers off and together we made up the substitute bed, using only the animals which didn't squeak. We knelt together, hands joined, before moving onto the makeshift bed, our lips meeting as our bodies joined as one.

I'm certain my toys, if they were alive, would need some serious counselling after what Adam and I did on them that night.

***

I woke the next morning to an annoying shaft of sunlight blaring through the part in my curtains, and deliciously warm arms surrounding me. The sight of Adam sleeping peacefully in the twisted sheets, and surrounded by stuffed animals which had managed to escape from beneath us, was simply heavenly. I wished I could capture it, and keep it forever. I slipped from Adam's secure arms, nature's call becoming more of a scream for relief. The soft pounding in my head cranked up a few notches when I moved, and would require the application of painkillers and a cup of tea. I slipped on a tatty nightgown to cover my nakedness before making an appearance in front of my mum.

I left sleeping beauty surrounded by my stuffed toys and headed out to the kitchen, the accusing glare of Percy, my stuffed toy unicorn seemed to follow me as I crept out. The house was still quiet, but Mum must have been in the shower, I heard it running when I left my room.

In the kitchen, I popped the kettle on and grabbed some painkillers from the cupboard above the sink where Mum kept the first aid items, plasters and antacid and the like. As soon as the kettle whistled, letting me know it had boiled, Robbie staggered in.

He was dishevelled, his hair was a mess and his shirt wasn't buttoned up right. He looked like he'd just rolled out of bed after a long night of shagging, but he'd come in through the back door.

"Morning sunshine." I said, nursing my cup of tea as I leaned against the bench. "Sleep well, or did you find someone to take you home last night?"

Robbie's cheeks flushed red. I was on instant alert. He *had* gotten some action last night.

"Morning," he mumbled.

"You look a bit shagged love."

He grunted and pushed me aside to get to the kettle.

The door banged and a cheery whistling drifted through before a familiar American voice called out. "Robbie, sweetheart, are you coming back?"

My eyes darted to Robbie who had the good grace to look abashed.

"Well welly well." I smirked as Zane entered, looking equally as dishevelled as Robbie. It didn't take a Mensa genius to put one and one together and get two. "Robbie, you skank." I giggled and nudged my brother playfully.

"Morning Mel," Zane grinned. "I must say, your brother has a particularly delicious ass."

"Eww, Zane, I love my brother, but I really don't need to know about his *delicious* arse. It is way too much information at seven in the morning, no, make that way too much information period."

I sipped tea while Robbie made Zane a coffee. Zane placed his arms around Robbie and kissed his cheek. I smiled as my brother leaned into his kiss. I knew there was more to them chatting on that gay dating site than either of them was letting on.

"Where's the bathroom?" Zane asked.

I nodded down the hall, "Second door on the right, but I think Mum's in there."

"I can wait." He took the coffee Robbie had made for him and sat down at the kitchen table. "This place is gorgeous, Mel. I'm amazed you left for LA, I mean look at this place, the charm!"

Robbie chuckled, I smiled as I sipped my tea.

Mum's sudden scream broke the camaraderie. We dropped our cups and bolted to where she stood at my door. I swear my jaw dropped through the old floorboards of the house and down to the core of the earth.

Adam was standing in the middle of my room. Naked and cradling Percy in front of his crotch. The toy unicorn's horn pointing upwards.

Mum swung towards me with a glare. "Melinda, why is there a naked man in your bedroom, and what the devil is he doing to Percy?"

"Uh… Mum, this is Adam Jacobs, my boyfriend." I moved to stand beside Adam, who was flushed pink with embarrassment.

He stepped forward, keeping Percy in place over his groin, and held out his right hand. "Nice to meet you, Mrs. Whittaker."

"Yes, you too, Adam. Please, call me Angie." Mum accepted his hand cautiously and they shook. "Will you be staying for breakfast?"

"Of course, you are staying for breakfast, right?" I gazed up at him.

"I'd love to spend the day with you, I don't have to be back for filming until tomorrow." Adam hugged me close.

"Well, that's lovely, but I would prefer if you dressed." Mum turned and stopped, noticing Zane. "And, who are you?"

"I'm Melinda's friend, from the states, Ma'am. Zane. I met your son Robbie last night."

Mum looked Zane up and down. "I didn't hear anyone come in last night, and Robbie's bed is still made, where on earth did you two sleep last night?"

"Who the bloody hell has been in the tool shed?" Uncle Leo's Scottish brogue boomed through the house.

"Uh…" Robbie flushed red.

I sighed, pinching the bridge of my nose with forefinger and thumb.

If this morning didn't make Adam run for the hills, I don't know what would.

Fuck. My. Life.

Chapter Forty-Two.

While our clothes tumbled around in Mum's dryer, Adam sat in one of Robbie's clean robes and I changed into something more becoming than my tatty nightie. Jeans and a long-sleeved shirt, topped with a pullover covered my former naked state. Adam still looked sexy in Robbie's nearly threadbare dressing gown.

"I think this should fit you." Robbie held out a selection of clothes for Adam to try on.

"Thanks, man." Adam smiled as I placed a coffee in front of him.

"So, laddie, how long have ye and our Mel been together?" Uncle Leo asked, sitting enjoying his own steaming cup of tea.

"Well, there's been a small separation, due to some misinformation." He gazed at me with a forlorn expression. "For which I'm sorry. I should have tried harder to get in touch with her, but my schedule was too hectic. I think my manager also had something to do with keeping us apart." He shook his head.

"Might be time for a new manager, one who doesn't mess with ye personal life, laddie."

"Yeah, I think so. I think he is only interested in the cash flow which comes with my name, and to hell with how I feel about anything." Adam scrubbed his hand over his face, sighed and looked to Uncle Leo. "I'd love to have something normal for once, you know? Like here." He spread his arms wide, indicating our property.

"Normal?" Leo chuckled. "There's nothing normal about life, ye just gotta take it as ye can. If ye get lemons outa life, add some vodka."

Adam laughed.

Robbie came back in from whatever it was he'd been doing, and joined us at the table. Mum and I served up plates of bacon and eggs to the boys.

"And ye, laddie." Uncle Leo pointed a fork at my brother. "Ye better get back in that tool shed and set it aright. Damn bloody mess in there, ye are lucky it 'twas me and not ye mam that went in there first."

Zane joined us after using the bathroom, his hair still wet from the shower. "Ooh, eggs 'n' bacon!" He rubbed his hands together.

"And ye can bloody well help Robbie." Zane looked up when Uncle Leo's statement was directed at him, he looked like a deer caught in the headlights of an oncoming truck.

"Me?"

"Aye, ye. Ye helped make that mess, ye can help clean up. That's how things work out here. Then ye can make yerself useful and help with the deliveries."

"Well, I'm heading in to see your father shortly." Mum wiped her hands and took the apron off. "Melinda, I think it prudent to introduce your new boyfriend to your father, but perhaps not in the same way as I was introduced this morning."

I glanced at Adam, who chewed on a piece of toast.

"Sure, Mrs. Whittaker. I promise I'll be dressed." He smiled happily.

I smiled too, unable to stop my grin.

"All right then, when you two finish and wash up, we'll head out. Your father is having a half day of rest today. He's being far too hard on himself in rehab, if he keeps pushing the way he does, he'll get sick again." Mum was unable to hide the worry in her voice.

Robbie stood and gave mum a hug. "You know what he's like, Mum, he wants to come back home as soon as possible."

I joined them, leaving our guests at the table.

"I'm lucky to have you both." Mum hugged us close.

Adam, Zane and Uncle Leo smiled at the family display. Mum looked to Adam and Zane. "I hope you boys have wonderful people in your lives as I do with these two."

Adam's gaze stayed on me. "I certainly do, Mrs. Whittaker." He winked at me before his face lit up with a charming smile.

***

The hospital didn't seem so gloomy today, not with Adam's hand firmly in mine. Mum had driven us to the hospital and was chatting to one of the nurses on Dad's rehab ward. Dad sat in a recliner, his wheelchair not far from his side.

"Hey Daddy." I held the bunch of flowers Adam and I had picked earlier before we left for the hospital. Dad's eyes lit up, and the good side of his face perked in a lopsided smile.

"Pop-Pop-Poppet…" he stuttered, and tried to lift his arms. There was more movement in them than I'd seen previously.

"Hi." I crouched down to hug him.

"Wh-who's this…?" He nodded slowly to Adam.

"Daddy, this is Adam Jacobs, my boyfriend." I looked up at my man from my kneeling position.

Adam reached out with his right hand to shake my Dad's trembling hand.

"A pleasure to meet you, Sir." Adam lifted Dad's hand into his and they shook.

"Adam Ja-Jacobs… from m-mo-movies?" Dad asked.

"Yes, sir. The very same."

I heard the whispering of the nurses before I noticed them, Adam had been spotted. He turned and smiled at the nurses. "Excuse me for just a moment." He released Dad's hand to my care and headed to where the nurses stood gawking. I heard him murmur something to the nurses, and the door closed.

I looked at him puzzled when he returned to our side. "Sorry, I get that everywhere. I explained, I'd be happy to do a couple of autographs and visit the children's ward after our visit, as long as we're left undisturbed while we visit with your father. I also asked that no one leaks my visit to social media until after we've left."

"Sounds good and the kids will love it."

Mum came in shortly after, and insisted I join her in the cafeteria for, what turned out to be, very weak tea. We left Dad and Adam to talk. I felt nervous.

Mum smiled over her cup. "Don't worry, sweetheart, your father only wants to make sure your new beau is right for you."

"Oh, God…" I moaned, hiding my face with my hands.

Mum chuckled. "Your father won't scare him off. I mean, if I didn't scare him off when I discovered him stark naked in your bedroom surrounded by your stuffed toys this morning, then I don't think he's easily scared. Your father just wants to make sure you're not going to be taken for a ride like you were with that other bastard."

"Mum!" I gasped, shocked at her sudden, and uncharacteristic, profanity.

"What?" she asked, looking innocent.

"You never swear."

"When occasion calls for it, darling, I have been known to toss a dirty word or two in. It can be therapeutic." She tipped her tea as if the bland brew was the absolute height of sophisticated English Tea.

All that was missing were the watercress and cucumber sandwiches. Our stale and slightly soggy ham, cheese and tomato sandwiches would have to suffice. I fidgeted with the crust I hadn't eaten as I thought over Dad's situation. He wasn't improving much, though his speech had improved, his physical movements were still a long way from normal.

"Mum…." I slowly spun the crust in my hand. "Dad's improving, isn't he?"

Something flashed in Mum's eyes. My heart sank, gut fell through the floor to join my jaw from this morning. She cleared her throat nervously.

"Ahem. Well, Melinda…" She began in a tone which once matched how she would tell us the pet guinea pig wasn't going to be coming back from the shoebox Dad had placed it in before he took it to the back garden for an unceremonious burial. She sighed, and my heart broke as a tear escaped.

"He's improved, but not as much as the doctors were hoping. It's quite possible …" She took a deep, calming and visually bolstering breath. "It's possible he may be confined to a wheelchair and need our help to do things for the rest of his life."

I stared at her, mouth open, catching flies.

"But, what about the nursery? It's Dad's whole life."

"It was your father's dream, honey. He got partway there. He's always loved plants and gardening. But you kids, his family, that's his life. As long as we are all here for him, he'll be okay. We will more than likely end up selling the nursery, I can't see how we can continue to run it if I'm taking care of your father."

The stale sandwich settled like a hard stone in my stomach.

I didn't know what to say, or what to do to help.

Poor Dad.

Poor Mum.

Poor Robbie.

They were going to give up something they all loved, for the one person who gave it all to them.

Fuck. My. Life.

Chapter Forty-Three

Two warm hands settled on my shoulders and a slightly stubbly cheek brushed against mine.

"Hey, beautiful." Adam turned his lips to my cheek and planted a soft kiss on my skin.

Mum smiled warmly at the display of affection and I swear I heard someone drop something breakable in the servery of the cafeteria along with whispers of:

"Holy shite, that's Adam Jacobs!"

"No, it isn't."

"Bollocks, it is!"

"Mrs. Whittaker, Mr. Whittaker asked if I would take you and Mel out for lunch today. Where would you like to go, my treat?"

I craned my head backward to catch his gaze.

Mum smiled, he flicked his eyes down to catch mine and winked. Relief flew through my system like a crazed European swallow on speed carrying a coconut on a line. His hands squeezed my shoulders gently, reassuringly. Dad hadn't gone to town on him.

"No, that's quite all right, Adam." Mum stood, leaving the rest of her sandwich on the plate. "I'm not hungry."

"Raincheck then?" Adam asked hopefully.

"Yes, raincheck." Mum shouldered her bag and moved to my side. "Now you two kids have fun, Oh, and Robbie has been told to get you a new bed. It's not going to be an expensive one, mind you, but you can't use that horrible old mattress anymore, the springs are ready to go on it."

Adam chuckled, and I felt my cheeks heat.

"Uh, yeah, they are well and truly stuffed. Thanks mum!"

She kissed me on the cheek, and squeezed my shoulder before Adam and I in the cafeteria.

"Ready to go? I need to stop by the children's ward before we leave. Oh, and if your mom isn't going to make it, would you like to invite your brother and Zane? We can go bed shopping instead of your brother." He waggled his eyebrows suggestively.

I laughed and playfully slapped at his hands on my shoulders. "You want to test it out once we get it back to my place." I stood slowly so as not to smack him in the nose with my head. The lump had gone down, and there was only site pain when I touched it. Adam pulled me into his embrace and softly kissed me.

"Oh, you have become wise to my evil plans: to get you into bed as soon as possible and ravish you." He imitated a British accent, the same as he'd adopted for the Duke character he was portraying in the film. "I shall have to find a suitable dungeon to keep you in, my princess."

"Oh no, don't go all *Christian Grey* on me," I giggled, sliding my arms around his perfectly muscled waist.

"No, no, I'm not *that* kinky." Adam slipped an arm around my shoulder and pulled me tight against his side as we walked out of the cafeteria.

Nurses smiled shyly as we passed, their eyes glued to my tall, handsome man. I was no arm candy and I knew it. It still boggled my mind as to why he'd chosen me. I wasn't a supermodel, I wasn't some famous actress. I was just me, plain old Melinda Whittaker, who buggered up almost everything she touched. Who was given the dubious title of 'Smelly Melly' in school and whose first love cheated on her with a woman of every race and was now marrying one of them. I glanced up at him as we walked, my mind trying to figure it out.

We turned the corner to enter the Children's Ward. When Adam spotted some of the children, he smiled, a genuine smile. Not one of those fake arse ones like a politician puts on for the cameras, but a true, genuine smile. I couldn't help but smile too.

The rows of children who were in the ward looked back at him, wide-eyed in amazement.

"Hi guys, mind if I visit with you for a while?"

Instantly, there was a rush of kids around him. Some had their parents bring their IV stands, while others waited somewhat impatiently for the nurses to bring wheelchairs to transfer them all into a brightly sunlit room where books and games were stacked neatly on shelves for the kids to entertain themselves while they got better.

Adam moved away and settled on a chair in the room, children surrounded him like happy, chattering little mites. "Okay everyone, pick a book and I'll read to you." Some of the children were able to move quickly, unhindered. Parents helped those who couldn't get to the bookshelves on their own because they were in wheelchairs. One of the cancer patients, confined to his bed, which had been wheeled in shortly after we arrived, asked one of the other children to choose a book for him.

The nurses brought around a tray of drinks and light snacks for the kids. The matron of the ward stood beside me and smiled, her arms crossed.

"We heard he was coming to pay our ward a visit. These kids are so happy, it's lovely to see such a big star taking an interest in his fans and offering some of his time to them." The matron wiped a stray tear from the corner of her eye before it managed to escape. "Are you a friend?" she asked me.

"Yes." I watched Adam open the first book in the pile the kids had placed beside him, and begin to read. Parents and nurses had turned on their phones and were recording the scene as he read each book. Children snuggled up to their parents, and one little girl curled up on his lap, sucking her thumb as he read her chosen book.

One of the nurses joined us, a mother following. "Oh my god, I think my ovaries have exploded," The nurse said with a chuckle. "That's got to be the sweetest thing I've ever seen, Kira Holsworthy is one lucky girl."

"Oh, he's not with Kira," I said, a little defensively, but trying to keep my tone off-hand.

"Oh, who is he with then?" the nurse asked, her eyes calculating the chances of hooking a big fish like Adam Jacobs. "Not that blonde cow who made a fool of herself on YouTube?"

I felt my face heating with embarrassment and anger.

"I don't know why he would bother with someone like that. I mean, did you read the interview with his manager quoting Kira and Adam were happy, and looking forward to marriage?"

I turned and punched the bitch, in my mind.

In reality, I turned and smiled at her. "Don't believe everything you read, lovie." I turned my attention back to Adam, who was finishing the second-last book in the pile.

The children had sat quietly, and watched patiently as Adam read to them, as enthralled by his presence as the parents and staff were. He had that effect on people. He drew you in, made sure you were okay. He was a good guy, the perfect guy. And already, I could feel the female sharks circling.

I'd have to defend my turf like a mama bear defending her cubs.

Only problem was, I was terrible at defence, and worse at confrontations.

Fuck. My. Life.

Chapter Forty-Four.

As soon as the sliding doors whooshed open, revealing the outside world, the flashes started. Of course, someone had tipped off the press that Adam Jacobs was visiting the local hospital. Paparazzis and journalists shouted questions and snapped pictures as we hurried to meet Adam's driver, who was waiting patiently at the kerb.

"Good afternoon, Mr. Jacobs, Miss Whittaker."

"Hello, Mike, we're going bed shopping today." Adam smiled at me as he bundled me into the back seat of the car first.

I checked my phone, it was almost three o'clock. "Looks like we missed lunch, but if Robbie's still about, we can catch him for afternoon tea."

"Sounds good." Adam clicked my seatbelt closed before he secured his own into place. He reached over and gathered my hand, enclosing it in his long, thick fingers. I shivered on thinking how magical those fingers had been last night, heat crept into my cheeks.

"What are you thinking, Miss Whittaker?" Adam leaned over to whisper in my ear.

The warmth of his breath tickled my skin and he pressed his lips against the shell, tongue sliding down to draw the soft skin of my earlobe between his lips. I giggled. I'd never had sex or fooled around in the back seat of a car, and thankfully the windows of this one were dark enough that there was little chance of someone taking a snap of our activities.

Mike chuckled and pressed a button, a small partition rose and closed off the back area from the front, I hadn't noticed the feature until now. The car was like a taxi, but more private. I turned my head, catching Adam's lips against mine and let his tongue slip into my mouth. He unbuckled his seatbelt, scooting over to the middle seat before he buckled up again.

"Safety first." He grinned.

"You're going to have me all hot and bothered before we pick out a bed." I giggled again, as his hands roamed over my body, tickling me as often as they aroused me.

"Ooh. I like the way you said *we,* does this mean I get to sleep in it with you?"

"Maybe," I replied cheekily.

"Maybe? Hmm, how can I change that to a *yes*?" He pressed his body against mine as his lips chased lines over my jaw, along my neck and shoulders. He tugged the neck of my shirt from one shoulder, so he could patter kisses on the skin there. I moaned softly as his hands found places to tease me into submission.

"Is that a *yes*?" His voice rumbled against my neck.

My body tingled with desire as I reacted to his erotic touch. "Oh Adam," I whimpered as a hand shifted lower.

He eased back, and studied me. "Yes, Melinda?"

"Yes," I whispered, "Yes, you can sleep with me in my new bed, anytime you like."

"Fantastic, we'll get new sheets and pillows as well as the bed, if you like?" He pulled away from my feverishly aroused body. "And, you don't have to worry about paying, I've got this covered." He winked.

I stared at him, surprised he didn't continue from where he'd left off. Instead, he put an arm around my shoulders and casually pulled my top back into place.

"So, all that was to get me to agree to let you into my bed?"

"Yup."

"You bastard." I laughed and playfully slapped him on the arm.

"It worked, didn't it?"

"Too well, I think I may need new panties, and poor Mike might need to wipe down the seat after we get out."

Adam laughed. "Damn, woman, you know how to leave a guy with a boner."

"Self-inflicted," I said as we pulled up at Hobson's Furniture. "I have no sympathy and I hope you have trouble walking." I clambered over him to get to the door Mike had opened. He'd parked in the side parking lot, beside the furniture store.

"I called the security boys, Mr. Jacobs. Considering we had a little trouble back at the hospital, I figured it was warranted. Your bodyguards waiting in front of the store." Mike said, after Adam adjusted himself and managed to climb from the car.

"Thanks, Mike, good thinking." Adam patted Mike on the shoulder before leading me to the front of the shop.

"You know, I've not done this before, bought new furniture. This is going to be fun." Adam rubbed his hands in gleeful anticipation

"Now, nothing too big, it won't fit into my room. Nothing larger than a queen size." I couldn't believe how excited Adam was. I grabbed his arm and drew him to a stop. "Wait, you've never bought your own furniture? Like ever?"

"Nope. I had a lot of third and fourth-hand crap given to me when I was starting out on my own, and then when I landed my first big contract, I was too busy to organise my housing, so my manager did it for me. From the choice of apartment, to the décor, it was all my manager."

"Please tell me you're joking, right? Can you at least cook?"

"Does Ramen and tinned peaches count?" He slipped an arm around my waist and pulled me close.

"No, really, you're having me on, right?" I asked as one of the big burly blokes from last night pulled the glass door open for us.

"Nope, I need you to feed me, woman. It's the only reason I hooked up with you, for sex and food."

"Pfft, then you're going to starve." I chuckled. "My cooking is terrible. Fish fingers burnt on the outside but still frozen on the inside and roast beef which is still mooing in the middle, just to give you a couple of examples. I can make a mean cup of tea, after all, being British – Tea is our thing."

"I'm sure we'll survive, there's always my personal chef. He's managed to keep me alive and healthy this long."

I laughed, unable to help it. We'd only been together a short while and already he was using 'we' in full sentences, like it was a foregone conclusion we'd move in together.

Wait?

What?

What exactly was he insinuating? My mind reeled as the store's owner approached us and showed us the different models of bed which were for sale.

Did he want me to move in with him?

Did I *want* to move in with him?

Were we going to last, or was I deluding myself? Did he want more than what I could give him? My mind worked overtime, almost to a point where I was insensate.

"Hey, baby, are you okay?" Adam's voice broke through the chaotic thoughts racing through my mind.

"Huh? Oh, yeah, I'm fine."

"It looked like I lost you there for a moment."

"Sorry, lost in thought, just worried about Dad is all."

Adam pulled me in for a hug. "He'll be okay, he's in the best place, and they are getting him better." He kissed the top of my head affectionately. "Let's pick a bed and get it delivered, I want to try it out as soon as we get home, you know, pick up where we left off in the car." He whispered the last, making my body revert to the horny state it was in not too long ago. I squeezed my thighs together in a vain attempt to get a little bit of relief.

I was in a bed store, surrounded by beds we couldn't use. With Adam Fucking Amazing Jacobs, my boyfriend, making me hornier than I'd ever been.

Fuck. My Life.

Chapter Forty-Five.

Just as we'd found the perfect bed and mattress set, my phone rang. I checked the caller ID, it was Libby.

"Hey!"

"Omigod, Mel, please tell me you haven't seen the paper today?!" Her voice sounded panicked, almost hysterical.

"No, why?"

"Okay, good. Don't look at the paper, any paper okay? I'll be at your house in an hour. It's going to be okay, I promise babes." Before I could respond, Libby hung up.

Adam moved to my side, planting a kiss on my temple as I stared at the phone blankly. "Well, that was weird." I dropped the phone back into my bag.

"What's up?" Adam slid an arm around my waist, slipping the fingers of his cuddling hand into the pocket of my jeans. I smiled at the little motions of his fingertips as they teased my arse cheek.

"Libby, my best friend called and told me not to read any papers today…" I looked up at him and shrugged.

"I might have been snapped by a pap last night, with a hot blonde," Adam winked.

"Libby does get protective over this kinda stuff. We grew up together, best friends since we were in nappies."

"Nappies?"

"Diapers."

"Oh." He smirked. "Hopefully we won't need those for a while."

I was lost for words.

"I'd like to keep you to myself for a bit first." He turned my face to his and kissed me, deep, long and sweetly, with as much passion as he could show without throwing me onto the display bed model we'd both picked and having his wicked way with me in the middle of the store.

Before I could make my naughty thoughts verbal, the store manager approached us, clearing his throat. "Well, everything is in order, Mr. Jacobs, we'll have the suite delivered today.

"Suite?" I thought we were only buying the bed.

"Yeah. I went ahead and got the entire suite, for you."

"Adam, you didn't have to do that!"

"I wanted to, because you're worth it." He held me tight against his body and turned his attention back to the store manager. "Thanks again, Paul, I appreciate your help." Adam shook the man's hand and led me back to the store's entry, where his bodyguards were waiting. Adam escorted me to the waiting car and opened the door for me, ushering me in.

"Home?" he asked.

I nodded. "Yes, I better get home, or Libby will blow a gasket if I'm not there when she arrives. She seemed a stressed on the phone, so I hope she's all right. I have to get a start on dinner too."

"Are your mom and brother going to be home for dinner with us?"

"Who said you were invited?" I retorted, but made sure to grin cheekily so he knew I was joking about his non-invitation.

"But, I was going to bring wine!"

"Well, in that case… Adam, would you like to stay for dinner? We are having lasagne."

"And dessert?"

"Sure, why not"

"Hmm... Dessert… Melinda covered in chocolate…" Adam leaned in, his tongue sliding over the pulse point on my neck. I shivered at the erotic sensation and couldn't stop the tiny moan which escaped.

"Oh god, I'd probably eat myself if I was covered in chocolate!" Yes, chocolate is an important food group.

"I'd eat you first." Adam pulled away from my neck to attack my lips with his own. In front, Mike tapped on the partition between the front and back of the car as Adam's hands reached around to caress my curves.

"Damn." He whispered.

I pushed back in my seat, setting my shit back to rights.

"Sorry to interrupt, Mr. Jacobs, but the Furniture store called and said they are going to deliver the bed suite to Miss Whittaker's home right away. They wanted to know if someone would be home to sign for the delivery."

Adam flopped back in his seat, placing an arm casually around me. "Yes, we will be there, I need to stop by a liquor shop to get a bottle of wine for dinner, then we'll head straight to Miss Whittaker's home." Adam pulled me in against his side, as much as the seat belt would allow.

"There's one not far from here." I gave Mike directions to the local liquor shop.

Mike drew the car to a stop in front of the store, and Adam handed him some money from his wallet to grab the bottle of wine before settling back in the seat with me. His hands roamed again, his lips not far behind as the temperature in the back of the car got a little steamy, and the windows began to fog up. If this were a movie, it might have been *Titanic*, the scene where Jack and Rose shag in the back of the car and she leaves a handprint on the steamed-up glass… it was that hot.

In my lust-driven haze, I heard the car door open and close in front, the engine fired up and we moved away from the kerb, onto the road. Adam's body was pressed against mine and I could feel how eager he was to get me home and into the new bed.

Reluctantly, I had to stop him after we left the village, and turned onto the road leading home. Adam looked as flushed as I felt, and I giggled as he adjusted himself.

"Well, let's just hold that thought until tonight." He grinned and kissed me again. His hair had been mussed up a little from where I had run my fingers through it in passion, and now, I ran them through the soft strands again, trying to set it to rights. My finger-combing attempt worked, sort of. Adam still looked like he had 'I just almost shagged my girl in the back seat of a town car' hair. The windows were still steamed up from the hot-n-heavy make-out session.

Mike pulled to a stop in front of the cottage, the delivery truck was already there and Robbie was talking to one of the workers. We left the car and Mike drove off, leaving the bottle of wine in my hands.

"Hey, you finally got rid of that crappy old bed?" Robbie asked, striding up to us, hands in his pockets.

"Yes, Adam figured the toys in my room needed some time to get therapy."

"Yeah, poor, poor Percy, he'll never be the same Unicorn he once was." Robbie laughed at his joke. "What's for dinner?"

"Lasagne." I replied while I watched Adam help the workers shift the bed frame out of the truck and around the back where there was a larger door to fit it through.

"Is he staying for dinner?"

"He is."

"Okay." Robbie looked pensive for a moment.

"Mel, if he hurts you, you let me know, okay? I'll have the entire gay community on his ass."

I laughed so hard at the picture of a bunch of gays taking on Adam, I began to choke on my own spit. Coughing and spluttering as Robbie whacked me on the back with the flat of his palm until I'd recovered.

"That might work, if the entire gay community didn't want his ass, but it's mine, all mine." I rubbed my hands together in the mimicking gesture of some evil villain who had achieved her goals. "He's not so bad, Robbie. We're working on this, we both want it to work. You know, he stayed at the hospital and read each kid a book in the children's ward?"

"Well, that may be, but if he hurts you Mel…" Robbie left the threat unvoiced, I nodded my understanding.

"Hey, Robbie, can you help me set all this up?" Adam called from the front door. "If you're not busy, that is?"

"Sure, just gimme a minute to wash up." Robbie raised his dirty hands in the air, he'd been working in one of the fields with Uncle Leo, removing old and dead plant stock and replanting with new seedlings.

"I'd better get dinner started." I leaned up on tippy-toes and kissed my brother on the cheek. "Be nice, don't go all British Bulldog on him." I turned and walked towards the cottage, Adam had disappeared back inside. I heard the *thump-thump-thump* of fast and heavy bass and the crunch of tyres on gravel as Libby arrived.

"Oh, thank fuck, you bought wine, you'll need it." She shouted through the driver's side window as she parked.

I wondered what disaster she was about to bring to my attention.

Fuck. My. Life.

Chapter Forty-Six.

"All right, so what's the big problem, this big thing you're so worried about?" I poured myself a cup of tea after putting the wine in the fridge to chill it before dinner. I started prepping for the lasagne as Libby sat at the small kitchen table.

"Okay… well... I guess there's no other way to tell you this but…" She sighed, it was almost like she was steeling herself to tell me something bad, something really, really bad. I had turned on the stove and poured a little oil in the frying pan, ready for the onions to sauté.

"Adam Jacobs was seen last night leaving the night club we were at, with some sexy blonde. Then, he was seen with the same blonde at a hospital, reading to a group of sick kids." She stood and came to my side where I had started chopping onions and garlic, the large kitchen knife was left mid-air when she broke the news to me. The tip of the knife was shaking, Libby reached over and took it from my hand.

"It's okay sweetheart, that bastard is a… he's a - a fucking bastard, you don't deserve a man like that, one who gives you something to hope for and then takes it and pisses all over it. If I ever come across the pillock, I'll fucking throw him in the river with a set of concrete shoes. What a bastard, I mean seriously. I honestly hoped he'd see you, be insanely jealous that you were dancing with such a hot guy, from what I remember of last night… and sweep you off your feet again… Ugh!" She hugged me tighter, my whole body was shaking, but not with anger.

"Honey, we'll get through this. Don't worry about Adam Jacobs, he's such a…a…"

"Bastard?" Adam's voice broke through Libby's tirade.

Libby spun around, her arms dropping like stones to her sides. Her face displaying her shock, eyes wide, mouth agape and ready for a fly-catching session.

"Oh… my… fucking… god!" Libby turned bac to me. "It's… it's…"

"Libby, this is-" I began, but was cut off.

"Hi, I'm Adam Jacobs." Adam smiled as he stepped toward Libby and offered his hand.

"I… I…" Libby stuttered, still shocked.

"Libby is unable to make articulate sentences right now Adam, she's just been..." I offered

"Putting my foot in my mouth. Oh, my god, I'm so sorry. I didn't know, I…" Libby glared at me. "You're the blonde, why didn't you stop me?"

I shrugged and burst into laughter.

Adam chuckled. "It's okay, I'm taking care of Mel. I promise you don't need to worry. And you're right, she does deserve to be looked after." Adam pulled me into his side, his strong arm wrapping around my shoulder. He turned his head and kissed me on the temple. "Hey, just wanted to ask, where you wanted your bed put? Space might be a little tight."

"Oh, okay, just a sec." I turned and lowered the heat on the stove, tossed the chopped onions and garlic into the pan, stirred them with the wooden spoon and left them to sizzle while I went with Adam to check on the work in my room.

The old bed had been taken out, as had my crappy old dresser with stickers and marker doodling all over it from my angst-ridden teenage years. Now, stood a handsome mahogany tallboy and dresser, two bedside tables and the four-poster bed I'd fallen in love with, but thought might not be practical considering the size of my room.

"Hmm, maybe we could put the tallboy in the living room for now?" I suggested.

"That could work." Robbie nodded.

I looked over the beautiful bedroom suite, I felt so fortunate.

Adam's hand slid into mine and he squeezed. I felt the warmth of his breath against my ear as he leaned in and whispered. "I can't wait to break it in tonight." His voice sent my mind back to our ride in the car, I licked my lips and grinned. Adam turned me to face him and kissed me, passionately.

"Oh god, you two, get a room," Robbie growled.

"Hey, do we need to video this? Robbie, we could make a mint!" Libby laughed as I flipped her the bird.

The back door opened and closed.

"What the bloody hell?" the Scottish brogue of Uncle Leo roared through the house. "Why is the frying pan on fire?"

At that same moment, I smelled the burning stench of onions and the smoke detector went off, screeching like a banshee.

Oh fuck. Adam broke free from me and ran to the kitchen, Libby, Robbie and I hot on his heels. We found Uncle Leo trying to put the flames out with a damp tea towel. We rushed in and watched as the flames reignited and jumped higher as Uncle Leo took the tea towel away.

"Here!" Adam grabbed the lid from the frying pan and covered it over, before removing the pan from the stove. Grey smoke drifted in the kitchen and the stink of burned onion permeated everything. Adam took the frying pan outside

"Bloody hell, Mel's back in the kitchen." Uncle Leo shook his head.

"Dinner might be a bit late," Robbie chuckled.

I groaned. Yep, showing off my domestic awesomeness to Adam was at the top of my priorities list. Nearly burning down the house wasn't.

Fuck. My. Life.

Chapter Forty-Seven

I awoke snuggled up to the deliciously warm chest of a very naked Adam Jacobs. We were cosy between a set of new sheets on a wonderfully comfortable new mattress, one guaranteed never to poke us in the arse with a broken spring, no matter how hard we bounced on it – and we did quite a bit of bouncing last night.

Dinner was saved by Adam's talent in the kitchen, which he had lied about, and Libby making golden syrup dumplings for dessert.

Our dreamy bliss was disturbed by Adam's phone alarm going off.

"Crap." He sighed. "I have to be in make-up and wardrobe soon. I've got a car coming to pick me up in half an hour. He grumbled, his voice rough with sleep and his hair dishevelled. He wrapped his arms around me, snuggling in tight. "Don't wanna go, don't make me go," he mumbled against my neck.

"Aww, honey, you can stay here if you like."

Adam sighed. "Wish I could, baby, I really do." He grunted as he sat up, keeping the covers over me so I'd stay warm in the chill of early morning. He switched on the bedside lamp, the warm glow illuminating the room and chasing away the shadows.

I lay on my side, head propped up on my hand as I watched him get dressed. His arse fit nicely into his blue jeans and the muscles of his back rippled as he slipped on a tight tee-shirt.

He turned and stared at me. "Are you checking me out?"

"Me?" I asked innocently. "No."

"You totally were, you little liar." Adam chuckled softly, climbing back onto the bed to kiss me. He groaned, breaking the kiss, and leaning his forehead against mine. "Are you delivering to us today?"

Every day we were delivering bouquets of flowers to the lead actors, and replenishing the prop stock with fresh arrangements. Uncle Leo and Robbie were both helping me this morning, as we had a few more orders from local florists to get out as well. The weekend had been busy with wedding orders, and we were slightly behind. But, Robbie and Uncle Leo were both confident we would catch up.

"Yes, Robbie had to let one of the guys go, he wasn't pulling his weight. He was lazy and mouthy to the customers."

"That's not good, you're a man down." He sat on the edge of the bed and pulled on a pair of socks.

I ran my fingertips over his back, feeling each muscular line beneath his skin and revelling in the feel of him against the tips of my fingers.

"Keep doing that and I'm going to be really late, or I'm going to have a lot of trouble fitting into my costume." Adam turned and faced me, his eyes bright with desire in the dim light of the bedside lamp.

I grinned wickedly and moved my hand lower, to the waistband of his jeans

"Now, don't you start, naughty girl!" Adam grabbed my descending hand and held the fingertips to his lips, kissing and nipping at them.

"You just wait until I get home, young lady."

"You're coming back here?" *Wait, he said - Home!"*

"Of course, If it's okay with you?" He took my hand in both of his, covering my fingers with his. "I don't want to waste any time apart from you, Mel." He kissed my fingers, the tips exposed between his hands. "I've lost too much time already, I don't want to lose any more."

I swear I melted into a fresh Melinda puddle right there. Our moment was broken with the beeping of his phone indicating a text message.

"Damn, he's early," Adam cursed. He stood and slipped his shoes on.

He leaned down and kissed me firmly, and lovingly, on the lips. "I'll see you later, okay?" He caressed my chin and jawline with warm and gentle fingers.

"I look forward to it." I watched him grab his wallet from the nightstand and leave my room. I snuggled under the covers, listening to the sound of the front door softly closing and the crunch of the tyres on the gravel drive.

I smiled.

Adam was certainly making himself at home, and I was not complaining.

***

"Come on, Robbie, hurry up." I called through the window from the passenger seat of the van. He was talking to Zane on the phone, organising a date night. Zane was running around London with Perry and the 'girls' for another week yet, before moving on through more of Europe on tour. Robbie flipped me the bird, such a loving brother. Pillock.

I was eager to see my man. It had been a very busy morning, as expected, and now I was dressed in my Whittaker's

Nursery uniform which I wore for deliveries. Robbie drove us to the Castle with the radio playing eighties hits on the local station. We pulled up and were signed in by the film set security, followed the fat guard in the golf cart as we had the last time we were here. There was more activity this morning, one of the biggest scenes was being filmed today, or so Adam had told me.

Robbie pulled up and we unloaded the main order for the ballroom. I noticed there were a few bees buzzing around the Castle's rose bushes, a sure sign of a healthy garden. Robbie and I left the arrangements in the hands of the props staff before we went to deliver the bouquet arrangements to the trailers housing the stars of the film.

"Here, take this to lover boy, and don't be too long. Mum wants us back in town to see Dad's doctor after we're done here." Robbie handed me a large floral bouquet. I'd picked most of these flowers this morning, along with a small group of employees. We prided ourselves on having the freshest picked blooms in our arrangements, having our own flower fields behind the nursery did help.

"Fucking insects," huffed the high-pitched and whiney voice of Kira Holsworthy. "Someone get me some bug spray."

I smirked behind the bouquet, secretly hoping a bee might sting her as I walked with the big bunch of flowers in my arms.

"Excuse me, Miss, where are you going?" a young brunette holding a clipboard asked me.

"I'm to deliver these to Mr. Jacobs' trailer." I explained, hefting the bouquet in my awkward grip.

"I'm sorry, we don't allow anyone in the trailers, I'll take them." She spoke huffily, reaching out for the flowers.

I frowned, bugger my luck.

"I'll take those, thank you Kaylyn." Adam's voice drifted dreamily from behind me. I felt the warmth of his hand on my back. "Hey, babe." He turned me, leaned in and kissed me on the lips.

The woman's mouth dropped open and her eyes widened in shock.

"Kaylyn, this is Melinda, my girlfriend." Adam spoke with ease while taking the flowers from me with one hand and hugging me close in his free arm.

She barely hid her look of contempt behind a mask of indifference. Adam may have missed it, but my girl senses picked it up in an instant.

"Oh, of course, Mr Jacobs, I didn't realise. I'll add her to the list of allowed visitors?"

"Yes, please, that would be great." Adam turned to me. "Kaylyn is my studio appointed assistant, she gets flustered when I try to do things for myself."

Kaylyn looked abashed at his words. "I only try to do my best, Mr. Jacobs, you're a very independent man. They want you back on set in thirty minutes, so I'll leave you to it. Please page me if you need *anything*." The glint in her eyes left the words *anything at all* unsaid.

I felt my hackles rise at the unspoken invitation for my man to stray.

Adam guided me to his trailer and ushered me in. He placed the flowers on a table to one side before turning to face me. His hands reached up to my face, caressing my skin as his fingers slid over my jawline and up into my hair. My peaked cap was pushed off my head, and his nimble fingers found the hair tie. It snapped free, unbinding my blonde locks. Adam's breathing became heavier as he approached me, his lips parted, eyelids low with desire as he caught my lips with his, kissing, licking and gently nipping. I was breathless and lost in his kiss.

"I've been thinking about you all morning." His voice was husky.

"I've been thinking about you, too." I'd been so distracted with thoughts of seeing Adam again, I'd made up a bouquet of Dutch Lavender when the order asked for English. I'd had to start again, and the Dutch bouquet was sent to the nursery store in the hopes someone might purchase it.

Adam's mouth was on mine again, his hands moving slowly over my arms and shoulders as he backed me against another table. There was a small double bed in the back of the trailer, a kitchenette and tiny living room-type space. Adam guided me away from the table and towards the back where the bed was awaiting.

"You wanna do it in my trailer?" he asked, grinning like a cheeky teenager. He certainly was acting like one. Not that I minded, mind you.

"Won't you get in trouble? You're still in costume." My voice was breathy and soft as he lay me on the bad, his hot body looming over me.

"Right now, I don't give a fuck." Adam lifted himself up slightly to unbutton and remove my jeans.

I reached down and struggled with the laces on his pants, he grunted as my fingers brushed over the bulge of excitement down there.

"It's going to be quick and dirty," Adam promised.

"Fine by me." A soft moan escaped my lips as his fingers brushed over a nipple under my work shirt. The trailer rocked slightly with the movement of our lovemaking, and he was right, it was quick and it was dirty, but bloody hell, it was spec-fucking-tacular!

We were getting dressed when a blood-curdling scream erupted from outside. "I was fucking stung by your goddamned bees. I'll make sure your nursery never has another contract in the film industry. I'll ruin you." It was the voice of her royal bitchiness, Kira Holsworthy.

"Nursery?" I whispered as dread washed over me. I finished dressing in record time, Adam not far behind me. I opened the door of the trailer onto the scene outside. Kira Holsworthy was red faced, with a swollen lip.

Poor Robbie was trying to placate her as she continued to shout about our business going down, and how she'd sue us for everything we were worth.

I knew the bitch would do it too. I looked to my brother, not knowing what to do, or how to help.

"Security, get these two morons off the set," Kira shrieked when she saw me standing in the doorway of the trailer, my hair dishevelled, and my clothing slightly rumpled from our rendezvous.

Robbie nodded to me, silently indicating it was time to go.

Adam reached out and squeezed my hand. "It will be all right," he whispered in my ear.

I wasn't so sure.

Fuck. My. Life!

Chapter Forty-Eight.

"Well, we have the results back from the latest round of scans. Mrs. Whittaker." Dad's doctor spoke with us while we all huddled around his bed. "Though there is some marked improvement in his speech, there has been less than optimum results in his movement, especially in his lower legs. I'm afraid he may never regain enough movement, or strength, to be able to walk again. His motor skills are severely lacking, and he will need assistance for most things in life. He has shown a determination to at least try, which is very good."

The doctor flipped over a page on Dad's chart.

"We are still going to keep up with his rehab, aren't we, Doc?" Robbie asked, his eyes showing the strain of the day. After having to deal with Kira Holsworthy, he'd been very quiet on the trip back.

When we'd left, her entire lower lip had been swollen. If the situation wasn't so serious, I'd have laughed. The threat of her suing us, and destroying our business, was still very real, and we both felt it. We'd not said a word to Mum or Dad about it, we didn't want to worry them. By the looks of things, we'd have even more on our plates now.

"We are going to be releasing your father in the next couple of days. We think being at home might help, but as you suggested, we will continue with physical therapy, massage to stop muscle atrophy and water therapy." He pulled a sheet of paper off the clipboard and handed it to Mum. "Here's a list of things you need to do to help the patient get around, bathroom modifications, wheelchair ramps and modifications to a van for wheelchair access.

"I'm n-n-not an in-in-invalid." Dad stuttered angrily. "St-s-stop t-t-t-talking ab-b-b-bout me like I a-a-a-m." Dad scowled, the right side of his face drooping badly.

I shared a concerned look with Robbie. This was worse than we thought. Our hope, best case, was that Dad would be walking and mobile, able to talk. But unfortunately, it didn't look like it was to be.

"I'll leave you to discuss what you need to do, then we'll organise for the district nurse to come and assist you with whatever arrangements you might want to make." The doctor closed the file on dad and left the room, closing the wide door softly behind him.

Mum sniffled, I'd not even noticed the tissues in her hand.

Robbie took Mum's hand, patting it gently. "It's all okay, we're here for you both." He kissed Mum on the cheek.

Dad looked sadly at Mum, and reached a shaking hand out to her. "Love you, T-t-tulip," he whispered, causing Mum to burst into tears as his hand took hers from Robbie's grasp. "N-n-not dead y-y-yet."

"We'll get everything done, but do we need to modify the car?" Robbie asked. "We could just use the van; a chair lift would probably make unloading the flower deliveries easier."

Dad shook his head, I could see he was getting agitated. "No. I c-c-c-can get in an-an-and out of the b-b-b-bloody car m-m-m-myself."

"Good on you, show those doctors they're wrong." I hugged him tight, he lifted his free hand and patted my cheek.

"We'll b-b-be ok-k-k-okay." Dad gave us a lopsided smile.

Robbie stood. "We'd better get back and started on this list." He took the sheet of paper from Mum's hands. "I'll get Uncle Leo to help us with the rails in the bathroom, and we'll build some ramps over the steps."

"Wait, Robbie, Melinda." Mum wiped her eyes.

I turned, and looked at her. "What is it, Mum?"

"Your father and I have discussed this at length, and we decided we may have to sell the nursery so there's no point in doing any of this."

"What?" Robbie's face paled. "You can't sell the nursery, it's Dad's dream." Robbie's voice shook with shock and anger. "You can't just bail on this, Mum, why would you? You both worked so bloody hard to get the place to where it is today, and you're going to throw it all away?"

"Robbie, your father won't be able to work, even he can see that. I'm going to take care of him, not some bloody nurse who will cost us more than we can afford." Mum's voice was raised.

"Yeah, so where does that leave me? Where does it leave Mel? What are we going to do? We won't have jobs, and we can't live with you forever." Robbie shouted in his frustration.

There was a knock on the door, an annoyed-looking nurse poked her head around the door. "Excuse me, but we have other patients who are trying to rest and recover. Please quieten down, or I'll have to ask you to leave."

Robbie responded apologetically, "Sorry."

"Thank-you." The nurse said before closing the door.

"Look, Mum, don't be too hasty to put the place up for sale. We'll work something out, I can take a course in business, go to night school or something. I'm certain I can do the job. I mean, I've been helping out since I came back, and I'm more than willing to stay on and do what's needed to keep your dream alive." I put my arms around Mum who had begun to cry again.

"Oh Mel, sweetheart, you can't do that," Mum sniffled

"Oh yes I bloody well can, you just watch me."

"G-g-good g-g-girl," Dad stuttered.

I turned to him, smiling. He looked so frail, but I knew he had strength in him, and it was still early days.

Robbie cleared his throat, and I could see the unshed tears in his eyes. "We'll be fine, Dad. I promise."

We left the hospital and headed home.

"We still have the problem of that actress bitch," Robbie reminded me.

"Yeah, I know. It's best if we don't tell Mum and Dad, they've got enough on their plates right now without adding more to their worries."

Robbie nodded.

"We'll have to wait and see what happens, cross that bridge when we get to it." I sighed as I looked out the window. "Adam said not to worry about it, but it's damned hard not to when everything else is falling in a heap around you.

"I know what you mean," Robbie agreed as he turned onto our drive. "Whose car is that?"

I looked up to see the strange, silver Mercedes in the drive. "No idea. It's not Adam's, his is black with tinted windows."

"Hmm I wonder who it could be." Robbie pulled into the carport. We stepped out as the passenger side door opened.

"Mrs. Del Rosa?" I looked at the older woman as she emerged gracefully from the car.

"Alison!" Uncle Leo's voice called out from across the front yard where he'd been quietly trimming the front hedge. "What are ye doin' here me lovely?"

Mrs. Del Rosa smiled at us all. "Not a social call, unfortunately Leo. I actually came to discuss the matter of Kira Holsworthy trying to sue Whittaker Nursery."

The world bottomed out beneath me.

"Oh fuck," I muttered, echoed quietly by my brother, word, for fucking word.

Fuck. My. Life.

Chapter Forty-Nine.

"It's all right, we've convinced her that if she goes ahead with this, it will look very bad on her part. We pointed out it would be particularly bad to sue a man who has just had a heart attack and a stroke. After all, you can't control the bees." Alison smiled warmly at us.

"Oh, thank Christ!" Robbie sagged against the door. "After the morning we've had, Mrs. Del Rosa, that news is very welcome indeed."

"I'm glad, but unfortunately, we're going to have to end the contract with you. I regret it terribly and I fought hard to try to convince the other producers to keep the contract. Your flowers are some of the best and most beautiful I've seen. Unfortunately, Kira has her hands in the 'pockets'...." She made air quotes as she said the last. "of the male producers and the director. And by pockets, I actually mean down the front of their pants, but you didn't hear that from me." She winked.

Uncle Leo stepped beside me. "Are ye stayin' for a cup of tea, Alison?"

"Yes, please, where are our manners? Come in." I left Robbie's side and removed a key from my purse. Alison followed me in while Robbie and Uncle Leo stayed outside to discuss the modifications to the house which were needed to bring dad home.

"So, how are you and Adam getting along?" Alison asked as I placed a plate of home-made biscuits on the table and started making a pot of tea.

"Good," I said, unable to keep the smile out of my voice.

"I'm very glad. He's a good man, a very good man." Her voice sounded wistful. I wondered what she meant by the strange intonation of her voice.

"Alison, is everything all right?" I set out the fine china and returned to prepping the teapot.

"Hmm? Oh yes, just demons of the past coming back to taunt me. I think it's coming time to do something about it."

Okay… that was mysterious.

"You know, I've known Adam since he was born, and he's never once been this taken with a woman." Alison smiled warmly as I poured her tea.

"Never?"

"No, there's been flings with supermodels and actresses. Personally, I've not approved of them, but you, Melinda… you bring the best out in him." She stirred sugar into her tea and added milk. "He's been fantastic on the set, happier than I've ever seen him. You're good for him, very good. We're wrapping up filming in the next week, and he's supposed to be heading back to the States. But, he's been talking about staying here, permanently." She lifted her cup and sipped. "That's how serious he is about you, Melinda."

My spoon clattered against the cup, Mum would have been mortified at the abuse of her good china. "He's talking about staying?" My shock could be clearly heard in my voice.

"He is," Alison confirmed.

"I don't know what to say. I have a connection with him, I can't stop thinking about him. Every moment we're apart, it doesn't feel right, but when we come together…"

"When you're together, you feel like you can take on the world." Alison smiled. "I know that feeling. You need to hold onto it, and never let it go." She placed her hand over mine. "Even if the world is falling down around you, if you hold onto that one good thing you have in your life, you will overcome any obstacle in your way." Alison sighed, setting her cup down on the saucer. "I wish I'd had the same advice when I was younger."

"Oh?".

Alison nodded, her eyes wistful. "Before I was married to my late husband, I had an affair with another statesman. It was scandalous, but we were in love. Unfortunately, my father found out and banned me from seeing him again, lest I dishonour the family in some way. Never mind the fact he was banging my younger brother's nanny at the time and my mother was a high functioning alcoholic on the verge of a fatal bout of liver disease. But, for me to be involved with a married man was the limit, until I discovered I was pregnant to the man I loved. As I said, demons of the past, they haunt you."

"Yes, they certainly do. What happened to your baby? I mean, if it's all right to ask?"

"I had to give my boys up."

"Boys?"

"I had twins." I saw the pain she felt in her eyes.

"Oh, I'm so sorry you had to give them away."

"It's all right. Though one died of a childhood illness, the other is doing quite well. I'm very proud of him, even if he doesn't know who I am." She finished her tea. "Well, I do need to get going, Again, I'm so sorry about the contract." She stood and picked up her purse. "The amount owing will be paid into the business account by the end of the day."

I too stood and walked with her to the door.

"Melinda." She stopped at the door. "Take care of our Adam, he's a very special man." She placed a warm hand on my arm.

Something about our conversation niggled at the back of my mind as I walked her to the car. Uncle Leo came out and spoke quietly to her, he smiled as she nodded before driving away.

"Well, looks like I got a date tonight, better get my good kilt out." He beamed with joy.

I laughed at Uncle Leo, he never wore his kilt unless it was a very special occasion, and for him to consider wearing it to a date, well, that was pretty special. He was clearly smitten with Alison.

"Leo and I are going into town to get some stuff for Dad, plywood for the ramps and some hand rails for the bathroom. Do you need anything?" Robbie asked when he joined us.

I shook my head, watched as the men climbed into the van and drove off. I turned back to the cottage, and then it hit me, everything Alison had told me. Her two sons, twins. Adam had a twin who had died when they were kids, and she was very interested in his life. She'd known him all his life as well.

Holy Shit.

I'd figured out Alison's secret, the demons haunting her past.

Adam was her son, one she'd had to give up.

It was a secret I was now privy to, even if it wasn't confirmed.

Do I talk to Adam about this?

No, I decided. It wasn't my secret to tell. It was up to Alison.

But still… it was one hell of a secret to keep.

Fuck. My. Life.

Chapter Fifty.

The week passed by slowly, Dad had come home after Robbie and Uncle Leo finished the modifications to the house and we were adjusting slowly. I'd applied for night school and was waiting on administration to sign me up for the online business course they offered.

Adam had come home to me every night. There had been stories in the newspaper about him taking an attractive blonde to his hotel one night, then a brunette and a redhead, all with pictures. I'd questioned him on it, though I knew the truth. He'd been with me, at my home.

"That's Frank, my body double, looks almost exactly like me." Adam explained with a laugh. "He's got the looks, but different voice. It's gotten him, and me, into a few scuffles before." Adam snuggled up against me in bed. "When we come back here for the sequel's filming, he'll take a more active role in scenes, playing the duke's twin, or the duke when I have to perform the twin's role."

"That's going to be hard, playing a double role, right?" I ran my fingers teasingly over his warm, naked chest

"Yeah, going to bring talking to myself to a whole new level of insanity, especially in the scene where the duke has to fight his twin." He chuckled.

I sighed happily and lay my head on his chest. This was our after-sex-pillow-talk. I enjoyed it so much more than what Asshole-Ex and I shared. He usually rolled over, farted and went promptly to sleep. Good luck to his new fiancé, she could keep him.

"When do you start your course?"

"I'm waiting for passwords and stuff to come through on my email address, but once it happens, I can start right away."

"That will be good, are you sure you don't want me to help you with the tuition?" Adam had offered when we'd spoken about my decision to take over Mum and Dad's business with Robbie.

He was excited for me, and offered to help out where he could and however he could. I was touched, but declined, this was something I needed to do for myself, for my family. Adam understood, he knew I wanted to have some independence and he was wonderful. He didn't go all alpha male on me and order me about like you see in some romance movies. He knew I needed to stretch my wings and get my groove back.

"I'm proud of you, Mel." He ran his fingers over my bare shoulder.

I hugged him tight. "Why?"

"You've gotten your confidence back. When I first met you, you were so unsure of yourself. It endeared you to me, but now, you're like this tigress, who goes and gets what she wants."

"A tigress?"

"Yeah, more kickass than a lioness. Independent, doesn't have to take care of the tiger, and doesn't take shit from anyone."

"Ha!" I laughed. "That's not quite me, but I'll take it." I lay my head back on his chest, and listened to the thump-thump of his heartbeat.

"Last day of filming tomorrow."

"Going to miss it?"

"Nah, I'll be back. I was going to tell you this tomorrow, but I think I'd like you to know now."

I sat up and studied his face. His eyes glittered and a big cheesy smile spread across his lips.

"I was looking at houses around here, there's one I thought you might like to come and check out with me." His eyebrows raised with hope.

"Well, sure, that would be great."

"And I'd like it if you moved in with me when I do get a place here."

I bounced on the bed in excitement. "Are you serious? You're not kidding me, are you? Not pulling my leg or anything, right?"

Adam grinned and grabbed my hips, lifting me over to straddle him. "Yes, Melinda Whittaker, I'd like you to move in with me."

I squealed and giggled, leaning down to kiss Adam soundly on the lips. There was a banging on the bedroom door.

"Would you two shut the fuck up? Gay man trying to get some beauty sleep here." Robbie's muffled, cranky voice came from the other side of the door.

"Sorry," I called back, before returning to ravishing my man with kisses.

"Are you going to come to the Castle when we finish filming? I want to take you out to celebrate," Adam asked when I came up for air.

"Absolutely, I'd love to."

"I'll get Mike to pick you up," Adam promised.

I snuggled down on top of him, laying my ear to his chest again as I listened to the beautiful sound of his heartbeat.

***

It was after four, and Adam's car still hadn't arrived to pick me up. I peered through the window again, checked my phone, nothing. Something wasn't right.

I heard the crunching of gravel as watched as a car pulled up. Adam stepped out, his face unreadable. My heart thundered in my chest. I opened the door.

"Hey." He moved past me and into the house.

"Adam, what is it? What happened?" I followed him to my room where he began packing.

"I have to go," He said softly.

"What? Why? After this morning, I thought…"

"It's not you, Melinda. I've just received some news I need to process. I have learned I'm adopted. My twin and I were given up by our mother… Alison Del Rosa."

"I bloody well knew it!"

Adam glared at me, his eyes blazing with anger.

"What? You knew, and you didn't tell me? Didn't say anything, didn't think I had a right to know?"

"What?" My heart beating furiously in my chest with the fear I might lose him. All because I had an inkling about something.

"I had my suspicions when she started talking about her early life, but she never said your name, Adam. Alison said that she was forced to give up her twin sons after an affair with a statesman when she was younger, before she was married. I suspected she was talking about you but didn't know for sure and it wasn't my secret to tell."

"When did she tell you this?"

"About a week ago, when she came out to tell us we'd lost the contract." I flopped down on my bed.

Adam raked his fingers through his hair in frustration. "It seems like everything I've been told is a lie. My mother is actually my real mother's cousin, my siblings aren't really my siblings, but distant cousins, and I have a whole other family I don't know." He sighed. "I'm sorry baby, I need some time to process this, I've also got another film to work on back in the States my manager just told me about. This is all such shit."

"I think you need a new manager." I climbed to my knees and laid my head on his shoulder.

"I think I need a new life." Adam kissed me on the temple. "I have to go. I'll call you when I land, okay?" He grabbed his bag, but stopped and turned to me from the door, he looked so lost. "Melinda, I love you."

"I love you too." He was gone by the time the words left my lips, the front door slamming and the crunching of tires on gravel sounding far too loud in my room. Something didn't sit right.

Why did Adam's "I Love you" sound like, "Goodbye?"

Fuck. My. Life.

Chapter Fifty-One.

Three weeks.

It had been three fucking weeks since Adam had sent me a simple text. *'landed safely. X'*

His "I Love you" was looking more and more like, "Goodbye."

I started crying in my sleep as I lay in the beautiful bed he'd bought for me, the one we'd shared for almost a month before he left.

Dad noticed my moods changing from happy to dour. When Robbie had remarked it must have been my time of the month, I snapped at him. For a week after, he'd been walking on eggshells around me until he found me quietly crying in amongst the orchids.

"He hasn't called?" Robbie asked.

I shook my head.

"No emails? Texts?"

Again, I shook my head.

Robbie pulled out a handkerchief and wiped my eyes. "It'll be okay, Sis." Robbie draped an arm around my shoulder.

"We got the offer accepted on the neighbouring fields, and the council has approved our plans for extending the nursery and building the café and playground." Robbie sat down on an upturned ceramic pot beside me. "Why don't you try designing the hedge maze? Uncle Leo thinks if we can plant it before the builders come in and get cracking on the café, the hedge will be matured enough to trim and be ready when we are open."

Dad's pension had been approved, the retirement fund also had a 'death or permanent disability' payment clause which we were able to use. We'd bought up the two blocks of land adjacent to the nursery grounds, and had consulted with Dad on what he wanted for the new and improved nursery. Much would stay the same, but with the addition of a Café, playground and hedge maze, we were hoping more people would come by and help us as well as bump up tourism for the village. Having the Castle nearby was good, but there wasn't anywhere near for people to have a nice cup of tea or use the bathroom. That was where we were hoping to come in.

"I know, sorry, I just…."

"You miss him, I know. Look I'm sure he's just going through some shit right now, it will be okay. You're perfect, he'd be an idiot to move on." Robbie leaned back against the shelves behind us. "Besides, I'll cut off his balls and shove 'em down his throat for hurting you."

"Since when did you get all aggressive?"

"Since my sister went through shite to get where she is today." Robbie stood up from his seat. "Come on, let's go have a nice cup of tea."

I followed him up to the cottage. Dad was sitting in the sunroom with the cat sleeping on his lap. "Hey Dad." I leaned down to kiss the old man on the cheek.

"P-Poppet," Dad smiled. His speech had improved, and he was only stuttering or slurring a few words here and there. He still tired easily, but he was pushing himself to walk, even though his legs didn't do what he told them to. He'd have to admit one day, that he wouldn't walk again, but until then he was damned determined to do it.

Mum was in the kitchen where the sweet scent of her biscuits drifted from the oven, warm and homely. My mouth watered at the thought of the thick, chewy centres. Robbie grabbed some off the cooling rack, yelping when they burned his hands.

"Serves you right," Mum scolded him.

"But they're better when they're hot, and still chewy!" he protested.

I had to agree with him, but I wasn't about to burn my fingers over a delicious biscuit… or was I? I reached for one, but mum smacked me with a biscuit dough-covered spoon.

"Ouch! Fuck, mum, that hurt." I whined, earning me another dough-covered smack on the hand, leaving sticky dough on my skin, which I promptly licked off.

"Don't swear," Mum chided me.

"Libby's been trying to call you, she said she's coming over, and don't look at any papers."

"Oh fuck…" Robbie said.

I turned to see what had caused his comment. The thump-thump-thump of Libby's overly loud stereo vibrated through the walls, and the crunching of skidding tires on the gravel reached my ears. Then, all sound vanished with the rushing of blood in my ears as it drained from my face and head, down to my feet to join my stomach and heart. On the table was a paper.

Front Cover.

Adam Fucking Jacobs.

With a beautiful blonde, and a two-year-old girl in his arms.

"ADAM JACOBS' SECRET FAMILY REVEALED!" the headline screamed.

"Mel! Don't look at the…" Libby yelled as she dashed through the door… "Paper. Oh bollocks."

"Oh, fuck." Robbie muttered.

I sank into a chair, my eyes filled with tears, sight blurring, heart breaking -no shattering into a bazillion little pieces. I heard sobbing, it was as if someone had died, who was it? My vision cleared for a second as a fat tear dropped onto the newspaper to splatter all over the happy face of Adam as he played with the little girl. She looked so much like him, the same eyes, nose and perfect lips I had kissed were mimicked in perfect miniature detail on the face of the beautiful little girl.

He looked happy. Happy with his family I'd never known about. Had he lied to me? Had he played me like a chess piece all this time, while back home, his wife (Yes, there was a wedding ring on that finger, and a flashy one at that) and daughter were waiting for him to come home to them?

I felt sick.

I ran from the kitchen as my stomach rebelled against me. My heaving sobs echoing down the hall as I forced myself to run to the bathroom where I collapsed before the toilet and prayed with such devotion to the porcelain gods. I heaved in between sobs.

My hair was pulled back, despite it being covered with vomit and a soft, calming hand was placed on my back. "Shh, sweetheart," Mum soothed. "It's all right baby."

"Why did he lie to me, Mum?" I hiccupped with sobs.

Mum flushed the toilet, washing away my stomach contents in a swirl of chemically blue water. "I can't answer that, sweetheart, but remember what the press is like, this could all be some big mistake, blown out of proportion."

"You don't know that, Mum. For all we know, he's been hiding me from them, not the other way around. Did you see how happy he was in those pictures? Why can't I have that?" I sobbed. "Why the hell can't I have that!" The ugly cry broke free of its prison. Tears, snot and saliva with tiny flecks of vomit dribbled down my face as Mum knelt on the bathroom tiles and rocked me like a child until my sobs subsided. She helped me to clean myself up. I breathed deeply, looking at myself in the mirror. Red nose and flushed cheeks with red-rimmed eyes was the fashion statement for today.

Mum left me to pull myself together. I took a few deep, calming breaths as I leaned against the vanity basin. "You are better than him," I whispered to myself. "So much better." I felt slightly more human, and headed back to the kitchen where everyone was waiting.

The looks of pity in their eyes was more than I could take. "I'm heading to the shed, got work to do." I didn't need their pity, didn't need them to be sorry for me. Didn't need Adam fucking Jacobs to have a family I didn't know about.

Didn't need for him to lie to me. But, he did. My life was shite, his was bloody brilliant.

Good for him, asshole.

Fuck. My. Life.

Chapter Fifty-Two.

It had been two months since I'd broken down. I'd slept on the sofa for a few nights, waking up each morning in my bed, and wondering how the fuck I'd gotten there. Stupidly, I'd refused to sleep in the beautiful bed Adam had bought me… us. At first, I thought I was sleepwalking back to bed, haunted with dreams of Adam and needing the comfort of his scent which still lingered on the pillow on *his* side. But, it was Robbie who carried my fat arse from the lounge room to my bedroom each night when I had fallen asleep.

Dad and I had walked the hedge maze we'd planted, well I'd pushed him in the wheelchair. We made sure everything was wheelchair friendly, not only for him, but for our customers as well. The café was ready, and Mum had been helping with the baking for the opening. We were offering free tea, coffee and biscuits for opening day. The new smell of the building was overpowered with the sweet scent of freshly baked goodies.

Robbie smiled at me as he looked around the place. "It's amazing, Mel, I'm so proud of you."

I'd finished my online course in record time, and now had a certificate in business. Robbie and I had officially taken over the business, but Mum and Dad were still a big part of it and listed as the owners. My mind was on the job during the day, working hard to get everything set up, and ready for this very day and beyond. Already there were cars waiting to park in the car park.

"Robbie, are you ready to open?" I checked the clock. It was just past eight, we weren't due to open until half-past, but looking at the number of cars waiting for us to open, it was going to be a very busy day.

"Sure am," Robbie grinned.

"Let's go do it then." Robbie took hold of Dad's wheelchair and pushed him out of the Café. Mum followed us, whipping off her apron and handing it to one of the wait staff we'd hired.

"P-p-proud of you, P-p-poppet," Dad said as Uncle Leo came and joined us. He took control of Dad's wheelchair from Robbie.

I smiled, trying hard not to cry as we approached the gates. There were a lot of cars waiting to come in, I couldn't believe it.

The Castle had been closed to the public again, the film crew were back and sightings of Adam Jacobs were yet to surface. I tried not to care, but the fact was, he haunted my nights, my dreams. Thoughts which distracted me throughout the day were all about him, what he meant to me, and how he'd broken my heart. For weeks, thoughts of him had kept me awake at night, and it was a miracle I was able to finish my course at all let alone in such a short time. I admit, I used the course to distract me from my distraught emotional state over Adam.

I watched as Robbie and Uncle Leo threw open the gates, letting the first customers into our new and improved Nursery. Robbie grinned at me and I smiled back, it was going to be a big day for all of us.

The joyous screams of children at play sounded across the fields of flowers. I ignored them as I ran my fingertips over the lavender heads, the scent lingering in the pores of my skin. A part of me wished Adam had been here to see this. Pillow talk with him had often brought up the subject of finishing Dad's dream for him, after he'd been told he'd never work or walk again. At times, I wanted to find him, call him, but I'd blocked and deleted his number in a fit of misery-fuelled rage one day. So that option was no longer available to me. I had to let him go. It was obvious he had done the same as more pictures showed up of him with his beautiful wife and child, on outings at parks, at society balls and functions, at movie premieres and so on.

I was done.

The two-way radio at my hip crackled.

"Robbie To Mel, come in Mel." Robbie's voice sounded tinny through the small speaker. We'd decided to have two-way radios due to the size of the property now, it made communication easier rather than using our phones.

I clicked the push-to-talk button. "Go ahead."

"Got a kid lost in the hedge maze, do you think you can come help us find her?"

"Yeah, I'm on my way." I'd designed the hedge maze along with Dad. In every dead end, there was a scene or interactive project from a fairy tale or English children's book. *Peter Rabbit, The Far Away Tree, Noddy, Winnie the Pooh and Paddington Bear* were amongst the classics we'd created in the maze. I knew the maze like the back of my hand. There weren't many places a little girl could get lost in, but we did have a crawl tunnel which led from one part of the maze to an adjacent part, for the *Alice in Wonderland* piece. It led to a slight upward incline and then down a slide to another section of the maze. It was easily found by parents, as we'd placed a sign above the tunnel to show where it ended up. That was likely where the girl was, and the parent was most probably panicking.

I hurried through the entrance to the maze, past children dashing around and giggling, talking about what they'd seen. From the description I'd been given, I was looking for a little blonde girl in a blue dress named Clara. I moved quickly through the maze, following each twist and turn, looking out for the blue dress.

I finally found her.

In the arms of Adam. Fucking Jacobs.

Fuck. My. Life.

Chapter Fifty-Three.

Standing next to the man who had haunted my dreams, ruined my life and who I still felt something for, was the blonde woman, his fucking wife. I felt like a homewrecker.

I watched as Adam handed the girl to his wife, she was the daughter in the pictures, I realised. He stepped towards me. I couldn't do this, not now, not ever. I took a step back, away from the scene of happiness I could never be part of.

"Mel." His voice was tight with emotion.

I shook my head, backing up and turning. I ran through the maze, my eyes blurred with tears as I sobbed. I raced near blind through the maze I knew so well, but I was lost in my utter despair at being face to face with the man I still loved. Damnit, yes, *loved!* I loved Adam Jacobs but he was with the family he loved.

"Mel!" Adam's voice cried out behind me as I slammed into one of the dead ends which held a picture of *Paddington Bear*. I felt my nose flatten against my face and the crunch of cartilage and instant pain brought fresh tears to my eyes.

"Go away, please leave me alone. I can't do this." I held my hands over my nose, and could taste and smell blood as it dripped sticky and warm through my fingers, and down my chin.

"Oh Mel, baby, are you okay?" I heard him speak as his warmth wrapped around me.

I cried harder. "Go back to your family, your wife, your daughter. Please, leave me alone."

"My wife? Baby, I don't have a wife. Not yet." He pulled me against his chest, my blood smearing red over the pristine white of his shirt. "I don't have any children, what are you thinking? Oh, do you think that woman is my wife? The girl, mine? Oh Mel…" he chuckled, shaking his head, a wry smile on his lips.

I pushed from his arms. "What? Don't lie to me, Adam Jacobs. It broke my heart seeing you together. So happy, on the front page of the paper. You didn't call me like you promised, never sent me a message. It's more than two fucking months since you left. I eventually got it. I got your message loud and fucking clear when I saw the papers." I tried to push myself away from him again, but he held tight to me.

"Papers? What papers?"

"The ones showing your new, or should I say, *old* family you've kept hidden away. Your wife, your daughter, it was all in the paper."

"All in the paper? Mel, that's bullshit. Ella is my sister, my half-sister, and that little girl, Clara? She's my niece."

The words penetrated my pounding head and pain filled face. "What?"

"Ella, the blonde woman with me, is Alison's daughter, my half-sister. The little girl is her daughter, my niece. They are the secret family, the ones I knew nothing about until Alison and I spoke the day I left. I was leaving to go and sort things out in my head. Everything I knew wasn't the truth, everything except how I felt, and still feel about you."

Adam pulled me tight against his chest, the scent of him mingled with the scent of my blood in my mangled nose. I was certain it was broken, it hurt like a bitch. Adam pulled away and took off his shirt. He took a bunch of material in his hand and gently pressed it against my bleeding nose. "We're going to have to get that looked at, it could be broken."

I whimpered in pain as he gently pressed the bloody cloth against my nose again. I reached up and held my hand over his.

"So, you still love me?" I asked him, hope flaring in my chest, but fear bleeding like my nose, that he didn't still care for me.

"Yes, these last two months have been torture. My filming schedule was ridiculously hectic. I couldn't get back here and I couldn't get through on the phone. I ended up firing my manager and was on the hunt for a new one. Fortunately, Ella is a manager and she's taken me on as a client."

"I blocked your number. So, that's why I've seen you together so much?" My voice sounded off with the nasally tone it had developed, I could feel my nose swelling.

"Yes, baby, and remember I did say not to believe everything in the papers?" He kissed my forehead. "My silly woman. I'd never intentionally leave you, baby. I meant what I said the last time I was here, I love you."

I searched his eyes and saw the truth in them. Our lives were so totally different, but I knew he loved me, and I felt the ache in my chest for him as well. I wanted to be with him for as long as I was able to be, the rest of our lives sounded damned good to me.

"So, you thought I had a secret family?"

I nodded, eyes downcast.

Adam chuckled, "And you got angry with me?"

Another nod in the affirmative.

"That's why you blocked my number?"

I tasted blood on my tongue and retched, before I pulled the cloth away from my nose and spat blood into the hedge. "I was an idiot, I was devastated, got angry, and that led to stupidity. I should have called you, I'm sorry."

"Baby." Adam tilted my head with a finger under my chin. "Look at me, Mel."

I complied, albeit a little reluctantly. I felt ashamed by the truth of my actions. It had hurt both of us. Instead of setting everything straight, I'd chosen to trust the media instead of the man I loved. "I'm sorry, and I know that doesn't even come close to covering it, but god, Adam, I'm so sorry I didn't trust you, trust in us enough to ask you first," I sobbed.

"Mel, It's all right, baby, I'm here now. We're good, we're together. I want to be with you forever, marry you, have babies together, grow old, deaf and senile in matching rocking chairs together. You and me, baby, it's all that matters."

I heard the pounding of footsteps behind us as the rest of the family caught up. Adam wiped the blood from my face and mouth before he kissed me, softly, lovingly. Certainty flourished in my heart.

This man loved me.

This man wanted to be with me.

ME.

I squeaked in pain as he kissed me again, his nose bumping mine.

"I think I broke my nose."

Despite everything which had happened before, I had the future to look forward to now.

Fuck. My. Life.… It's going to be awesome.

Epilogue – Adam.

She was so beautiful, radiant. *Glowing*.

The bright lights of flashing cameras only added to her sparkle. The blue dress she'd picked out from a new, and previously unknown, student designer hugged her body in a way which made my own ignite with the need to hide her away from prying eyes and do decidedly wicked things to her.

From the first moment I'd first seen her, drenched in coloured water and shocked she'd made such a fool of herself, I was smitten. She was just as gorgeous covered in fake punch as she was in casual clothes. I had to find out who she was, and though I wanted to stop her as she ran off the set in tears, I knew she needed her space. I gave it to her, until the next day.

I smiled at her, we'd been through so much. From her father's stroke, to discovering I had another family which had been kept hidden from me all my life. We'd come through it all, tears and anger, love and laughter. In the end, it cemented a foundation of love and trust which made our relationship so much better.

I smiled as she draped a hand over her stomach. Kira was in front of us, she was such a jaded bitch. I really despised her. She stopped directly in front of us, and had been doing it all along the red carpet. We were here for the premiere of *A Duke to Remember*, the film where Mel and I had first met though she didn't know it was me in the shadows, offering her my empathy at the time.

I pulled up a step or two away from Kira. Mel, however hadn't been watching and bumped into her. Kira swung around and snarled.

"Watch it, bitch," she growled under her breath.

Mel simply stared at the woman, not rewarding her nastiness with a response.

Kira huffed and turned away, striding from us. Mistake. Big, huge mistake, as Kira didn't realise, that Mel's foot was on the train of her dress. There was a ripping sound, and her ivory-white, floor length dress ripped away to reveal her dressed in very little underneath. She squealed as the camera flashes almost blinded us with the intensity. Kira screamed again, trying to cover herself. She had no bra on, and only a skimpy little G-string which really did nothing for her.

Laughter competed with the clicking sounds from digital cameras and phones of anyone who could get a clear view of Kira.

I looked at Mel.

She shrugged. "Oops." She stepped off the material which had previously trailed behind Kira as part of the dress. I hurriedly ushered her away from the scene.

"Whittaker!" The shrill scream came from behind us. "You, bitch!"

Mel and I both turned to face Kira, who had gathered the ruined dress and wrapped it around her near naked body. "You slut."

She raised her manicured had to slap Mel, but before I could intervene, my wife stepped up into her face. I was so proud.

"You'd hit a pregnant woman, really?" Mel glared at Kira, who looked stunned.

"You're pregnant?" I asked Mel, my heart thumping in my chest.

"Twelve weeks today." Mel smiled at me.

I gathered my beautiful wife in my arms and kissed her senseless. Kira huffed and stormed past us, leaving us in the blinding flashes of the paparazzi taking another money shot.

A baby!

Fuck, my life was about to get even better!

The End.

Scarlett J Rose.

Dedicated to My partner-in-crime, and in life.

Steve. ♥

With special kick-arse thanks to:

Susan Horsnell, Joanne Effendi, Cheryl Riddell, Helen King

And you, my readers! For without you, there'd be no book to be read!

Other books by Scarlett J Rose:

<u>Independent books:</u>

The FML Series:

FML

WTF

OMG *(Coming soon!)*

Redemption of the Fallen Series.

Demon's Embrace

Angel's Redemption

Demon's Bargain (*Coming Soon!*)

Maelstrom MC.

Firestorm.

Broken Flowers:

Desert Rose

<u>Evernight Publishing:</u>

The Trenin Alliance:

Subject 26-A

(2017 Evernight Publishing Reader's choice runner up in Science-fiction Category)

Fallen Star

Romance on the Go Standalones.

Guarding Her

The Indecent Proposal of Mrs Cortez

More to come!

*'Like' Scarlett J Rose on Facebook for upcoming releases and
more information!*

www.facebook.com/scarlettjrose/

Chapter One

"Gorgeous"

Click.

"Just lean against him a little."

Click.

"Okay, one more in that position."

Click.

"Great! Now the mums and dads, if you can come and join the bride and groom?"

I looked up from prepping the Polaroid camera for my boss Danny, as the families of the happy couple joined the bride and groom for their photograph. Danny was in his element, but I wanted a little more from my life than just taking photos and happy snaps of happy families.

It was all a fucking illusion; my shitty childhood had taught me that. I knew there were people out there who were happy. Two such examples were my best friend, Mel and her husband, movie star Adam Jacobs, and Mel's parents, who owned the nursery and gardens we were shooting the wedding photos in.

My own romantic endeavours basically revolved around Friday night hook-ups and the subsequent 'Walk of Shame'—or in my case the stagger of shame—early on a Saturday morning.

Danny reached out behind him for the Polaroid camera. I quickly handed it to him, grabbing the digital camera he'd used, and connected it to the work laptop to upload and backup. I looked over the gorgeous pictures, knowing that Danny had an eye for detail, one he'd said countless times that I possessed, despite my obnoxious scoffing.

Okay, so I had an eye for when the lighting was just right, juxtaposition of things, took some great action shots, and my prints had sold well to the tourists when we had the local craft market.

But I wanted more. To *be* more. To learn more. To become kick-arse and awesome. Yeah, I was a lil' spitfire, who went on weekly benders up the local pub, had a bigger-than-life attitude and flipped the bird at life if it pissed me off. This shit was normal to me. Nothing in life was easy, I knew that, but I didn't want it to be so fucking hard that I was going to be forced to live a life of mediocracy in a place where I was conceived, born and dragged up.

A place where my grandparents and parents couldn't get out of…well Dad got out, if you call dying in prison getting out. And my mum? She checked out years ago, dotty as fuck, decades of alcohol abuse rotting her brain until she overdosed at one of her boyfriend's places. I knew if I wasn't careful, I'd end up just like her and the old man. My 'lovely' parents were one of the reasons why I only bended on Fridays.

I heard my phone's message notification go off. While the camera uploaded the shots to the laptop, I checked the phone. Mel had messaged me, letting me know she was back home. I was headed to her place after this shoot to get ready for a date later that night. I'd been going around with this bloke for about three weeks. So far, so good. Shagging him was pretty fucking awesome. He had a few special 'tricks' that I hadn't had anyone else try before. He told me he had something special planned for tonight, and if my pink bits weren't excited, then I wasn't a red-blooded woman.

Some might call me a slapper, or a tart, skank, ho-bag—all those lovely names for a lass who just wants to have a bit of fun with a bloke. Yeah, blokes are players, women are sluts. Hooray for equal fucking opportunity! Honestly, I didn't give a shit what anyone thought. I lived it hard when I was a kid. I deserve a bit of fun. And if anything happens? I deal with it, like an adult, or I kick them in their bits. Either way works fine.

I smirked, Mel wanted me to swing by early if I could. She was having issues dealing with being 'fatter than a bloody whale', otherwise known as so preggers she was almost ready to pop. Her firstborn was due in a month, or just under, and Adam was away shooting some multi-bazillion dollar chick flick that would have some crazy stalker bitches after his very sexy body. Yes, I look, but I do not touch. That's a big fat fucking deal breaker. I'm not going to be labelled a homewrecker or a cheater.

I texted my bitch back, telling her I'd be there ASAP, with her choice of sweeties, as well as a box of chips n' gravy from the cafe in the village. It would mean a quick trip into the village, instead of heading up the small drive beside her parent's cottage to the gorgeous house that Adam had built for their main home here in the UK, but hell, Mel was my best friend, and had been there for me for so much of the shitty parts of my childhood. We were practically sisters.

With my pre-date plans set, I finished the upload to the laptop while Danny finished with the polaroid as the wedding party moved back towards the vintage Rolls Royce cars they'd used for the wedding.

We packed everything away. Danny would be continuing his photographer duties at the reception. I'd been given the rest of the night off, which was lucky, because I'd already told him I had plans, and thankfully, Danny was an accommodating boss.

I loaded my own cameras and gear into my trusty little car and jumped in. As soon as I turned the key, the *Dead Sinners*

Society pounded their fucking-awesomely-kick-arse Death Metal through my skull via my speakers. Yours truly had been most fortunate and honoured to have been the meat in the sandwich with Lars and Jorgen, lead singer and drummer from the DSS. And damn, if it weren't one fucking awesome one-night stand. I still have very, *very* fond memories of that epic night… It was also the night that Mel reunited with her true love, Adam… Yeah sappy shit, but hey, she's happy and that's what matters.

I drove down the country roads, swerving around farmers in slow-moving tractors until I came to the village centre. Lisa Cunningham, one of the local coppers was waiting in the chip shop for her order. She grinned at me when I stepped up next to her after placing my order.

"Hey Lis." I grinned, she'd also gone to high school with Mel and me. She was considered one of the really geeky kids back then. Who knew, that years of being called names because of her braces and glasses, would drive her to become a cop? And one heck of a cop too. This chick was fearless.

"Hey Libby, how was that wedding you were shooting at?" she asked with a grin.

"I give 'em six months, tops. The groom was too busy checking out the maid-of-honour's tits in the low-cut gown she wore, to notice than his own bride was giving him death glares."

"Ha! That'll teach him. Bloody men, eh? Ya can't live with 'em, can't bury em in the backyard, eh?" Lisa grinned.

I chuckled with her. "That's the truth there."

"Yeah, well, unfortunately, I'm showing a new bloke the ropes today. Comes from London. Poor bastard is gonna die of boredom here."

"Well, this isn't the most exciting place. I mean we do have our little break-ins here and there, usually the kids from the village getting into the whisky. But nothing too bad." I grinned.

"Yeah, poor bugger probably just wants a nice holiday from the shite going down in London these days. Be nice for him to have a normal life for a bit I think."

"Define 'normal' these days?" I snorted.

"Good point." Lis chuckled. She reached over to the drinks fridge and cracked open a bottle of cola. "How's our favourite superstar wife these days?"

"Beautiful, and about ready to pop too, I think. Maybe another couple of weeks, but this is her first, so anything goes." I didn't like to gossip too much about Mel's life. People wanted the ins and outs and minute details, when really, they should be looking inwards on their own pathetic excuse, not living vicariously through someone else.

"Well, let her know we're all thinking of her," Lis said as my order was called.

"Will do." I grabbed the butcher-paper-wrapped parcel of greasy chips and the plastic container of gravy and headed out to my car... Where a cop was writing out a ticket and slapping it on my front windshield.

"What the fuck?!"

Okay, so apart from being royally pissed that some arsehole cop was writing me out a ticket for being a SINGLE FUCKING INCH over the parking line…claiming I was 'double parked', this guy was hot… And not just hot, but, fuck me, he was so fucking hot I swear my knickers just spontaneously combusted, leaving me with third degree burns all over my pink bits.

"What the fuck are you doing?" I asked him as I stormed up to my car, my package of chips tucked up under my arm. "You seriously gonna give me a ticket for being a teeny bit over the line? What are you, some kind of fucking parking Nazi or something?" I could feel my blood boiling. I never got a ticket in this town, I drank with the local coppers regularly on a Friday night, I'd even shagged constable Lee Donahue a couple of times. I was good with the local cops.

"Libby? Everything all right? Oh, I see you've met Senior Constable Richard Handcock." Lisa gestured to me. "Richard, this is Elizabeth Hastings, one of the local photographers."

"Nice to meet you, Dick." I said with a sneer as I shoved the offending ticket in my bag.

"Richard." He corrected me as I opened the car door and slid into the driver's seat and shut the door.

"Yeah, but you'll always be 'Dick' to me." I smarted off as I turned the key in the ignition and let the bass drown out anything else the tosser might have said.

I pulled out, almost colliding with Mrs Tompkins, who really shouldn't have her licence at her age. Poor old bat could barely see over the steering wheel, and her glasses were so thick, you could use them as astral telescope lenses.

"Fucking cocksucker, I mean, seriously, a ticket for not even an inch over! That wanker won't last five minutes in this town." I griped to myself as the soothing pounding base and sexy, raspy voice of Lars thumped through my head.

I left the village, heading back to the nursery and gardens, behind which Mel lived. She had taken over the business with her brother, providing florists with beautiful blooms, and backyard gardeners with all their plant needs. She'd been living in LA with Zane, a gay friend of hers, until her father had a severe stroke.

Poor Mr Whittaker was going to be wheelchair bound for the rest of his life, and still had a bit of a stutter, but he was always in the workshops, helping to set up florists' orders or slowly wheeling himself through the gardens that Mel herself had designed, complete with a hedge maze and playground for the kids who visited with their parents.

I turned off the road, just before the nursery drive, and in to Mel's parent's property. They had a small road that led behind their cottage and back down to Mel's property.

I typed in the security code at Mel's gate and waved at the camera. Adam had a bit of security here, mainly to keep their privacy, something I could completely understand. I mean, when you're married to one of the hottest, most fucking sought-after movie stars on the planet, then, yeah, I'd want security too.

I pulled up in one of the parking spots, right next to Mel's car, a new model Range Rover. One she never really drove, unless she absolutely had to… Mel was an absolutely woeful driver. She was so bad, that Adam had hired her a driver for her birthday, whom she hardly used.

I got out of my car and headed up to the front door. Before I could reach the handle, it opened, and Zane stood there with a smirk on his face.

"Hey Slag." He grinned, his American twang making the word sound strange.

"What are you doing here, Fag? I thought you'd be cruising for the local 'talent'." I chuckled, knowing he wouldn't take offence to the word. Since Robbie and I contacted Zane to organise a surprise visit for Mel's birthday two years ago, we'd become pretty chummy. I had become one of his coveted 'Fag-Slags', along with Mel, and another of her friends back in the states called Fiona.

"Oh, you know, tending to 'Madam Whale'." He sniggered.

"Hey! I heard that!" Mel's voice called out from the entry.

"Oops," Zane said with a wry grin.

I shook my head. "You'll learn one day, my lad, that teasing a heavily pregnant woman will get you squashed." I smiled at Zane, hoping I came across as wise and knowledgeable.

"Hey Slapper, how are you feeling?" I asked Mel.

"Like a bloody beached whale," she said, placing her hands at the small of her back. "I swear if I start laughing I'm going to wet my pants." She looked at Zane and then me, her face serious. "So, no larks, got it?"

"Got it!" Zane said, placing his hands up in a surrendering gesture. Mel smiled and turned, waddling back inside the house. "She's testy today," Zane stage whispered.

"I heard that!" Mel shouted back.

I entered the beautiful home of my best friend. Zane took the bag holding my little black dress from me as I passed him.

"Ooh…pretties!" He squealed like a teenaged girl who had come across her superstar crush all alone in a parking lot.

"Take care of that, it's my most prized possession…after my cameras. Cost me a fucking arm and a leg, and most of my lady bits too."

"That's okay sweetheart, I won't harm your *precious.*" Zane imitated Gollum from *The Lord of the Rings*.

"That right there, is creepy as fuck." I shook my head as we walked up the stairs to the guest rooms where Mel had already run me a bath.

"Did he do Gollum?" Mel asked, poking her head out of the guest room door where we were headed.

"Yes! This guy is seriously freaky, where did you find him again?" I asked her as I entered the room. The scent of rose and lavender bath oils drifted through from the ensuite bathroom.

"Los Angeles," Mel said, lowering herself on to the bed with a sigh.

"Oh, weren't those some decadent times?" Zane giggled. Mel smiled and flipped him the bird.

"Everything is your fault, you know." She grinned.

"Yes, yes, It's my fault you're in this condition." Zane leaned down and gave Mel a chaste kiss on the temple. "But it's not all about me tonight, tonight…" He spun around dramatically and faced me. "It's all about Miss Libby here." He grinned wickedly. "She's going to get good and fucked."

"I think the term you're looking for, Zane is: 'shagged rotten.'" Mel supplied.

"Abso-fucking-loutly." I agreed.

"Right, get your ass in that bath bitch," Zane said, giving me a friendly push towards the bathroom.

By the time I'd finished, my body shone with bath oils, I was wearing a light, but expensive perfume, courtesy of Mel, and my little black dress had been accessorised to the nines by Zane, who had gone from movie extra, to phone sex operator, to webcam model, to drag queen and was now between professions. The drag queen dream had ended spectacularly thanks to Mel, during what was now deemed 'DragGate'. Two years ago, on Mel's birthday, we had surprised her by taking her to a Drag Queen show that Zane was debuting in and had been touring around the UK from America. Mel, in one of her famous clumsy moments had accidentally tripped over on stage, where she was being serenaded by the Drag Queens for her birthday, and had caused some seriously major wardrobe malfunctions for the two drag queens on either side of her.

There were plastic titties everywhere.

Zane had dubbed it a tit-tastrophe, and the Drag Queens had refused to speak with him ever again, except for their friend, Perry, or Miss Periwinkle, who was aware of Mel's infamous two left feet.

I left Mel and Zane, who were going to have a girl's night in, due to Mel's condition, and watch bad romantic movies all night long with popcorn.

In hindsight, I probably should have joined them instead of going to my date.

I found him sitting at our table, with another woman. Whom he introduced as his wife, and introduced me as his girlfriend *to* his wife.

Then, the pillock proceeded to invite me to a threesome with said wife.

"What the Fuck?"

Chapter Three

I looked at my 'date' and his wife.

"Are you fucking kidding me right now?" I asked, my voice rising. "You're fucking *married?*"

"Come now, Elizabeth, don't cause a scene, dear. Let's all sit down and discuss this like adults, we can have a lot of fun together." He had the audacity to smile at me.

"My name…you fucking arsehole, is *Libby*. I don't fuck married men, and I ain't into bitches." I grabbed the glass of water that sat innocently on the table and tossed it in his face before I stormed out of the ritzy restaurant.

I was so fucking angry with that tosser.

How dare he think that I wanted to fuck him *and* his wife? How the fuck did I miss that he was married? I went through it all in my mind as I got in my car. The signs were there. But I didn't read them right. The phone call he'd had on our first date that he'd had to take outside, the slight lightness of skin on his ring finger and the way he kept saying I was 'perfect'. I grumbled under my breath as I unlocked my car door and slid inside, slamming it shut.

I didn't need this shite. I could have been helping Danny at work, instead of chasing a dick for a good time. I started the car, the noise of *DSS* pounding through my car and body. It looked like it was going to be a 'good vibrations' kinda night with Handy Andy, my vibrator. He would do in a pinch, or when desperation got the better of me.

I lit up a cigarette and inhaled the acrid smoke, enjoying the burn in my lungs. I'd been good around Mel, never smoking around her, and not because she asked me to, but because I knew she was going to be a worry-wort all through the pregnancy and I didn't want my best friend stressing any more than I knew she would.

Pulling out of my parking spot, I drove down towards the main street of the village. Anger at the arsehole burning in my gut. I slowed briefly at a stop sign before I rolled on through, making sure there were no other cars coming. I accelerated through the streets, but the tell-tale flashing blue and red lights blazed through the night, illuminating my little car's interior.

"Great, just fucking great." I grumbled around the cigarette as I pulled over and parked my car out of the way. I wound the window down, letting the heavy bass pound through the quiet streets, setting the neighbourhood dogs barking and howling. Lights started to come on in the dark houses along the street. I looked in the mirror and watched as the flashing lights caught the figure of the copper as they came up to my window.

"Good evening Miss. Can you turn down the stereo please?" A male voice asked just loud enough to be heard over the falsetto screaming of Lars.

"Sorry, can't. Knob's broken," I shouted, taking a drag on my cigarette. I blew a smoke ring. A thick arm reached in and turned the ignition off. I glimpsed a tattoo of a girl's name *'Daisy'* surrounded in the white flowers of her namesake, in the shape of a heart on the hairy forearm of the officer. The noise of my stereo died with the engine as the officer took my keys.

"Hey! I need those back!"

"Step out of the car, please, Miss." The voice seemed familiar. I looked up at the copper as I got out of the car, stumbling a little on the old cobblestone road in my high heels.

"Well, Constable Dick." I grinned, pronouncing 'constable' as *'cunt-stable'*. "We meet again."

He eyed me with an eyebrow raised at the obvious insult, but said nothing about it. "Licence please," he said, holding out his ticket book and scribbling in it.

"Sure. It's in my car," I said, turning around and leaning back into my car. Again, stumbling on the damp cobbles in my heels.

I reached in and grabbed my handbag, backing up a little too quickly, and felt my ass connect with him. His hands gripped my hips, fingers digging into the flesh as well as something else.

"That's not what you think it is." Came the strained voice behind me.

"That better be your taser," I said straightening slowly, as I moved a step forward.

"It is," he assured me, taking my proffered licence. "Ah, yes Miss Hastings, I do remember you now. Got that parking ticket sorted yet?"

I gave him a deadpan glare.

"Have you had any alcohol this evening? You seem a little unsteady on your feet."

"Nope, no alcohol, though the night is young." I huffed, hoping this wouldn't take long.

"You know what a stop sign is?" he asked, writing down my details in the ticket book.

"Yes, I know what a fucking stop sign is." I grumped.

"Good, then you'll know the reason I'm giving you a ticket then." He smirked, ripping the ticket out of the book and handing it to me.

"You're fucking kidding me right now?" I sighed, and ran my free hand over my face, before putting the cigarette back to my lips and reading over the ticket.

"Have a nice evening miss, and get home safely. Oh, and remember the road rules, or you'll be seeing a lot more of me."

"Oh, I'm sure I will…*cunt*-stable Dick," I muttered as he walked back to his car and jumped in, he pulled up beside me as I got into the driver's side of my own.

"And Miss Hastings? You'd better get your stereo fixed, or you might end up getting pulled over again for noise pollution laws."

I snorted as he drove off and went to turn on my car—but the bastard had taken my fucking keys!

"What the fuck!"

Chapter Four

I got out of my car and watched as his tail lights turned a corner.

"Fuck, fuck, fuck, fuck, fuck!" I shouted, stamping my heeled foot for emphases. It fucking turned on the cobblestones, my ankle twisting painfully as I went down like a sack of shite.

I huffed a lock of hair out of my face as the heavens opened and fat, cold drops of rain began to fall. "Fuck," I grumbled as a got up and locked up the car.

Moments later, I was hobbling along the wet footpath, each step agony to my swelling ankle. Alcohol was certainly called for. I hobbled to the nearest pub with full intentions of getting good and stonkered. I'd have to come to the police station tomorrow to pick up my keys once I was sober enough, but fuck it, after tonight's disastrous date and the thieving copper stealing my keys, I needed a shot of vodka…followed by a pint of lager, then a few more shots of something. I got all that, but after the last few shots, it got a little blurry.

I remember having a couple of guys try to pick me up, and even one or two women who eyed my cleavage with hot looks, but I stand by my principles, and sexuality choices…not that I haven't experimented a little bit in community college. I didn't find myself attracted to my own gender like some of the other girls. I like dick, not pussy. I don't judge others if they do like their own flavours, but I'm a happy hetero.

The pub was getting rowdy by my seventh drink. The place was a bit wobbly, and I didn't feel the pain from my ankle, which was fucking fantastic.

"Fuck you all, cocksuckers and motherfuckers!" I cheered, standing on the bar, raising my vodka shot to the bar patrons.

"Okay, I think you've had enough. Get off the bar, miss," the bartender ordered me.

"Nope! I'm queen of the fucking pub! These, these are my people!" I slurred.

"Miss, you need to get down or I'm going to have you removed." The bar keeper commanded me again.

"You don't tell me what to fucking do…" I slurred. There seemed to be another bartender, who looked exactly the same as the first…but slightly to the left and a bit blurred.

The doors to the pub opened as the bartender tried to get me down again.

"That's okay, I've got her." I peered through the alcohol haze at the blurry blob that approached my perch. I was swept off my feet and carried out of the pub.

"Robbie?" I was surprised that Mel's brother had come into the pub.

"Yes, it's me, your prince charming, come to rescue you."

"But, I can't fucking leave yet! They have to hear my royal speech!" I cried… Somehow it was really important that the patrons of the pub heard my speech. "I'm the queen of the pub!"

"Sorry, your majesty, but you've been cut off, and you're lucky I was swinging in for a pint with a friend and saw you. What the hell are you doing here anyway? Weren't you on a date?"

"The bastard is fucking married," I bemoaned as Robbie set me down.

I squealed as pain shot up my ankle, I lifted the offended leg and held it, hopping unsteadily on the good foot.

"Shit, Libby, what happened?"

I couldn't help it, but started to babble as he helped me to the van. The diatribe of drunken words tumbled from my alcohol-numbed lips.

"Robbie, why can't I find a nice guy?" I said, the alcohol doing its work and bringing me down from my drunken high.

"I don't know, love," he replied, kneeling in front of me. "But let's get you home, get some ice on that ankle, and get you out of that damp dress and into something warm. Where are your keys?"

"*Cuntstable* Dick took them," I said, leaning against the back of the passenger seat as Robbie eased the shoe off my injured foot.

"Who is '*Cuntstable* Dick'?" Robbie asked me with a frown.

I hiccupped before I felt my stomach rebel a little. "He's an arsehole," I mumbled against the headrest of the passenger seat.

I was sleepy. Robbie tossed the shoe he'd removed from my foot into the van and reached over me, pulling the seatbelt across and clipping it in. I was dozing by the time he'd gotten into the driver's seat and started the drive out of the village and back to the Whittaker's place.

I vaguely remembered him pulling up at the front door of Mel's place, and carrying me up the steps and to one of the guest rooms. The bed was like a fluffy cloud of awesomeness and I crashed out into the drunken world of nod.

I woke up with a pounding head and a desperate need to puke. I opened my eyes and looked around, desperate to find where I was, and the location of the nearest loo. I recognised the room as one of Mel's guest rooms. As soon as my feet touched the floor, I fell down, one ankle swollen and throbbing with pain as I cried out, trying to hold back the wave of nausea that threatened to embarrass me.

I crawled on hands and knees to the bathroom, barely making it in time to lift the lid and seat of the toilet and evacuate the contents of my sour stomach into the blue chemical treated water of the toilet.

"Ahh… Our queen is awake!" Robbie chuckled from behind me as I felt a cool, damp cloth pressing over the back of my neck. "Good thing you've got a pixie style cut, Libby." I moaned in response and lifted a middle finger in salute to him. The fucker laughed.

"Sorry love, your pain is self-inflicted. You'll get no sympathy from me." He sighed, as I heaved again. "So, I'm heading into town soon on the afternoon delivery runs, if you want to get your keys from the police station. I've called already, and they have them waiting for you to pick up. Someone named Constable Handcock said he'd meet you when you came in."

"*Cuntstable* Dick…" I groaned and heaved again. Surely my stomach was empty by now!

"Oh dear, our sleeping beauty has awoken." Zane's American twang hit my pounding head.

"Fuck off, I'm dying here." I moaned.

"Yes, I can see that. Oh Libby, you are just like our Mel, before she got in the family way."

"Taught her everything I knew." I groaned, reaching to the back of my neck and pulling the damp washcloth over my face. I wiped my mouth, ignoring the putrid stink of undigested alcohol and vomit. "Now, gentlemen, if you'll excuse me, I need to take a shower. Zane, can you grab my emergency clothes from the bag in Mel's wardrobe?"

"Ah, you mean the 'Libby got drunk and crashed at Mel's place' bag?" He smirked.

"That'd be the one." I nodded, then groaned as another pulse of pain throbbed through my head. "Okay, evacuate the bathroom…" I groaned as I pushed myself up from the temple of the porcelain gods and flushed my offering. Robbie smiled and turned the water on in the shower for me before he left. Zane had already left to retrieve my emergency clothing. I stripped and stepped under the warm stream of water, letting it pulse over my aching muscles as I washed the sweat and stink off my body and out of my hair. I luxuriated as long as I could under the warm spray before I decided I was just going to start pruning like some old biddy and got out.

Zane had left my bag on the rumpled bed. Along with a nice tray of toast with marmalade, tea and orange juice and, god love him, aspirin.

And a note.

Constable Richard Handcock is on his way to pick you up. – Robbie ♥♥♥.

PS- He sounded sexy as fuck! If he's as good looking as he sounds, I'd do him in a heartbeat!

I choked on the orange juice.

What the Fuck?

From my vantage point at the top of the stairs, I heard the front door open and Robbie welcome someone inside. *Cuntstable* Dick had arrived.

I wasn't nearly ready yet, still clad in my sports bra and a pair of boy-short style knickers, but I was curious to see why he had decided to come all this way out here from the village to pick me up and take me back to my car. Maybe he wanted to get a glimpse of Adam, who was filming in Scotland, so he had no chance there.

Mel was due back from a Doctor's appointment with her mum at any minute. Her due date was getting closer and she was getting worried, first time mum jitters. It didn't help that Mrs Del Rosa, Adam's birth mother, and her own mother had been fluttering around her. This was Mrs Whittaker's first grandchild.

I leaned over the railing a little, catching a glimpse of *Cuntstable* Dick in regular clothes. He wore a tight black tee-shirt that seemed almost painted on his body, and a pair of jeans that hugged his arse.

"Oh, My God! Sandbags required…like yesterday." Zane whispered beside me. I squealed in fright and pushed him back away from the railing. I grabbed his wrist and dragged him in my hobbling gait back to the guest room where I shut the door a little louder than I intended to.

"You little shite!" I slapped him playfully on his chest. "You scared the absolute fuck out of me. Fuck you and those fucking ninja skills." I stopped, then placed my hands back on his chest. "Holy fuck Zane, have you been working out?"

He grinned. "Maybe…"

"Oh God, don't tell me you've been thinking about that body building idea again?"

"Nope." He smirked. "I'm going to be the next top model." I rolled my eyes. "Don't you scoff at me young lady! I *was* going to ask if you could help me build my portfolio, but now, I'm not so sure." He took on an offended air about himself, sticking his nose up in the air.

"Oh, come the fuck on, Zane. I'll be happy to help you with your portfolio. Besides, it would help my own, especially if I want to get into runway and model photography. We can help each other."

Zane squealed and clapped his hands together in such a rapid motion it was a blur of sight and sound. "Yay!" he cheered. "I'm going to be a model!" He clasped my hands in his. "Oh, you won't regret this, at all! I have contacts back in LA, and we can get you started over there whenever you're ready." He looked me over. "But, sweetie, you need to get dressed, I don't think your constable is ready to see you nearly naked." He smirked. "Or maybe he is…"

I scowled. "*Cuntstable* Dick won't be seeing me nearly naked or otherwise anytime soon, if ever." I raised a finger to punch my point home.

Zane wrapped an arm around me and kissed me on the temple. "Darling, he can try, but I know you've got the resolve." He got up and moved to the bedroom door. "Now, you wait here, and I'll get you something nice of Mel's for you to wear."

"What's wrong with my clothes?" I asked, picking up my singlet top.

"Darling, have you seen those rags? They don't fit anymore. You've lost more weight this year. You need to eat a little more."

"Ugh." I moaned, flopping back onto the bed. Zane was back within a few minutes, holding up a skin-tight pair of jeans and a low-cut top that put my not-so-ample cleavage on display.

"You're kidding me, right?" I asked him. Zane grinned and shook his head. "I fucking hate you, Fag." I grumbled, laying back on the bed and pulling the jeans up my legs. They stopped at the curve of my arse and refused to go any further. "They don't fucking fit!" I tugged again, my hand slipping off the hem.

"Here, let me help!" Zane said, helping me to stand. I kept my weight on my good foot, favouring the injured one while Zane gripped the hemline of the wretched jeans and tugged, jostling me up and down against his body. I faced him, chest to chest, my poor little c-cups smacking him in the face with each jostling attempt to get in my pants.

The door opened, and a throat cleared. Both Zane and my faces turned to see Robbie and *Cuntstable* Dick staring at us with looks of amusement and confusion.

"Gee, Zane, here I was thinking you were gay," Robbie said with a smirk. "I didn't think you batted for the other team."

"Oh, bite me, darling," Zane said poking his tongue out.

"I already did." Robbie retorted.

"I remember."

"Uh guys? Excuse me, half-dressed woman getting shoved into jeans that don't fit here… A little privacy please?" I said, turning away from the eyes of the boys. I had noticed that

Cuntstable Dick's eyes had been riveted on me the whole time, almost like he wanted to shove Zane aside and do the job himself.

And you know what the stupid thing was? I'd have been more than happy to let him. Despite the fact that he was an arrogant arsehole, who gave me two tickets in one day, stole my keys, and then came to my best friends place to pick me up and take me back to my car.

I watched his arse as he turned away, my eyes glued to the jeans-clad glutes of the sexy pillock. My naughty mind went through the fantasies of what I could do to that body. My own started to respond to those dirty, naughty thoughts.

But seriously, brain? Have you lost all sensibilities? This guy was an A-Grade arse, and here I was fantasising about licking his pecs and abs while I dug my fingernails into his delectable arse.

Robbie closed the door with a smirk.

"Don't worry, darling, I was thinking about his sexy arse too." Zane grinned.

What. The. Fuck?!

I had changed from the jeans of death into a more comfortable pair of sweatpants, the kind I used when I was having a girls' night in with Mel and we'd be slumped over each other on the couch watching some silly comedy, like Monty Python or some sappy girly shit. But right now, I was sitting in the passenger seat of *Cuntstable* Dick's car as we drove through the beautiful countryside back towards the village.

"So…" he began, the awkwardness levels in the car were rising at an exponential rate.

"So…" I said back to him. The silence between us grew. He seemed to grip the steering wheel tighter.

"Okay. So, I may have come across as a bit of a pillock yesterday, but in all fairness, I am a police officer, and I was on duty. I was just doing my job," he said as he stopped at an intersection and turned on to the road that led to the village.

"Right," I said, not intending on saying anything more.

"In London, we do things a lot differently than here."

"Well, here's the thing, you're not in London anymore, Toto," I said, gazing out the window. "We are a bit more relaxed here, not everyone is out trying to break the law intentionally. You need to get that big spiky stick out of your arse and stop being such an arse. You'll last a bit longer than the last London copper that came through here."

"Why, what happened to the last transfer?"

"He went bonkers and ended up in Middlefield Mental Hospital."

"He what?" Dick looked at me, surprise on his face.

"Yup. Farmer Dawkins had an old, World War Two German bomb, from The Blitz, in one of his fields. Everyone knew about it, and it had been disarmed years ago, but he wanted it left there as a souvenir. This copper had given him five tickets in one week for parking his tractor in town while he went and did the shopping, he had no car you see, and the poor old farmer knew he couldn't afford to pay, so he called up the station and asked specifically for that officer to come over to his farm to help with something urgent." I paused in my story as we entered the town, looking around.

"And?" Dick prompted me.

"And the town heard about it, and all came out, even the off-duty coppers. He wasn't too popular with them either. Everyone watched while this poor sod started to look over the bomb, Dawkins even gave him a pair of wire clippers and told him he had to disarm it. The silly bugger reached forward with a hand and as soon as he touched the bomb, the onlookers all shouted *'BOOM!'*"

I giggled at the memory. I was one of those onlookers. Nearly everyone there had had a run-in with that particular tosser, and none-too-pleasant ones at that.

"He jumped so high, pissed his pants and ran screaming into the woods." I reached down and adjusted the bandage that was wrapped around my ankle. "It took us a day or two to find him. He was covered in dirt and manure and trembling like a leaf. Poor bastard kept mumbling about bombs and evil towns and the Germans. The doctor had him committed." I grinned wickedly. "So, the moral of the story, is don't piss off the townsfolk." I noticed we were pulling up beside my car. Dick smiled and handed me my keys.

"I'll remember that." He grinned, before he unbuckled his seatbelt and got out of the car. He came around to the passenger side as I opened the door and held out a hand. I eyed it a moment before taking it, letting him help me up. I hobbled a little, getting my balance.

"Are you going to be okay driving with your sore ankle?" he asked, helping me over to the driver's side of my car. His body was warm against me, and his scent was masculine and delicious. *Down girl!*

"I should be. I only live a few streets over," I said as I unlocked my car. Dick held open the door for me.

"I'll follow you home," he said.

I gave him a curious look, not sure what to make of his decision.

"To make sure you get home okay. I promise, I'm not one of those crazy stalkerish type cops," he said as I settled in my seat and put my seatbelt on.

"Oh-kay then…" I said slowly, still unsure as to what to make of him. He smiled at me as he closed the door and stepped back, letting me start my baby and pull away from the parking space where I'd abandoned her for the night. The pounding of the music set the local dogs off again. I checked my rear-view mirror to see him pull out in his sedan behind me.

A few turns later, we had pulled up in front of my row of flats. I was on the second floor, and not relishing the idea of climbing the steps to my flat. I got out, with *Cuntstable* Dick holding the door, and a hand out for me.

"Well, fuck me, chivalry ain't dead after all." I smirked.

"Was just raised to be a gentleman, I guess." He grinned.

"Oh, so it was the police force that turned you into a bit of a dick then?" I couldn't help myself.

"Nope, people in general did that," he said, closing my car door for me. "Which one is yours?" He looked up at the row of small flats.

"Number six," I said, nodding up to the one on the end of the second floor.

I began to hobble towards it. Dick was there in a second, his arm slipping under mine and around my back, as he tried to support me up the stairs.

"I'm injured, not fucking invalid." I snapped, feeling slightly insulted that he felt the need to burden himself with me. Still, he didn't let me go. And in some twisted fucking way, I was grateful. I was still unsteady as fuck on my injured ankle.

"I could carry you caveman style." He smirked, waggling his eyebrows.

"Fuck off." I groused. We made our way to my door where he finally released me, as I unlocked the door to my crappy flat. My cat, Lord Psycho, heard the keys and instantly began yowling for food.

"Okay, so here we are. Thanks for everything, except the tickets, and taking my keys," I said so quickly my words almost blended together in an unintelligible mash.

"I am sorry about the keys, but the tickets… I was—"

"Only doing your job, Yeah, yeah, I know." Lord Psycho, or LP, as I called him, yowled again, making a horrendous noise.

"Look, I feel we got off on the wrong foot here. You only get to make one first impression, and I feel like I've bollocksed it up." He sighed, running a hand over his shaven head. "I'd like to make it up to you. Would you like to come out for a coffee with me?"

It was cute, how he was trying to endear me to him, almost puppy-dog like with the eyes he was making at me. Pity, I was a cat person…and with LP, I was on my way to crazy cat lady status.

But seriously? After all that? He wanted to take me out for coffee?

What. The. Fuck?

I was flummoxed. "Uh…okay, sure, I'll call you when I have the time," I said, quickly opening my door and letting myself in before he could see what a state my flat was in.

I shut the door behind me, pressed my back against the cheap plywood panelling and hid like a coward until I heard his heavy footsteps recede down the concrete walkway that joined the flats on the upper floor. I stayed like that until I heard him pull out of the driveway, peeking around the window like someone who had something to hide.

I so totally didn't. I watched him turn the corner, unable to tear my gaze from him driving away from me, out of my life. A small part of me hoped he'd call, but then I realised I didn't have his number, nor he mine. My mind began to drift with thoughts of how I could give him my digits. However, considering my track record with guys, was I really wanting to start a relationship with someone who was a bit of a pillock? The town copper?

It wouldn't work. There was no happy ending for me, the cards of fate just weren't ever right, I hated my family with a passion that I should have reserved for the stuck-up bitches at school. The ones who would bag me out for my high-school goth style, or my baggy clothes that hid the bruises after Dad threw me across the room in a drunken rage blaming me for Mum's infidelities and drug abuse.

My one escape had been Mel and her family. I was practically adopted by the Whittakers. There'd been more times than I could count that my parents had been at it. The music of fist against flesh, and the screams of drunken anger that caused me to flee out my window, risking the thorns from the scrabbly climbing rose that choked the rusting drainpipe I used to shimmy down to get out of the house in the darkness and across the fields, pushing my way through hedges and risking being shot at by farmers who thought I was a wild dog. I'm sure I looked wild enough with bloodied arms and legs, twigs wild in my unkempt hair. My pain was worth a little bit of love and normalcy from a family not my own.

My own family were arseholes. I seemed to attract the same.

A sharp claw jolted me away from my forlorn thoughts.

I was already in a relationship with an arsehole. A fucking cat who 'owned' me.

"What? Oh, fuck LP. Okay, okay, I got you," I said picking up the four-legged feline I had been cursed with and getting him something to eat.

I'd found him as an abandoned kitten on one of my last nights living under my parents' roof. The scrawny, near feral kitten had snuck into my dad's run-down shed. I'd had enough and wanted to finish my life using weed killer or, faster, and probably less painful, the axe cutting across my wrists, having hit my lowest point.

I'd acted out as a teen, gotten into some alcohol one night at a party and wound up sleeping with two guys…one who hadn't worn a condom. By the second month of not getting my period, I knew…well, that and the 'stomach flu' I seemed to have. I went into town, after swiping some drugs from my mum's secret stash, she didn't think I knew about, sold them to some kids I knew were into the ecstasy pills Mum had hidden from 'Daddy dearest', and went to the local pharmacy, where I purchased my first pregnancy test.

My bitch of a mother had found the pregnancy test, and told Dad, who then proceeded to 'beat the little bastard out of me', as the fucking prick so eloquently put it. Dad threw me in the shed and put a lock on it. In the tiny pinpricks of light that shone through the nail holes in the shed, I discovered I was bleeding. I cried, I was ashamed, but I wanted that poor baby to have a better life than I did, and I had been determined to make sure it had that.

Because of my cunt of a father, I was not going to be a mum. But I could give this scrawny little kitten what my unborn baby could never have. Love, and a safe home to live in.

I managed to break out of the shed using one of the older metal walls, which had begun to curl away from the old wood, snuck into the house where the arseholes, who were my parents were sleeping off their drunken states, packed my shit and began living in an abandoned warehouse taking Lord Psycho with me. Mel had given me a camera for Christmas, one of those cheap polaroid type ones, and she'd given me extra film for it too. She'd even offered to let me live in her room with her. I declined. I needed to find myself, discover who I was, for me. I still loved her, still needed her as my best friend.

It was my eighteenth birthday when Danny came into my life. He had been my saving grace. I was taking photographs of areas around the village, scenic spots, while avoiding the poor side of town where I knew my asshole parents still lived. I took pictures until my camera film ran out, taking each polaroid and shaking it in the air to let it develop before I checked it over and slipped it into a stolen plastic sleeve for protection.

I sold my better ones for a few pounds, so I could get something to eat, most of my meagre dinners were dumpster dives, and LP managed to get a few rodents in our abandoned warehouse to keep him a happy kitty, though he did mooch off me a little bit.

Danny found me in my little warehouse, tracking me down, after he bought two of my polaroids. I was sceptical of him at first, this stranger offering me a job, in which I didn't have to lick, suck or fuck anything, just take pictures, and he'd teach me how to become a professional photographer.

He saw potential in the scrawny girl who stank to high heaven, and clutched a wriggling cat in her arms like he was a safety blanket, no matter if he scratched up her face.

I owed Danny so much.

I had my career to think of. I went to the door of the small bathroom that also acted as my dark room. It was perfect, no windows to allow that pesky sun in, and decent ventilation from the ceiling exhaust fan when I was working with chemicals. I had a few pictures hanging up, left drying from my last shoot, ones I was happy with and going to sell at the market on the weekend.

Though there was something not quite right, the bathroom door was ajar, I know I'd closed it when I left yesterday. I slowly pushed open the door and switched on the light.

I gasped in horror.

The pictures had all been shredded. Great jagged strips torn from the photographic paper. There was only one culprit who could be so dastardly as to do this.

And the tabby little fucker was contentedly licking his paws after a good meal of sardines.

"LP!" I shouted, turning to face the guilty party. I'm sure my face was a picture of insane rage at the furry little fucker.

"WHAT THE FUCK!?"

The fucking cunt of a cat! I ran at him, anger fuelling my mind and clouding my judgment. Of course, being uninjured and having full use of four legs, *and* being a cat, the little sod managed to evade my hobbling gait and snarling promises of turning him into a fur rug to sit in front of the little fan heater that barely heated the place, but shot my power bills up to the fucking moon in winter.

I chased him around until I gave up. He was too quick, nimble and smart for me. I fell face-first on the sofa, my legs kicked up behind me as I groaned. I was hoping to have these pictures framed and ready for sale today. It seemed like my luck was running out.

Unlucky in love – check.

Unlucky with work – kinda check.

Unlucky in general – check, check-fuckity-check.

I lay there, my face buried in the pillow that was covered in a fine layer of cat fur. Thank fuck I wasn't allergic or the little fucker would have never stood a chance. I felt the sofa cushion in front of me dip suddenly, a soft purring and the tip of a small, wet nose pushing against my exposed forehead, before the rest of LP's face pushed against me in that affectionate way cats had of rubbing themselves all over you.

"You're lucky I love you, you fucker," I said, looking up. I instantly regretted it. I was greeted with LP's favourite pose. 'The-cat's-arse-in-the-human's-face'. Oh, how many times had I woken up to that sweet little view in the morning… That or a claw-n-paw to the face.

"*Really* lucky I love you," I grumbled to the pussy's pucker.

A few hours later I sat at my tiny kitchen table, the shreds of photographic paper laid out on a stiff, piece of white cardboard canvas. With a stick of glue in hand, I worked painstakingly on the pieces, but I didn't glue them back together, instead I let my inner artist have at it.

I finished the picture and within, it seemed like I saw a part of my soul. I hadn't realised, that in the background, I'd inadvertently captured the old two-storey cottage where my parents had lived, where my hellish childhood had drawn out, long and desolate. The house had been torn in two by LP's savage claws. It seemed poetic, that I was trying to put back together that which had been shattered in the first place, my childhood home.

I'd left space between the jagged pieces of the picture, like pieces of a puzzle that would never fit again, bits missing, the heart and soul of the place gone forever, or perhaps it was never there to start with. I gazed at the black and white image, shiny photographic paper against dull canvas. It was raw, gritty, and showed the reality, with the fantasy of my life, washed white behind the lies my parents told the police, the school and the social workers.

I felt the first hot, angry tear fall. I hadn't fucking cried in a long time. Not over those fuckers, not over that fucking house where I was supposed to feel safe, but where I had nothing but fear and loathing burning through my veins each time I had to push the rusty gate open after school.

My parents no longer lived there. Dad had drunk himself into liver failure and then died in prison after assaulting a police officer, and Mum had left him to be with one of her 'boyfriends' shortly after he went to prison. I'd learned she'd overdosed a few weeks after he died. I didn't attend their funerals, nor did I attend the reading of their wills. I didn't want anything from them ever again.

I still had the unopened letter from Mum's lawyer. Mr Montgomery had even come to my flat, telling me I now owned the cottage, as the last living descendant of my mother's line.

I didn't want it. Never did. Now it stood empty, and abandoned. Like my heart.

I should sell it, be done with that part of my life. But something within me, just couldn't bear to part with it. It was still part of me. My pain, my suffering. The loss of my baby. Mel knew about so much of my agony, but not about my miscarriage. Only I knew about that. I'd never told anyone about it. I still felt the shame, the failure of not being able to protect my unborn child from the wrath of a drunken cunt of a father, and the vindictiveness of a bitch of a mother.

Every time I looked at that house, I felt every strike of that cunt's fists. Every visit from the police or the social workers, every lie they told to keep me there, so they could get the most out of a system that supported the abusive fuckers that they were. To hell with the poor girl inside who hid the bruises beneath the baggy clothes that her sodding excuses for parents said were the fashion she liked.

I looked at the picture. The more I looked at it, the angrier I got, and the happier I was that LP had destroyed that one picture, that in another person's eyes, would have been so beautiful, so homely. All I saw, all I felt, was hate. I picked up the piece of cardboard canvas, stomping out of my little boxy flat and down the steps, ignoring the ache on my injured ankle and down to the dumpster out the back. I shoved the attempt at...whatever the fuck I was trying to accomplish deep down into the dumpster.

I had no idea what was going through my mind when I tried to fix the past. But ya know? I tried, but seriously,

What the Fuck?

Chapter Nine.

"Okay, so we have Mr and Mrs Flannigan's Gold Wedding Anniversary coming up. They want us to re-create their wedding pictures. Though I think there's about three members of the wedding party who aren't alive any longer, but we do have pictures of them available to us, so we can photoshop them in with the permission of the family members." Danny looked up from the appointments book. I nodded, taking notes down. I had learned a bit of photoshop, enough that I knew I didn't like the 'modern' day thing of 'photoshopping' shit in.

"Friday, we have the local debutante ball. Saturday, we have three weddings, so we'll have to split for the first two in the morning. Then we have the big one in the afternoon. Sunday," he paused, looking at me…

"Sunday, I have the market booked," I said, shifting my feet off the desk and stomping the carpeted floor under my chair.

We were sitting in Danny's office, actually a converted conservatory in his little row house cloistered amongst the others in a cul-de-sac off the main road. The week had progressed slowly, I'd taken my SLR and Polaroid cameras out and about, shooting bits and pieces of the countryside, houses that were favourites, bridges, cows, the usual nature-y shit that sold at the markets to the touristy types.

I'd been visiting Mel a few times through the week, taking the last of her progressing pregnancy photographs. Adam had come back from Scotland, and was back at the Castle, filming the third movie in the 'Duke' series. The set of the first one was where he had first met Mel, who had become the unlucky recipient of a broken heel and a bowl of chilled punch, a result of said heel. The subsequent, and leaked video of her spectacular fall from grace had brought them closer together, and from that disaster, and a few others, they lost and then found each other here in England after Mel's dad had a stroke.

The photographs that they selected, were then given to me to 'officially' sell to the media. Thus, I was technically their official photographer. I took some happy snaps, candid shots, the usual stuff. Shots of them before they got into their limo to go to gala events, charity fundraisers all that fucking superstar jazz that Mel now had to deal with.

I loved seeing her happy though. It was something I didn't think I deserved, despite her telling me I did. With all the shite I'd gone through, I highly doubted it. Hell, I hadn't even seen *Cuntstable* Dick over the last week, and I knew he was out and about, because there were a few people griping about the 'new copper' on the local beat. I smirked at that, then felt my body flush at the memory of him in that tight shirt… Fuck, I needed to get laid. My vibe was out of batteries, and I was overdue to any kind of satisfaction, even if it was just battery-operated satisfaction.

"Libby? Are you listening to me? Earth to Libby?"

"Huh?" I asked, jolting out of my daydream.

"The local Fireman, Paramedic and Policeman's ball committee wants a photographer to work at their annual ball in two weeks' time. I've got a visit planned with Lonnie then, so I'll have to get you to do it for me.

"Oh… Uh… Okay, no problem." I knew Danny tried to spend as much time with his sweet little three-year-old as he could. He and his girlfriend, Shelly, had separated not long after Shelly had discovered she was pregnant with Danny's baby. Despite them trying to reconcile for the sake of little Lonnie, it just never worked out, so they separated again. When Shelly moved back to her parent's place, over three hours away, it almost broke Danny, but he was determined to live his life and keep Lonnie in it, so they figured out a compromise. They both drove an hour and a half to Danny's Mum's home, where Danny and Lonnie would stay for a weekend before Shelly would come and pick up Lonnie.

"Chin up, old duck. You might find yourself a nice sexy policeman or a hot fireman, maybe even a paramedic to restart that heart of yours."

I scowled at him and flipped him the bird. He knew all about my encounter with *Cuntstable* Dick. The fucker had even laughed harder when I told him about my keys being nicked by the dick.

"Right," he continued. "So, you have the keys to the gallery. The exhibits are all ready to go, but the big question is, are you ready for tonight?"

I sighed. Tonight was not going to change my life, but having pieces in an exhibit that we'd put together with the local artist community was a big deal, at least for me.

I'd never had any of my photographs up for others to see, well, other than the customers of course. But Danny, being the awesome fucker that he was, went through my old portfolio of landscapes and candids and demanded that I put them in the exhibition.

"I guess," I mumbled, picking at the fraying armrest of the chair I sat in. I sighed. "Yeah, okay I'm ready." I didn't sound too convincing, even to myself.

Danny leaned forward, his deep blue eyes piercing beneath the mop of dirty blonde hair.

"Listen, Kid," he said, using the nickname he branded me with when he found me shivering with cold in the warehouse with

LP clutched against me for a semblance of warmth, despite the threadbare blankets I had wrapped around us to keep us warm. "You got this. You have a talent I've not seen in a long time. You have an eye for detail and beauty that is unmatched by any other photographer I know." He put a reassuring hand on my shoulder. "You got this, Libby, I know you do. You need to put all your doubts out of your mind." He grinned. "And if no-one buys your work, then you know what? Fuck 'em."

"Yeah, fuck 'em," I muttered, still not one-hundred percent sold on his enthusiasm. I downed my cup of tea that had been sitting, cooling on the desk and stood up. "Right, I guess I'd better go get tarted up then."

"I'll see you later. And you'll do great."

***

I smiled at the people who milled around, looking over sculptures and artworks in the form of paintings, prints, textile weavings and my photographs. There was a large group of people milling around one of my pieces in particular, though I knew all of the pieces that were in here, there was one that I knew I hadn't submitted… The one that everyone was 'ooh-ing' and 'aah-ing' over. I walked up to the group, slowly pushing my way through so I could get a better look at it.

My heart fell through the pit of my stomach and I felt sick.

It was the carboard canvas piece that I'd unceremoniously dumped in the rubbish. And it had a 'sold' card sticking against the frame.

For three hundred fucking pounds!

What. The. Fuck?!

I spun, pushing my way out of the crowd. I couldn't breathe. I needed air, needed to get the fuck out of the little former corner shop-turned-gallery. My heart pounding hard in my chest as I bolted out the door, hearing Mel and Adam calling out to me, Danny's voice floated by as I bolted. My feet pounded the pavement beneath me as I escaped into the night.

Hot, angry tears traced down my cheeks at the thought of people seeing the place where I was hurt so many times in my youth and childhood. Seen as a piece of art, that someone liked so much they'd pay that amount of money, hell any amount of money to buy it. It felt like every harsh word, every strike of my father's fists against my body were there again, tenfold.

I felt the pain in my stomach, my heart, my soul all over again as I lost the baby. I ran blindly through the streets until I came to the one place I never wanted to set foot in, or see again.

The cottage.

It stood forlorn in the dim moonlight. My breath was ragged as I pushed open the rusty gate. Its hinges, unoiled and weathered through the years screeched harshly, as if the monsters within the house could be awoken again. I knew they were no longer alive in the old clay brick and mortar cottage, nothing but ashes in the wind, and bones beneath the ground; but the fuckers were well and truly alive in my mind. Their claws had secured their place in my soul and even though I knew they couldn't hurt me anymore, I still felt each and every cruelty they unleashed on me.

I looked over the hated dwelling. My fingers curling and twitching. I stumbled over a chunk of concrete, hand sized and perfect. I knew no-one lived there, after all, I owned the place and refused to rent it out. The waist-high grass was a testament to the fact that this house had become as abused, neglected and unloved as I had been. I gripped the chunk and hurled it at the house. It hit one of the windows that hadn't been broken or boarded up already. The shattering of the glass sounding loud in the cool darkness of the spring night. It was the sound of my first chain breaking. I laughed, a dry, throaty chuckle that bordered on near-fucking hysterical insanity.

I walked to the shed, it was already half-collapsed with the weathering it had endured. I knew there was an old axe in there. I had considered using the sharp blade to cut my wrists and end it all as I lost my baby. I pushed through the place where the corrugated iron had separated, ignoring the nails that tore my dress and scratched my skin. My goal was in sight.

The holes where the roof of the shed had collapsed had exposed the axe to the weather. The head was rusted and no longer sharp. I didn't need it for the cutting edge. I needed it to destroy the house that held me prisoner for so long.

I started with the shed. My body swinging the axe like a sledgehammer, my muscles bunching and releasing with each heavy, soul-freeing strike. I cried out as the axe head struck the rotten wood of the shed and destroyed it with vigour.

My face was wet from the tears I'd shed, the sky above was clear, the stars and the moon were my only witnesses. Sweat ran in rivulets down my body, over my neck and between the cleavage of my breasts as I heaved and swung the axe again, and again, and again, destroying the place where my heart and soul had finally shattered. Destroying the chains that kept me in the one memory that haunted me. The fucking shed.

"Libby…" A voice called to me through my emotional pain. I fumbled with the axe, splinters burrowing their way into the flesh of my palms. I sobbed, my legs trembled with adrenalin and exhaustion, both emotional and physical as I sank to the dew-damp grass.

Warm hands caressed my shoulders as I broke.

"It's okay, Libby, I got you." I heard the voice of *Cuntstable* Dick, warm and soothing.

His hands left me for a moment, and I sobbed, bereft of the contact, before he gently took the axe from my hands and covered my bare shoulders with his jacket. I was lifted into his strong arms and carried to a car. I settled, quietly sobbing in the passenger seat, as he drove us away from the cottage where I tried to break free of my demons. Through the haze of my misery, I heard him speaking on the phone. I ignored the world until he slowed.

He pulled up outside a small block of flats. I knew them to be the temporary residences that belonged to the police station, for new officers who didn't have families and the need for a permanent home just yet. It meant that maybe *Cuntstable* Dick wasn't staying as long as was first thought. He helped me out of the car, and before I could protest, he swept his arm under my leg and carried me bridal style to his flat, unlocking the door and carrying me inside.

He jostled me slightly in his arms as he flipped the light on. Warm, yellow light illuminated the darkness as my blurry eyes adjusted. The place was spartan, there were still boxes stacked against one wall of the small flat, obviously unpacking wasn't a priority for him.

He settled my feet on the floor and guided me to the kitchen table, noticing my hands were curled up in pain from the splinters I'd taken.

"Have a seat, I'll just grab the first aid kit," he said, leaving me to move to the bathroom.

"That's really not necessary," I said, my voice tight from my hysterics.

I must have looked a fright. I knew my mascara had run, my eyes felt red and puffy, and my nose was running like a faucet. I absently wiped the back of my hand against my nose, leaving a smear of snot on my skin. Dick came back with a box of tissues, a warm damp wash cloth, and the white box with the green first aid symbol on it.

He carefully took my chin in warm, with his slightly calloused fingers, and wiped the mess from my cheeks and upper lip with the wash cloth.

"You had quite a few people worried about you, Libby," he said softly, taking the cloth and wiping my smear of snot from the back of my hand.

Carefully he turned my hand over and looked at the redness, and the little black splinters that had embedded themselves in my hands. He took out a pair of tweezers and some antiseptic wipes, placing them beside my hand on the table.

"Okay, this will hurt, but you're a tough girl. I mean you sure showed that shed what for." He smirked, taking up the tweezers. I winced. "Oh, come on, I haven't even started yet." He grinned, before he pressed the nose of the tweezers against my skin, pushing the first splinter out.

I whimpered, and sucked in a breath at the sharp pain "Didn't know you were such a sadist," I griped.

"One of my more endearing qualities, I assure you." He smirked, taking the splinter and wiping it off the tweezers onto a tissue, before going for the next one.

"Your friend, Danny said he'd come collect you shortly. I just want to make sure you're okay before I hand you over." He looked at the big splinter in the tweezer's grip. "That's a big bugger."

I nodded, biting my lip against the sting.

His eyes locked on mine. "So, why were you destroying that shed?"

I paled, my throat closed up and I began to tremble a little.

"Libby?" His eyes showed his concern. "It's okay, you're safe." Dick had gone back into policeman mode. "No-one is going to hurt you, okay?" he asked, his hands gripping mine. I yelped, there were still a couple of splinters in there.

"Oh, fuck! Sorry." He lifted my hands to his lips and kissed them… He fucking *kissed* them. I sat there, my mouth agape, surprise must have been scrawled all over my face in permanent marker. Dick stopped, pulled my hands from his lips. "Oh, uh…right." He blushed. "Sorry." His cheeks flushed sweetly. He was silent as he went about, plucking the rest of the splinters from my flesh until Danny arrived…With a certain picture tucked under his arm.

"Hey Richard, here's your purchase, thanks for finding our girl."

My eyes went wide as I saw that fucking photograph. I almost stopped breathing as Danny handed it over to *Cuntstable* Dick.

"Thanks." He smiled. "It's really a beautiful piece, perfect in its imperfect form."

I gaped, looking at the fucker who had bought a piece of my shattered past and said it was perfect.

What. The. FUCK?!

"I can't fucking believe you did that, you're a fucking arsehole." I snapped at Danny as he drove us back to my flat. I'd left *Cuntstable* Dick's place without saying goodbye, or thanking him for taking the splinters out of my aching hands. "I threw that fucking piece of shite picture out for a reason, Danny!" The pillock just let me rant at him, his hands resting easily on the steering wheel as he drove. "And then you *sold* it to that fucking *Cuntstable*. Seriously, Danny! You know what that place means to me, you know about the shit that went on in that house. Why would you fucking do that? I never wanted to see that picture again."

"That may be, Libby. But it was, as he said, beautiful, perfect in its imperfection. You are a broken soul, still putting yourself back together. Sure, there might be a chip off here or there off your hard-won veneer, but Libby, you are an artist. And how many artists have had a broken soul? Their imperfections are their saving grace, their healing comes out in their creativity." He turned a corner, entering my street. "You have a gift, borne of tragedy and heartbreak. Don't throw it away." He reached into his pocket and handed me over a thousand pounds in notes and cheques. "That's from your sales tonight." He smiled. "Get yourself something nice." He stopped at my drive. I got out of the car and turned to face him.

"You're still a pillock," I said softly. My head had started to pound with a slight ache from the emotional stress.

"I know." He grinned. "Now go get some rest."

I nodded, turning away as he drove off. I noticed the front light was still on at my front door, which was expected, but I didn't expect the lights to be on, glowing behind my closed curtains. I slipped up the stairs to my front door, slowly sliding the key in and unlocking the door, knowing the click would alert any would-be robber to my return. I pushed the door open quickly, a girlish squeal erupted from one of the two figures making out on my couch.

"Jesus fucking Christ Mel! You scared me half to death," I said stepping inside my flat. Mel quickly pulled the skirt of her gown down over her knees,

"Sorry, Libby, we were waiting for you to come home, Adam—"

"Adam didn't want his heavily pregnant wife roaming around the countryside hunting for her best friend in the dark, so I convinced her to come here and wait," Adam said, not even bothering to fix his unbuttoned shirt.

"Then…the pregnancy hormones kicked in…"

"And you've been hornier than a bitch in heat, I get it," I said, flopping down in the mismatched armchair. "But seriously? On my fucking couch? You know how much I could sell that for now, right? 'The couch that Adam Jacobs made out with his pregnant wife on'," I said with a dramatic wave of my hand, as if I was imagining the words on a billboard to advertise said couch. "It'd sell for millions." I smirked.

Adam chuckled. "Yeah, maybe billions. You'd be rich beyond your wildest dreams.

I laughed. "Yeah, right. Only if you left a little white stain or two on there."

"Eww! Libby! Don't talk about my husband's white stains, he'll get a big head on him."

Adam leaned forward and whispered something against her ear. Mel blushed and slapped him playfully on the chest.

"Nope, so don't want to know what he said." I pushed myself up from the sunken cushion of my armchair and headed to the kitchen. "Tea?"

"Decaf for milady, and I'll have a coffee if you got it."

I snorted. "Coffee." I pulled three mugs from the cupboard. "What do you think this is? A fucking Starbucks?"

Fortunately, I did have coffee, and I did have decaffeinated tea bags just for Mel. Mel had come and visited me often while Adam was away on set. We'd sit on my shitty couch and watch crappy movies, LP snuggled up between us, purring contentedly.

I made my guests their hot drinks, and brought the cups out with a plate of biscuits.

"Okay, so tell me, what the hell happened tonight, Libby?" Mel asked, clutching her tea in her hands while Adam sat back with an arm draped over Mel's shoulders.

"The fucking cottage," I said, sighing as I sat back against the lumpy backrest.

"The cottage?" Adam asked, curious.

"Yep, the fucking cottage. The place where I grew up, or was dragged up, depending on how you see it."

I didn't know what Mel had told him, from the look on her face, it wasn't much, and I was secretly pleased about that. It meant that my best friend, my confidante, still held my absolute trust. I sighed, then began to tell them about the picture I'd taken, how LP had destroyed it, and a few other pictures that weren't salvageable, and how I'd tried to piece back together the shattered past in an image that seemed to haunt me, just as much as that *fucking Cuntstable* Dick did.

Mel listened and didn't judge. She'd been there so many times in our youth, helping me up through her bedroom window, pulled out a box of band-aids, iodine and cotton balls, she'd kept under her bed for my visits, and tended to me like a nurse. Then we'd both curl up in her bed and talk about things that mattered, things that didn't remind me of my hell back at the fucking cottage.

She knew it all, except for the one thing that I kept to myself.

"But why the shed? I mean I can understand smashing the window, but why did you destroy the shed?" Mel asked.

My throat closed up, memories of laying curled up on the dusty concrete floor after the miserable fucking excuse I had for a father locked me in, after beating me and kicking my stomach until I was near insensate with the pain, then the sticky, wetness that bled out from between my legs. Mel could see there was something about the way my eyes shimmered with tears.

She turned to Adam. "Honey, can you give us a moment?" she asked, then pushed a little bit to get herself up off the sofa, Adam helping her, supporting her.

I was desperate for someone to show me the affection he showed her, but I knew I was too damaged for that.

Mel held her hand out to me. "Come on, I think you've been hiding something from me for a long time, and you need to let it out."

The sadness in Mel's eyes showed me she had an idea about what I wanted to tell her, I was so afraid. But as soon as the door was closed, and we settled on the bed. My loss, which still haunted me, so many years after the fact, pushed its way past my final barriers, breaking my heart all over again, shredding my soul.

I sobbed against the swelling of life that waited in my best friend's belly as she held me.

"I knew your dad was a bastard, but seriously…" Mel said, as she stroked my hair, the next words spoken summed his actions up perfectly.

"What the fuck?"

Adam stood at my bedroom door. "Sorry, Libby, Sorry, Mel. I just wanted to make sure you were okay, I didn't mean to hear the last bit, but fuck," he said softly, lowering his head.

I knew he was worried about what kind of father he'd be, especially after finding out he was adopted not too long ago. It was one of the things that had Mel doubting his fidelity, especially when pictures of a beautiful woman and a child popped up in the papers with him. The woman and child turned out to be his half-sister and niece. I'd tried desperately to stop Mel from looking at the pictures, but it had been too late, and she'd had a category eleventy-bazillion meltdown.

"Honey, I'm going to stay here tonight," Mel said, huffing as she sat up a little on the bed, her arm around my shoulders, fingers stroking my arm.

"Okay, baby," Adam said. "I'll crash on the couch."

"No, you guys don't have to do that. That's not fair to you two," I said up, wiping my eyes. "I'll be fine."

"Shut up Libby," Mel said with a smirk. "It's what best friends do. Besides, you'll be called upon for babysitting duties soon," she said, rubbing her hand over her swollen belly. "Oh, he's kicking!"

She grabbed my hand and placed it over her belly. The flutter became a jolt as the baby kicked hard enough for us to not only feel it, but to see the lump of movement under her tight dress. Mel's eyes met mine.

"You'll be a fucking awesome mum," I said, knowing it would be true.

"So will you, one day," Mel promised me. Adam left us in the bedroom, I heard him pottering about in the kitchen, washing the mugs we'd used and putting them away after drying.

"You got him well trained then?" I asked.

Mel giggled. "Very well trained." She sighed. "Sorry about that pillock and his wife. Plenty more fish in the sea for our madam shark to devour." She grinned at her nickname for me.

I'd gone as a nurse shark to their last Halloween party…a slutty nurse shark. It was a tacky costume, a shark costume with a naughty nurse getup I'd bought as a lark at an adult store in London, but heck, it worked. I had a very good night, picked up a very sexy American footballer, who was dressed as a fisherman, and I'd let him hook and reel me in all night long. I couldn't help but laugh at the memory.

"See, got you to smile." She made a fist and gently nudged me with it. "Slapper."

"Tart."

"Skank"

"Ho."

We grinned. I hugged her. She was my best friend, and she knew all my terrible secrets, my shame, and she didn't judge. She had mourned with me now, knowing about my loss. Some might have said it wasn't to be, some might have even been so cruel as to say it was only two months along, it wasn't really there, but to me, as soon as I knew I was pregnant, I wanted it. I kept my hand on Mel's baby bump, feeling the restless little bugger shifting until he settled.

"This kid is going to be one very loved and cherished child."

"Especially by his Godmother." Mel grinned, giving me a knowing look. As far as I knew, they'd not asked anyone to be the godparents yet.

"Wait… What?"

"Adam, can you come in here a minute?" she called out. Adam was there in seconds.

"Everything okay, baby?" he asked, concern on his face.

"Yes, just want you here for this," Mel said, patting the side of the bed. She took his hand in hers when he sat beside her, before taking my free hand in her other hand. "We want you to be our baby's Godmother."

I couldn't believe it. I opened and closed my mouth a few times before I took a deep breath and gathered myself.

"I'm… Wow, speechless. Of course, I'd be fucking happy, and honoured to," I said.

My smile split my face, all previous sorrows forgotten for the moment as we enjoyed the happiness that my friends had given me. Mel hugged me tight, an awkward embrace with her belly in the way.

"Do you have some blankets and a spare pillow? I'll take the couch. You ladies share the bed," Adam said standing up.

"Guys, like I said, that's not necessary, go home. You'll both be more comfortable there." Mel looked at me, seeing I was determined that they shouldn't stay, especially as my bed was comfortable to me, but not quite to Mel in her delicate condition.

"Libby…" she said slowly.

"Mel…" I said shaking her head. "I'm a big girl, I'll be fucking fine."

"There you have it, she's almost back to normal." Mel grinned.

"Fuck normal." I grinned. "Look, you two get going, before the paps have a field day when they discover you're visiting a friend. God forbid you do something 'normal' like you know, us regular folks?"

I stood up, Adam helped Mel off the bed.

"Are you sure?" she asked, still looking at me with concerned eyes.

"I'll be fine. Besides, I have LP with me," I said, nodding to the cat, who was fast asleep in his basket.

Mel looked at Adam, then back at me. "Okay then," she said, as she gathered her bag, and Adam helped her with her jacket. "But if you need us, call, and we'll be right back, okay?"

"I will, I promise," I said letting them out of my home.

I watched from my door as Adam helped Mel down the steps, down to the black Range Rover that Mel never drove. I waved as they pulled out, Adam tooting the horn a couple of times in farewell. I headed back inside and settled down on the couch, dozing off to some terrible late-night telly.

I was woken with a fright when there was a banging on my door. I checked the time on my phone, it was after midnight.

I gripped my trusty cricket bat that I kept beside the front door, peeping through the eyehole before I unlocked and opened the door.

The multicoloured highlights of Zane's wild hair blazed under the front light.

"Zane!" I greeted him, with a speck of confusion "It's after midnight," I said, stepping aside to let him in. He carried in bags of junk food, and a couple of DVDs.

"I heard you needed some company. I couldn't sleep, so, I thought I'd come around. You look like you need some crappy, sappy Rom-Coms and lots and lots of chocolate."

I smirked, closing the door behind him. "Aw, what the fuck."

After that first night, Zane had been around almost every night that week. He even came by to help me set up for this morning's market, before he saw a guy, who in his words was, 'OMG, that guy is so fucking HAWT!', and he went on the prowl. His mission: to see if he could get the guy's number, leaving me alone at my stall with all my framed and unframed photographs. I had cards and flyers set out as well, advertising Danny's photography business.

The spring morning sunshine beat down on the market. Tourists, who were here to see if they could catch a glimpse of the famous movie stars who were filming at the Castle, milled around the stalls of local produce and crafts. Our little village was having a bit of a boom time, even some of the local cafes were doing a great trade, and there were plans to renovate the local fish n' chip shop, upgrading the old fryers and the warped, laminated tables that were fixtures from at least the fifties.

I was helping a little old lady look over some of the photographs of the local area when I saw him. *Cuntstable* Dick. He was on duty, patrolling around the markets on foot with Lisa. He smiled when he saw me at my stall.

I glared.

He gave me puppy dog eyes.

I still glared.

He moved on. Lisa walked past, while he slipped around another stall. Then I saw the reason they had split, a young man had slipped his hand into a woman's bag and lifted her phone and purse from within, slipping the phone into his jacket pocket, and quickly slipping the notes from her purse before he dropped it and kicked it under a stall. I watched, while trying to make a sale with the old biddy, as Lisa and *Cuntstable* Dick moved to where the pickpocket was trying for another unsecured handbag. I returned my attention to my customer.

I looked up from the pictures that the old lady was looking at as shouting caught my ears. The pickpocket was running through the market, back towards my stall, arms and legs pumping as he pushed his body in a burst of adrenalin-fuelled speed.

"Excuse me, just a moment," I said to the lady, as I stepped out from behind my stall into the path of the pickpocket.

He was too busy looking behind him to see how far behind Lisa and Dick were to notice I had stepped in his way. I casually put out a foot as he barrelled past, catching his foot and tripping him up. He stumbled and fell, face planting the cobblestone-styled bitumen of the blocked off street with an *'oomph!'*. I watched as Lisa and Dick slowed down, and stopped next to the pickpocket. *Cuntstable* Dick sat on the pickpocket's lower back, straddling him as he cuffed the criminal. Lisa pulled on a pair of gloves, ready to search him.

One of the other stall holders came over with the pilfered wallet that the pickpocket had kicked away to hide it.

Cuntstable Dick looked at me with a smirk as he hauled up the now hapless crook. "Good job, Libby. You'd make a pretty decent police officer," he said with a wink as Lisa started to search the guy.

I snorted and rolled my eyes, turning back to the old lady who was now more than happy to purchase a framed print.

"OMG, what did I miss?" Zane asked, coming up beside me with a bag of popcorn as I wrapped the framed print in an old newspaper to protect the frame for the old lady.

"Libby was doing some freelance police work," Dick said, with a smirk as Lisa finished checking over the pickpocket. All in all, they'd found a large sum of cash, credit cards and three phones on him.

"This looks like one of the guys we've been after for a while. Good job, Libby," Lisa said with a grin as she checked over the pickpocket's ID.

Cuntstable Dick nodded. "We'll need you to come down to the station to make a statement," he said to me.

"I can come later this afternoon, when we've packed up." I had no intention of doing this with him in a small interview room, plus I had a wedding shoot this afternoon.

"That's okay, I'll take care of your stall sweetheart, you just go with the nice officers," Zane said, pushing me towards Dick in a not-so-subtle way. I gave him my absolute best *'I'm gonna fucking kill you'* look.

"Great, we'll see you at the station in about half an hour." Dick smiled as he and Lisa hauled the pickpocket off towards their patrol car.

I turned slowly, with deadly precision. "Zane. You are a bitch."

"Why, thank-you sweetheart, now you better go get sorted, you look a little flustered. Go make yourself look absolutely sexy for that gorgeous policeman. I'm sure you'll break your nookie drought very soon." Zane grabbed my backpack and shooed me away from my stall.

I just stood there and looked at him, mouth agape, and with, what I was certain was a shocked look on my face. "Zane! Seriously?"

"Oh, come on, like I can't see the signs. You need to get laid, sister. And in such a bad way too. You've been twitchy, bitchy and totally hormonal. If I didn't know it wasn't your time of the month, I'd have guessed it was!" Zane chuckled.

"What…?" I gasped.

"Oh honey, I've known you for a while now, and I'm damned well attuned to you, and my girl Mel. If I was a chick, we'd totally be in sync with each other."

"Ugh, Zane, can you stop talking about that, like really?"

"What? It's a perfectly natural occurrence in a woman's biology. Besides, you seriously need to get some 'Dick' in you," he said with a wink.

"Zane! What the fuck?"

I trudged up the brickwork steps to the police station, my backpack slung over my shoulder. I'd left the market reluctantly, after Zane assured me he'd take care of everything, including packing up the stall and having Robbie pick him and my stock up in the van to take back to Danny's studio, where we usually stored my market stock.

I pushed open the glass doors, the smell of paper and tea strong in my nose as I walked up to the desk.

"Hi Kev," I said with a smile for PC Kevin Harris. He was a red-haired bloke with freckles across his nose and a youthful look about him, though he was in his later thirties.

"'Ello Libby, hear you been trying to do some police work of your own, eh?"

"Yeah, I was asked to come in and make a statement. Is Lisa about?" I asked, hoping that I wouldn't have to deal with *Cuntstable* Dick.

"Ah she just popped out for lunch, but PC Handcock, who was with her is available. Said he was expecting you." Kev smiled. "Have a seat, and I'll just go get him."

"Thanks," I said, really not feeling all that thankful as I went and settled in on one of those crappy plastic chairs that were in sets of four, and favoured by hospitals everywhere to make an uncomfortable wait even more uncomfortable.

Thankfully, I didn't have to wait long. One of the doors to the back section of the police station bleeped as its electronic lock disengaged, and it opened, revealing *Cuntstable* Dick.

"Miss Hastings?" He smiled at me, as he opened the door wider and gestured for me to come through.

I got up, pushing from the moulded plastic chair and walked across the linoleum, discoloured in spots from the sunlight that shone through the windows. The old police station needed a little bit of renovation in places, but it was still functional, and hadn't seemed to warrant much attention in regard to maintenance or upkeep of appearances.

I'd only been here once, when I'd been out after my father had attempted to beat me for not keeping the house clean, and I'd been caught roaming the streets with no reasonable explanation as to why I wasn't at home, tucked up 'safe' in bed. The back sections hadn't changed all that much.

Cuntstable Dick lead me to one of the interview rooms, where two cups of tea were waiting.

"I took the liberty of getting you a cup of tea," he smiled, pulling out a seat for me, before he took the one opposite.

"That standard procedure?" I asked, a little snidely.

Dick grinned. "Nope, just thought you might like a cup of tea." He settled in his seat and opened a clipboard with a lined notepad clipped to it

"Uh, okay. Thanks, I guess." I reached for the steaming foam cup and slowly pulled it towards me.

Dick grabbed his and took a sip. "Okay, so in your own words, can you please tell me what happened today?"

He picked up a pen and began to write down the details of the meeting.

I leaned forward, my hands clasping the cup as I began. "I was working my stall at the local Saturday market when I saw this young man in a white shirt reach into a woman's purse and pull out a phone and a wallet. He quickly took the money out of the wallet and dropped it, kicking it under Farmer Trotter's produce stall before moving on. I noticed you and Lisa—"

"PC Smythe," Dick corrected me, scribbling down on the notepad

"Right, PC Smythe…" I said with a touch of ire in my voice at being corrected. "…following him and keeping an eye on things. I continued to work at my stall until you tried to stop the young man, who then turned and fled, running back towards me. I then decided to try and help, don't know why, just did it. So, I walked into his path and tripped him up, allowing you and *PC Smythe* to catch him."

"Okay, and did you see anything else, any other thefts?" he asked, the pen scratching over the lined paper.

"I did see him slip his hand inside someone else's bag and take another phone just before you tried to get him." Dick nodded.

"That was all?" he asked.

"Yep." I picked up my cooling tea and sipped it, leaning back in the chair.

"All right. Let me just read this back to you, and I'll get you to sign and date your statement."

I nodded, listening to him read back what I'd said in my statement as I sipped at my tea. It was sweet and still slightly hot, but that perfect temperature to be enjoyed.

"Sounds about right," I said, finishing my tea.

"Excellent," *Cuntstable* Dick said, sliding the pad over to me, and handing me the pen. My fingers brushed against his as I took the pen, feeling a little jolt of static electricity as I took the metal pen from his fingers. He smiled warmly as I looked up at him, before diverting my full attention to my statement and signing on the dotted line.

"All right, now that's done, I'm pretty sure I owe you a drink." He grinned. "How about I pick you up at seven tonight?"

Ah…so that's your game? I shook my head in bewilderment. "Can't. I have a wedding to shoot this afternoon, and I'll be shooting at the reception till late."

"Raincheck?" he asked, his eyes hopeful.

I sighed. "Listen, I don't know what you're playing at, but I don't think I'm your type of girl." I leaned forward. "Seriously, I'm not sure I like you, you were a real arse to me the first time I met you—" I held up my hand. "I know, I know, you were doing your job." I crossed my arms on the table and leaned over on them. "And yes, you did buy a picture that I had actually thrown out, *and* paid too much for it in my opinion, and then you found me at my weakest, and you still want to take me out for a drink?" I leaned back, leaving my hands on the table, my eyes searching for an answer in the look he was giving me. "I'm damaged goods Di— *Richard*," I said, actually using his proper name felt weird. "What could you possibly want from me?"

"Libby," he said softly. "I like you, you're smart, witty, funny, beautiful. I would love to get to know you better, start out as friends, maybe even see where that goes." He reached forward, a large hand reaching forward tentatively, fingertips caressing my knuckles. "And you're not damaged. You are just, maybe, a little lost. I want to find you."

"Uh…ok-ay…" I said, pulling away. I got up and walked out the door, leaving him alone in the interview room, my mind a maelstrom of thoughts.

He wanted to get to know me better? To *find* me?

What. The. Fuck?

The next day went by without sight nor sound of *Cuntstable* Dick. For that, I was kinda glad.

I vegged out on the couch as the photos from the evening before developed in my bathroom-come-darkroom. Several had already developed and had dried. I'd laid them out on the kitchen table and let LP in from outside at about midnight, before I lay down on the sofa again.

I'd been watching some silly soap opera and had drifted off when a sound woke me… The unmistakable sound of a cat in the first stages of throwing up.

I bucked up off the couch, my legs flying upwards, as did my torso, just enough to see over the back of the couch into the kitchen where LP was. The poor boy was hunched over, back arched as he retched, bobbing his head as if he were in a sickly cat mosh pit. The worst part wasn't that I knew he was going to be sick. The worst part was that he was perched atop the kitchen table. Right on top of the beautiful photographs I'd taken of the bride and groom. The ones they'd specifically asked to have ready tomorrow for their bridal breakfast.

I struggled off the couch, my feet thumping on the thinning carpet towards LP in a desperate effort to save the photographs that had already been paid for, with a damned guarantee that the pictures would be delivered to them in the morning. I reached for my poor pussycat just as his mouth opened. I cried out in abject horror as his lips pulled back in a rictus, his jaw opened, showing his sharp little fangs, and curling tongue as stomach acid and congealed feathers erupted from his mouth to splatter all over the photographs of the smiling bride and groom.

"No!!!" I cried out, as I ran from carpet to cheap linoleum. My bare foot squelched in something that felt warm, and disgusting…and reeked of cat vomit.

This wasn't the first of LPs pukes this evening. I skidded in the small pile of puke and landed hard on my arse with a grunt as LP retched once more and then jumped off the table, darting towards the bathroom where he liked to hide behind the toilet or the washing basket if he knew he was in trouble.

"Seriously? Come on!" I bemoaned to the heavens. "Fuck me, not even Mel has this much bad luck." I thought for a moment on that statement. "Okay, maybe she does." I groaned as I sat up, rubbing my butt only to discover it too was smeared with vomit. "Really, LP? Seriously?" I felt my stomach churn at the bits of badly digested blue bird feathers that were stuck to my hand. "Cat. We seriously need to talk about your eating habits." I peeked over the top of the table. "And your opinion on my photography."

I hauled my arse up, ignoring the squishy stuff on the bottom of my foot. I hobbled over to the bathroom and turned on the light. A pair of green eyes looked at me from behind the washing basket. "You do realise I'm going to be really fucking late with this order now, don't you?" I asked him.

I sighed, stripping my clothes and dumping them into the basket. My washing day would have to be bumped up from Tuesday to as soon as the pictures I'd have to develop a second time were dry.

I finished scrubbing the parts of my body that had been in contact with LP's stomach contents before I left the bathroom to clean up the mess he'd made. I wasn't great with cleaning up vomit, especially when parts of it were still identifiable with whatever had been eaten.

I finally finished cleaning up, and disinfecting the kitchen table, the floor and my body. Then I set to work on getting the reprints done. My eyes felt like someone had thrown coarse sand in them and I felt like I needed another shower by the time I was done a few hours later. But I finally had the last of the photographs dried and in their frames, which fortunately, had not been on the table. I carefully placed them in the gift bags that the bride and groom had provided, which also had escaped the vomitus attack from my feline.

I checked my hair and makeup in the mirror beside my front door, before I realised how bloodshot my eyes looked. I groaned, before I headed back to the bathroom where I scrounged for my old friend, Mr Clear Eyes. I sighed softly as the lubricating eye drops did their job, easing the gritty feeling from beneath my eyelids. There was a soft knocking at the door.

"Who the bloody hell could that be?" I wondered to myself.

I opened the door to find Mrs MacDonald, one of my elderly neighbours at my door. The poor old dear was hunched over with arthritis, and osteoporosis, but she had somehow managed to get up the steps from her flat on the ground floor to my one at the second floor. No mean feat for a woman who kept to herself and only left her flat for her doctor's appointments. Realistically, she should be in a home, as her family didn't come around to see her often.

"Good morning, Elizabeth. I'm so terribly sorry to bother you so early, but it seems that Porridge has gotten out," she said in her sweet, little old lady voice. "You haven't seen him, have you?"

Porridge…her blue budgerigar. My mind flashed back to the disgusting mess of congealed *blue* feathers that LP had puked up all over the kitchen floor and dining table.

Oh shite.

"No, I'm sorry Mrs Mac, I haven't seen him. But if I do find him, I'll try to bring him back to you." I promised her.

"Oh, you are such a good young lady." Mrs MacDonald smiled, taking my hands and patting them with affection. I smiled back, though it was so forced that I was afraid I'd break my fucking cheeks.

I closed the door and turned around to see LP smiling at me, the smug little fucker had the audacity to lick his chops before he began to clean a paw so nonchalantly it made me shake my head. "Really, LP? Of all the fucking birds you could have devoured then puked all over the kitchen, you chose Porridge the budgerigar?" I set my hands on my hips and shook my head again.

"What the Fuck?"

I was ninety-nine-point-nine percent certain that LP had killed, eaten and then regurgitated Porridge the budgie. So, after I dropped off the photographs to the grateful couple, without their knowledge that they were a second batch. I said my goodbyes to the loved-up and happy couple and then headed to the local pet shop.

My mission: 'Operation Replacement Porridge' was a go.

I entered the pet shop where the chirps and squawks of birds, the yips and howls of puppies and the yowls and cute squeaking mewls of kittens reached my ears. The ice in my heart began to melt a little as a Husky puppy bounced around the little Perspex-box pen they'd placed him in. There wasn't nearly enough room in there for a large puppy, but no-one had bought him yet. He licked the Perspex where I had placed my hand, his little paws scratching to get at me, then he sat on his haunches and howled. If I had the room, and the money, I'd probably have taken home a new pet to terrorise LP.

But, instead, I was here for an entirely different purpose. Regretfully, I left the cute bundle of mischief, and steadfastly ignored the other little babies looking for their forever homes and made my way to the aviary, where the brilliantly coloured feathers of the caged birds awaited me.

"Hi, can I help you?" The young shop assistant came up beside me, her mouth moving like a cow's as she chewed a piece of gum and popped it between her teeth.

"Uh, yeah, my cat decided to make a meal out of my elderly neighbour's budgerigar, and I wanted to get her a replacement," I said, eyeing the birds off. There were some really pretty budgerigars. In a variety of colours from white pied, right through to an almost iridescent lavender.

"Okay, male or female?" the girl asked, putting her hands on her hips in a casual and relaxed manner, as she continued to chew and pop her gum. I kinda sympathised with the chick in *'Chicago'* who killed her husband for popping his gum. That shit was annoying as fuck and would drive anyone to murder.

"I think Porridge was male," I said, racking my brain to remember.

"Right, and what colour were you thinking of?" The girl moved to a section of cages that was marked 'Male Budgerigars'. Her mouth worked again, then seconds later it came *POP!* I shuddered a little.

"Uh…blue.," I said, feeling a slight wave of nausea come over me as I recalled the blue feathers that LP had brought up. I was getting a little bit irritated at the amount of questions the girl was asking, though she was trying to be helpful. My lack of sleep and lack of food was making me one cranky arse bitch.

"Okay, juvenile or mature?" she asked. *Chew-squish, chew-squish, chew-squish, POP!*

"Look, I just want a fucking blue budgerigar. One that goes chirp-fucking-chirp, and that my fucking cat won't eat and then puke up all over my flat." I stared daggers at her. "Is that too much to fucking ask, or are you going to continue to chew and pop that fucking gum in my face all morning?" I had raised my voice, feeling like I wanted to explode. All the animals in the store were deathly quiet as soon as I had finished.

"Ahem, is there a problem here?" The gruff voice of a man entered my tired and grumpy mind. I looked up. The gum-popping girl had backed away and a burly, fat man stood before me, arms crossed and an unimpressed look on his face. I dared a look at his name badge. 'Larry – Store Manager'. Just fucking great.

"I just want a blue budgerigar." I sighed. "Look, I'm sorry, I have had a very stressful night, which included my cat eating my neighbours pet bird, then vomiting its remains up all over my kitchen, destroying some work I'd laid out on the table, and I have barely slept at all trying to get it finished for my client by this morning. I just want to replace the poor woman's fucking bird and get it home to her, so I can go to bed and get some sleep."

"We can't help you. We have no birds for you."

"But you've got fucking blue budgerigars right there," I said, indicating to the cage filled with the little blue fuckers who all eyed me with suspicious beady little eyes.

"Not for you, we don't. I'm going to have to ask you to leave." He pointed to the door.

"You're fucking kidding me, right? I'm wanting to buy a fucking bird from you, and you're not going to let me?"

"That's exactly right, now get the hell out of my shop!" Behind him, the girl popped her gum with a smirk. I turned and stormed out of the shop, the animals started their noisy calls behind me.

"Arsehole." I grumped, turning to flip him the bird before I turned and stormed out. Three steps later, and not watching where I was going, I collided with a tight, muscled chest.

"Oof!" I grunted, butt-smacking the pavement. With all the mistreatment, my arse was going to be black and blue

"Hey, Everything okay?" Robbie asked, helping me up.

"Fuck no." I sighed. Shaking my head as I got to my feet. Robbie, Mel's brother was so kind, a gentle soul, and a gentleman, I would have loved to have him as a boyfriend, if I were his type. He was more Zane's type, and from what I knew, especially from

'Uncle' Leo's grumbling about it more two years after the 'event', Robbie and Zane were no longer allowed in the tool shed alone together.

"Come on, Mel's in town, she was going to call in to see you on her way out. Let's go get a cup of tea with her, and you can spill."

"Fuck, that would be just what I need right now."

"You certainly look like you need it. You look like shite, old duck."

Robbie put an arm around my shoulders and we headed to Rosie's café, a place where we had hung out many times, and our usual table was often available. The one with the crude pictures of cocks drawn on the cracked vinyl. Rosie had left them there in honour of the 'artist', Ollie, a high school friend who was killed in a car accident. I smirked, running a hand over the cracked vinyl, my painted fingernails tracing one of the black lines of the cocks, which included hairy balls, and a few drops of cum dripping from the exaggerated tip.

Mel waddled in from out back where the bathrooms were and sat down with a slight wince.

"Hey Mummy, how's things? Ready to pop?" I smiled.

"Yeah, been feeling a bit weird all day, hardly slept last night, I have a very sore back," she said, reaching behind awkwardly to rub at the sore spot.

"Should you be out and about?" I asked.

"I'm fine," Mel said, as Rosie came over and placed a teapot and three cups in front of us.

"Decaf for you, love." She smiled, placing a smaller pot down in front of her.

"Thanks Rosie." Mel smiled as Rosie placed a hand on Mel's shoulder.

"All right, so what's wrong with you? Looks like your cat died," Mel said, pouring her tea. I noticed her wince a little bit as she lifted the teapot.

"I got that," Robbie said as he reached over and took the pot from Mel.

"Well, you're not far from the mark," I muttered, relaying everything that had happened.

Mel gave us a funny look. "I think I need to…" Her mouth dropped open as the sound of liquid splashing on the floor silenced the café.

"I…oh shit… Uhm… Robbie, can you call Adam…"

"He's in Scotland, Mel," Robbie said, giving his sister a strange look.

"I know, dear brother," Mel said, her face going pale. "I think my water just broke, is all, and I think my husband would LOVE TO KNOW THAT!" She near shouted the last.

"Oh my God! Mel!" I gasped my heart pounding. "Robbie fucking go and call Adam!"

"Right now?" Robbie asked, incredulously. "You're having the baby now?"

"Yes, right fucking now!" Mel gasped as a contraction hit she looked up, her eyes flashing as if possessed by some demonic spirit as she reached out and grabbed Robbie's shirtfront. "In fact, if you don't fucking hurry up and get him here, I might just drop this baby right here, right now!"

"Okay! Okay, I'm dialling now!" Robbie said, pushing away from his sister, I pushed Robbie out of the way and went to Mel's side. "Okay Slut, we're going to take a nice, deep breath, then we're going to get the ambulance here to get you to the hospital, okay?"

"Please, hurry." Mel gasped, her hands clutching her swollen belly, as if that might stop her from giving birth. I quickly dialled the emergency services.

"Hi, my friend is in labour, we need an ambulance right away," I said, once the operator picked up.

"What's your location?"

"Rosie's Café, King Street, Miltonford."

"Okay, you might have a bit of a wait, there was a large accident on the motorway, we can get you an ambulance, but it's about an hour or so away."

"You're fucking kidding me, right? An hour? She's having this baby now!"

I'm sorry Miss, I know you're under a bit of stress right now. But that's all we have, I'm afraid. You may have to get your friend to the hospital yourself, or see if there's a local police officer available to escort you under lights and sirens."

I looked up as she said that, Mel whimpering as another contraction hit, they were coming quick. A familiar figure was writing out a parking ticket as Robbie was talking on his phone, animatedly, his body language panicked. I knew what I had to do. My pride was swallowed.

"Mel, I'll be right back!" I said, as I hung up the call to the emergency services.

They say pride goes before a fall, and my friend needed my help, and the help of the man who was writing that parking ticket.

What the fuck.

"RICHARD!" I cried as I ran out the door of Rosie's Café, the little tin bells tinkling as the door swung. Robbie shrieked like a little girl as I burst out the door. *Cuntstable* Dick turned, his face surprised to see me in my flustered and exhausted state. "I need your help! Mel's gone into labour, we need to get to the hospital now!"

I stopped just short of bowling him over. He put his hands on my arms to steady me, and I swear I fucking *swooned* just for a moment in his grip.

"Did you call an ambulance?" he asked, tucking his ticket book back in his Batman-like utility belt.

"Tried, but there's been an accident on the motorway. The closest ambulance is about an hour away. If you can get us to the hospital, I'll be forever grateful. I'll take you out for coffee, dinner, drinks, dancing whatever you want!" I waved my hands like a madwoman.

"Okay, go back to Mel and wait for me. I'll bring the car around. Tell her to keep as calm as she can, we'll be there in no time," he said, placing a reassuring hand on my arm.

"Thank-you!" I said, tears threatening to break free in gratitude.

I turned and bolted back into the café. Robbie was there, holding Mel's hands and wincing when she gripped him with a vice-like grip.

"Did you call your parents?" I asked. Robbie shook his head. "Go do that, Can Leo bring them in?"

"No, I got the van, Dad will need it to get to the hospital."

After his stroke, Mel and Robbie's Dad, Gilbert Whittaker. had lost most of the mobility in his legs, had had been confined to a wheelchair. Robbie had their Nursery's work van modified to accommodate their father's change in mobility, and it was their primary way of getting him around when he needed to leave home, or the nursery.

"Call them, then go get them. They'll want to be here, oh and Mrs Del Rosa too!"

I knew the family well enough that everyone would want to be nearby for the birth of Mel and Adam's first baby. Robbie nodded and ran out the door like the hounds of hell were on his arse. I turned back to Mel, Rosie had come over and was helping her to settle back in the bench seat covered in cocks.

"Libby… I can't do this…" She whimpered, her face showing how scared she was.

"It's going to be okay, Mel. Your baby is ready to come and meet you," I said, feeling the sting of tears prickling behind my eyes.

"What if something goes wrong?" She sobbed, whimpering as her body tensed with another contraction. Rosie had brought out some tea towels and had laid them under Mel to help soak up some of the fluid.

"You'll be fine, love." Rosie smiled, patting Mel's hand.

"I want Adam, and my Mum!" Mel sobbed.

"I know skank, they're on their way," I soothed, looking up over the table to see the flashing blue lights heralding our chariot had arrived.

"Hi Mel," Richard said, striding in like a hero, and yes, I guess he was. "I'm PC Handcock, a friend of Libby's here. I've

got a special ride for you, ever been in the back of a police car?"
He grinned.

Mel choked out a half-sob-half laugh. "Nope, but I'm sure the Paps will love that."

"Yeah." I agreed, "Just remember, I got the rights to the official photos of you and your new bub." I grinned.

"All about the publicity, isn't it?" Mel huffed through another contraction.

"Your contractions seem to be coming a bit quick. We need to get you to the hospital now, else Rosie will have something else to have this bench be famous for." Dick said. "Let's get you up, okay. This is going to be nice and slow, a bit of a shuffle to the car. I'll be on one side, and Libby on the other, okay? Rosie, can you get the back door to my car please?" Dick asked Rosie, who nodded and ran to the door of her café, holding it open for us to help Mel out and to the car.

"Okay, Mel we're going to turn you around and you'll sit back in the back seat of my car, then I need you to do a backwards butt-shuffle to the other side so Libby can sit in the back with you." Mel nodded, whining with the pain as another bloody contraction hit. "Okay let's get you in."

Dick and I helped Mel into the back seat, she did her best to shove herself backwards, gasping as her body complained with the process of labour.

"You're doing great, Mel," I said as Dick shut the doors and got in the front.

"Fuck you, just fuck you." She huffed.

"Atta girl." I grinned, letting her grip my hands. Her response was a pain-filled wail broken by a heartfelt sob and plea for Adam.

"He's on the way Mel, I promise. It won't take him long, he's had a private jet on standby just for this occasion, you know that. He'll be here in about an hour, okay?"

"This is taking forever!" Mel whined as we rounded a corner, the lights and sirens blaring.

"If it's any consolation, Mel, my sister took three days with her first baby." Richard offered, *Dick*.

"Not helping, Dick!" I grumbled.

"Sorry!" He chuckled.

He pulled up outside the hospital's emergency ward entrance. Mel huffed and puffed like the big bad wolf in the back seat, while Dick ran inside to get a wheelchair, or gurney, or some sort of mobility device to get Mel's pregnant arse inside.

"That's it Mel, you got some sexy doctors and nurses coming to help ease your pain."

"Yeah, how about a sexy PC to help ease yours?" Mel said with a sweaty smile.

"Don't you go playing matchmaker on me girl." I grinned, turning to open the door, and finding that Dick was on the other side already pulling it open. Two orderlies waited with a wheelchair, along with a nurse and a doctor.

"Hello Mrs Jacobs. Looks like we're ready for you to have this baby, eh?" the doctor said with a grin. I recognised him as Mel's OB/GYN.

I scrambled out and let the men help Mel into the chair. Her hand reached out for mine and I grasped it. "I'll be right in, Mel," I said, my eyes catching Dick's.

Mel's fingers stayed touching mine until the distance they took her in the wheelchair became so great that her fingers slipped from mine.

I watched her as she was pushed through the sliding doors and ran a hand through my short hair. I turned to face Dick… *Richard.*

"Richard, thank you…" I said, and without thinking. I leaned forward and kissed him.

Right. On. The. Mouth.

What.

The.

FUCK?

Tiny little fingers curled around my index finger as the baby boy snuggled against the blanket the nurses had swaddled him in. The cheeky little bugger had waited until his panting and exhausted father was seconds inside the door before he made his grand entrance, screaming blue murder and covered in blood and gunk.

Adam was slumped, exhausted on an easychair, soft snores coming from him, while Mel dozed a little from the medication they'd given her. They'd had to cut her a little bit to get the boy in my arms out, as he had a big head and broad shoulders on him. Considering he was his father's son, it wasn't surprising. But for poor Mel, it was an ordeal.

I looked down at my beautiful Godson's face and wondered what my own baby might have looked like. He grumbled a little in my arms, becoming restless—until I gently rocked him in my arms and quietly shushed him, leaning down to press a kiss against his warm forehead, breathing in the scent of a newborn.

Mel's room had been a constant revolving door of visitors. The vast number of flowers, stuffed toys and blue balloons that decorated the place made the room feel like a florist shop and not a private room in a hospital.

There was a soft knock on the door. I looked up as it opened. Richard entered, carrying a bunch of flowers and a small blue-wrapped parcel.

"Hey, that's a good look on you." He smiled.

I couldn't help it, I felt the tears rolling down my cheeks.

"Yeah, he's beautiful," I said, as Richard came closer, placing the flowers on a rare empty space, and keeping hold of the blue-wrapped box.

"PC Handcock," Mel said softly from the bed, her voice tinged with tiredness.

"Hello Mrs Jacobs. Congratulations, he's a fine-looking lad." He smiled.

Mel raised her arms, gesturing for me to return the slumbering bundle. I did, with a little reluctance. I wanted to hold him forever, I knew I'd be a big part of his life, but he needed his Mummy bonding time. Time my own bitch of a mother obviously never had with me.

Adam yawned and stretched in the chair, slowly coming awake.

"Adam, this is the officer who drove us to the hospital." I introduced him.

"Wow, I can't thank you enough for taking care of my family."

"Think nothing of it. It was Libby here who told me what was happening. Unfortunately, we didn't have enough ambulances to come pick her up, what with a seven-car pileup on the motorway."

"Damn, hope nobody was hurt."

"Unfortunately, there was one fatality. But we believe he had a heart attack while driving, which caused the accident, so it was believed he passed before the crash."

"Wow, that's not good."

"No, but we at least got your wife to the hospital in time." He grinned. "Here, this is for your son." He handed the blue-wrapped parcel. "From the Miltonford Police Department." He turned and picked up the flowers from their spot. "And this is for you, Mrs Jacobs."

"Mel, please call me Mel." Mel grinned, taking the flowers, inhaling their sweet fragrance and placing them beside her. "They're lovely."

The sound of wrapping paper being torn apart directed our attention to Adam, who was ripping the carefully wrapped blue paper to shreds like a big kid. "Oh wow, a Police Bear!"

"That is an official Bobby Bear," Richard said, nodding to the boxed bear.

"That is so cool. He even has a little ID badge!" Adam was transfixed with the stuffed bear, decked out in full police uniform.

"I think you might need another bear," I said to Richard, leaning in and shoulder bumping him slightly. He turned his head to me and grinned. "Maybe." He cleared his throat. "Anyway, I was wondering if I could steal Libby away for a little bit? I believe she owes me a coffee."

"I do?" I asked, innocently.

"I believe your exact words were, 'coffee, dinner, drinks dancing or anything.'" He grinned, before he leaned in and whispered. 'I'll take all five, if the offer is still there."

I looked at him as he leaned back and smiled warmly at me.

"Okay," I agreed. "Coffee." I turned to Mel, who was smiling knowingly, while Adam was looking at the back of the Bobby Bear's box.

"Hey, babe, the profits of each bear sold goes to the families of police officers who've lost their lives in the line of duty," Adam said with a hint of awe in his voice.

"Go, he'll be going over that for hours, then the next thing you'll know, we'll have a collection of Police bears from all over the world." Mel shooed us out the door. I smiled at her, catching a sly wink as I closed the door behind us, leaving me alone in the corridor with *Cunt*—I mean Richard.

"So…" I said, suddenly at a loss as to what to say.

"Coffee…" He grinned, offering his hand to me.

"I thought you only drank tea?" I asked, taking his hand and suppressing a delighted shiver as his fingers wrapped around mine in a somewhat possessive but protective grip.

"I do, but on occasion, I do drink coffee, but I think you're right. Tea it is."

He led me out of the maternity ward and out of the hospital, where his car waited. Like a gentleman, he opened the door and helped me in, waiting until I was seated and buckled in before he closed the door and went to the driver's side.

"Any place in particular you'd like to go for tea?" he asked, starting up the car.

"Rosie's is good, and I think she'd want to know Mel is okay.

"Rosie's, it is." He grinned and pulled out of the hospital parking lot. We drove in a somewhat comfortable silence, though I was a little bit nervous, well, fucking antsy would probably be closer to the truth. His aftershave danced through my senses, and the warmth he exuded was comforting after a long, and stressful twenty-four hours at the hospital.

"So, I take it everything went well?" Richard asked.

"Yes, though not without a few funny incidents that we'll no doubt be telling the boy about when he's older," I chuckled, as I recounted the events in the delivery room and maternity ward.

Mel's labour had been hard on everyone, but obviously most of all, on Mel. Her parents had come in after the as-yet unnamed boy was born, Robbie rushing in with his father's wheelchair, minus his father…whom had been left in the van due to Robbie's panicking mind going completely blank. He'd received an ear bashing from his mother, when she'd calmly wheeled their father in a borrowed wheelchair through the maternity waiting room doors to find Robbie standing with his father's empty wheelchair.

Richard chuckled as he pulled to a stop outside Rosie's. He got out of the car and rushed to the passenger side as I opened the door to get out. His hand offered to help me up, and I took it. I'd never been treated in such a genteel manner before. It was fucking odd.

He opened the door to Rosie's for me, and led me to a small table, set out of the way and secluded from everyone. Rosie had set it up for two, with a clean tablecloth and one of the nicest china sets I'd seen on her table.

"What's all this?" I asked, looking at him.

"Tea, for two." Richard smiled, placing a hand on the small of my back and guiding me towards the table.

"Right…" I gave him a quizzical look, but he just smirked. The cocky bastard.

He settled me down, pulling out my chair for me, more behaviour I wasn't used to, before he settled in across from me.

Rosie came and poured our tea for us. Richard just kept a level and easy gaze on me. It felt uncomfortable for the first few seconds, but soon, it felt…*normal*. Natural, wanted. I felt my heart beating a little bit faster as I stirred sugar and milk into my tea.

"So, tell me a little about yourself, Richard? Why did you come to Miltonford?"

"Well, I was so good at my job in London, they asked me to come here. I have an excellent arrest record, but they felt I was taking too much away from everyone else."

"Like the film, *Hot Fuzz*?" I asked.

He chuckled. "Yeah, kinda like that, but at least, I don't think there's a secret society of folk in the village happy to kill people to keep their village the way they want it."

I leaned forward conspiratorially. "How do you know there's not?" I asked with a sly grin.

He snorted, his tea dribbling down his front. "Smart arse." He grabbed a napkin and dabbed it down the damp spots where he'd spilled his tea.

There was a sudden fluttering noise, sounding suspiciously like wings and a disgruntled chirping noise coming from beneath the table.

"What was that?" I asked, frowning a little.

"That?" Richard smirked. "Well, a little birdy told me you were trying to replace a little birdy…"

He reached under the table and pulled out a small cage with a blue bow on the top. Within sat a little male budgerigar, his plumage a pretty sapphire-like blue. He eyed me with beady little eyes.

"What the fuck?"

After Rosie's, Richard had suggested we take Porridge the Second to his new home. I was more than happy to have him accompany me, mainly because I was worried that Mrs Mac might get so upset she'd have a fucking coronary.

Thankfully, she was an understanding lovely lady.

I knocked on her door a little hesitant about the possible confrontation. Richard stood behind me, holding the cage with a little blue bow tied to the handle.

"Hi Mrs Mac, I've got some news about Porridge," I said, smiling a little sadly.

"Oh! Did you find him?" Her eyes brightened with hope.

"Ah…sort of," I said.

"Oh, that's wonderful!" She beamed. "But where are my manners? Please, come in and let's have a cup of tea. You can set Porridge down on the table there. I'm so glad he's home."

I followed her in, Richard closed the door behind us. Her little flat was cosy, music played from the fifties on a CD player, and the entire pace smelled like old lady and tea.

Little knick-knacks were carefully arranged on the many bookshelves that lined her walls, along with a collection of Harlequin and Mills and Boon romance books the likes of which I'd never seen. It was obvious that Mrs Mac was a very lonely woman.

Richard set the bird cage down on the coffee table. The little blue feathered fucker flapped and fluttered around, squawking with indignation at being shuffled around in such a way. We both settled on the loveseat, leaving the worn-looking armchair, that was obviously Mrs Mac's favourite spot, for her to

take. While she bustled about in the kitchen, Richard looked at me
and smiled. He placed a warm hand on my knee and gently rubbed
his hand back and forth. I felt little tingles shooting up and down
my leg. I slowly placed my hand over his, my fingers intertwining
with his.

"Here we go, dearies," she said, settling a tray on the
coffee table with trembling hands that made the teacups rattle on
their saucers.

I pulled my hand away from his, almost feeling like I'd
been caught with my hand in the biscuit tin, especially with the
way my cheeks flushed.

Mrs Mac settled down in the armchair and looked at the
bird. "Wait… That's not porridge…" she said softly.

"Mrs Mac, I can explain," I said, shifting forward on the
couch. "I think my cat got him. I let him in the other night, and he
was sick in the early morning. There were blue feathers, and I
think he might have eaten Porridge." I sighed.

"I went to buy you a new bird, but I hadn't had much sleep,
and I was under a lot of stress, and got angry with the girl at the
pet shop, so they threw me out. Then, my best friend went into
labour while we were having tea at Rosie's, so, we had to rush her
to the hospital, and then Richard here," I turned and smiled at him,
my body warming when he smiled back, "who is one of the local
police officers, came by the hospital, took me out, and revealed
that he knew what had happened. He'd gotten a replacement bird."
I finished in a rush

"Oh, he's a sweetie," Mrs MacDonald said as she looked
into the cage.

"Again, I'm so very sorry about Porridge, Mrs Mac."

"It's nature, my dear. Cats will eat birds, and though Porridge will always have a place in my heart, he was an older budgerigar, probably not far from falling off the perch himself."

I sat on her floral loveseat, Richard beside me as we nursed fine china cups of tea in our hands. We chatted a little while longer, until Mrs Mac finished her tea and took the cage in her hands. She busied herself with setting the bird on the bench beside the forlorn-looking empty cage which once housed Porridge, all the while cooing at the bird in the cage.

"Well, I think it's time to go," I said, pushing up from the loveseat, Richard following my lead.

Mrs Mac turned and smiled. "Thank you, my dears. Again, I'm so thankful you told me about Porridge, and thank you for bringing me my new little friend."

"That's quite all right, Mrs MacDonald," Richard said. He smiled as the sweet little old lady wrapped her arms in a motherly hug, completely dwarfed by Richard. I couldn't help but smile.

"And you too, Elizabeth, dear." She pulled me in to the hug, I smiled as I felt Richard's hand slide along the small of my back, his pinkie fingers dangerously close to the top of my arse.

"Now, you two make such a lovely couple," she said, pulling back.

Richard still had his arm around me, and pulled me against his side as soon as Mrs Mac was clear. I didn't correct her, but I knew there was really no hope of us being together, despite the fact that Richard wanted to 'get to know me better'. I was still too broken inside, unfixable.

We left Mrs Mac's place, and headed up the stairs to my flat.

"Well," I said, unlocking my door. "I can't thank you enough for everything, Richard."

"I'm glad to see I've been promoted from '*Cunt*stable Dick to Richard, but you can call me Richard, if you like, Libby." He smiled, even my name on his lips gave me tingles of illicit pleasure.

I ducked my head, lowering my eyes in embarrassment. "Well, yeah. Look, I am sorry about that, but you really pissed me off when we first met." For whatever reason, I couldn't meet his intense gaze.

"I understand," Richard said. "But, I'm glad you've forgiven me, it means I can do this…"

He reached under my chin and lifted it up, so I was looking into his eyes. They mesmerised me, and made my body tingle with his touch and anticipation of what he was about to do—yeah, I know, I was thinking some sappy fucking shit that was more appropriate in Mrs Mac's bodice-ripper collection.

He leaned forward and pressed his lips against mine. I smelled him, felt the scratch stubble of his chin and upper lip abrading against my skin like sandpaper, the soft, but slightly insistent press of his tongue against my lips, asking me to invite it in for a cup of tea, or a roll around my mouth. I parted my lips just enough for him to get a peek in. Richard put his arms around me, pulling me flush against his body. I couldn't help myself, I fucking put my arms around him too. I felt him pulling away, part of me didn't want him to go, but the insistent ringing of his phone broke through the haze of lust that was roaring through my ears.

"Damn, I'm sorry Libby. I have to get this," he said with a regretful smile as he pulled his phone from his pocket and stepped away.

"That's fine," I murmured, my lips humming from that *fucking* kiss!

If I somehow fell down the stairs and broke my neck, at least I'd die a happy girl…well kinda happy. I'd felt the man's body while he was pressed up against me, and fuck me sideways with a rusty mace, it made my lady bits cry out like there had been a disturbance in the Force.

I needed to get laid, and something told me that this fine specimen who stood at the end of the walkway talking animatedly was the only one who could scratch that itch.

Relationship? Nah.

Beast with two backs? Bit of the old in-out? A bit of how's your father? Fuck yes!

I waited by my door, wondering if I should bang him over the head and go cavewoman style on him, drag him into my flat and have my wicked, wicked way with him. He ended his call and sighed, before he walked back to me.

"Come in for a cuppa?" I offered, giving him a sultry smile.

"Sorry Libby, I can't something has come up, I really wish it hadn't, but I have to go," he said, regret showing in his eyes.

"Oh, okay, that's fine," I said softly, feeling the sting of rejection.

"It's not like that, I promise," he said, reaching up to caress my face with his warm hands. He leaned forward and gently pressed his lips to mine, reminding me that he really wanted to be with me.

"I'll see you next weekend at the ball, right?" he asked, breaking the kiss.

"Sure," I said, with a smile that didn't quite feel genuine. I still felt like I was getting rejected.

"Save me a dance, okay?" He grinned then pulled away from me.

He walked past a very stunned looking Zane, who had witnessed the kiss. I slumped against the door frame as Richard… *Dick* headed to his car. There was definitely something going on that I couldn't put my finger on just yet.

Zane's face, however was priceless, I could see the shock and surprise written all over it with the perfect 'o' on his lips. "Girl…" he said, giving me one of his 'spill it' looks.

"What the fuck?"

"Okay, so just relax, lean down a little bit, and give me a soft pout," I said, peering through the lens of the camera. "Right there, that's perfect." I snapped a few shots on the old SLR before switching to the digital camera and taking a few more.

Zane was posing perfectly, and the shots were going to look great in both our portfolios. I was slowly building up my own for consideration in a few upcoming London fashion shows that Danny had suggested I put in for. He had a couple of mates in London who were fashion photographers, and he knew it was one of my dreams to work as a runway photographer. But now, I was in the beautiful gardens at the Whittaker Nursery and Café, with Zane stealing the limelight, as we took shot after shot, after shot of him posing and primping. He'd been working out a little in Adam's home gym while staying with Mel and Adam. I was going to go there later and work with them on the 'official' baby photos with them and baby Aaron.

They had finally decided on naming him after Adam's twin brother, who had died after losing his battle with an aggressive form of Leukaemia. Adam's biological mum, Mrs Del Rosa was visiting her new grandson, which, of course, meant Uncle Leo was visiting Mrs Del Rosa.

They were the worst kept secret.

"So, what time is the policeman's ball?" Zane asked.

"This evening, starting around seven," I said, taking a few natural snaps of him.

"You going to wear something dressy?" He settled down on the white concrete edge of a medium sized fountain. Mel had designed the entire garden and café complex that had brought their family's business up a notch.

"You mean like a dress?" I asked.

"Sure." He smirked, running his hands through the water. I quickly took a few snaps.

"Don't have one."

It was true, I really didn't I was going to wear some fancy dress pants and a nice top.

"Oh hell, no." Zane pulled his hand out of the water, shaking the droplets free. "We are going to go and raid Mel's wardrobe." He eyed me up and down. "I think you'll fit into some of her gowns."

"I can't do that! Do you even know how expensive her things are?" I saved the last pictures on the digital camera and began to pack away my gear.

"Mel will be fine with it, besides, she's married to 'Mr Rich and Famous.' He'll buy her more shit."

"Fucking hell Zane. I don't want to wear a gown."

"What? You don't want ease of access for Mr Hottie McCopper?" Zane said with a wink.

"It's not that!" *It's totally that!* "I'll be working, and besides, I don't think he's really all that into me." I carefully placed my digital camera into the bag and zipped it up.

"Uh…*excuse me?*" Zane shook his head in utter disgust. "Honey, even a blind man could see he was into you. The way he was playing tonsil hockey with you. Hell, I'd have me a piece of that if I thought he swung my way!" Zane moved up beside me and placed a hand on my shoulder. "Honey, trust me. He wants you. And after I'm done with you, he'll be all over you like a fat kid on a cupcake." He smirked.

Fucker.

"Fine." I relented. "Let's go get this gorgeous baby shoot done, then you can have at me."

"Squee!" Zane giggled.

"Uh, did you fucking 'squee' just then?"

"Maybe." He giggled.

"Ugh really?"

"Come on, sweet cheeks." Zane picked up my camera bags and *thankfully* was careful in how he handled the delicate equipment. "Let's get you sexified, after the cute widdle baby pictures!" He imitated a babying voice at the last. I rolled my eyes.

"Fucking wanker," I muttered as we walked through the gardens and up to the security gate at the back that led to Mel's place.

An hour, and hundreds of photographs later, and Aaron was getting fussy. I'd tried to keep the flash off as long as possible to keep his little eyes safe, but there was only so much I could do. I could see he was getting tired, and Mel was fussing almost as much as her baby.

Zane came up behind me as I was packing my cameras away for the second time.

"Okay, so, let's get our Cinderella ready for the ball."

"What ball?" Mel asked, as she rocked Aaron in her arms, the little mite making gurgling and cooing noises as he started to drift off.

"The policeman's ball," Zane said with a wink.

"Actually, it's the fireman's, paramedic's and policeman's ball," I said,

"Do you have a dress?" Mel asked.

I shook my head in the negative, as Zane came up behind me and placed his hands on my shoulders, before ducking his head beside mine and pressing his cheek against mine.

"I was going to ask you if Libby could borrow one of your gowns?" Zane asked with a raised eyebrow.

"Of course, hmm...maybe the sapphire blue one?" Mel suggested.

"Exactly the one I was thinking of." Zane grinned.

"What sapphire one?" I asked. Zane had already literally run out of the nursery where the majority of the photos had been taken. He dashed back in carrying a garment bag. With a flourish, he unzipped it, revealing the floor length slim gown that would undoubtedly hug my skinny-as-fuck body.

"Wow, that's...amazing," I said. Zane nodded with a wicked grin.

"Now, how are you with grooming down below?" Zane asked, holding up a home-waxing kit.

"Uh...?"

"Are you 'bare down there'?" he grinned.

"What the fuck?"

I could have fucking killed Zane. His 'home waxing kit' was more like a 'home fucking TORTURE kit.'

I smiled at the handsome men as they moved around the local church hall, tuxedoes and bow ties and cummerbunds—oh my! My cameras clicked and flashed as I took each photograph, ignoring the burning pain of my hair follicles around my thighs, and up between them, having been ripped out. I had to get help with my underarms, Zane had obliged, and nearly fainted when he saw the little pinpricks of blood.

Wasn't my bloody fault that I'd never waxed before.

I watched from the sidelines as the attendants of the Miltonford Emergency Services Ball swung their dance partners around the dance floor to old timey songs.

I had a glass of wine in one hand and my digital camera in the other. I'd also set up a photography area in one of the small rooms in the hall. With the backdrop and most of the portrait gear set up, I'd already had one session early on when everyone was arriving, but had been asked for a second session later on by the organisers.

I took a sip of my wine just as a hand ran over my back and around my waist.

"Good evening, Miss Hastings. Might I say, you look particularly gorgeous tonight." Dick's voice drifted over the music against my ear, his breath warm against my cheek. I swallowed the wine in my mouth before I turned to him.

"Good evening, Mr Handcock," I said, turning to face him.

He kept his hand on my waist as I spun, bringing his other hand to pluck my glass from my hand.

"Will you dance with me?" he asked, his eyes hopeful.

"I…" I held up my camera. "I am kinda working right now," I said, using my job as an excuse.

"That's okay, I think you can do with a break." He grinned, taking my camera out of my hand and placing it beside my glass.

"What if someone steals it?"

"In a room full of cops?" He chuckled. "Not likely," he said, guiding me to the parquetry of the church hall's floor where other couples were dancing closely to their partners.

He swung me around to face him once more, my body pulled against his, my heart starting to beat faster in my chest at the closeness of him, his scent, his *maleness*. My stripped bare pink bits tingled in a good way, not the stinging aching sensation of total and utter follicle distress.

I sighed as he took my hand and began to lead me around the dancefloor.

"I've been thinking about that kiss," he murmured against my ear.

"Oh? What kiss?" I asked, feigning innocence.

"You don't remember? That scorching as fuck kiss we shared at your apartment?"

I felt naughty, and daring as fuck. I shook my head. "Nope." I leaned forward and pressed my lips to the shell of his ear. "You might have to remind me." I leaned back and looked at him, the heat of lust smouldering in his eyes as he grinned like a schoolboy.

Richard leaned forward, nuzzling his nose against mine at first, rubbing the tip down the side before his lips met mine. I parted my lips at the insistence of his tongue, letting him in, breathing in the scent of his cologne as his mouth ravaged mine on the dancefloor. I felt everything in my body respond to him. I felt his movements stiffen a little bit, and something else in his pants stiffened too. I moved against him, working a little 'dirty dancing' of my own into the innocent-looking waltz we were supposed to be doing.

"Libby." He broke his kiss, groaning against my neck as I slid my thigh forward, rubbing against his crotch. "Oh fuck, if you don't stop, I'm going to have to take you off the dancefloor to somewhere more private."

I smirked, rubbing again.

He groaned, his hands tightening on my body. "That's it, you asked for it," he grunted, gripping my hand and leading me from the dancefloor.

I snagged my digital camera as we passed the table it rested on. He walked past other officers and people who called out greetings to him, nodding or grunting a greeting like a caveman as he pulled me through the hall. Most of the rooms were locked, and his agitation became apparent. He whirled on me, pulling me against his body before he kissed me madly again.

"Fuck… I need to find somewhere quiet and make love to you Libby, this is killing me." He moved his lips to my neck, kissing, licking and nipping the sensitive flesh there.

I breathed hard, wanting the same thing… "I have a room…my camera gear is in there…" I gasped as he bit a little harder on my neck, before softly licking the mark. "We can lock the door, and if we're quiet, we won't be disturbed."

"Let's do it." He smiled, breathing hard and heavy.

"Okay," I said, my words breathy as my chest heaved with the need to take in as much air as possible in preparing my body for what it so desperately needed... *Sex* and lots of it!

I led him to the door and unlocked it, letting him in, with a surreptitious look around the hall. Everyone was minding their own business, dancing, drinking, hob-knobbing, all ignored us as we slipped into the room.

No sooner had I locked the door, then Richard was on me, his hands sliding over the bodice of my dress, slipping around my back until nimble fingers found the hidden zipper. Each tooth that was freed from the zip vibrated down my back right to my needy core. I let the dress fall from my body, getting caught at the widening of my hips. The cold air caressed the swells of my breasts.

I felt Richard's lips press against my shoulder, fingers trebling as they caressed the lines of scars that I'd ever revealed to anyone else… "Oh, baby… Who did this to you?"

I quickly pulled the dress up, back over my naked chest, I turned, trying to hide the shame of my messed-up childhood, the evidence still visible so many years later.

Oh shit.

I'd forgotten about the scars my father had left me… what the fuck was I going to say?

What. The. Fuck?

Chapter Twenty-Two.

"I…" I stopped, unable to formulate any kind of fucking articulate sound. The sensual heat that had suffused my body only moments ago was flushed away with cold dread. I could feel the rejection now, even before he voiced it. I was prepared for the pity, the disgust, the rejection, I wasn't prepared for his anger.

"Who fucking did this to you?" He pulled me into his arms, ignoring my weak attempts to push him away. He pulled me back against him. "Shh… It's okay sweetheart. I got you." He held me as I began to softly cry. We both sank down to the floor together, the warmth of his body against the chill of the air conditioning that pumped through the vents in the ceiling kept me from shivering with cold.

"I understand if you don't want me… I get it," I said, feeling broken. Just another victory for the monsters in my head, and those who were dead and buried, yet still haunted me through their actions in the past.

"I never said I didn't want you, and this changes nothing. I still want you, and I hope you want me too," he said softly, his hand stroking up and down my bare back, fingers sliding over the bumps and lines of my back, fingertips tracing the roadmap of scars that adorned my skin. "When you are ready to, you'll tell me who did this to you, then, we'll deal with them, I promise."

"It's too late, they're dead already."

"Who?"

"My parents," I said, my voice thick.

"Your parents did this to you?" he asked, surprise and anger in his voice.

I nodded, sniffling, and knew that my makeup, so carefully applied by Zane, was now a total disaster zone. "Yeah, my fucking parents. Mother and father of the fucking year. Even when I was really little, they kept telling me how they never wanted me, then as I got older, it turned physical."

"Were you ever…" He paused, as if trying to find the right words. I knew what he was asking, if I'd been sexually abused by my parents.

I shook my head. "No, never got to that, thank fuck. If it had, I'd have fucking killed them both," I said with absolute certainty.

Richard let me cry it out. Speaking softly to me, giving me words of encouragement as I told him of my childhood, the beatings, the verbal and psychological abuse. The stupid thing was, my parents were really intelligent people. Really smart fuckers. They knew how to play the system. They knew how to work everything in their favour. It's a pity that their intelligence was wasted on such fucking horrible human beings.

"I don't ever want to be a person like my parents, if I ever have kids, they'll be loved, cherished…" I sniffled, I'd not told him about losing my baby. That was far too deep a wound to open up again. Richard pulled me against him, his lips softly kissing my shoulders.

"Libby. I'm here for you, always, if you need me, you just call. I'll be there in a heartbeat. Even if I'm on duty. You're someone who I want to be part of my life, even if we are just friends. God knows I want it to be more, but if you're not ready, I can wait."

I turned to face him, my fingers trembled as I reached up and caressed his clean-shaven jawline. "What if I don't want to wait?" I asked, gazing into his eyes.

I smiled at the happiness I saw in their depths. He pulled me down to him, his hands sliding reverently over my body, pulling the long, sleep skirt of the sapphire-blue dress I'd borrowed from Mel up over my hips until I bunched up at my waist.

"Are you sure? I don't want to rush you," he said.

I smiled, laying atop him, I could feel how ready he was. "I'm sure," I said, leaning down to kiss him.

All thoughts of everything else forgotten as we made love in the small room they used for the children's playgroup on Tuesdays, Bible studies on Thursdays, and illicit, powerful, soul-mending lovemaking. Because, you know, what better place to heal our soul through sweet, scintillating sex than on holy ground?

After, I straightened myself up to the best of my ability, Richard lay there, atop the pile of his clothes. I smirked, enjoying his nakedness. I picked up my digital camera and turned it on, taking a few personal snaps.

"Those going in the official photographs?" he asked with a chuckle.

"Maybe not the official ones…" I grinned, leaning back down to kiss him. I moaned softly as his tongue slid over mine. "You'd better get dressed, I have another photo session in about ten minutes." I kissed him again. I got to my feet and saved his sexy pictures to my private folder on my laptop before I deleted them from the digital camera's memory.

I unlocked the door once he was decent and not looking so dishevelled. The room had a little sexy funk to it, but it aired out quickly once I'd left the door open. People started to filter in and out, and Richard stayed by my side, watching the others having their photos taken for the photo books that would be produced and left in the police, fire and ambulance stations.

The evening ended, and Richard helped me to pack up. I sighed as I felt his arms slipping around my middle.

"Come home with me…" he whispered.

I turned, my eyes meeting his. I could see the need, the desire in them. "All right…" I agreed.

We had everything packed in my car in record time, and I followed him back to his place. As soon as his door was open, we were embracing, kissing, fondling, touching… We only made it as far as his couch that first time… Then later the bed, then the shower, then finally back to the bed, where I collapsed atop him in a sweaty, sex-fuelled exhaustion.

The next morning, the sunlight streaming from the open curtains in his bedroom woke me. Richard was already awake and watching me. As soon as I smiled at him, he pulled me into his arms for another round.

As I lay there in a post orgasmic haze, h kissed me once more and got up. I snuck a glance over my shoulder as he stood up, his back to me. He had ink. A beautiful scrollwork with two doves and wedding rings, *'Olivia & Richard always and forever'*, was inked on his right shoulder. I wondered at its meaning, it was obviously some sort of marriage thing… But was it his? He hadn't said anything about being married, and there was no wedding ring, nor wedding band tan on his ring finger.

But still…

What the Fuck?

Over the next week I spent time working on getting new photos and prints ready for my stall, having lunch with Richard, when we could find the time, spending time with Mel and her new family, and getting more shots of Zane for both our portfolios.

I'd also decided on the fate of the old cottage.

"Okay, so you sure you don't want to fix it up? You can get a lot more for it you know," the estate agent said, as he looked around the front of the property.

"No, list it as a renovator's dream whatever, I just want it gone."

"You have the key? Mind if we take a look inside?" This was the part I wasn't looking forward to.

"Uh… Yeah," I said, fumbling in my pocket for the old key that my lawyers had kept hold of in one of their safety deposit boxes, kept in trust until I was ready to face the old demons that resided there.

If anything about my blossoming relationship with Richard had taught me, it was that in order to grow, I needed to let go. He was there for me when things got dark in my mind, talking to me about things he was doing that day, or taking me to places that I'd been before, but was now seeing through new eyes.

My photography work had changed too. I was taking less photos of dreary places, more light and happy ones, and that was helping the sales at the market stall as well. I had a wedding coming up that was taking place at Mel's family gardens. I was looking forward to it. I loved taking photographs in the gardens. Mel had worked so hard on the place, and it was going to be featured in *English Garden Monthly Magazine*. Quite a prestigious thing for Mel.

But now, I had to face the darkness of the cottage. I pulled the key out of the denim pocket of my jeans and unlocked the door. The hinges creaked noisily, and the dust flew as the air shifted. The estate agent waved his hand as the dust drifted in the shaft of light offered by the open door. He pulled his phone out and activated the small LED light in his torch app, the beam cutting over the abandoned furniture. The scurrying of mice sounded overloud in the house and the smell of animal droppings permeated the air. I ignored it, as memories of my time in hell resurfaced. The estate agent pulled a handkerchief from his pocket and put it over his mouth.

"Upkeep on this place hasn't been kept I see," he noted. Small piles of garbage were still in the corners from when my parents still lived here. There were no pictures on the wall, nothing to indicate this was a happy home, just a place of ghosts and demons.

"It wasn't a priority to me, I never really wanted to set foot in this place ever again." The only response I got was a grunt.

"Well, you'll have to clean it out before we even consider listing it."

I nodded as we left the house. We'd only been able to get in as far as the living area, but that was far enough for me.

"Yeah, I understand." Oh, fuck yeah, I understood, but I wasn't happy about it.

"This could get a good price at auction, if you put a little into it."

"I can't really afford to put a lot of money into fixing the place up. Cleaning it won't be a problem, I can do that. But repairing it? Going to cost me too much." I shook my head. "Look, I just want a quick sale once I've got the place cleaned out."

"All right, once you have this mess sorted, we'll come in and get some pictures and get the auction set up."

"Right." I sighed, wondering how I was going to accomplish this.

I guess I'd need a little help from my friends, and a few days later we began.

I'd called up for a dumpster to be delivered to the cottage, and it was already halfway to being filled and we hadn't even gotten a quarter of the way through the living room. I'd waded through garbage and broken furniture to push open curtains that fell apart in my hands with rot and age just to let in a semblance of light through the grubby windows. I avoided my parent's room until the last. The scent of my father was stale, but still there and sent shivers down my spine. Richard came with me, holding my work-glove covered hand in his as we stepped over the broken remains of my childhood home.

Robbie was going through some old paperwork that we'd found, when he called out to me. I picked my way back through the broken furniture and garbage until I came outside into the bright, cleansing sunlight.

"What's up, Robbie?" I asked, already feeling emotionally wrung out.

"I found your birth certificate, Libby."

"My birth certificate?" I scowled. "Mum said they lost it, years ago," I said shaking my head. Yet more lies I was told.

I reached over and took it, looking over the details… There was one thing that stuck out like a pair of dog's balls.

The name of my father did not match the name of the man who raised me.

I guess I now knew the reason why my 'father' was such an arsehole to me. I wasn't his daughter.

"What the fuck?"

The sun shone down on the wedding party as the bride made her way to the small altar that had been set up in the Whittaker's gardens.

The bridesmaids wiped their eyes as the bride kissed her father, who had escorted her down the grassy aisle between the neatly-lined seats decorated with white, frilly and fluffy buntings. My camera clicked as I got more shots of the beautiful woman as she approached her bridegroom. The soft murmurs of appreciation came from the congregation of guests as the softly playing harpist finished their piece. Behind the groom, the tinkling of the fountain where Zane had posed for me took over as the natural background music for a beautiful wedding setting.

"Dearly beloved," the vicar began, "we are gathered here today, in the sight of God, to join Gloria and Andrew in holy matrimony…"

I snapped a few more pictures shifting into position in front of the fountain, so I could get a shot of the couple and their guests in the background, not noticing the movement at the end of the grassy aisle as two police officers approached.

"Andrew McKenzie…you are under arrest!"

The shocked gasps of the guests and the shouts of indignation rose as Richard and Lisa approached.

"Shite," the Groom muttered, turning and pushing past the vicar as he bolted… towards me.

I stood in shock as he pushed past me. I lost my balance, toppling into the fountain that was right behind me. The shock of cold water made me drop my beloved digital camera, and unfortunately, my old, trusty SLR was attached to the neck strap, and nestled on my chest as well, ready for use…and not a dunking as it too was currently getting.

I coughed and spluttered as I broke the surface, slogging my way out of the fountain with my poor precious and now ruined cameras in hand. The wedding itself was in shambles. I hauled myself out of the cold fountain and watched as the groom made a break for it, leaping over the small hedge borders, kilt flapping in the wind exposing his very pale arse cheeks with Richard in hot pursuit. The bride wailed, her mascara trailing down her cheeks as she screeched.

"I told him not to do it!"

I sat on the edge of the fountain, letting the water drain from my precious cameras. Hours of hard work gone into the fountain. I shook my head. This could, and probably would ruin me if I couldn't get my cameras replaced. I'd spent pretty much all of my savings on clearing out the fucking cottage, and fixing some of the dire repairs, such as the broken windows and a hole in the roof.

"Fuck," I muttered.

I looked up as a shout from the chase grabbed my attention. Richard had tackled the groom, his kilt flying up unceremoniously over his arse with the impact of runner and earth. There was a small struggle as the groom attempted a futile escape, and Lisa ran to help her partner. Another two police officers arrived to help with the arrest, letting Richard get up and dust himself off. I looked forlornly at my cameras, the digital one wouldn't even turn on, and the SLR had a cracked section in the film compartment casing, which had undoubtedly let light in to ruin the film within.

"You okay?" Richard asked, kneeling down to check on me.

"Bit wet, but I'm okay, my fucking cameras, however…" I sighed. "They're totally and utterly fucked."

"You want to press charges for assault and reckless damages?" he asked.

"You think I'd have a chance at some compensation?"

"You might, but I don't know, depends on the judge."

I sighed heavily. "I won't bother. I can't afford the lawyer fees anyway. Guess I'm about to become an unemployed photographer."

"What makes you say that?" Richard asked, reaching up to push my sopping fringe out from over my eyes.

"These were the only fucking cameras I own." I held them in my hands like dead puppies. "I am ruined." I looked up to see the wailing bride. "And I'm not the only one who's had a shit of a day." I sighed. "You need me to come by and make a statement?"

"I can get it from you now, if you like."

I nodded, letting him lead me away from the bride who began to screech as her groom was led to the police van. I gave Richard my statement. He guided me to the police car and, like the gentleman he was, drove me up to Mel's place where I had my car. Seeing that he was the arresting officer, of course, he had to head back to do paperwork and process the groom.

I walked into the laundry door of Mel's place. Mel, Adam and little Aaron were in Scotland. Adam was wrapping up filming there before he came back for the final shots of the movie being filmed at the Castle.

I pulled off my sopping wet clothes, tossing them into the washing machine and grabbing a towel from the clean laundry basket and wrapping it around myself.

As I headed towards one of the guest rooms to make use of the shower, I heard a strange noise coming from the door. A grunting…squeaking sort of noise. I frowned as I put my hand on the handle and opened the door… To be greeted by another bare arse, and four bare legs…and a kilt on the floor.

Oh fuck…

Uncle Leo was paying a visit to Mrs Del Rosa…

The worst kept secret was shagging on the bed in the guest room I used.

What the Fuck!

After turning tail and heading to another bathroom to clean and wash my eyes out with bleach, astringent and soap to hopefully erase the image of a naked, humping Scottish arse, I emerged, clean, warm and wrapped in a guest robe. My clothes had been in the wash for a little while, and soon they'd be tumbling around in the dryer. I headed down to Mel's kitchen to make a cup of tea.

A bright, cheery tune was whistled before the bright cheery orange beard of Leon McLeod emerged with a towel wrapped around his waist.

"Morning sunshine." I smirked. "Alison on good form, is she?" I swear the bear of a Scot jumped ten feet high when I spoke. Obviously, he wasn't expecting company.

"Jeezus lass! Give a lad a heart attack won't ye?"

I giggled as he settled down and headed to the refrigerator.

He pulled out a bottle of water, took the cap off and took a long pull of the cold water. "What are ye doin' here Libby me lass? Everything all right? Where are yer clothes?"

"I could ask you the same." I smirked as I sipped my cup of tea.

I swear, his cheeks almost matched the colour of his beard. "Ah, well, I had tae use the shower…"

"Leo, are you coming back…oh!" Mrs Del Rosa's voice drifted through to the kitchen, she'd obviously spotted me sitting at the breakfast bar with a steaming cup of tea.

"Afternoon Mrs Del Rosa." I smiled politely, ignoring the fact that she was wearing a bedsheet wrapped around her body.

"Hello, Libby." She blushed.

"Well, I just need to grab my bag of spare clothes from the room… Then you can have it back," I said, downing my tea and giving them a sly wink. "Don't you two kids do anything I wouldn't do."

I rinsed my cup and left the stunned couple in the kitchen. I dashed up the stairs, ignoring the funk of sex in the guest room as I grabbed my bag and ducked back down the stairs to slip inside the downstairs bathroom and change into dry clothes.

I sighed as I left the beautiful house. Now I had even more reason to sell the fucking cottage. I had to get new cameras. I started my little car and listened to the soothing, pounding bass and drums of *DSS*. Death metal at its fucking finest. I headed back home with my wrecked gear and a heart heavy with worry about what I was going to do.

Back at my flat, I knew the cameras were truly wrecked when I had a better look at them. The Digital still wouldn't turn on, and still dripped water, even now. The SLR was definitely broken too. It rattled when I shook it gently. My cameras were now expensive paperweights.

I fixed myself some dinner and settled in on the sofa, with LP settling on my lap and clawing at my thighs mindlessly, as though they were a pair of pillows for him to plump. I yelped as one of his claws sunk in deep and shoved the pillock off my lap. My eyes went to the coffee table where the damning birth certificate lay. I picked it up and looked at the name of my biological father on the birth certificate.

Lachlan Monroe.

I picked up my laptop and opened up a browser. I typed the name into a search engine and hit enter, results in nanoseconds.

The name hit a few million results, as expected. Most were dead ends, a couple of Facebook profiles of guys who were my age or slightly older, and in no way, could have been my biological father.

There were a few hits though, on recently archived news articles from before I was born, that hit right in the village where my mother had been born. I only knew this, because the place of her birth was listed on the birth certificate. She'd never spoken to me about her own childhood, nor where she'd grown up. And, knowing I'd be in a world of hurt for asking, I never asked. And now, I knew why.

Father Lachlan Monroe had been charged with child sex offences dating back thirty years, and had also been accused of sexual assault of his female parishioners. He was now serving time in prison after having gotten away with it for so many years. I let my mind do the math… It had to be true. There was no other conclusion I could come up with, and it certainly explained why my mother had acted out so much, especially with drugs and getting married to my abusive…whatever the fuck he was to me.

I looked at the picture of the man on my laptop, then pulled my phone out to stare at my own picture, one of me and Mel. We were both smiling in our photograph, the picture of youthful happiness. The image of the man on the laptop was dour, old, he knew he'd done wrong and he knew his time had come to pay for those transgressions against the innocent.

We had the same nose, the same eyes. I had my mother's dark hair and pouty mouth.

My mother had been a victim of sexual assault, rape, which was how I'd come about.

No wonder she hated me.

No wonder she couldn't bear to look into my eyes when she spoke to me.

No fucking wonder she didn't want me.

In all truth, I probably should never have been born.

What. The. Fuck.

A knock on my front door startled me out of my doom and gloom musings. I set my laptop down on the coffee table, along with my birth certificate. I pushed my skinny arse up off the sofa and headed to the door. Peering through the peephole, I saw Richard on the other side, smiling. My heart warmed at seeing him. I definitely needed to be wrapped up in his arms, to feel loved, like I mattered. I unlocked and opened the door.

"Hey," he said. "You're looking less like a drowned rat now. Glad to see you got home okay." He leaned forward and kissed me softly, keeping his hands behind his back.

I nodded. "Yeah, I am, but my cameras are ruined." I nodded to the drainer on the sink where they were still draining. "They are now some very expensive paperweights."

"Well, maybe these will help." He pulled a gift-wrapped package from behind his back. Wrapped in silver paper with black and purple ribbon, it was obviously two boxes, one smaller one stacked atop a larger one but professionally wrapped.

"Richard, what have you done?" I asked, stepping back into my flat, looking back to him as he followed me.

"Just taking care of my girl." He smiled, settling down on my sofa. "Open it."

I sat beside him, shifting the paperwork from the fucking Cottage out of the way.

I carefully opened the gift wrapped present. I gasped. Sitting amongst the paper were two cameras, two brand-new cameras.

"Fuck! Richard, these would have cost you at least three grand!" I turned to him, shocked that he'd spent that much. "I- I can't fucking accept these!" I shook my head in amazement.

"Yes, you can, and you will," he said, taking the boxes out of my hands. He clasped my hands in his own, bringing them up to his lips, kissed my knuckles. I couldn't help it, I started to fucking cry. "What's wrong?" he asked, concern on his face.

"Other than Mel, no-one else has ever done something like this for me." I sobbed, ugh I hated crying. I'd wasted so many tears over the years on my arsehole parents, but now I was happy. I didn't want to cry because I was happy.

I was pulled awkwardly into his arms, being held was still a little strange, but comforting, and I needed that now. I sniffled as I snuggled into his arms, feeling warm, safe, secure…*loved*.

"I'll pay you back, I promise." I pulled away, wiping my eyes.

"No, you bloody well won't. They are a gift to my girl."

I smirked. "Your girl."

"Yep. Like that huh?"

"Maybe." I ran a hand over the box holding the SLR. I turned to smile seductively at him. "There's something else I might like though…"

"Oh, and what's that?" He smiled. I pulled my legs up underneath me and gently, but insistently pushed on his shoulder, laying him down on my sofa. I gripped the front of his button-up shirt and ripped it open, buttons flying everywhere.

"Hey! I liked that shirt!" he said in mock-distress.

"I'll fix it." I leaned down and kissed his slight six-pack, my hands going to his belt, looking up at him, my eyes caught the decadently sinful lust burning in his eyes. "Besides, you should know, cameras make me kinda horny, especially when I get them as gifts from sexy police officers." I ran my tongue over my lips before I unzipped his pants and slid a hand inside.

He moaned before his hands gripped my hips and he somehow managed to flip us, so I was now underneath him. "Sweetheart, I'll buy you all the cameras in the world if this is what happens!"

His lips crashed against mine, and we made sweet, frantic love on my sofa as Lord Psycho watched, his green eyes widening as we writhed, butt naked on the sofa finding our own fucking Nirvana within each other.

Later, I lay snuggled up on the couch, spooning with Richard while we watched some old television show. His discarded pants started to vibrate. He was asleep behind me, I reached forward and snagged the belt loop of his pants and pulled them towards me. He grunted in his sleep and tightened his arm around my middle. I sighed, dropping the pants to the floor. The impact had jostled his phone out of the pocket and I saw the screen all lit up with the name 'Liv' on it, with a picture of him and another woman snuggled up together and smiling for the selfie before the call rang out and the screen went dark. I leaned back, my face curling into a slight scowl. I wasn't sure exactly who that was, could she be a sister? He hadn't said anything about his family, she could be anyone.

But my mind went back to that fucking tattoo on his back… *'Richard and Olivia, Always and Forever'*

Olivia… *Liv.*

It couldn't be coincidence… Was he married? Was I his side chick? Could my life get *any* more complicated?

What. The. Fuck.?

I said nothing to Richard about the phone call. I had to work things out first. He left my flat, after we arranged to go out to dinner the next day. I had nothing else to do, so I called Zane, and we arranged to go out to a local park for another shoot, with my new cameras. I took my time in setting them up while Zane chatted to a gorgeous and obviously gay couple. I took some candid snaps to test out the cameras. They were beautiful, professional quality, and though not quite top-of-the-line, they did a fantastic job.

Over the next couple of hours, I took some fantastic shots of Zane, with high quality pictures on the digital camera, and some excellent shots on the SLR that would make Zane and my portfolios—as Zane put it—'sparkle'.

"So…" he said as we settled into the infamous 'Cock Booth' at Rosie's for a cup of tea, well coffee for him, tea for me. "I have a friend in LA, who wants to help me kick start my modelling career, and she's looking for a new photographer." I set my cup down.

"Really?" I asked.

"Yep. I kinda suggested you, and kinda sent some of your shots to her, and she was excited. She wants to meet you, or at least chat via Skype." Zane grinned. "You know I'm heading back to LA in a few weeks. Can't stay here, this fucking English weather has destroyed my Man Tan."

I laughed, he was starting to look a tad pasty. "What about you and Robbie?" I asked.

"Robbie and I have had fun, sweetie. I'm all for fun, you know that. But we are great friends, with benefits, and that's what we're comfortable with. He knew I wasn't staying here. LA is my home, while this is his."

"You know, I do work, and Richard and I are together, right? If I do accept, then how's that going to work."

"Long distance relationships do work, you just gotta put some effort into it. I mean look at Mel and Adam, he's not home most of the time, but they're always chatting on the phone or Skyping." He stirred his coffee absent-mindedly. "And you did say Danny owes you some vacation time, right?"

Yes, yes, he did, about four months' worth of it… Which would work out perfectly if I took this job and didn't like it. "That's different, they're married. This is all new, we've just started out really."

"Oh? And how many times have you done the horizontal tango with him?" he asked.

"Ahem… A few…." I said, clearing my throat in embarrassment.

"So, it's all fizzle and no bang?" he waggled his eyebrows

"What? No! The sex is pretty damned great, I'll have you know."

"Ew! TMI girl, way TMI!" Zane put his hands over his ears. "I'm gay, remember. Va-jay-jays gross me out, like, totally, blergh!"

"You don't wanna know, then don't ask." I shook my head in amusement while Zane made a show of downing his coffee then reaching for the coffeepot for a refill.

I nursed my teacup.

"So, he bought you those pretty new cameras?" he asked me.

"Yeah there's over three thousand pounds worth of gear there."

"You're getting them insured this time, right?"

"Yes, I most certainly am." Yes, I had been an idiot and not had my old cameras insured, but this time, I'd make sure they were properly covered by insurance, lest I have another camera-tastrophe.

Inside my backpack, my phone rang.

"Hang on a sec," I said, reaching down to my bag. "Ugh, estate agent, I gotta take this."

I hauled myself out of the seat and answered the phone. I stepped out into the street and walked around the side of Rosie's into the small but clean alleyway.

"Hello, Libby speaking," I said as I answered the call.

"Hello Miss Hastings, this is Ernest Young from Young and Bold Real Estate, we just want to arrange the final viewing dates for your property before it goes to auction next weekend?"

Fuck, I'd almost completely forgot about that. "Uh, yes, sure, so this is you guys coming though and then the next day the public viewing, right?"

"That's correct, Miss Hastings, yes."

"And do I have to be there for the viewings?"

"I'd like you to come to the first one, just to make sure you're happy with the process, but the public one, no. You don't need to be present for that."

Inwardly, I sighed, I was glad for that. I didn't want to step foot in that house ever again if I could help it.

Over the last few weeks, we'd finished clearing out the rooms, pulled up the carpets, torn down the old, ratty curtains, cleared the garden of the shed I'd destroyed, and cut the long grass and brambles that had taken over the place. I was surprised at how nice it looked, even without the carpets in it. If I didn't have so many horrible memories associated with the place, and if I had the money, maybe I could have turned it into a nice home for myself…and Richard. Wait…was I really considering long term with him? I sighed, as I ended the call. Maybe I was. Maybe it was time for Libby Hastings —'wild child', to settle down.

In part, I think I was a little jealous of what Mel and Adam had. Happy life, beautiful baby boy, strong marriage and love, lots and lots of fucking love.

Yes, I fucking wanted that. All of it. Maybe, with Richard, I could have it.

I headed back to Rosie's and sat opposite Zane. The look on his face was not good.

"What?"

"Honey, don't panic, but Richard just went across the road to the jewellers."

"Okay, why would I panic?"

"Because, he just walked in there, hand-in-hand with another woman."

"What. The. Fuck?!"

I watched, hidden inside Rosie's as Richard walked out with the woman beside him. The pretty lace curtains that covered the lower half of the windows kept us hidden as we peeked over the curtain rail like a pair of naughty children waiting for a glimpse of Santa on Christmas eve, only this time, it was the Grinch.

"Oh, my fucking God," I said softly, watching as they shared a kiss.

My heart broke, shattering into a million pieces as she hugged him and caressed his face lovingly before they walked off, hand-in-hand towards his car, where he, being the fucking gentleman he was, opened the car door for her, then closed it once she was safely inside.

"Breathe honey." Zane had come over to my side of the booth and was rubbing my back as I felt the start of a panic attack settling in. My chest tightened, my vision lured with tears and I trembled in sheer emotional agony.

"Did… I … Just… Fucking... See that?" I gasped, rocking slightly as I hunched over.

I tried to calm myself. It had been years since I'd had a panic attack, fucking years! The last one was when Danny had shown me the death notice of my 'father'. I don't know why I had panicked then, but all the emotional shit that he'd put me through had raced back through my body, rendering me near insensate with panic. Danny had been there for me then, and I knew he would be there for me again and again, just like Mel, and Zane.

I had a good, tight circle of friends. I could get through this latest shitstorm.

"I had a feeling something was up," I said, finally getting control of my breathing. I sniffled, wiping the tears away.

"Oh?"

"He's got a tattoo, '*Richard and Olivia forever and always*'. Got wedding rings and doves on it, all that lovey shit. There were times when he'd take phone calls and leave the room, and we were asleep on my sofa the other day and his phone rang. I saw who it was. 'Olivia'. There was even a picture of them, all loved up on the screen." I put my hands over my face, trying to stop the stupid flood of fucking tears. "How could I have been so fucking naive? Seriously? Why the fuck can't I find someone who isn't married, like do I have a fucking sign on my forehead that reads *gullible bitch*?" I sighed. "Fuck this, and fuck him. You know what? Call your friend Zane, she if she'll give me a shot."

"OMG! Really?" Zane asked, clapping his hands together so rapidly they were a blur. "Oh girlfriend, you can stay with me! Mel's old room is empty, and I was going to start looking for a roomie bitch as soon as I got back to LA, but squee! This is epic!" he paused, looking at my distraught face. "But honey, you sure you want to do this? I mean, you are in a tizzy right now, and might not be thinking clearly…"

"Oh Zane, everything is fucking clear to me right now. But first, I'm going to go and confirm what my eyes, and you have told me. I'm going to sell that fucking hell hole, then I am so fucking out of here."

"What about Mel?"

I smiled at him. It was sweet he considered our best friend, and how she'd take my leaving the UK for LA. I knew she'd be sad, but she also knew that I had to spread my wings, especially when she heard about this latest fan-fucking-tastic development in my love life—or now, lack of love life.

"Honey, Mel has a whole village to look after her and baby Aaron, Aunty Libs will be back for Christmas, his birthday, her birthday all the rest of those really important milestones."

"And, so will Aunty Zed." He smiled, texting on his phone.

"Uh, no, do not call yourself 'Aunty Zed'. That right there is a *Pulp Fiction* reference that will haunt that baby for eternity. Aunty Zee sounds much better, or fuck even Aunty Zane."

"But it's 'Zed' in the UK, so I'd be literally correct." Zane smirked. I flipped him the bird. But I was secretly glad he'd managed to divert my attention.

His phone pinged with a message.

"Oh! Libby! Laura Rose got back to me! She said you can start as soon as you get here! I said you'll be there in about two weeks!" He squealed like a rabid teenager at some fucking famous boy band concert.

"Well, I guess there's nothing else for it then. Time to give Danny my request for leave. Oh wait, what the fuck am I going to do with LP?"

"See if Mel will take him," Zane said, finishing his text to Laura Rose.

"Hmm, but she's got the baby."

"True… What about Leo?"

"Well…" I smirked, "I do have something that might convince him to take the cat on." I grinned.

"Oooh juicy Goss! Give it up bitch!" Zane demanded. I shook my head. "What and lose my bargaining chip? Not fucking likely." I sighed, pushing up from the bench. "I got a fucking load of stuff to get done now, Zane." I grabbed my backpack, picking my phone up from the table. I noticed there was a message from Richard. "Fucker." I muttered reading it. He'd fucking cancelled our dinner date. I knew why. That was fine, I now intended to pay him a visit this evening, and tell him to fucking sod off.

I sent him a message, alluding that everything was ok, and that I'd see him later.

He had the audacity to send me back a message filled with sappy fucking hearts.

What. The. Fuck.

I pulled up in Zane's car, mainly because my little boom-box on wheels would have alerted my prey to my presence. I lifted my hand, fisted to knock on his door and rapped my knuckles against the wooden panels.

"Coming. Just a sec." A female's voice called out form the other side. I heard the words. "Pizza delivery is early." Muttered as they unlocked the door. Pizza, eh? Not quite.

"Hi." I smiled at the woman who had been with Richard earlier this afternoon. "Is Richard here?" she looked slightly uncomfortable.

"Uh, yes, but he's in the shower."

"That's okay, can you give him these for me? Tell him I don't want them anymore, and he can go fuck himself. Though it's obvious, he's fucking you too." I shoved the cameras, boxed back up in their original packaging and turned away from the stunned woman. I heard the door shut, then ten seconds later it opened as I walked down the drive.

"Libby?" His voice cut me like shards of freshly broken glass. "Baby? What's going on?"

I couldn't turn to face him. I kept walking to Zane's car. I felt his hand on my shoulder. "Libby, damnit talk to me!"

He turned me. I was faced with his eyes, confusion blazing in them as he stood naked but for a towel, still dripping wet from the shower.

"Fuck you, you fucking, lying piece of shit! Why didn't you tell me you were fucking someone else huh? It's not so bad that I have my entire existence fucked by the fact that my real dad was a fucking child rapist, and that my childhood was so fucked it would fill a psychiatrist's filing cabinet, but oh no, I have to fall for the one guy who gave a shit about me, only to find he's fucking *MARRIED!*" He stopped, looked at me, realisation on his face. "That's right, *CUNTSTABLE DICK*! The registry of Births, Deaths and Marriages has a public records section you know that? Imagine my surprise when I did some research on you tonight, after Zane told me you'd gone into a jewellery shop with your *wife!*" I pushed away from him when he tried to reach for me. "Do you think I'm so fucking stupid? So fucking gullible? What am I? Something to keep your dick wet while you waited for the little fucking wife to move here? Huh? Well, fuck you, I hope you live fucking happily ever fucking after." I pushed him again, causing him to stumble backwards. "You fucking cunt!"

"Libby!" Richard tried to grab me again as I turned, his hand warm on my shoulder, his voice desperate. I pulled back my hand and slapped him as hard as I could, ignoring the stinging ache in my hand at the impact. I'd done something I'd sworn never to do to someone I cared about, I raised my hand to them.

"Just leave me the fuck alone, Richard. We're done." I sobbed. "Go back to your wife."

I spun on my heel and ran to Zane's car, sliding quickly into the driver's seat and pulling away from the kerb so fast the tires squealed.

I was a mess.

My life was a mess.

Everything was a complete and utter fucking mess.

I screamed and belted the steering wheel, letting my emotions out as my body trembled with anger, sadness, desolation. I drove, ignoring the blurring in my eyes, being mindful of the speed limits, despite my fractured emotional state. I left the village behind, heading for the one place I knew I could find sanctuary, Mel's.

I pressed the buttons on the keypad, fucking up the code at least twice before I pulled myself together and got it right. The lights were on in the front room as I pulled up, and I knew Mel would be up with Aaron, who was still having a little trouble settling down at night. I pulled up next to her Range Rover, locking Zane's car up before I headed to the front door. Zane was there, standing at the open front door wearing nothing but boxer shorts and an open robe.

"Hey honey," he said, offering me a cup of hot chocolate. "Mel is in the media room with Lil' A-A-Ron."

I giggled through my snotty, teary face. "Oh, I'm sure she loves you calling him that."

Zane smirked, rubbing his shoulder. "Yeah, Good thing we're leaving in a couple of weeks." He reached under my chin and turned my face to the light. "I see you ended it?"

I nodded, feeling my throat tighten again as the tears threatened to break free. I felt my legs weaken and slid down to the front stoop. Zane followed me, sitting next to me and sliding an arm around my shoulders, hugging me against him.

"Has he tried to call you?" Zane asked. I unzipped my backpack and pulled out my phone. He'd been blowing it up with messages and calls, and even now, there was another call coming in. I rejected it, before I turned the phone off. I sighed.

"Honey, it's all going to be fine. We'll get through this, besides, in LA, you might find yourself a nice, sexy movie star, or even a hot rock star."

"Done the rock stars already, though they were death metal, and I was meat in the sandwich," I said with a wink.

"OMG! Who?"

"*DSS*," I said with a smirk, as I wiped yet more fucking tears from my eyes.

"Get the fuck outta town!" Zane playfully slapped me on the arm. "Lars and Jorgen?"

"Yep."

"Ho-lee shit-balls girl! OMG, I would so swap my dick and balls for a Va-Jay-Jay just to get into their pants."

"I thought you said 'Va-Jay-Jays were gross?"

"They are! But I'd go the sixty-four-thousand-dollar question for those two!"

"Who is getting a sex change now, and why are we discussing this on my doorstep where little ears can hear?" Mel's voice drifted over to us from the front door. I turned.

"Hey, Mummy."

I hauled my sorry arse up from the tile steps to hug Mel, being careful of baby Aaron who rested in his swaddle, secure in his mother's arms. I pulled away, looking down at my best friend's baby, he was so adorable.

Zane and I had gone to Mel's after I'd had my near meltdown in Rosie's. Mel had even offered to pay for my flights to LA, which I'd flatly refused. I had enough to get over there, and had put in the paperwork to organise my work visa, with the information that Laura Rose had supplied. The woman was damned efficient. Danny had been sad that I was leaving, but after

I explained things, he understood, promising that there'd be a place for me when I got back… *If* I'd told him, if I came back.

"Come on in, you two," Mel said, rocking the baby as he started to fuss again.

I got up from the step, with Zane's helping hand and we headed in to the media room where a movie was on pause. The smell of buttered popcorn and hot chocolate made my stomach growl, and I remembered I'd not eaten since yesterday.

"Here, before the Libby monster breaks free and devours us," Mel said with a smile, as she handed me the bowl of popcorn.

I settled into the large, plush leather recliner and we chatted about LA while the movie played on. After a while, Mel's phone buzzed, she picked it up.

"Hello?" she said, sitting up. I was holding Aaron, who slumbered peacefully in my arms. "She is, and she's safe…" I tensed, knowing who she was talking about. "Well, that's up to her if she wants to speak with you."

She looked at me. I shook my head. "No, she's not interested in speaking with you right now…" Another pause. "Okay, I'll pass on the message, drive safe, Richard." She ended the call. "Wanna talk about it?" Mel asked, looking at me. I shook my head. "Okay, I'm here when you are ready, you know that."

I nodded. I couldn't believe the arsehole had driven all the way out here to try to see me. Seriously, after the scene I'd caused, and the stinging slap I'd given him as a parting shot…

What. The. Fuck?

For the next week, I hid out at Mel's, only heading out to attend the final viewing of the fucking cottage. I was glad that one tie to my childhood was about to be severed. My plane tickets had been 'gifted' to me by Mel, along with a new Digital SLR camera as a 'going away present'—bitch. And I had gone to my flat in the dead of night, or when I knew that Richard was on duty, to pack up my shit. I'd managed to 'convince' Leo to look after LP while I was away. The big, burly Scotsman took one look at LP and I swear he was in love. So was LP. Fucking traitor cat.

Today was Auction Day. The day that I was going to be free of the shackles of my childhood. Finally, I'd be free of that fucking house where my miserable life started.

I'd turned my phone back on the morning after I crashed out at Mel's place, after I'd ended it with Richard to find so many messages on my phone that the storage was full. I deleted them without reading and then blocked his number. I had to move on. Right now, I was trying to do just that. I waited for the phone call from the estate agents to find out if the place sold. I wasn't expecting a lot of money from the sale, I'd be happy to just get rid of it.

I waited anxiously with Mel while the auction began. I didn't want to have a direct line open to the auctioneer's assistant to hear how the bidding was going. I didn't have a reserve on the place, hoping that that little fact might make it go faster. It would sell for whatever anyone was willing to pay for it, and good riddance.

Little Aaron sat in the baby bouncer, blowing spit bubbles and kicking his chubby little legs around in pure innocent abandon. It made me sad that I'd miss so much of him growing up, but I'd be back in a few months, in time for Mel's birthday.

This time, we wouldn't be having a major pub crawl like we had the last two years. The first time, Mel hooked up with Adam for the final time, ending in where we were now, and last year, the Paps had a field day. After that, Adam had put the foot down, no more pub crawls for Mel. Mel falling pregnant with Little Aaron had put a stop to that anyway. I had a sneaking suspicion that his conception that night was Adams unwitting birthday present to Mel.

My phone rang on the kitchen bench, making both Mel and I jump with fright. Mel tittered nervously, I shook my head and grinned, the sudden ringing had given me a jumpstart to the heart as well. I picked up the phone.

"Hello, Libby speaking."

"Hello Libby, this is Abbigail Asterley, with Klein-Mercer Auctions. I'm please to tell you that your house sold at auction this afternoon, with a sale price of two hundred and forty thousand pounds."

"I'm sorry, what?"

"Two hundred and forty thousand pounds."

"You're fucking kidding me?" I sat back down on the stool, totally stumped.

"I'm certainly not kidding you, there was a bit of a bidding war between a London developer and a local buyer. His name is…" I quickly cut her off, not caring who bought the place, all I cared about that it no longer loomed over my head

"Stop! I don't want to know who bought it, thanks. So, do I need to come in and sign the paperwork right now, or?"

"Tomorrow will be fine," Abbigail said.

"Right, see you then, thanks!" I ended the call, Mel looked at me expectantly.

"How much?" she asked. I was still in shock, I couldn't believe the shitty old cottage went for that much.

"Libby? How much?" Mel prodded again. I was still speechless. Something hit me on the head and dropped to the bench, it was one of Aaron's stuffed toys.

"Libby, for fucks sake, how fucking much did it go for?" Mel's swearing had returned, she'd managed to curb it since Aaron was born, and had even incorporated a swear jar in the kitchen.

"Two pounds Mel."

"What, it went for two pounds?" Mel shook her head, "No way it could have gone for that fucking much."

"Three pounds." I smirked.

"What?" she realised what she'd done. "Fuck."

"Four."

"Shut the fuck up."

"You're up for a fiver now." I grinned. She flipped me the bird.

"Okay, so how much?"

I took a deep breath. "Two hundred and forty thousand."

"Fuck me, you are fucking kidding me? That's fan-fucking-tastic! I'm so fucking happy for you."

"That's nine."

"Fuck." I shook my head at her profanity… Though I myself had added to that jar quite a bit. "I had to make it an even ten, besides, I've been a good girl." She grinned, going to her purse and pulling out a tenner. I watched as she reached up above the fridge and slipped the note into the swear jar. "Aaron is going to be so spoilt when this is full." She smiled.

"He's going to be fucking spoilt anyway.

"That's one." Mel grinned. I shook my head and pulled a tenner out of my own pocket, I could afford it, so…

What the fuck.

Over the next couple of weeks, I'd started to get messages from an unknown number, but I knew who it was.

Please, I know you're leaving, don't leave because of ME, we can work things out.

I love you Libby, please, don't end this!

It's not what you thought, please meet with me so I can explain things!

I ignored the messages, I'd heard them all before.

It was D-Day, as in departure day, time to go to LA and the start of my new life. Robbie was driving Zane and me to Heathrow. Mel, baby Aaron and I were snuggled up in the back, Aaron's baby seat taking up most of the room, so it was a little squishy for both Mel and me on either side of him. My phone rang in my pocket, I pulled it out, not looking at the number.

"Hello, Libby speaking."

"Libby, please, please don't hang up the phone." My heart hammered in my chest.

"Why shouldn't I? You broke my heart, Richard."

"I know, I'm so sorry baby, please, where are you? I want to talk."

"About a half hour out of Heathrow." I stared out the window, not really seeing the scenery that passed.

"The airport?"

"Yes, the airport. I'm leaving for LA today. So, goodbye."

"Libby! No, wait!"

I ended the call and sniffled, fucking tears had started to march towards freedom. Mel reached over and put her hand on my arm.

"You okay?" she asked.

"I'm ok." I nodded, my phone started to vibrate with another incoming call, I ended it before it started to ring. I switched it off and pulled the SIM card out. "Well, guess I'll be getting a new number then." I sighed.

"You'll need a new number in the States anyway," Robbie said, as he slowed down to navigate a section of roadworks.

"That's right, and only those who you want to have your number will have it," Zane said, turning in his seat and smiling back at me.

"You'll have fun living with Zane. Just make sure to lock your door, as he likes to wake you up my jumping on your bed of a morning. Oh, and don't let him take you to any movie studios for extras casting!" Mel advised.

"Bitch, turned out fine for you." Zane stuck his tongue out at Mel.

"That's one!" Mel and I both chorused in the back seat. Zane grumbled and fished out a pound and handed it to Mel for the swear jar, as the rule was, when little ears were around, you still had to pay the penalty for swearing.

"In the end, but the middle was hell," Mel admitted as she pocketed the money.

"Yeah, how many times did I tell you NOT to look at the paper, because things weren't as they seemed?" I smirked.

"Too many to count." Mel sighed. She was thoughtful for a moment. "Libby," she looked at me. "Is it possible that you might be taking things out of context with Richard?"

I shook my head. "No, Mel, everything was clear as day. He kissed her in public, on the street for everyone to see. Then, he cancelled our date for that night, so I went to confront him about what I'd seen, she was there, he was in the shower, she answered the door in a robe thinking I was a pizza delivery."

"So, you put two and two together?" Mel asked.

I nodded "Yep. Seems pretty clear to me." Mel sighed. "What?"

"I don't know, it's just, something doesn't add up."

"Yeah, he fucking lied to me."

"That's one!" Zane and Robbie sang from the front.

"Fuck." I muttered.

"Two!" Robbie laughed, checking me in the mirror and holding out two fingers in a peace sign.

"Buttheads," I grumbled, handing Mel two pounds.

"That's…" Zane started

"Not a swear!" I cut him off.

"Cow." He smirked. Oh yes, this was going to be fun.

A short time later, Robbie pulled up in the short-term parking section, and got our bags out while I went and grabbed a luggage trolley to put all our crap on. I had about three large suitcases and two carry-on bags, while Zane had two suitcases and one backpack. Mel had Aaron loaded into his stroller and we headed to the international terminal where our flight was departing from.

We checked in at the front desk and booked our luggage in before we headed over to one of the small cafes to wait until boarding time.

"You'll love LA," Zane said, a wistful look in his eye.

"You miss it, don't you?" I asked, taking a sip of my tea.

"Yeah, but we'll be there soon," Zane said, slurping his coffee.

I finished my tea and nursed Aaron, snuggling with my Godson until the time drew near to head to our gate. We passed through the passenger lounges to a secure section where Mel and Robbie had to leave us. I was teary eyed as I said goodbye to my best friend.

"Oh stop, you'll set me off. You'll see me in two months, my birthday, remember?" she said.

I nodded. "Yeah, I know."

Zane moved in and hugged Mel and then Robbie.

"You take care of each other, okay?" Robbie smiled as he hugged me. I stepped through the security gates.

"LIBBY!"

I turned, hearing my name being called by a familiar voice.

"No," I said softly, shaking my head.

"Come on, sweets, let's get to the gate." Zane put an arm around my shoulders and led me away.

"LIBBY, STOP!" Richard's voice reached me as Zane walked me away.

"Sir! You can't go through there without a ticket!" The voice of the security guards reached me as we moved ever closer to the gate as the boarding call for our flight was announced.

We handed over our tickets and moved to the door just as the shout carried over the noise of the airport

"Libby! She's not my wife!"

What.

The.

Fuck?

I showed the security guys at the door my company identification card as they searched through my bags. Going through a metal detector was always fun. I had a couple of piercings that seemed to show up, especially the belly button one, and the toe ring on my left pinkie toe. I hopped on one foot and tugged my boot off followed by my sock to show them the toe ring. I was finally let through, after they'd gone through all my bags, and left me to repack everything. I headed to the studio where Laura Rose was working.

Everything was so flashy, it was busy and bustling with activity. I was amazed at how much was going on, from hair and make-up, to wardrobe changed right there in the middle of the floor.

"Seriously, can you not give me one fucking good pose?" The voice of my employer screamed at a hapless model.

I approached her carefully. "Uh, Laura?" I said moving up slowly, so as not to startle the beast

"Who is addressing me improperly?" She turned and gave me such a scathing look that I almost cringed. "I am called Laura Rose, you will call me as such."

"Right, sorry. I'm Libby."

"Ah, yes Hastings. You're late." She sneered. "Right. Those digitals over there need to be uploaded to the computers, then our boys will touch them up. Then I want you to get the next lot of digitals ready for the next model, back up those files in triplicate, one to the laptop, one to the desktop and one to the hard drives under files with today's date and session one. Then format the SD cards, then get me a coffee, skinny Cappu-latte with caramel and stevia, three stevia, not two, not four, but three." She sniffed, and I noticed the tiny crusts of white under her nostril.

Oh great, a fucking coke head. It was obvious the fucking bitch didn't even remember me from our skype conversations. So much for her being super organised. I wondered if Zane knew she was an addict.

"Well. Get fucking on it girl. I'm not paying you to stare at things."

I nodded, so this was me getting experience as a fashion photographer… Back to doing the shit work that some punk kid intern could be doing, instead of learning the finer points of fashion photography from someone who knew what they were fucking doing. I worked through the day, my feet killing me, my head hurting from the constant flashes of the damned camera's studio equipment and my stomach grumbling from the ache of not having any lunch.

And of course, all through the day, Laura Rose ducked into the bathroom for a line of coke when she started to come down. I staggered into the apartment I shared with Zane, exhausted, I collapsed face first on his three-seater sofa.

"Hey Miss Photographer! How are you doing, sweetness?" he asked, leaning against the kitchen doorframe.

"Rough first day?" he asked. I grunted. "You'll be fine, sweetie, you'll get used to it."

I only hoped he was right. I grunted again. "Yeah, it's gotta get better."

The next few weeks went by in a blur of screaming, crying models and orders for stupid caffeine drinks that went cold, and then I was screamed at for letting it go cold. I was screamed at for uploading the pictures to the wrong files, even though I'd done *exactly* as she'd asked me and named the fucking files *exactly* as she'd fucking told me to. By the end of the fourth week, I was a wreck.

I was having trouble sleeping, I'd lost weight from not eating right and I swore I was coming down with a cold.

I was right.

I woke up on the Saturday with a bad cold. I coughed so much that I was sick, and I was barely able to drag my sorry arse out of bed to go pee. My phone rang, the ringtone of one of *DSS's* hits *Kill the bitch* was appropriate for the caller… Fucking Laura Rose.

I answered, my nose all stuffed up and my hearing dulled form the sinus blockages.

"Hello…"

"Where the fuck are you? You know we have a runway shoot today. You'd better get your fucking ass here or you'll be finished in this industry, you hear me? Fucking finished!"

The bitch hung up before I had a chance to tell her I was sick.

"Honey… Are you okay? You look terrible," Zane said as I dragged myself out of bed and into the kitchen for some cold and flu medicine.

His Aunt Jessica and her wife Claudia were both visiting. They'd adopted me as their British niece and had kept be entertained with stories of Zane's youth. Jessica worked at a local youth centre, helping homeless kids find a place to stay.

"I'll be okay. Just drug me up with some cold meds and I'll be fine. I have to get to work," I said, even my voice was dulled in my ears, so chocked up with snot and swollen form the infection.

"Libby, honey, you can't go to work like that." Jessica looked at me, concerned.

"I have to Aunty Jess, I'll get the sack otherwise."

"Libby…" Zane started I put a hand up to stop him.

"Zane, I gotta do this," I said, closing the cupboard door and opening another to grab a glass.

I poured some juice and downed the pills, followed by a swallow of juice that felt like I was swallowing razorblades. I showered and dressed, catching a city bus to the fashion show just as the cold shivers of fever racked my body.

Laura Rose was in her element, screeching like a fucking banshee at everyone. Her eyes seemed to glow with wicked glee when she saw me. "This is your last fucking warning, Lucy. Don't think I won't hesitate to have you on a fucking plane back to Australia, and so help me, if you even think of fucking up today, I'll have your job."

I'd had enough. "You know what?" I stood taller, even though my muscles screamed in agony with the cold. "Fuck you, you fucking slapper skank coke-head bitch. I've put up with your fucking shite for weeks. You make people cry, tell them they're fucking no good, when I can see a fuck load more talent in the people you bring down than you have in your fucking little toe." I scowled at the bitch. "Just because you're behind the camera doesn't mean you are the bee's fucking knees, I got more out of working at weddings and debutante balls than your miserable arse. You know what? Take your fucking job and suck it. You were the one who looked at my portfolio and asked Zane to bring me here and work for you, when I could have been living back home where the sun doesn't burn me to a fucking crisp, where I could spend time with my best friends, and try to work shit out with the man that I love…" I stopped, my sickness and anger bringing out the home truth. I began to cough, a harsh, wracking cough that stole my breath and made my stomach cramp.

I turned, leaning up against a table as I felt dizziness take over.

"Fuck…" I mumbled as the room spun around me and I fell to the floor before black spots danced before my eyes before they joined up and darkness took me out for the count.

"Wha… what the fuck…"

I woke up in the hospital. Zane and his aunt Jessica sat up and watched me worriedly.

"Oh sweetie, are you okay? You gave me such a fright." He reached over and rubbed my hand.

I reached up and touched a sore spot on my head, wincing when I felt the plaster on it, covering a small gash.

"Yeah, head hurts, still feel like shite." Yep, my head was still there, it was fucking pounding.

"No wonder, you took quite a nasty fall, bumped your head on a table on the way down."

"Ahh, I see Ms Hastings is awake." A female doctor entered with a kind smile gracing her lips. "Now, we've run some scans, and you'll be pleased to know your baby is fine."

"Wait… Baby? Doc, what do you mean, 'my baby is fine'…?" I sat up, panic starting to rear its ugly head at the sudden news. "What baby?"

"You weren't aware you were pregnant? You are about six weeks along," the doctor said, moving to my bedside. She took my wrist in her hand, checking my pulse.

"Hmm." She said, looking down at her wristwatch as she checked the seconds hand against my pulse "Your pulse is elevated. I know this is a bit of a shock, but I need you to calm down a little bit for me, okay?" I nodded. Zane looked at me, shock written all over his face. "You haven't been feeling queasy in the mornings?"

"Nope."

"When was your last cycle?"

"About four weeks ago."

"Normal bleed?"

"Eww…" Zane groaned.

"No, very light, actually."

"It's not unusual for a woman to have a small period once she is pregnant. Any previous pregnancies?" She asked me.

I was quiet for a moment, reliving the pain before I answered

"A long time ago." I said softly. Zane's eyes widened a moment.

"Miscarriage, or aborted?"

"Miscarriage," I said softly.

The doctor gave me a sympathetic smile. Zane's eyes went wide for a moment then softened in sympathy.

"I know this is a surprise, but, you're intending to keep the baby?"

"Abso-fucking-lutly," I said, fierce determination in my stuffed-up, nasally voice.

"Okay, so we're going to start you on a course of vitamins that are going to bring your levels up and help your pregnancy, and I want you to start eating correctly."

I nodded. The doctor turned her attention to Zane

"And you, young man, you need to take care of your girlfriend. I take it you're the father?"

"Me? Oh no honey, Libby's my best friend, but she's so not my type. That male nurse from earlier, though, I'd play doctor and nurse with him any day of the week," he said with a wink, the doc chuckled.

"Yes, Ethan is popular with both ladies and gents." She smiled back at me. "Libby, you have a life changing event coming up. Children are the best thing to happen to a woman." She smiled. "You'll be fine, just rest, get over this cold, eat well, reduce stress and in a few months, you'll be welcoming your baby into the world."

I nodded. "Thanks Doc."

"We'll have you out of here tomorrow. Just need to make sure everything is good before you leave. You had a nasty bump to the head."

"Oh, Doc, I'm heading back to the UK in a few months. Is there going to be any problems with me being pregnant and flying?"

"A long as you're healthy, then no, you should be fine to travel." The doctor left us in the ward. I sighed, rubbing the bridge of my nose.

"So, it's Richard's?" Zane asked, already knowing the answer.

"Yep."

"Gonna tell him?"

"I don't know. I guess, I just… Fuck this is complicated," I growled, before I started to cough again.

"Easy, don't stress, just relax," Zane said, standing and grabbing the glass of water by my bedside.

"I just… A baby? Shit Zane… I… I wasn't expecting this. I was certain that I was up to date with my shot, what am I going to do? I think I told Laura Rose to shove her job…"

"Actually, she said you told her to suck it." Zane smirked. "She was crying when she called me, said you'd collapsed, and was unconscious, she called the paramedics. You actually made her cry…"

"Bitch made everyone else cry, she had it coming."

"Yeah, I know she was extreme, but she said there was still a job for you. She needs to take some time out and reassess her position. She said she knew she had a problem with her drug use, wants to get help, but couldn't find the way out. I think you gave her the fright, the shove she needed."

"I don't know if I can work for her again, Zane…"

"I understand." Zane smiled. "You rest, we'll talk more later, okay?" he said, turning on the TV above my bed.

We watched some cheesy, crappy soap operas until visiting hours were finished and the horrible hospital food was brought around.

Zane picked me up the next morning when I was discharged. I skyped with Mel as soon as I got home.

"Hey!"

"Hey, Zane said you had an 'incident' yesterday and ended up in the hospital? Hell woman, I knew going to LA was going to be good for you. Is this one of those 'you should have seen the other bitch' kind of incident?"

I chuckled. "Nope, but, I kinda got some news," I said, looking away abashedly and rubbing the back of my neck.

"Ooh, I got some news for you too! But what's yours?"

"Oh, no you tell me yours first." I could tell Mel was keen to tell me.

"Ok, ok, it's big!" She grinned unable to contain herself. "We're pregnant again!"

"Oh, my god! Congratulations! Seriously, if I could reach through that screen and hug the fuck outta you girl I so would do it!"

"Oh, and more to tell you… Your old crappy shithouse cottage? The new owners have done it up, you'd not recognise it, but they have turned it into a bed and breakfast! Richard and Olivia…" she stopped. "Oh, fuck…uh…" I felt my heart clench again. Obviously, he lied to me at the airport when he said she wasn't his wife.

"It's… It's okay," I said smiling sadly. It really fucking wasn't ok, but hey, I can't control things in the world. "So, I guess I know who bought the cottage then."

"Yeah, they redid the gardens with plants form the nursery. Looks nice, I guess," Mel smiled, trying to work out how to save the conversation.

"I'm not angry, Mel," I said. "I promise you that, not with you. I just…" I sighed.

"You wish things worked out different, I know." She sighed. "Well, why don't you call him?"

"Can't, I don't have his number, remember?"

"Libby… I have his number." Mel offered

"I… I can't call him, not yet."

“Why not?”

“I don’t know how to tell him my baby is his…” My voice was a whisper, but I knew Mel had heard when she blurted out…

“WHAT THE FUCK?”

Mel looked at me aghast. "What the fuck do you mean 'the baby is his'?" She shook her head in bewilderment "What fucking baby?"

"That's two!" Adam's voice jeered in the background.

"Shut the fuck up, babe, I got a fucking girlfriend emergency, it's called for, completely and utterly fucking called for." Mel turned her head as she shouted back at him.

"I… I guess, when we did the horizontal mambo, we forgot protection…"

"You *forgot* protection?"

I felt shitty enough as it was, though I wanted this baby, this was in a way my second chance at something I'd been denied all those years ago… *Motherhood.*

"Mel…" I said softly, my throat closing up as her barrage continued.

"How could you forget protection! I mean, come on, out of all the guys you've shagged in your life, you never once forgot to get him to cover his knob! How the fuck do you do something like that? How are you going to be able to support yourself and a baby?"

"Mel…" I tried again to get her attention.

"Of the two of us, I mean, come on, Libby… You're a career girl, always have been! What are you going to do? Abort? Adopt? Like seriously, you can't take care of a baby, hell girl, you can barely take care of yourself after a Friday night. How are you going to cope with poop and vomit and screaming, and late fucking nights, especially when the father isn't there?"

It seemed Mel was projecting her unvoiced problems onto me. But still… It made me think.

She was fucking right. *How* did I expect to be able to take care of an eating, screaming poop and vomit machine?

"Well?" Mel asked, seemingly impatient to have an answer right then and there.

"I gotta go…" I said as I ended the connection, the skype logo stared back at me, not as accusing as Mel had been. I put my hands over my face and cried.

Zane came in shortly after, and closed the laptop lid.

"Hey, sweetheart, here, you need this." He smiled softly, handing me a cup of tea. I took a sip.

"Blergh… What the fuck is this?" I said, scrunching my nose up in distaste.

"Decaf."

"Ew… It's toxic, I need my caffeinated tea back…"

"Sorry sweetie, after living with a pregnant Mel for so long, its second nature, nothing but good food and decaf tea and coffee for you now. You've got another life to care about now so you gotta be eating right."

"Great, just fucking great," I groused, but my sneaky hands slid around my middle.

"Just wait until you crave pickles and ice-cream with horseradish and chocolate sauce on top.

"Get the fuck out, that's disgusting!"

"Mel swore by it."

"She never told me that," I mused.

"That one wasn't her finer moments, but she got it. I guess she was embarrassed about that particular selection."

"What, and the sardines with port wine jelly and custard wasn't?"

"Oh my god, if you *ever* pull that one on me… I'll… I'll disown you woman!" Zane made a gagging sound as he walked out of the living room and towards the bathroom. "Fuck, just thinking about that makes me want to puke!"

I laughed my arse off as he slammed the bathroom door and began to retch.

****

I lay back on the sheet covered reclining seat, or whatever the fuck they called it. A tiny little peanut shaped thing was on the screen, blurry, but fucking there. And the heartbeat… Sweet fucking hell, I was in love as soon as I heard it. The ultrasound tech printed off a copy of the ultrasound for me, and circled the peanut-shaped thing that was my baby in a red marker.

I gazed at the image back at the apartment. I was now on the edge of my first trimester. I'd been lucky that my morning sickness was minimal, the same couldn't have been said for poor Mel. She suffered terribly, according to Zane. I didn't want to speak to her yet, not after our spat. I wasn't ready. But damnit, I knew I was ready for this baby.

I'd been working at Laura Rose's studio, doing photoshoots for her while she was in rehab for her cocaine addiction. I worked differently to how she did. I used the technique's I learned when I was working with nervous brides or debutantes, and the models loved it. Calm music played, giving them a more natural look, which didn't need to be 'photoshopped' as much. The atmosphere was definitely calmer, no shouting, no stress. And the rise in pay was fucking helpful, to say the least. But I wasn't really happy there.

My heart lay elsewhere. It was back home, in the UK.

I looked over at Zane… "I need to go home," I said softly.

Zane smiled. "We're almost there, sweetheart."

I put a hand over the small bump that would undoubtedly grow bigger in the weeks to come.

"No, Zane… I want to go *home*."

Zane smirked. "Took you long enough."

"What the fuck?"

I shook my head. "You knew all this time, didn't you, that I wanted to go home."

"Well, you kept watching the BBC channels on the cable service, plus you are always looking at the UK newspapers online. And I've spotted you checking out Mel's website for the nursery too many times. You're pining for home, I understand."

"I miss her." I admitted.

"Anyone else?"

"I…" I closed my mouth. I didn't want to admit it, but fuck, yes, I did miss Richard, but I wasn't about to get my heart broken all over again. I'd avoid him. Danny knew some people in London where I could get work as a photographer. Maybe I could even go back to selling my prints, even set up a website to sell them from. After all, I was going to be a single mum soon.

"It's okay, sweets. Mel says she can't wait to see you."

"Really?" I asked, tears pooling in my eyes…

Stupid fucking pregnancy hormones, I fucking cried at the stupidest things… Commercials, puppies, sunsets, homeless bums who stunk of piss and alcohol—those Zane steered me far, far away from. If it was even *remotely* sad, I bawled. I also started to have weird cravings, like Krispy Kreme doughnuts with mustard smothered all over the sugary coating, Ben and Jerry's ice cream— any flavour, partially melted with sardines to dip and devour… I think Zane is forever off any kind of ice cream after he caught me doing that and licking my fingers afterwards.

"Oh my god, it smells like bad porn in here…" he'd groused coming home and catching me sucking melted ice cream and sardine juice of my thumb. "Libby. What the hell are you *eating*?"

"Stuff."

"Stuff that smells like a porno grandma who hasn't showered in weeks." Once he saw what I was eating, he spent the next twenty minutes with his head over the loo while I simply dipped another sardine into the ice creamy, gooey-goodness.

"I got the ultrasound done today," I said, waving the little picture at him when he returned to the living room.

"Can I see?"

"Of course, you can, Aunty Zed." I smirked, patting the sofa beside me after I shifted the empty tins of sardines and the near-empty ice cream bucket. Zane squealed and snuggled up beside me. "There's the head… I think… And there's the arm…"

"Honey, you sure that's an arm? Looks an awful lot like…"

"I won't know the sex for at least another month, that's *if* I want to know," I said snuggling up to him as he slipped an arm around my shoulders.

"I still think that's a weenie…" He smirked, pointing at the spot.

"Arm…"

"Baby's arm holding an apple."

"Wanker…"

"It's a boy, and what a boy!"

"I bet you it's a sweet little girl, and not an icky fucking boy."

"Okay, I'll take that bet." Zane smirked, sticking his hand out.

"What? That it's a boy?"

"Yep, now you tell me what you're going to front for that bet."

"What?"

"Yep, put your money where your mouth is momma."

"Okay… I bet…" I thought for a moment… "Fifty pounds."

"Pfft. Come on, for a big, lifechanging thing like this…. Fifty pounds…"

"Okay smartarse… A big bottle of cognac?" I offered, knowing his penchant for the liquor.

"The good stuff?" His eyes glimmered.

"Like I can fucking afford a three-hundred-pound bottle of that crap. I'm an expectant mother!"

"Oh no, honey, this one is an 1862 cognac. It's like a thousand bucks or more."

"Seriously?" I asked, amazed that someone would pay that much for a bottle of alcohol.

"Absolutely, the *really, really* snobby stuff can go for the price of a new house."

"I'm an expectant fucking mother, you think I'm going to be able to afford a thousand-dollar bottle of booze? Fuck I'll probably need it after giving birth and the first few days of motherhood."

Zane chuckled.

I sighed. "Okay, then if I have to front you some expensive fucking grog, then you have to sort me out with a crib, a changing table and a rocking chair."

"Ooh! You're in the nesting phase already?" Zane squealed with giddy abandon.

I rolled my eyes at him. "No…" I denied, but secretly I was thinking about where I was going to live. I'd given up my flat's lease and my furniture was all in storage, so I'd need to find at least a two-bedroom flat to live in and then I'd have to see if Danny had work for me, like he promised. Fuck, this was going to be hard.

"So, got any idea on where we're going to live when we get back?" he asked.

"We?" I looked at him.

"Yep, 'we'. There's no fucking way I'm going to let you live on your own while 'up the duff'. Anything could happen." Zane put an arm around me, pulling me tight against his side. I sighed, enjoying the warmth of my friend's body.

"Thanks Zane."

"Anything for you, sweetie."

He reached forward and grabbed my laptop, pulling it towards him he flipped the lid open and turned it on. "Now, let's have a look at three-bedroom houses to rent."

He instantly searched for Miltonford properties, there was one that was perfect three-bedroom, two bathrooms and a little conservatory.

"That's perfect." Zane smiled.

"But Zane, that's for sale, not rent."

"I know," Zane replied, sitting back with a smirk.

"And there's already an offer on the house…" I pointed at the little red flag scrolling across the top of the listing."

"I know." He continued to smirk, leaning back against the couch, putting his arms behind his head in a relaxed pose.

"Zane…" I shook my head, trying to figure things out, until it hit me like a bell from above.

"You fucking bought the place?"

"Yep." He grinned at me. "I put in an offer on the place about two days ago. They need to update the website. The offer was accepted this morning. We own a house!"

"But…but… How can you afford that?"

"While we were back in merry old England, my father passed away," Zane said, his eyes showed a touch of sadness.

"Oh, I'm so sorry." I reached over and wrapped my arms around him in a consoling hug.

"It's okay. He was a rich old bastard who didn't approve of my 'lifestyle choice'," he said, putting the last two words in finger quotes.

"Oh."

"Yeah, basically told me to get my 'faggoty ass out of his sight and never darken his doorstep again'. When I came out at sixteen. I was homeless for about two weeks before my aunt Jessie found me and took me in. She and her girlfriend were very understanding of my situation, having gone through the same with my grandparents." Zane sighed, putting an arm around my shoulders.

"My aunts looked after me until I was eighteen, then I left and moved out to LA, away from all those bigoted fuckers back home. My aunt told me he'd died while I was over at Mel's place, just before Aaron was born. She'd said that no-one was named in his will, so she took some papers to court to claim the inheritance on my behalf, saying she was his only living relative, and then deposited the old man's money into my bank. So, you can imagine my surprise when she sent me a message, saying there's something in there from my father's estate, and it was pretty much all of his money."

"How much?" I asked, then realised how rude that sounded. "Oh, never mind, forget I asked."

"Three-point-four million," Zane said, as if it were nothing.

"Three-point-four million dollars?" Holy shit… I was snuggled up to a gay millionaire.

Who had just bought us a house in England.

What. The. Fuck!

Chapter Thirty-Six

I looked at myself in the mirror, rubbing my hands over my swelling belly.

Yep, there was a definite bump there, and it was growing.

I was now at my twenty-fourth week. I'd been away from home for almost five months now, and I was feeling homesick. Though we had planned on going to the UK two weeks ago, Zane's Aunt Jessica had discovered she had stage three breast cancer, which had sadly progressed to stage four. After they'd found the first lumps, it had spread through her body at a rapid rate.

Zane had spent many hours at her bedside as the fucking disease took another good woman down. His aunt's wife sat on the other side, softly weeping as her beloved slowly succumbed to the pain.

I kept vigil with them when they both were too exhausted, both emotionally and physically, letting them go and rest, or shower or eat.

"Libby," Jessica called to me as I sat reading a pregnancy magazine while Zane and Claudia, Jessica's wife both went and refreshed themselves.

"Yes, Jess?" I leaned forward, reaching out and taking her frail, pallid hand.

"I want to ask a favour of you."

"Anything."

"I want you to take some photos of us, of me and Claudie, and Zane. Can you? I don't want them to remember me in this horrible state."

"Of course," I said, my mind quickly going over everything I'd need. "When do you want to do this?"

"Soon, but not here. I don't want to die here." She sighed. "One of the orderlies here, he helps terminals like me pass easily. I have the drug that will ease me out of this pain and let me die with some dignity." She sighed softly. "But I don't want to let Zane or Claudie see me suffer. I want to go out on my own terms, happy, free, loved. I want a good day. Can you help with that?"

I nodded, feeling the tears prickle against my eyes as I closed them. "I can, and it would be a pleasure and an honour to help you."

"Good. Thank you." Jess lifted my hand to her lips and kissed the back, before she pressed it against the dry skin of her cheek. "Can you organise a few things for me? There's a park where Claudie and I got married, I'd like to be there when it is time. I'll convince her to take me out of this hole for a day, get the paperwork done."

"You know, this can implicate me in your death," I said, whispering the words.

"You didn't know a fucking thing about this." She smirked. "I only asked you to give me a good day and be my photographer, so my loved ones can have some good memories before I die."

I nodded. "Okay, one good day coming up." I smiled.

"Hey, you two. What are you up to?" Zane asked, coming in with a decaf tea for me and a strong cappuccino for himself.

"Nothing. Aunty Jess was just telling me what a shit you were in your teens," I said, reaching for the decaf, though it wasn't normal tea, it was still hot and sweet, and almost perfect.

Jess laughed. "Wasn't he just." She smiled at the memory. "I want to tell you how much I love you, Zane. If I had been able to have kids, I'd have wanted them to be as wonderful as you. It doesn't matter how you were raised, Zane, it's how you became the person you are today. A good, generous and loving young man, who deserves more than he got in life."

Claudia entered, her hair was still damp from her shower, and wearing clean clothes.

"Right, now we're all here," Jess said. "I want to get the fuck out of here. I want us to have a nice day together. Libby is going to help with her photography skills. Zane I want a nice picnic lunch, Champagne, oysters, the works! And Claudie, I just want you there with me." She gazed lovingly at her wife who looked ready to burst into tears.

"When did you want to do this?" Zane asked.

"In a couple of days, then, we can all rest." She smiled softly.

****

The next couple of days went by in a blur, the knowledge that Jess was going to leave this world by her own hand this afternoon bore down on me, but I had seen the pain in her face, the darkened circles of exhaustion and pain under her eyes. I'd seen the weakness sapping her strength as the horrible disease that is cancer took days, weeks, months and years from her life.

Now, at her choice, she had only hours.

The sun was bright, the day beautiful, warm but not too warm. One of the make-up artists I knew from my job working for Laura Rose had come over and managed to give Aunt Jess some colour to her face. Her eyes were even brighter than normal. She revelled in the warmth of the sunlight, breathing in the sweet, fresh air.

Just getting out of the hospital had been an effort. At first the staff were dead set against it, until she managed to convince her doctor that it wouldn't do her any more harm than what the cancer was doing already, and that she needed one good day before it all went to shit. Her doctor agreed, and we were allowed out of the hospital. Aunt Jess changed into a nice pants suit, and the IV of pain medicine hanging from a stand attached to her wheelchair as we left the sterile and impersonal hospital environment.

Three flute glasses of champagne and one of orange juice (for me) were clinked, and toasts were made as we sat underneath the tree where Jess and Claudia had taken their vows five years ago. Jess slipped the drug into her glass. Though we all saw it, we would deny it.

"It's time," she said softly.

"Time? What was that you put in your glass, Jess?" Claudia asked.

"You know what it is, baby. It's my last hurrah." Jess smiled, she downed the champagne. "I've got about five to ten minutes left. Now, come, let me hold you until I go."

Claudia's eyes brimmed with tears, she let out a sob before she slipped in behind her wife's back and held her, speaking softly. Zane and I kissed her on the cheek, our final goodbyes, before we stood, and left the two women alone in Jess's final moments.

I watched as Claudia hugged the stull body of her beloved wife, sobbing, heartbroken.

"I wonder if I'll ever have a love like that?" Zane asked the cosmos.

"She told me she was going to do this," I said, feeling my own tears break free. "Maybe I should have told her no, but, you know, she was ready."

"What the Fuck?"

Zane looked at me, aghast. "She told you she was going to do this? Why didn't she tell me?"

"I don't know, Zane," I said, packing away my cameras. "Maybe she didn't want to stress you out."

"But you're pregnant, Libby. The stress of this knowledge, not to mention any repercussions of this, you could go do jail."

I held up a hand, stopping him. "Stop. She wanted this. She did this because she was suffering, Zane. Watching you and Claudie enduring her death was killing her emotionally, she didn't want that."

I turned and looked at the couple, one holding the other, who lay as still as a stone. I knew the drug had done its work.

"Go to your Aunt Claudie, she needs you, Zane," I said, placing a hand on his shoulder. He nodded, pulling me in for a hug before he turned to comfort his desolate aunt.

****

The funeral was a week later. Zane held up well, and there was nothing said about her death away from the hospital. Apparently, it was done quite a bit by other terminally ill patients who were nearing their end. A final, good day with their loved ones, then a sip from a poisoned cup, and oblivion. Unconsciously, I kept my hands protectively over my baby bump, though protecting my unborn baby from whom, I still didn't know.

We left for the UK a week later, finally setting foot on the plane, Zane getting us first class tickets. I felt nauseous on the flight over, plus I had to pee, like, every half an hour. Added to that, I couldn't take a crap, and, to make things worse down that end of the world, I had fucking haemorrhoids! It hurt to fart, and I didn't trust a burp. Heartburn was kicking my arse.

I was miserable.

Until I felt that first flutter.

"Oh my god…" I said, sitting up, putting a hand to my big belly.

"What?" Zane jerked awake, spilling his packet of nuts everywhere.

"I felt something."

"What? A contraction? You're too early!" Zane began to panic, reaching up and pressing the call button for the stewardess to attend his seat.

"No, you tosser." I smiled. "The baby kicked." I grabbed his hand and placed it over my bump. "Wait hang on…" the flutter came again, stronger

"There!" I smiled. Zane had a curious look on his face.

"Fucking. Wow." He smiled, his eyes as wide as saucers.

"Is everything all right?" The stewardess asked as she stopped by Zane's seat.

"Oh, yeah, sorry, false alarm," Zane said sheepishly

"Baby's kicking, and he thought I was having contractions." I smiled, shaking my head.

The stewardess nodded. "No, problem, would you like some more nuts?" She indicated to the scattered remains of Zane's snack.

"Oh, yeah, uh, sorry." He leaned down to scoop the scattered snacks back into their packet, before handing them to the stewardess.

"No problem." She left.

"Oops," Zane chuckled.

"Arse." I snorted, before I settled down and tried to sleep. The baby kicked again, right in my bladder. "FUCK!" I got to my feet. "Move, now, out the fucking way, pregnant lady, gotta pee!"

"But you just peed, like ten minutes ago." Zane got out of his seat to let me and my belly past.

"Yeah, I did, but the little bastard just kicked me, and now I gotta pee again!" I stumbled slightly, as the plane hit some slight turbulence.

The seat-belt sign dinged.

"Ladies and Gentlemen, this is Captain Franks. We're heading into some inclement weather, and the seatbelt sign has been turned on. We'd like you to please, fasten your seatbelts, as this could get a little rocky. Nothing to worry about, it's a very mild storm but we are expecting some turbulence."

"Oh, great," I grumbled as I held a hand under my belly to try to pull up some of the weight from my bladder.

"Miss, you'll need to return to your seat," a stewardess said, stopping me from moving forward.

"I need to use the lavatory," I said, trying to move forward.

The stewardess put a hand up. "I'm sorry miss, but you have to return to your seat."

I saw red. "Look lady, I am twenty-six weeks pregnant, I'm peeing like a racehorse every half hour, and right now, the baby just kicked me square in the fucking bladder. If I don't get to the lavatory right now, there's going to be a mess, and I'm not sodding cleaning it up."

The stewardess sighed. "Fine, but the first-class lavatory is out of order. Someone clogged it up, so you'll have to use one in the economy section. It's down the back of the plane."

"The back?"

"Right up the back."

"Shite," I muttered as I waddled down the aisle towards the curtained section that separated first class from the unwashed masses.

Children cried with ear-piercing wails and men who were almost as fat as I was, were squished against poor little old ladies. I groaned as I waddled through, my body screaming out for release as I held tight. The door to the lavatory in the back was in sight. But so was the 'engaged' sign.

"Nooo!" I moaned as I waddled up to the lavatory door. I knocked as politely as I could.

"Someone's in here!" A man's voice called.

"Yeah, fuck off!" A woman's voice joined in followed by moans and rhythmic thumping against the door. The fuckers were joining the Mile-High Club just as I was trying not to piss my fucking pants

"You've got to be fucking kidding me." I whimpered as I crossed my legs as a bit of turbulence jostled the plane. "Hurry the fuck up, pregnant lady, gotta pee!" I banged my fist on the door.

The banging got harder, the moans louder. My urge to pee became uncontrollable as the baby kicked again, hitting my bladder.

"Oh… Oh no…" I moaned as I felt my body give in and the sweeping warm wetness covered my crotch and thighs. "No, no, no, no, no, no!" I cried softly at the state of my light-coloured pants, which now had a dark, damp patch in the crotch.

"Yes, yes, yes, OH GOD EDDIE! YES!" Came the scream of rapture from the lavatory as the thumping finally finished.

The door opened a moment later and a dishevelled redhead and a portly bald man in a cheap business suit ambled out. "All yours doll." He winked.

"Fuckers," I grumbled, heading in to the lavatory to try to clean myself up. I closed the door only to find they'd left a 'present' in the sink. Their used condom.

"What the Fuck…"

Chapter Thirty-Eight.

Thankfully, the stewardesses were helpful, and Zane was able to grab a spare pair of pants and underwear from my carry-on. I sobbed at my misfortune in the privacy of the lavatory, holding myself up against the wall to counteract the turbulence. Of course, little mini-me decided to settle down after my lavatory fiasco and I rested uncomfortably for the rest of the flight while Zane slept soundly.

We landed at Heathrow a little bit delayed by the storm, which was worse than the pilot had told us. We'd had to fly around it, all the way down to Wales before we were able to get a path into Heathrow.

I was exhausted, having barely slept or eaten on the flight.

I noticed the pudgy asshole who had joined the Mile-High club kissing and embracing a woman with three sweet little girls. I stalked over to him.

"You've got a lot of fucking nerve, shagging some redhead slapper in the lavatory while your wife and daughters are waiting for you," I said with a snarl.

"What? Eddie? What's she talking about surely you've not gone back to her again?"

"Oh, again. Eh, Eddie?" I turned to the wife. "Sweetheart, once a cheater, always a sodding cheater."

I turned away from the man who was now redder than one of Mel's roses with embarrassment, and the haranguing he was getting from his good wife.

Zane had watched from the luggage carousel, collecting our bags. He laughed as I returned to his side.

"Libby, that was the fucking best!" he snorted with laughter, piling our bags onto the trolley.

We passed through Immigration, the customs officers stamping our passports. A joyous shout erupted as we passed through the doors to British soil.

I looked up to see Mel, Robbie, Adam, who held little-but-not-so-little Aaron, and Mel's parents. Robbie and his mum held a "Welcome Home Libby and Zane" banner. I smiled.

"Oh wow. This is f—," I stopped, remembering I'd have to pay up if I dropped the F-bomb, "flipping amazing!" I smiled.

Mel rushed forward, her belly slightly bigger than mine. We bumped bellies like a pair of idiots wearing those ridiculous inflatable sumo wrestler suits.

"Oh, my god, look at you!" Mel gushed.

"Look at me? Nuh-uh Mel! Look at *you!*" I smiled.

"Oh, you've seen me like this. So tell me, twenty-five? Twenty-six?" She pulled back from my preggers-hug attempt and looked down at the swollen belly that I sported.

"Six, almost seven." I sighed. "It gets easier, right? Please, tell me it gets easier?"

Mel laughed. "You were there the last time, remember?"

"Uh, yeah kinda." There were some things I was struggling with remembering, like where I put the car keys, and appointments that I'd made but forgot about until my phone reminded me.

"Got baby pics?" Mel asked.

"I do." I reached into my purse and pulled out a few copies of the few ultrasounds I'd had.

"Oh my gosh!" she pointed to the questionable limb "is that a…?"

"La-la-la-la-la-la I can't hear you, no it's not a weenie la-la-la-la-la!" I sang, putting my hands over my ears.

Zane laughed. "We have a bet going on, if it's a boy, I get a three-hundred-pound bottle of cognac, if it's a girl, I get her baby furniture."

"Well, we will just have to wait and see who wins then," Adam said, bouncing Aaron in his arms.

"It's a boy." Mel smirked.

"Oh fu-*fudge*, not you too!"

"I'm having another boy." Mel grinned.

"My sympathies," I said without any real sympathy.

Mel looked at the ultrasound. "Can I keep this one?" she asked.

"Sure, I have a couple of copies spare."

"I did that too, made copies."

"I know, you gave them out as cards for your baby shower, remember?"

"That reminds me! We are having a double shower, you and me!"

"What? A double baby shower?"

"That's what I said!" Mel smiled, as she linked her arm in mine and we waddled through the airport.

"When?"

"In two weeks, then the week after, we celebrate me getting another year older!" Mel cheered.

"Bloody hell, you're in good spirits."

"I got my best friend back home where she belongs!" Mel grinned, pulling me in for an awkward hug. I felt the familiar fullness in my bladder that heralded even more doom for my pants if the loos were all occupied again

"Ugh, I gotta pee, and I'm dying for a shower."

"Yeah, we don't want another accident like you had on the plane. I don't think we have any more pants that are in easy reach." Zane smirked.

"Why? What happened on the plane?" Mel asked.

"Zane…" I warned.

"She peed herself, while a couple were joining the Mile-High club in the only working bathroom on the plane."

I felt my jaw drop. "Zane!"

Oh, my fucking god, I was mortified. Seriously?

What. The. Fuck?!

Zane, Robbie and Adam had left us girls to prepare for our double baby shower. Mel's mother had fluffed and fussed around us while we drank mocktails and 'helped' by bitching about our pregnant bodies.

"Oh my god, I need to burp and fart, but I'm too scared to," Mel said.

"Why?" I asked, resting my feet on the ottoman. My ankles were swollen and my back ached, and perched under my arse was one of those doughnut pillows to rest my weary haemorrhoids.

"I'm scared I'll shit myself."

I snorted my mocktail and ended up laughing and coughing so hard that I almost peed myself—almost.

"Well, that was a little too close for comfort. I'm heading to the loo."

"Not if I get there first, bitch," Mel said, hauling herself up with a grunt.

"Like hell woman. I'm not as fat as you. I got speed on my side!" I hauled my own pregnant body up out of the chair, the pillow under my ass sliding to the floor at my feet.

Mel and I waddled with as much speed as we could awkwardly muster towards the nearest bathroom. Though there were plenty in the house, Mel's place being a fucking mansion and all, it was still the thrill of the race and the taste of victory that spurred us on in our childish dash to the toilet.

"Don't be too long girls, our guests will be here any minute!" Mrs Whittaker called.

"Yes Mum!" Mel shouted behind me.

I squealed and giggled as I tottered on my swollen ankles towards my goal, the silver-trimmed handle of one of the downstairs bathrooms.

"I win!" I shouted, as I turned the door handle and flung myself inside.

"Cow!" Mel teased banging on the door good naturedly before she shuffled off to the next nearest loo.

I spent a little more time than I anticipated in the bathroom, nature's callings and all that. I finished up and headed back to the living room where the party was starting. There were several unfamiliar faces there, though one that was vaguely familiar, but I wasn't sure where I'd seen her. I settled back down on my seat, Mrs Whittaker had placed the doughnut pillow back in its place for me before I eased myself back down.

I nodded and smiled to those women I knew, and smiled in what I hoped was a friendly manner to those few I didn't. Mel squealed and hugged the strangely familiar woman.

"I'm so glad you could make it, thanks for coming."

"I wouldn't miss it, after all, you've done so much to help us these past few months."

"Well, we're all here. Excellent!" Mrs Whittaker smiled as she came in with a box.

"What's that, Mum?"

"Oh, it's a cake that Alexandra dropped off for you. She said she was sorry, but she had to deliver a birthday cake to a ten-year old's party, else she'd have been able to stay."

"Well, I'm sure she outdid herself, like she usually does." Mel smiled, while Mrs Whittaker put the cake down on the coffee able. "We'll dig into that soon girls, first, let's play some games!"

"Okay so first game up is called: 'My Water Broke!'" Mrs Whittaker smirked, holding up a tray of cups. "We have these cute little plastic babies in ice cubes, these represent the time it takes for a baby to come along, now, we each take a cup, and the first one that melts wins!" She began to hand out the cups. "We have some beautiful chocolates as prizes. This one takes a while, so we'll get to our next game: 'Baby Price is Right!'"

We watched as Mrs Whittaker pulled away a tea-towel that covered a bunch of baby items, along with hand-written price tags that were lined up neatly in front of the items.

"Now, we need to guess which item cost what! Who wants to go first?"

After a few rousing rounds, Mel's mother began the next game, though it was a little icky, it was still ridiculously fun, 'Test the nappy.' We each had five nappies, and each had a gooey-brown mess within. We had to taste the contents of each nappy and identify what it was.

"Chocolate Pudding!"

"Milky Way!"

"Marmite!"

"Gravy—or I hope it is!"

"Choc-hazelnut spread!"

"What the hell are you crazy women doing?" Zane's voice carried over the laughter.

His face was priceless, he gazed at the crazy women in the room, each of us holding a nappy, some had brown gooey stuff on their face, Mel had chocolate pudding on her nose and a huge grin on her face. I licked the gravy from my lips.

"Well, how else do you expect us to figure out what the baby's been eating?" I asked, standing up with a huff. "Here, try it, tell me what you think." I grinned, offering up the nappy to Zane.

"You all are just crazy." He shook his head.

"Anyway, Adam said there was cake?" Zane reached for the box and flipped open the lid. His girlish scream echoed down the halls of Mel's mansion, had Aaron not been sleeping, he would have been woken by 'Aunty' Zee's girlish wail.

"OH MY GOD! WHAT THE FUCK IS THAT?" Zane was posed dramatically, his hands on his cheeks in shock, his eyes and mouth wide. "That's—oh my god, so disgusting. Even worse than the poopy diapers you were licking! I can't believe you're going to *eat* that!"

He retched and ran towards the bathroom I had raced Mel for not two hours before. Every woman got up and peered into the box.

The cake was an imitation of a woman giving birth. Showing the most intimate parts with a doll's head poking out. The uproarious laughter filled the room as Mel and I both hefted the cake out of the box and together we cut it, taking the doll's head off first, before we cut into the delicious cake beneath.

We all took a piece and settled out in the garden, enjoying the late afternoon sunshine.

The strange woman approached me. "Hello, you must be Libby? I've heard so much about you." She smiled, offering her hand. "I hear you're a wonderful photographer. I was wondering if you'd do some work for me?

I quickly dabbed the crumbs from the cake off my lips with a paper napkin and took the woman's offered hand. "Yes, that's me. Sorry, I didn't catch your name?"

"Oh, Olivia, Olivia Handcock."

Olivia fucking Handcock

Richar- *Cunstable* Dick's *wife* was here, was talking to me. Did she know? Did *He* know? Were they going to try to claim custody of my baby? My heart rate went up a few thousand beats per minute.

"Nice to meet you. If you'll excuse me, I'm not feeling too well." I was suddenly feeling pretty fucking poorly.

What the fuck was she doing here? I headed back inside and glanced back once I was in the shadows of the kitchen. She and Mel were chatting like old chums, even hugging and smiling,

Mel... The woman who was supposed to be my best friend was hugging the woman who was married to the man who had ripped my heart out.

What. The. Fuck?

I hid in my room for the rest of the day while the party wound down. My hands swelled up and I was so hot that I lay in my underwear on top of the bed with the overhead fan whirring away silently above me. I felt dizzy and nauseous and generally crap.

I'd drawn the curtains to shut out the world and its betrayers, and curled up in what was my best guess at a foetal position, my legs and arms protecting my baby from the woes of the world.

"Don't you worry, baby, Mumma's here. Mumma's going to make sure you are loved and cherished."

Unlike my own childhood, I was going to give this kid everything they'd need to be happy and healthy.

A few hours later, Zane knocked on the door. I'd been sleeping, trying to get rid of a headache that was verging on becoming a nasty migraine.

He flipped the light switch on and looked at me. I winced covering my eyes with my arm.

"Bugger off, Zane."

"Nope. Mel was worried about you, Okay? Apart from that gross ass cake, everything at the baby shower was fine, what gives sweetheart? Are you getting bitchy this far in your pregnancy?" he asked me before moving to my bedside.

"I'm really not feeling well, Zane," I muttered, another round of vertigo hitting me. I moaned. "Oh god, get the bucket."

I felt my stomach churn as Zane ran and grabbed the bin from the en suite bathroom, holding it under my chin as I puked up the cake and everything else I'd eaten.

"I thought your morning sickness was over?" Zane asked. "Honey, are you coming down with something? Your face is swollen a bit."

"Dizzy…" I moaned, clutching the edge of the bin as I heaved again.

"Stay right there, I'm going to get Mel." he said, leaving me in my misery.

Mel came soon after, followed by Adam who was holding Aaron.

Everything was blurry, and I just wanted everyone to stop talking so loud.

"Shh, not so loud, I have a splitting headache," I moaned.

"Honey, we're not talking loud at all. I think we need to get you to the doctor, you might have preeclampsia," Mel said, pressing a cool cloth to my head. She turned to Adam. "Baby, can you call ahead and see if Doctor Forrest is on tonight?"

I barely noticed Adam nod before Mel was bustling around my room, gathering a nightgown and a robe and getting Zane to help me get dressed. I felt floppy and dizzy and everything was just blergh.

Adam and Zane carried me 'chair style' to the jeep, while Mel called her mother to come and care for Aaron while they took me to the hospital. Zane sat beside me in the car, an ice cream bucket at the ready in case I was sick again.

The hospital admitted me after running a few tests, and the doctor determined that I indeed had preeclampsia. The next two days were a battery of tests and ultrasounds to ensure the baby was okay.

"Pee into this cup."

"Let's take your blood pressure,"

"How are you feeling today? Any changes?"

"This gel will be cold."

"Here, take these, they'll lower your blood pressure."

I was so sick of hospitals, but at least I was able to pee on command, thanks to the melon sitting in my belly. Finally, I was being released back into the wild, with orders for bed rest and to take things easy until the baby was born

Zane was wheeling me out of the hospital entry in the required wheelchair when an ambulance came screaming up to the emergency entrance. A police car came screaming in to the car park, parking in the police parking space and none other than *Cuntstable Dick* got out. He didn't even spare me a glance as he raced inside, following the paramedics and the unfortunate person on the gurney.

"Get me home, please Zane," I murmured.

"Okay sweetheart."

"Hey, how long until we get the new place?" I asked him.

"Not long now, another month then we can move in."

"Good, I can't wait. I don't like being underfoot at Mel's place," I admitted.

"Oh honey, she loves having you there, you know that. Besides she's missed you."

I grunted, it certainly didn't fucking seem like it the way she was hugging and laughing with Olivia fucking Handcock.

I was quiet on the drive back to Mel's and we came into the kitchen to a sombre mood.

"What?"

"Lisa was injured and has been flown to London," Mel said, sitting at the table with a cup of tea.

"How?" I asked, settling down with a grunt in the seat next to her.

"Apparently, she and Richard had stopped a drunk driver. He tried to get away and he ran her over."

"Oh my god," I said, feeling horrible for the poor woman. "That must have been them at the hospital," I said, looking to Zane.

"We're going to send her some flowers and a card, though there's not much we can do right now, just wish, pray and hope for the best," Adam said, rubbing his wife's shoulders. He turned his attention to me. "You need to go rest, I've set up some movies in the media room for you, there's popcorn and chocolate, Mel, you should go join her."

Mel nodded and we both stood up. I took my best friend's hand and we waddled to the media room, where the title screen of a movie was waiting on the rear wall, the light from the roof-mounted projector shining in the darkness.

"She'll be okay." I said to Mel.

"Yeah, I hope so, she's such a wonderful person, gives her all to the community. So is Richard," she said trying to steer the conversation away from the morbid subject.

"Mel, don't."

"You need to tell him, if you don't." She paused.

“If I don’t tell him then what? You’ll tell him?”

“No, Olivia will.”

“What the fuck?”

Chapter Forty-One

"She knows, Libby. She even saw the ultrasound."

"Where the fuck did she get the ultrasound?" I asked, feeling my blood boil.

"From me," Mel admitted.

"Mel…" I stood up, the movie forgotten. "You fucking didn't."

"I did, Libby. He deserves to know. It's for your own good. You know this. You'll regret it otherwise."

"Yes, he does, and I'll tell him soon," I said.

"But when? When you're pushing that kid out? When it's his first birthday? When he asks who his daddy is?"

"When I'm good and fucking ready!" I shouted.

I turned and stormed out of the media room and up to my guest room I packed my shit and made some calls to a local motel. I wasn't going to fucking stay here any longer.

"Libby, what are you doing?" Zane asked.

"I'm fucking leaving. I've had it with everyone here. Everything they do, they say, or believe is for my own good. You know what? My fucking parents said that every time they beat me, every time my weak cunt of a father put his joint out on my arm. I know when I'm not welcome, Zane." I zipped up my bags and hauled them from the bed, feeling a slight twinge in my back. "Fuck," I moaned.

"Libby, stop right now, you'll hurt the baby," Zane said sternly.

I stopped and looked at him. In my anger, I hadn't even considered the little one growing inside me.

"Oh fuck." I sat down heavily on the bed, the bag forgotten at my feet. "I'm a terrible mother." I burst into tears.

"Libby, no, you're not a terrible mother." Zane sat beside me, his arms going around my heaving shoulder as I sobbed. "You're going to be a kickass mom who loves her kid to bits."

"What if I tell him, and he doesn't want to be a part of the baby's life?" I sobbed, my words broken between trying to breathe through my snotty nose and the tears that cascaded down my cheeks.

"Then that's his choice. You can't say you didn't try, unless you don't try at all." He hugged me tighter. "Listen, we have Mel's party coming up next week. He's going to be there, why don't you tell him then?" I nodded.

There was a soft knock at the door. "Libby? Can I come in, please?" Mel's voice was as broken as mine.

I nodded. Zane got up and let Mel in, leaving us alone.

She looked as bad as I felt. "Fuck I'm so sorry, I should have told you before. At the baby shower, Olivia, she saw your ultrasound, you know, they have your name on it. She knew you and Richard were together, so she put two and two together and realised it was his baby. She promised she wouldn't tell him, but you have to tell him yourself." She placed a hand on my belly. "And soon. Don't leave it too long, he's already missed out on a lot with you. He loves you, so much."

"He's married to her though, what if they want to take custody of the baby once its born?"

"No, he's not. They were separated, and their divorce came through last week. They wouldn't dream of taking your baby away from you. They aren't that kind of people, Libs."

"Then why is she here?"

"That's something you'll have to ask her, but for now, I think we both need to rest. You've had a bad trot over the last few days old girl, we don't need you to have that baby early."

I nodded and settled down on the bed. Zane came back in and put my clothes back.

****

Bed rest totally sucked, though I did sneak down to the kitchen a few times and helped peel potatoes for dinner, until Zane ushered me back with the clucking of his tongue like a disgruntled matron. He could see how utterly bored I was, so he brought up baby and House and Garden magazines, hoping I'd find ideas for the nursery.

I couldn't wait to move into our new house—I picked neutral colours, lemons and pastel greens. I still hadn't asked the baby's sex, even though the ultrasound technician could easily tell what it was by this point. I didn't want to know, after all, if it was a girl, I'd have some lovely new furniture from Zane for my little princess to enjoy. Otherwise, Aunty Zee would be getting an expensive bottle of cognac.

We'd also heard that Lisa was going to pull through, though it would be some time before she would be able to return to work, for that, I was thankful.

****

I relaxed in a garden lounge watching Aaron playing in the garden. The little bugger was growing so fast and was crawling on chubby hands and knees. I looked forward to a similar scene about a year from now, watching as my own child played in our garden.

Mel came over with a glass of juice in each hand, passing me one, while the boys set up the portable marquee for Mel's birthday bash. I'd been having a few twinges in my back recently, and was having more trouble sleeping, though I was now at the thirtieth week, the time seemed to be ticking by fast. Mel was due two weeks before me, and was bigger.

We took our 'supervisor' roles very seriously, cajoling and teasing the men as they set up the marquee, and trestle tables. Caterers from London were arriving and setting up. Mel's party was going to be a nice affair, but I felt exhausted and my back ached terribly. "I'm going to go lay down for a while," I said.

Mel nodded. "Okay, I'll send someone up to check on you later."

I nodded as I headed back inside, waddling slowly up the stairs to my room where I collapsed onto the bed and snuggled up to a pillow, supporting my body against its fluffiness.

I woke to a kiss on my cheek and a scent that was familiar to me. "Hmm?" I murmured.

"Libby." Richard's voice came to me in the dark.

"What?" I sat up, just as a searing pain ripped through my belly.

"Oh fuck…" I whimpered, clutching my belly.

"Are you all right, Libby? Why is the bed all wet?" Richard's voice sounded a little panicked.

"Wet?" I asked, looking down. Sure enough, the bed and my dress were soaked.

"Oh shite… It's too early."

"Too early?" Richard asked, looking confused.

"Richard, my water broke. I'm having our baby."

He paled. "It's coming now?" he asked.

"I nodded, wincing as another contraction bit into me.

 "What the fuck?!"

"Oh my god, oh my god, oh my god!" Zane chanted as Richard held my hand in the back seat of Mel's Range Rover. Robbie drove like a maniac to the hospital where I was whisked away to a delivery room.

"Richard! I want Richard and Zane!" I begged, I was terrified for my baby.

"Who is the father, honey?" a nurse asked.

"Richard, but I want Zane here too. He's my support person." I moaned as another contraction hit. "It's too fucking early, way too fucking early," I cried.

A nurse came and dabbed my tears. Two panicking males burst through the door, surgical masks and gowns covering them as they ran to my side. Richard on one, Zane taking the other as I huffed and moaned with each contraction getting closer and closer.

"How far along are you honey?"

"Just at thirty weeks," I panted.

"She has preeclampsia," Zane said. "She was in the hospital for it only last week."

The nurse nodded. "Well it looks like this little one wants to come early."

She moved aside for the doctor to examine me.

"You're just about ready Miss Hastings," he said. He turned to the nurse. "Have the NICU ready."

"Yes doctor." The nurse moved out of my line of sight, but I could hear everything happening, the beeping of the heart monitor they'd hooked me up to, Richard's fast breathing, the way he gripped my hand.

"Richard." I panted. "I'm sorry I didn't tell you before… I was so afraid."

"I know, it's all right. We have a second chance here Libby. If you want to take it, I'll be here for you, and our baby." He pulled his mask down and kissed my hand. I gripped his fingers tight as another contraction hit, it was a big one.

"Okay, Miss Hastings, I think we're ready to bring this little one into the world. On the next one, I need you to push."

He looked up over my splayed legs. I nodded. I felt it hit me like a fucking Mack truck. I squeezed Richard's fingers and cried out as I pushed, sweat beading on my forehead as I worked to bring my baby into the world. Another two more pushes and I heard the mewling of our son.

"Oh… My god…" Zane whimpered before he collapsed into a dead faint on the delivery room floor.

"Looks like we have a fainter," the doctor chuckled. "Hey mum and dad, here's your baby boy."

They placed him gently on my chest before they whisked him away to the NICU.

Richard looked at me, tears shining in his eyes. "Libs, he's beautiful, he's perfect, he's ours." He leaned forward, and kissed me, his lips so tender and filled with love that I began to weep. I raised my hand and pulled him closer against me.

"I'm sorry," I sobbed.

"Shh, it's all right, we have a lot to talk about," he promised, leaning back and wiping my eyes.

"Huh? What happened?" Zane asked groggily as a nurse waved something under his nose to rouse him.

"You fainted, you pillock," I chuckled.

"Really? Damn. What was it?"

"A bottle of cognac."

"Woohoo!" Zane cheered.

"A bottle of cognac?" Richard asked, confused.

"Zane and I had a bet, if it was a girl he'd buy the furniture for the nursery and put it together, if it was a boy, I'd buy him a bottle of cognac."

The doctors finished up with me cleaning me and checking me over for any issues from the preeclampsia, which I was assured would clear up now I've had the baby, and I was wheeled out to the maternity ward.

"When can I see him again?" I asked. Richard walked beside me, his hand clasped with mine

"We'll have him in there for a little while, until we know he's grown a little bit more, a few weeks, more depending on if there's any complications."

Richard nodded. I felt my heart rate spike. "Complications?"

"Your son is premature, but hopefully he'll be fine. He might have a few little things that might crop up here or there, but neonatal medicine has come a long way," the nurse said as the orderlies helped me into bed. "Now, we want you to rest."

I nodded and closed my eyes. Richard lay his head down on the bed beside me, and I rested my fingers over his hair, stroking softly until I drifted off from exhaustion.

I woke up alone.

"Richard?" I called softly, trying to not disturb the other sleeping mothers.

A nurse looked up from the nurses' station across from my room. She came in and smiled. "You're looking for your husband? He's with your son in the NICU. Did you want to go visit him too?"

I nodded, eager to get to my boy. The nurse helped me out of bed and into a wheelchair. She called for an orderly who wheeled me down to the NICU, where Richard was sitting beside a clear plastic crib, a hand inside the ports, and our son clutching a finger.

The orderly wheeled me in.

"Hey," I said, looking in on our baby.

His red wrinkled skin made him look like a miniature old man who had spent too many days out in the sun. He had a small tube in his nose, affixed with a clear tape to his tiny cheek. He looked so small, so fragile

"This is a gift, Libs, you can't understand how precious this is to me," he said, softly, with tears in his eyes.

"I'm so sorry I didn't tell you."

"I understand, you were afraid. Mel told me you saw Olivia and I going to a jewellery store." He sniffed.

"I did. I saw you hug and kiss her, and I know she called you a few times."

"We were going through a separation and divorce. I wasn't there for her when she needed me." He paused, as if trying to find the courage to say what he had to, to help me to understand.

"We had a daughter, her name was Daisy. She was beautiful, but she died when she was two months old. She died from SIDS." He wiped his eyed again, keeping his gaze on our son. "After the funeral, I lost myself in work, never thinking on how it affected her, only caring about my next big job, the next arrest. I came home one night to find dinner on the table, and her things all gone. She left me, and I deserved it."

What. The. Fuck?

Chapter Forty-Three

"You didn't deserve that, you were both grieving in your own way."

"We went our separate ways, and she filed for divorce. Then, shortly after I'd met you she called me, asking for help. She'd wanted to find a nice little place to set up as a Bed and Breakfast. It was always one of her dreams. I owed her for being a shitty husband, and she had no-one else to turn to. Her parents were both dead and she was an only child. So, I helped her. Gave her a place to stay while we looked at properties, and then your old cottage came up, and it was perfect, I know this because, well, I'd helped clean it up, remember?"

I nodded, remembering I watched the sweat glistening off his muscular arms, and wanting to find a nice, private, shady thicket and have my wicked way with him.

"Then we were lucky enough to get it at auction. It went for a good price too, even if I say so myself. After you left, I worked on helping Liv get the bed and breakfast set up, fixing the cottage, doing the gardens. You wouldn't recognise it now. Mel kept me up to date with you in LA, and I can't tell you how many times I wanted to jump on a plane and come see you, to try to get you to come back so we can work things out." He looked at me, eyes hopeful. "Tell me, please, Libs, is there still a chance for us? Even if there's not, I still want to be part of his life."

I took his free hand, not wanting him to lose the connection to our boy. "Yes, Richard, I never stopped feeling for you, thinking of you even when I felt like you'd ripped my heart in two. It still was, and always will be all for you, even if you were a bit of a dick to start with."

He chuckled. "I know, and, well, I was just doing my job."

We were distracted by a soft knocking at the doorjamb. A nurse stood there with a soft smile on her face.

"Sorry to interrupt, but would you like to hold your son?"

"Abso-fucking-loutly." I smiled, Richard gently pulled his finger free of the baby's grasp and pulled free from the crib.

The nurse took our boy out and gently picked him up, cradling him a moment before she settled him into my waiting arms.

"Oh my god, he's so beautiful."

"We had to put a nasal-gastric tube in, so we could feed him." The nurse explained. "He'll be ready for a change of nappy soon, did Daddy want to do that?" she asked Richard.

"I've already done one." He said with pride.

"What? When?"

"While you were asleep, he needed a nappy change."

"You've been here with him all this time?" I asked, my heart melting.

"Between you and him, yes." He looked down at the little one I my arms. "Have you thought of any names yet?"

"Nope." I shook my head. "I didn't even know the sex until he came along."

"I'm sure we'll think of something soon." Richard smiled. A few hours later, we left our boy back at the NICU and returned to my room.

We had visitors. A room full of flowers and balloons had materialised. Zane was sitting in one of the two chairs, sipping coffee while Mel sat in the other. Adam, with little Aaron, Robbie,

Mrs Whittaker, and Mr Whittaker in his wheelchair, even Olivia, were all settled in my small room, the women perched on the bed.

"What's this, a bloody mother's conference?" I asked.

"That's one," Mel said, dropping a pound into a new jar before she handed it to me.

"What's this?" I asked.

"Well, you never let me give it to you at the baby shower, so this is as good a time as any." She smirked. I looked at the jar, in glittery letters, the label read 'Libby's Swear Jar'.

"Oh, come on, I don't swear that much!" I protested good naturedly.

"Honey, you swear more than a sailor on payday. That baby boy in there? You know what his first words will be? It's going to be Fu-." Zane said.

He stopped as I held the jar out to him, shaking it so the one pound rattled against the glass.

He poked his tongue out at me. I flipped him the bird. I turned to Olivia.

"I need to apologise to you for my behaviour."

"No, you don't," she said.

I shook my head. "Yes, I do. I wasn't aware that you and Richard weren't together anymore. I've had bad experiences in the past, where I've been the 'other woman' and hadn't realised it. I've treated you badly, based on a misconception, and I apologise."

"Libby, I don't want you to stress over it, it's fine. Richard should have told you before what was going on. I'm surprised he didn't. But I can understand, maybe he was afraid of what you might think, might do. We were both hurt before, by each other after we lost Daisy."

I stopped her. "He told me about that, I'm so sorry."

"Thank you, she's still part of us. I hope one day, Richard will tell her brother about her."

"I'll make sure he does, and besides, you're still part of the family, right?"

She looked at Richard, slightly confused.

"I'm not sure, I don't know what you mean."

"Well, I'd like you to be." I turned to Richard. "If that's fine with Richard?"

"Of course, Olivia, you'll always be part of the family."

She smiled. "Thank you, both so much." She hugged me, and then Richard. "Well, I'd best be off, I have some guests arriving tonight and I need to finish getting their room ready."

She said her goodbyes and left. I turned my attention to Mel.

"Did I ruin your party?" I asked her.

"No, actually, it was winding down when Richard came screaming down the stairs calling for help." She giggled. "How is he? Do you have pictures? A name?"

"Oh, no, I didn't get any pictures of him." I said, realising that I had done nothing of the sort.

"That's okay, I got a few." Richard smiled. "He's perfect, they think he'll be in there a few weeks until he's strong enough for the outside world, but with a mum like Libby, he'll be out sooner," he said, passing his phone around to show them the pictures of the baby.

Zane scooted off his seat and came to sit next to me on the bed. "When we get home, I got a surprise for you."

"Oh god," I said, knowing what some of Zane's surprises were like.

"You'll love it, I promise."

"Oh, now that makes me *really* scared to see it."

"Trust me." He winked.

'Trust me'

Really, Zane?

What The fuck?!

We left the hospital a month later with baby Andrew safe and secure in his carrier. Richard had spent almost every day at my bedside or at little Andy's while we changed and fed him. His nasal-gastric tube had been removed and he was still getting used to being breastfed, though the doctors were pleased with his progress and deemed him fit and well enough to go home, as long as we ensured we made weekly visits to his paediatrician and the maternity nurse to make sure he was growing enough.

Richard drove past the turn off that left town and would take us to Mel's place.

"Uh, you missed the turn," I said to him.

He smiled, taking my hand in his. He brought it to his lips and kissed it gently. We'd grown closer again since being reunited, and I felt the love beating in my heart every time I looked at him, and our son.

"No, I didn't." He smirked.

"Yes, you did, this isn't the way home."

"Oh, yes, it is." I shook my head in exasperation.

He turned another corner and pulled into a driveway. The house was familiar, then I realised, it was the house Zane had bought. "Oh crap, the cognac!" I had completely forgotten about it.

"I got you covered love." Richard leaned back and pulled a brown paper bag out from behind the front passenger seat.

He got out of the car and, like the gentleman he was, opened my side for me and helped me out. I moved to the back door, juggling my purse, the baby's nappy bag and the bottle of cognac in my arms.

"I'll get Andy out." He smiled, leaving me to right myself with my armloads.

With everyone and everything unloaded from the car, we made our way to the front door Zane opened it as we hit the first step.

"Welcome home, you two." Zane smiled, handing Richard the keys.

"Wait, what?"

"Zane has given us this house."

"Uh… He what?"

"It's yours sweetheart, my gift to both of you, well all three of you." He leaned down and grinned at Andy, who was fast asleep.

"Zane, you can't just do that."

"Yes, I can."

"No, you can't."

"Libby, shut the fuck up and take the damned keys," he said crossing his arms.

"Fine, take your damned cognac," I said poking my tongue out.

"Very nice." Zane grinned, checking the bottle over. "Good price, a house for a bottle of cognac." Richard chuckled. "Come, I want to show you the nursery."

We followed him through the house, past the kitchen and towards the back hallway where there was a row of doors, all closed.

"Bathroom is in there," Zane said, pointing to a door in the middle. "Mommy and Daddy's room here." He pointed to the door on the right of the bathroom, and opposite that, was another room. "Mommy, won't you do the honours?" Zane asked, taking my armful of crap.

I gripped the handle and opened the door. I gasped. Oh my god, Zane, this is… It's gorgeous."

The nursery was fully furnished, a beautiful wooden crib waited for Andy to sleep in, a change table and rocking chair and tallboy sat in prime positions around the room. The walls were painted a soft robins-egg blue, and lacey curtains and a pull-down blind with a rocking horse motif adorned the windows. I wandered deeper into the room, looking over the mass of stuffed toys sitting in the corner. I looked over the tallboy, pulling open drawers and seeing the clothes inside. I turned around and saw Richard on one knee, a white box in his hand, open to show a beautiful diamond ring inside.

"Libby, I want to spend the rest of my life with you, will you do me the honour of becoming my wife?"

I felt the tears in my eyes break free as I stepped to him. we'd come a very long way, through love, hurt, separation and our beautiful miracle that brought us back together again. I wanted everything he had to offer me, and I was willing to give him everything else in return. I took his hands in mine and looked into his eyes.

What the fuck?

"YES!"

THE END.